# THE PLANTATION

*a paranormal historical novel*

By

## JULIE JONES

*The Plantation: a paranormal historical novel*
by Julie Jones


©2021 Julie Jones
Printed in the United States of America

# DEDICATION

This book is dedicated to the memory
of my parents, Jim and Betty Proffitt.
Thank you for your love, guidance,
patience, and the examples and
standards that you set. These were
invaluable gifts that allowed me to
become the person I am today.
I hope this book is a success
that fills your hearts with joy.

This novel contains graphic sex, slavery, and violence. It is historically accurate and depicts a true account of The American Civil War at the same time engaging a paranormal story full of ghosts, curses and voodoo. I hope you enjoy reading the story of The Plantation. It is written "old style" with a great deal of historical detail and colorful side characters.

# PROLOGUE
## "Bronze John" 1853

illery Louise Ashford paced the cypress floors of her father's townhouse in the fashionable Vieux Carré of New Orleans; her unkempt gown showed the strain she was bearing, as did the tangled mass of honeyed curls hastily tied with a golden ribbon at the nape of her slender neck. Lingering over her father's bedside, she searched for and found the tremulous flutter of a pulse which was the only sign of life he yet possessed since his recent and violent siege of yellow jack.

As the ormolu clock on the dresser struck twelve a shrill scream pierced the muggy night air. Running swiftly down the hall, she collided with her nursemaid, Isis, who with tears still shimmering on her tawny lashes, looked sadly down at the thirteen-year-old Hillery whose aunt had been in labor these past many hours. "She's gone, ma agneaue, ma petite," the quadroon wept softly, "She and the babe both."

In that moment, Devon Ashford, strapped by the hampering bedclothes, called out in his sleep, "Mariette! Mariette!" he croaked, his cries melting into thin sobs as the rage of his delirium broke free. Tossing in sick despair, his addled mind was haunted by memories of his deceased wife.

Mariette had died thirteen years before in the aftermath of a childbirth that had presented him with a proud female infant. Or was it her body lying cold in the next room? Devon's mind was playing tricks.

"Hillery?" his moans were piteous, "Hillery, my girl? Where are you?

Are you...are you gone from me too?"

"Oh, papa, no, I'm here," the girl soothed, lovingly mopping the beaded moisture from his aged, damp brow. She bent to kiss the withered cheek and felt the faint stirring of his breath in her ear. A chill rippled through her at the sign of a vapor rising steadily from his lifeless body. It hovered a moment overhead then ascended more rapidly to merge with the ceiling.

# PART ONE

# CHAPTER ONE

he ocean vessel moved steadily toward shore, and the anticipation felt by passengers and crew alike was a thing contagious. It had been a long, uneventful journey. Now upon entering port, the excitement grew beyond bounds. Hillery took the arm of her new and dear friend, Natalie Michaels, and the two strolled quickly to the ship's rail. Standing on tiptoe, they strained to catch a better glimpse of the buzzing port. They had become fast friends the second day out to sea after meeting briefly during a tour of the ship. Theirs was an inquisitive nature full of curiosity and bouncing with energy. Sharing the age of eighteen, they made a well-bred, well-educated, and startlingly good looking pair.

Close behind came the almost silent footsteps of Natalie's grandmother accompanied by the familiar rap-tap-tap of her slender ebony cane. Turning, the girls looked into sharp blue eyes dancing with vitality and excitement. Her eagerness showed, for Gran was as anxious as a child to be home again. White haired and smiling, she was a tiny woman with a charming nature. As the three women and their luggage were helped to shore, Gran's bird-like countenance was alertly scanning the crowds for a sign of her grandson, Stuart.

"You'll love my brother," Natalie whispered to Hillery, a secretive smile on her ripe lips. She didn't mind playing matchmaker. In fact, she enjoyed it very much! Over the years, she had seen the many sketches of her brother's dream girl. This same face with an elusive energy kept cropping up. Natalie had thought her brother had imagined her, but this girl, this face, looked a great deal like her friend, Hillery. And Stuart had thought to keep her to himself. Yet Natalie, who had always tagged along after her big brother, gave him little privacy.

"Stuart! Oh, Stuart! Over here!" Natalie cried bolting straight into the arms of the most handsome man Hillery had ever seen! He had hair as black as night and deep-set blue eyes set off by a thick fringe of dark lashes. Unlike so many men of the day, his face was cleanly shaven and emphasized by two flashing dimples on either side of a perfect white smile. Tall and slender, he stood slightly stooped to embrace the sister he so obviously adored. Nearly as tall as he, she fell only inches short of his six-foot, one-inch frame. Their heads bowed together in a wave of unruly black hair, and they shared the same fathomless blue eyes as well.

Gran quickly joined in the greetings, and Natalie, seeing Hillery standing alone, pulled her forward for an introduction. This was quickly accomplished, and for a timeless moment the two stood entranced; she, lingering on his dark, finely chiseled features while he was lost in her radiance. He seemed so familiar; she had a strong feeling of deja vu, yet knew they had not met. He touched a long, slender finger to her cheek, feeling the softness of down while examining her beauty with a burning intensity. He had seen this face many times in his dreams. He had attempted to capture the essence of it only to fall far short of his expectations. He knew at once that he would paint her, that indeed, he must capture and put to canvas her deeply haunting quality. He was mesmerized by the depths of her huge violet eyes shimmering with golden sparkles and long, curling lashes. She had a small, straight nose and full red lips that seemed to beckon in invitation, but there was an innocence about her in the tiny pointed chin and blushing pink cheeks. Her honeyed hair, shot through with gold, was swept up on top of her head with tendrils falling free to curl about her neck and face creating an ethereal effect. Of medium height, she was not nearly as tall as Natalie and was of a lean build with a tiny waist, yet a surprisingly full bust.

While he helped her into the carriage, he noted the delicate turn of her ankle and the slight trembling of her hand. "Will you be staying with us long?" he asked hopefully.

"A few weeks, perhaps," she murmured.

"Have you visited Washington before?"

"No, I've never had the opportunity, monsieur."

"How long were you in France?"

"Five years, monsieur. My home is in Louisiana."

"Well, then I shall escort you while you are with us. We must make sure you stay long enough to see all the sights."

"Merci, thank you," she smiled as the carriage set off at a sedate pace. It rolled unhurried into the heart of the city where the air became putrid. There were scavenging pigs everywhere, the sound of their high-pitched squealing escaping nearby slaughter houses. Stagnant ponds adorned the roadside, each of them covered by clouds of mosquitoes. Swarms of flies were everywhere feasting upon the dung left to dry in the streets.

"It isn't all like this," Stuart strove to assure her. "However, the dust is beginning to thicken. You had better take this," he said, handing her a white handkerchief with his initials monogrammed in one corner. Gran and Natalie had already covered their sensitive noses. Hillery joined them as the dust began to roil in great clouds. Men with scarves about their faces were working on the roads, pouring gravel and digging ditches. New buildings were emerging slowly, but it was difficult to see them clearly.

They continued at a snail's pace until at last the carriage pulled in front of a large brick house painted pale yellow with billowing white curtains in all the windows. Its tall pediment, Palladian front was topped by a wide balustrade roof, while the yards seemed to overflow with an abundance of every imaginable flower and shrub. There were clusters of purple lilacs, all colors of blooming roses, daffodils carefully scattered – with a touch of pansies peeking through, and violets shyly hiding throughout the grasses. Added to these were double-flowering tulips, double-flowering almonds, and a whole section of primrose and prickly lantana. Surrounding all this beauty were weeping willows (reminding Hillery of home), clusters of redbud trees – their pink blossoms sweetly fragrant, dogwoods, and several of the gnarled-trunk, flowering crepe myrtles.

"As it is getting quite late, I'll show you the kitchen garden and the fruit orchard tomorrow," Stuart suggested with a grin. "I'm sure you're tired."

"Oh, yes! I'd like that, sir! Thank you."

"Stuart," he laughed as if enjoying some private joke.

"What?" she responded, confused.

"My name," he chuckled, twin dimples flashing. "You've called me nothing but sir or monsieur!"

"Ah bien, Stuart," she remedied. "It is a difficult habit to break."

"Hey, come on you two!" Natalie called, making her way up the front walk. "Maman!" she squealed as an incredibly beautiful, tiny lady in her mid–forties appeared in the doorway; she was a younger version of Gran with sparkling cornflower blue eyes and thick copper tresses pulled back in a chignon at the nape of her neck. Swathed in a gown as copper as her locks and decorated with tiny seed pearls across the skirt and sleeves, she gave the impression of a perfect china doll. Her voice was rich and melodious in response to her daughter's greeting as she gave both Gran and Natalie a hug, keeping one arm about each all the while. "Nat, my darling, how I've missed you!" she cried. "Mother, how are you after your long journey?"

It wasn't until at least half of her questions had been answered that she noticed Hillery for the first time standing with Stuart behind the gate. When Hillery glanced up, Rachael sensed vulnerability in this beautiful child-woman that sent her maternal instincts flaring. "Why, I don't believe we've met," she went to her warmly, "Nat, who is your charming friend?"

"Oh, excuse me, maman! This is Hillery Ashford. Hillery, this is my mother. Hillery and I traveled all the way from France together. We've become great friends. She's on her way home to Louisiana, but as she would need to change ships here in Washington, I thought perhaps she could spend a couple of weeks with us first?"

"Of course, dear, welcome," Rachael extended a porcelain hand. "You must stay as long as you wish!"

"Thank you, madame." The girl murmured, tears misting her vision. It had been a long time since she had been welcomed anywhere, and she wanted to be a part of this household if only for a while.

"It's Rachael, dear. You must call me Rachael," the older woman responded with a merry shake of her hand. "We don't stand on formalities here."

The ladies all bustled into the house. Natalie showed Hillery to a room across from her own. The walls were covered in pale gold damask with heavy velvet draperies hung in the windows. There was a thick bronze carpet upon the floor and two delicately carved French armchairs in the style of Louis XVI upholstered in plush green brocade. The bed à la polonaise was easily the focal point of the room with its elaborate rococo frame richly draped in tones of green and gold. Hillery paused by a Bonheur du jour to admire an intricate toilet service and dainty collection of cologne bottles.

"It's enchanting," she sighed after she had examined almost every article in the room.

"I hoped you would like it. Papa furnished most of the house himself. He was our ambassador to France for many years, so he had ample opportunity to acquire a fine collection. Upon retiring he decided to come back to Washington. He died five years ago."

"I'm sorry."

"Me, too, but you know, sometimes I feel like he is still here." Hillery shivered at Natalie's words. Her skin chilled as she caught the strong scent of Cavendish in the air. "At least I like to think so," Natalie continued unawares. "We keep his portrait in the library. You'll have to see it after awhile. Well, I must go. I'll have a bath sent up to you right away. Dinner won't be for at least an hour yet, so you'll have plenty of time. If you need anything, I'll just be across the hall."

"Thank you."

A short time later, a sturdy mulatto woman of indefinable age entered the room. She carried a large bucket of steaming water and two fluffy white towels, the latter draped unceremoniously across the thickness of her shoulder. She was quickly followed by a grizzly old Negro man lugging a porcelain tub. He set it on the indicated spot, emptied the bucket into it, and then retreated as quickly as he had come for a second and third bucket.

"Thank you, Cecil," the woman spoke in guttural tones. Cecil grinned and bobbed his head before shuffling mutely away. "I'm Annie," the woman continued, this time addressing Hillery. "I does the cleanin' and sewin', and if you need help with your hair, I does that, too." She wiped her rough, work-worn hands on her apron and nodded at the door. "That," she said, "was Cecil. He was a runaway till the old sir took him in, tended his wounds, and kept him hid out till the ruckus boiled down. Then he up and give him some papers what told him he was free. Had something to do with the fugitive slave law Miss Rachael said. That was just before the old sir died. Lands! Old Cecil been here ever since, lookin' after the family, tendin' the gardens, doin' all the heavier chores. Yep, he's old, but he's strong too. And smart!" she shook her gray head sadly. "Folks don't always notice that because he cain't talk, you see. His old master cut out his tongue for aidin' the young mistress to escape. He said if'n he wouldn't tell where she went, he wouldn't talk no more!"

"Yes, ma'am, he's had plenty of hard times, but he's well enough now, I guess. Has himself a cottage out back with plenty of food and clothes – and books! Lands! That man is quick! Mister Stuart taught him to read so he could learn to express himself in a new way." Nodding sagely, she pulled a bar of lavender soap from her apron pocket. "Cecil and I, we understands each other. Do you need anything else? Want some help with your hair? I could suds it up real fine!"

"No, everything's perfect! Thank you," Hillery replied, but upon seeing Annie's rather obvious pout, she added with a coy shake of her curls, "You could come back later and help me dry and style it."

"Consider it done!" the mulatto said triumphantly. "I'll be back shortly."

Gratefully, Hillery sank into the hot suds soaking her weary back and shoulders. She had become accustomed to bathing and washing her own hair at the Convent of the Sacred Heart in Paris. With her mind skipping back over the events of the day, she curled her toes and thought how very much she loved this family. They were all such extraordinary people – Gran and Rachael, Natalie and Stuart. Most of all Stuart, she thought with a blush. Natalie had warned that she would love her brother. Strange how the very thought of him could make her cheeks burn!

Dinner was a grand celebration that evening. With Natalie's and Gran's return from the continent, and Hillery's welcome to the household, Cook had truly put her skills to test. On the food-laden table were marinated beef steaks in an onion and tomato sauce, fresh fish fillets rivaling smoked Virginia ham, simmering crocks of pole beans opposite plates of buttered carrots, and scalloped potatoes in a thick cream sauce with a garnish of fresh parsley. After all this was consumed, Cook presented a dish of black raspberries lavishly topped with a heaping mountain of whipped cream and her own famous hot apple pie a' la mode. It was with snug bellies and warm hearts that the family retired for the night.

While Natalie slept late the next morning, Hillery arose early. She had been awakened by a ghostly figure at the foot of her bed. Though, to her, it was a trivial event, she was unable to return to sleep. Dressed in a pale green morning gown and matching kid slippers, she brushed her waist length, tangled curls and tiptoed down the stairs with an itch to explore the dew-drenched gardens.

"Ah, I see you're up with the sun too," a deep voice drawled from behind the winged shelter of one of a pair of "sleeping chayres". Drawing closer, she smiled at the debris of scattered news sheets across the floor at his slippered feet. An empty coffee mug perched atop one spatula-like arm while a set of five sensitive fingers drummed along the other. "Would you care for coffee?" Stuart asked politely. "I'm afraid Cook is still asleep, but I make a pretty fair pot."

"Oh, no, thank you. I hope I didn't disturb you. I had thought to take a stroll in the gardens before breakfast."

"All alone?" he shook his head reproachfully. "Such a lovely lady should have an escort."

They took the back way out and walked arm in arm down the bricked garden path. Hillery's face was alight with silent awe at the regal beauty surrounding her. Everywhere she looked, life was unfolding, from the symmetrically patterned vegetable gardens with their brick walkways in between, to the thickly twining grape vines and rows of blackberry bushes. And beyond all this, she could see the fruit-filled tops of the ever-stretching orchards. There were apple, cherry, and peach trees, plums, pears, and even pecans. It covered a vast area for being within a city and was enclosed by an ivy-clad brick wall creating a sort of quiet utopia.

They sat beneath an apple tree, munching its fruit and discussing their lives and homes, each at ease with the other. "I love it here, Stuart," Hillery expressed with enthusiasm. "It's so peaceful and happy."

"You make it seem so," he smiled.

"Oh," she laughed, pleased with the compliment, "it's just that this whole place is simply wonderful. It's gorgeous."

"So are you," he said, drawing closer to her. "I felt it the first moment I laid eyes on you. You've a special quality, ma petite. A temptress, yet an innocent," he whispered huskily into her ear. And before she could respond, before she realized what he was about, his lips brushed her fingers. She blushed, her senses reeling. She was speechless. She knew that she ought to protest, or at least leave now before sinking any further beneath his spell. But this was a newfound joy and contentment, and she was happy just to bask in it. He grinned as she ducked her head. At length he rose, pulling her up behind. "You must sit for me, little one," his eyes crinkled at the corners, "soon, starting today."

"Sit...for you?" she stammered, confused.

"I want to paint you! I must capture your beauty on canvas," he stated firmly, thinking of all his many attempts to capture her likeness from his dreams. He had failed miserably, he acknowledged to himself.

"Oh! You're an artist!" she exclaimed. "Nat didn't tell me."

"Yes, I am an artist," he chuckled. "It is what I do. As soon as we have eaten breakfast, I intend to paint you! With your permission," he smiled, "of course."

The family was gathered in the Italian Gothic dining hall, its furnishings bought in Italy during the 1830's and transported to the United States to be wedged within the carefully measured space that the Washington house had to offer. Each member sat enthroned in a gilded lion-pawed chair, while the frescoed landscapes glimpsed throughout the room were seen through the simulated ogee arches on the walls. Upon the crocketed table were smoked ham and bacon, scrambled eggs with chives, fluffy wheat biscuits with homemade jam, and a fresh pot of strong, hot coffee. Drawn by the luscious aroma, Hillery discovered a huge appetite in spite of the fresh fruit she had eaten earlier.

The studio was located at the rear of the home, just beyond the library. As Hillery had not yet seen this wing of the house, she paused to gaze at the many volumes of books shelved from the lowest point upon the Savonnerie carpet to the height of the twelve foot ceiling. Centered above a large marble hearth at one end of the room hung a pair of portraits. Easily recognizing the slightly more youthful image of Rachael, she realized the other must be Stuart's and Natalie's father. She had a subtle awareness of another presence in the room, and remembered Natalie's words from before. She also noted that Stuart seemed both conscious and comfortable with the energy. Again, there was a subtle hint of Cavendish. And a ghostly memory from earlier that morning!

"They're beautiful," she breathed entranced, noting the scrawled signature in the corner. "You are an artist! Natalie made a reference to your father's portrait earlier," she exclaimed, "but didn't tell me you had painted it. They are both simply exquisite!" She caught sight of Stuart's pleased, yet slightly flushed, expression. Why, he's embarrassed, she thought to herself, asking yet another question to ease the awkward silence. "What was his name, your father?"

"Thomas Maurice Michaels," his answer rang out proudly.

"You miss him, don't you?"

"Very much," he agreed soberly, brightening almost magically a second later as with a single sweep of his sinewy arm, he directed her through the next door. "My studio, my lady!" he bowed comically.

"Merci, monsieur," she laughed in gay abandon.

The studio was a very large, airy room with windows filling an entire wall. There were paints, brushes, and canvases cluttered atop a nondescript table in one corner. The wall opposite was lined with chairs, tables, and settees of every description, ready and waiting for any required setting. It was here they passed the morning – and many mornings after – with Hillery posing and Stuart painting, a strong bond growing between them like the chords of a perfect harmony.

Most afternoons Hillery spent shopping or visiting family friends with Natalie. They would sit and chat for hours in the coffee shops, sipping the hot brew and nibbling sweet cakes. Evenings were usually social events for Washington had its share of balls and cotillions. On these occasions Stuart would accompany the ladies, always claiming Hillery's first dance.

One such cotillion was meant to take place in a narrow brick house on Sixteenth Street, only a few blocks from the White House. It was a particular honor as the hostess was none other than Mrs. Rose O'Neal Greenhow, an active member of the Democratic Administration and a prominent social leader. The Michaels' held the Greenhow's in long-standing esteem and were only too eager to accept the invitation. It was even rumored that President Buchanan might attend. It was said he frequently visited the widow.

With some trepidation Hillery prepared for the evening ahead. She selected a violet silk with an extremely daring décolletage with tiny puffed sleeves that completely bared the shoulders. The heavily flounced skirts were ribboned and bowed in a deeper shade of purple. She wore a matching pair of slippers of the same hue. Annie arranged her hair in cascades down her back, leaving only a few wispy curls about her face. Stepping back to admire her handiwork, she pulled a pair of glimmering violet stones from somewhere beneath her apron, and said, "Miss Rachael say for you to have these. They're gonna match your dress just perfect!"

"How sweet," Hillery replied, already slipping the little silver posts through her shell-shaped ears. "They're lovely!" With one final pat to her hair, she walked across the hall and tapped on Natalie's door. She, too, had just completed her toilet, looking ravishing in a soft yellow gown of plush velvet. Her rich black hair was dressed on top and laced with pearls.

"You're gorgeous, Nat!"

"So are you. But you seem a bit nervous. What's wrong?"

"Oh, Nat, I am nervous! What if she doesn't like me?"

"She'll like you all right. After all, she's a true Southerner, and despite your years in France, you still sport more than a hint of a Southern accent."

"I hope you're right."

"Of course I am! She'll probably take you under her wing. There aren't that many soft-spoken Southerners left in Washington these days."

As the two descended the stairs, Stuart announced the barouche was ready. Rachael sat waiting in a nearby chair, beautifully at ease in her finery. With admiration in her eyes, Hillery thanked her warmly for the earrings, remarking at the same time on Gran's absence. "Unless I miss my mark," Rachael answered all poise and etiquette, "she is probably waiting on the rest of us. By now, she has no doubt driven the coachman mad!"

"Quite so," Stuart agreed, elegant in his tailored black suit and snow-white cravat, with hardtop black boots shining at his feet. Reaching for his top hat, he grinned as he said, "But even Gran will have to admit, you three were worth the wait!"

# CHAPTER TWO

pon arrival at the house on Sixteenth Street, they were ushered inside and regally greeted by their hostess, a tall slender woman of sublime beauty with olive skin, dark eyes, and sleek black hair. Though pulled tightly back in a chignon, the severity of the style did nothing to lessen her naturally good looks. With a deep red rose tucked behind one ear, she was a middle-age woman in all her glory. And because of her political position, she made it her business to become acquainted with all newcomers regardless of social background, to Washington. A smile curved the full red lips when she first looked into Hillery's young face. But it was the touch of a Southern accent that ultimately won her heart. There were introductions to many prominent citizens and even members of the president's staff, but no sign of Buchanan himself. Earlier that evening they had viewed the White House down gas-lit Pennsylvania Avenue. The Capitol building was still incomplete without dome. Political conversations were buzzing but not outnumbering the social entertainments. Many young gallants of quality and charm surrounded the girls – to Natalie's delight, and Hillery's despair! She had eyes for Stuart alone, but he was caught up in the dance with another.

As soon as the music faded, it began anew. The young men closed in, and through the swarm of admirers, Stuart appeared. Sweeping Hillery away in his arms, he held her a bit too closely, enjoying the soft fragrance that wafted from her and the womanly feel of her body next to his.

Rose stood watching them move gracefully across the floor. She had enjoyed meeting this young lady of whom Stuart Michaels was so fond, and before the evening was spent, it was her intention to give a small tea the following week in order to know her better.

During the next few days, Natalie, Hillery, and Stuart were seen together constantly. The threesome had become a familiar sight, though most mornings were reserved for the couple alone, either working in the studio or sitting beneath their favorite apple tree. They discussed their childhoods, families and goals. There was so much to learn about the other! Hillery told of her plantation home, and the gracious, lovely lady who had been her mother emerged theatrically through the stories her father had woven in her youth. She recounted the sorrowful details of her papa's death that long ago summer in New Orleans and admitted her fears and loneliness ever since, guarding her words nonetheless.

"Are we talking about *The* Plantation? The one that is reputed to be haunted, even cursed?"

"I was afraid you would say that," she said quietly.

"It's okay to be honest with me. You have come to mean a good deal to me, and I believe the feeling is mutual?"

"Of course," she sighed, appearing a bit more relaxed. "It's just that I never know how much to say. I didn't want to," she shrugged delicately, "run you off. Maybe make you think I was a tad bit crazy."

"I know better than that," he stated firmly. "I have spent my life looking for you! Now that I have found you, nothing can stand in my way."

Hillery was grateful for his understanding. She was well aware that there was much gossip about her home. It was still something of a shock as to how widespread that gossip actually was! Her time in France had been occupied by labors in the convent, but filled, too, with a solid classical education tempered considerably by European cultures, music, and language. She spoke seven languages in all but only five fluently, and though her musical skills were not outstanding, she was fairly proficient at the piano. None of this made up for the fearful looks cast her way when her home was open to discussion.

Stuart had spent most of his boyhood in France, studying the arts with a passionate inclination. He had furthered his education in England and Italy as well. He spoke of his interest in the works of

Gainsborough, and his keen obsession with the art of Watteau and Fragonard.

His father retired in 1848 when Louis Philippe was deposed. Upon deciding to return to the United States, he shipped home to Washington his precious collection of European furniture along with his son's many books and art supplies. Five years later, he died.

Now, in 1858, Stuart was twenty-nine years old with a childhood filled with European memories. Natalie, however, had left her French home at the early age of eight, thus yearning to return and rediscover her girlhood fantasies on this most recent tour.

On the afternoon of the tea the women all dressed with care, then set out for an hour of gossip and sweet cakes. There were only two ladies present to whom Hillery had not yet been introduced: Sarah Dorcel, an outstanding social leader, was ill the night of the ball. In her mid-fifties, she was of medium height and slightly plump. Her graying hair was arranged in ringlets about her flushed, round face, and the wrinkles around her mouth and eyes could not belie the perpetual smile she wore.

"Good afternoon," she gushed in a high-pitched voice. "It's so nice to meet you, dear! I was terribly upset that I missed the ball last week. I was quite ill, you know," she confided in a hushed tone, "Quite ill."

"Good gracious! Do be still," groaned Crystal Fleece, the other woman as yet unknown to Hillery. Crystal was a young beauty of twenty with a statuesque figure and a glorious skein of pale blonde hair. Her flawless features were no less than perfect, and she held herself with obvious pride. Looking up to no one, she set her goals high. Marrying into a wealthy Washington family was definitely her ambition.

"Do sit down, Miss Ashford," Crystal purred, patting the damask seat beside her own flow of turquoise skirts. "You look a little peaked."

"Oh, no, I'm fine, thank you. But I will have a seat," Hillery replied, innocently missing the competitive gleam in the other's eyes.

"My, we've all heard so much about you!" the blonde continued. "You must simply be lost in this big city!"

"No, not at all," she spoke quietly. "Actually I feel quite at home."

"And that's as it should be, dear," smiled Sarah, giving Hillery a reassuring pat with the backside of her dimpled fingers.

"Oh, bother," Crystal muttered, leaning forward to display her ample bosom. She was positive that her lush figure was by far the ripest, and in any case, a man like Stuart Michaels could not possibly be interested in some country girl from a convent! "How is that handsome brother of yours, Natalie?" she asked as though the thought had just popped into her head. "You know, he promised to paint my portrait this summer. I'm to be next, after that silly landscape with which he's been so engaged." At that, she turned back to Hillery, a sugary smile widening her already carnal mouth. "We're very close, you know," she said with a wink.

Natalie folded her hands in her lap, steepling her fingers with pretended concentration. "I'm afraid you'll have to wait until he is done with Hillery's portrait, Crystal," she grinned slyly. "You know how fickle artists can be. Anyway, he's been finished with that 'silly landscape' ever since I've been home."

Crystal's face turned a shade too pink as she spat with ill repressed venom, "Well, I suppose he does have to humor your little guest! What else could he do?"

Hillery stiffened her back preparing for battle as Natalie intervened once again. "My brother doesn't have to do anything. He works where he finds inspiration, that's all. Yours would be a paid consignment. It's not at all the same."

"Hmm," Crystal curled her lip, her china blue eyes raking Hillery's form insultingly. "It's easy to understand how a little convent miss like you could set her cap for a man like Stuart," she hissed, "but do yourself a favor, honey," her laugh was brittle, "and forget it! Stuart needs a real woman, not some little twit he has to paint just because she's a guest in his house."

"Ladies, Ladies!" Rose interjected, her tone smooth, but the message sharp. "Shall we take tea? Lily has brought such nice cakes and pastries!" she gestured toward a Chippendale tea service whose silver platter was overladen with sweets. "I will pour, Lily. Thank you."

She smiled serenely.

Lily nodded and ducked shyly through the door. She was a small, wispy woman, plain of face and seemingly without character. Yet she was an extremely devoted servant and loved her mistress dearly.

It was left to Rose to carry the conversation to safer ground. After inquiring after Sarah's health and Natalie's recent trip to France, she coyly shifted the subject to her own beloved homeland, the South. Taking deep pleasure in sharing the memories with another true Southerner, she reveled in discussing the beauty of the land. She spoke of the flowering magnolias and weeping willows, the rich black soil of the bayous, the outstanding climate and of course, the splendid architecture. But their thoughts divided, and met with friction at the inevitable mention of slavery. To Rose it was a necessary part of an ideal society, an accepted institution in the South.

Hillery, however, intensely disliked human bondage and though she would never be rude enough to openly dispute the subject with her hostess, her young face showed all too clearly what her manners would not permit her to speak. Raised in a household staffed with servants, she completely understood the cruelty and degradation involved. Though her father's people had been fairly treated, she knew that many others had not. In the hands of a lesser master, their fates were mercilessly sealed. She had worried often over the character of her guardian who now reined lord and master at The Plantation. Had Devon Ashford been alive today, he would have been exalted by the remarkable resemblance between her and his beloved Mariette. Nearly a mirror image, Hillery had flowered into the very replica of her mother. And Mariette's kindness and determination to help the underprivileged was no less apparent in the daughter.

Squaring her small shoulders, she set her chin. A stubborn crease puckered the corners of her rosy mouth. Not a word escaped. The two women spent long moments sizing each other up. A hush fell over the little group. Sarah Dorcel nervously bobbed her turtle-like head setting her ringlets to jiggling, and the only sound that invaded the silence was the gleeful chortle that sprang from the lips of Crystal Fleece.

Seeing the pink serpent within flick over that moist slash with delightful relish, Rose ended the tense uneasiness with a warm smile and outstretched hand. "I like you," she said to Hillery. "You have manners, grace, and charm. Yet you have a mind of your own. We may not agree on all, but I think we are birds of a feather."

Hillery accepted the proffered hand, dimpling at Crystal's ill-concealed scorn.

Days later, after the tea, Crystal Fleece came rolling up the Michaels' avenue in her open landau. Tripping daintily to the front door, she snapped impatiently at her driver. "Wait here, boy!" she called crossly. "And don't you wander off!" Her face, flushed with the crisp air of excitement, softened visibly upon sight of Stuart. "Oh, Stuart," she pouted prettily with an effective swipe at her teary eyes, "I've been so lonely! Why haven't you come to see me?"

"I'm sorry, Crystal. I've been busy," Stuart's reply was absent.

"So I've heard," she fumed at his inattention. "Have you forgotten your promise? You did agree to do my portrait, remember?"

"But of course, Crystal. As soon as I have completed Hillery's, I would be delighted."

"That's not fair!" she screeched, "I was to be next!"

Stuart's face registered shock. "Crystal, don't be foolish," he pleaded. "We are still friends. We always have been."

"Friends," She screeched, "I don't want to be friends!" Her movements were frantic. "Haven't you guessed? I want to be your wife! You'll see. You'll see how much better I am," she hurled herself into his arms, fingers twined possessively throughout his raven hair. Suddenly her face was only inches from his. She met his lips, mashing, sucking, and clinging wildly! Thrusting her pointed breasts into his chest, her hips began rocking, undulating in a sensual rhythm of urgent invitation.

"I thought I heard…" Hillery stood spellbound in the doorway. Eyes wide, flashing first pain, then anger, her voice wavered, "I had no idea!" She stumbled backward, and before Stuart could disentangle the entwining limbs that bound him, she had fled back inside.

Crystal laughed with evil delight. "She's as cursed as that plantation of hers, didn't you know?" Her words seemingly fell on deaf ears. But Hillery had heard.

"Hillery, wait!" Stuart's cries whipped hoarsely throughout the house. "Don't run from me! It isn't what you think!" Whirling her about where she stood by the stair rail, his hands bit into her slim shoulders. "It isn't what you think," he repeated more slowly, his voice raspy with irritation.

"Well, I know what it looked like!" she bit out unfairly, sinking pearly white teeth into a trembling lower lip. Stormy blue eyes clashed with violet, dark and murky, the eyes of an angry sea witch.

"I can see you won't listen," his words cut deeply as he flung her from him. "Think what you will."

Sobbing relentlessly, she ran to her room and lay beneath the towering green and gold canopy, a silent witness as the darkness snuffed out the light of day. Hours passed before a soft rapping fell upon her door. Before she could move, it swung open and there in the shadows a dark figure loomed lean and muscular.

"Stuart!" she gasped, ashamed of her mussed appearance and previous burst of petty jealousy.

"Shh," he pulled her into a gentle embrace, kissing first her eyes, cheeks, and hair before ever so slowly reaching her mouth. As he withdrew, his fingers lovingly caressed her lips stilling the flow of apologetic words. Taking her by the hand, he led her down the dimly lit hall around the staircase to his studio below.

"Come my love," his sweet breath fanned her face. "This is my gift to you. My hands have created what my lips cannot express. I have made you eternal, ethereal beauty of mine. I love you so," he whispered, kissing both her palms.

Speechless, Hillery gazed at her own likeness. The luminous pools of lavender looking back at her reflected immortality, while the mane of honeyed hair that flowed about her face might well have been a halo. It was more than a painting; it was a work of art. An offer of eternal love, for only love could reflect such a quality.

"Oh," she breathed, enthralled. "It's magnificent, Stuart! I am truly sorry. I should never have doubted you."

She was pressed against him, her lips ripe beneath his when Gran blustered into the room, her small body bent with fatigue. "What's the racket?" she railed. "Don't you young people keep track of the time?" Perceptive as usual, her plaited head swiveled in the direction of the canvas. She clattered with the aid of her spiral cane to stand before it. "It is your masterpiece, Grandson," she nodded, eyes suspiciously damp, "Your masterpiece!" Glancing up, she smiled placidly. Old bones don't lie, and hers were telling her that she had not seen the last of this Louisiana beauty.

Then came the day for Hillery to pack and begin her long journey home. She had made all the necessary arrangements, had written to Charles, her guardian, and had even purchased her ocean liner ticket. Yet somehow her leaving seemed unreal. She had come to love this house and its people, feeling a part of its odd solidity. But most importantly, she had come to realize just how dearly she loved Stuart.

# CHAPTER THREE

hey didn't speak of it that morning but sat quietly in each other's arms staring blindly at the surrounding fruit orchards. By dinner, her bags and trunks were stationed in waiting near the front door. Gran kept sniffling, claiming to have caught cold. Rachael smiled sadly and Natalie lost all control with impetuous hugs and tears.

Stuart and Hillery sat miserably facing each other throughout the meal. After picking at their food, they set off for a walk in the gardens. They moved briskly at first, then more slowly as their agonized words tumbled forth.

"I don't want to leave you!" she cried, her heart swelling with pain.

"Then don't," he answered, "Stay with me and be my wife. I love you."

"And I, you," she sighed, holding him near enough to feel their mingled heartbeats. "I'll come back as soon as I am able, and I will be your wife."

"Can't you wait until I can go with you? It could be dangerous for you to go alone."

"No, I mustn't. It is my home. I have waited far too long already. There are so many legalities to attend. I must be certain my father's wishes have been carried out. All of the people depend on me," she thought of her people, the family she loved. They might not be blood related, but they definitely shared a special bond. "I have an obligation to fulfill," she finished.

"How long?" he demanded. "I would marry by Christmas. And you are unsafe with each New Year." He was referring to the curse, and the sacrifice of the first healthy baby girl born after New Year's Day.

"I am not the target of the curse," she sighed, thinking how frightened her people would be if she could not free them before the end of the year. It was a very real fear they faced and she must put an end to it. "And I will be away no longer than necessary, I assure you."

"Then write to me, and if you need me I will come," he promised. "Autumn is almost here. I will come for you before the holiday if you have not returned. Agreed?"

"Agreed," she sighed, "but I will return before winter sets in." She smiled sadly as she looped her arm through his, "But now, my love, we must go back to the house. After all, your mother has gone to a great deal of trouble to throw me a farewell party. We mustn't disappoint her by being tardy. And we mustn't show any fear. I think she is suspicious of the rumors, but is trying to believe they are only that."

"Hmm, I'm sure you are right," came the muffled reply, "but I can think of a much more pleasant way to say farewell." Nibbling her neck, he blazed a trail of kisses down her throat, not pausing until he had brushed the tops of her heaving breasts. Her pulse was racing. He could feel it beneath his lips as his hands continued their slow assault. His fingers wanted to explore the ripe mounds beneath the bodice. They were eager to dislodge the lace fishue that would bar his way. She trembled slightly and he visibly straightened. He badly wanted to massage each swollen globe. He settled for the imagery, knowing one day she would be his.

"Master Stuart! Master Stuart!" Annie called from the path ahead of them, disrupting their rendezvous with a show of frantic hands. "The guests is arriving!" she scolded, guessing at their previous sport by the blush that bloomed on Hillery's cheeks. "Miss Rachael, she already be receivin'. You two oughta be there with her!"

"Okay, old girl! Don't panic," Stuart laughed. "We'll be right there."

"Shame on you, Master Stuart!" she huffed, "The young miss is a lady! Your mama would want you t' member your manners," she mumbled under her breath as she retreated back up the path.

The guests were indeed arriving when the couple returned to the house. Sarah Dorcel was aptly delivered in a gaudy orange carriage with waving purple plumes. She chattered gaily as she bobbed up the front walk in full possession of Hillery's arm. Many of Natalie's friends arrived together and the house soon rang with laughter and song. Rose came bearing a mysterious package for her young friend, one she was persuaded to open immediately. Hillery did so, gingerly tearing at the tissue-wrapped box. Therein, she discovered a fragile gold chain of intricate design supporting at its length a red rose pendant.

"It's my namesake," Rose smiled candidly, "so you won't forget me."

Crystal arrived last and like a gust of winter wind blew coldly into the ballroom. She stood in the entrance, gaining the attention and praise of every man present, waltzing over to Stuart with a snide glance at Hillery. He'll soon be mine, her eyes seemed to taunt. Hillery bore it all with grace even as Crystal pressed her charms. She was recalling what Stuart had told her a few days before. He had said that his father and Crystal's had been close friends, but there had never been anything between the two of them. There was a hint of mental instability with a family background of volatile neurosis on her mother's side. Even so, it was a tremendous relief when the evening had dwindled to an end. Hillery was tired of enduring the other woman's jibes and a headache had formed in the base of her skull from an excess of champagne. Her speech felt slightly slurred. She worked hard to hide that. She was embarrassed. And she was so sleepy! It was good to feel the strength of Stuart's warm body when he helped her to her room.

When Annie came to assist with her gown, Stuart lingered in the door catching a glimpse of swaying petticoats. The creamy round breasts he had yearned to fondle earlier strained tantalizingly against her chemise. In his imagination her lips beckoned his before he retreated down the hall.

Nursing his desires with a bottle of imported brandy, he sat brooding in the study. God! He could still see those perfect orbs fairly bulging from the scanty underwear! And her rapturous face in the half-light of the room! She looked so inviting! Unbidden, his fingers curled more tightly about the bottle he held, his mind raging with indecision. He knew what he was thinking was wrong. He was also aware that his actions in the garden were unseemly, and that a gentleman would never have lingered in that hallway taking advantage of the view. He knew, but he could not change the direction of his thoughts.

He quietly climbed the staircase and pushed wide her door. She was lying on her back in the moonlight, her face half hidden by the glorious mass of her hair. Through those tangled tresses he caught sight of a filmy gown of a near transparent weave. It had ridden up around her thighs exposing their creamy perfection, and one ripe mound as white as alabaster had nearly escaped the daring décolleté.

Groaning, he eased in beside her. He told himself he would remain a gentleman. He was only there to look. He meant to feast his eyes upon her exposed beauty, for in the morning she would be gone. He did not think he could bear it. He had only just found her! For years her beautiful face had haunted his dreams! Yet he had searched for her in every crowd, every city. How could he let her go? These were troubled times. What if she did not return? What if something happened to her?

He hadn't meant to touch her, but found himself lightly stroking her hair away from her face. She moaned softly in her sleep, roused slowly. She breathed in the scent of him as she opened her eyes. With one look at his face, she saw a world of emotion. She uttered a soft cry as she reached for him, and they melted together in a passionate kiss.

"I want to make love to you," he whispered in her ear. "But I will respect your feelings. I have no right to compromise your innocence. If you will allow me, I would hold you through the night."

She sucked in a deep breath, and for a single long moment he thought she would deny him. The feeling was torture. Then she stroked his handsome face, letting her fingers trail to his muscled chest. She wanted to bare that chest, to taste his skin. She wet her lips with her tongue, and he knew he was lost. His lips took hers. His fingers trembled, wanting to roam free, but he held his resolve.

She undid the buttons of his shirt in awe of the muscles that rippled beneath her questing fingertips. She felt awkward in her innocence, but allowed her tongue to flick lightly over his chest. The salty taste of him pleased her immensely. He groaned in pleasure, and returned the favor, running his fingertips lightly across her décolleté. He did not bare her flesh.

She didn't stiffen when his hand smoothed down the front of her gown, and through the light fabric, his fingers touched her most private part. Instead, she sighed and allowed her thighs to part ever so slightly. "Dear God," he breathed, "I love you so." Then rubbing softly, she moaned and arched her back.

His manhood hardened instantly causing her to gasp as he pressed against her. The shock somehow cleared her mind, and he saw both embarrassment and fear of the unknown in her beautiful eyes.

She heard Stuart's answering moan as he straightened. "We have taken it far enough," he said, his voice husky. "I would never force you."

His kindness and good manners restored her faith in him. She knew when she first laid eyes on him they were meant for each other. And she also knew this would not be happening now if they were not forced to part. No, he would have waited until they married. But she must leave, and the very thought of parting for even a while was far more painful than any hurt he would do her.

"You would not be forcing me," she whispered, and though he burned for her, he held her apart from himself and slowly closed his shirt. After what seemed a very long moment, he took her in his arms. He kissed her forehead, then her nose. They shifted into a safer position and held each other through the night.

"Get some sleep, my beauty," he whispered. "You have a long journey ahead of you, and I would not further tire you."

With the morning sunshine streaming through the window, she awoke. She lay quietly back against him, seeking the shelter of his arms. Soon she must leave.

When the last trunk was placed on the carriage after breakfast, the family gathered to bid farewell. Rachael's face was sorrowful as she drew the younger woman into a snug embrace. "Do be careful, dear," she mothered. "And be sure to write."

"I will," Hillery promised, tears sparkling on her lashes. "Here, I almost forgot to return these," she fished a package from her reticule. "Thank you for the loan."

"Keep them, dear," Rachael glanced at the glimmering violet earrings. "They match your eyes so perfectly." They hugged again then

Hillery turned to Gran and Natalie.

"Now you take care of yourself, Missy," Gran ordered a little too gruffly. "And don't you forget to hurry on back here. My grandson is going to be lost without you!"

"Oh," Hillery bit her lower lip trying desperately not to cry.

"She's right, you know," Stuart said softly as she swiftly gave the old woman a hug before turning away.

Next Natalie stepped forward to claim a hug. She clung to Hillery, her eyes filled with unshed tears. "I'm going to miss you so much!" she whispered, clinging tightly.

"I'll miss you too. You are my best friend!"

At the harbor, Natalie sat alone in the landau, watching as her brother and her best friend went strolling beneath a sprawling sycamore, hands locked and bodies close. With one final, lingering kiss they parted, unaware of the time and trials that were destined to separate them.

# CHAPTER FOUR

nce off ship, Hillery hired a brougham to take her from the murky black waters of the gulf to her home on Chartres Street in the Vieux Carré of New Orleans. There had been no word from Charles these past years aside from an occasional inquiry of her health. She could only hope that her step-uncle had kept the townhouse and plantation in good order.

After paying the driver, she stood staring at the graceful white Italianate house, bracing herself for the hurtful memories it was sure to unleash. It was here she stayed with her father during those long-ago trips to the city. And here that she had lost him forever. Now gazing at the lacy iron balustrade, she jumped almost fearfully when an austere man of color dressed in scarlet livery appeared in the door. He was tall with broad shoulders, displaying not a hint of familiarity in his cultural features.

"Miss Ashford, I presume?" the man queried in a wave of rich baritone. "The master has informed us of your arrival and bade that we make you comfortable in his absence."

"His absence?" she spoke softly. "He isn't here then?"

"No madam. You will have to await his convenience, but I should think he would be here soon."

"What of Benny and old Adam? I should have expected them to greet me."

"Dismissed, madam," he said succinctly. "Five years ago."

"I see," she replied, and she did, "thank you…um…"

"Higgens," he supplied, bowing slightly at her discomfiture. "And now if there is nothing else, I shall show you to your room," he continued as he began to climb the stairs, leaving her no choice but to follow.

"There must be some mistake," she gasped when they had traveled the corridor to its very end. "This was my father's room." It was indeed the room her father had chosen for himself after the loss of his wife. He never entered the master suite again. It was in this room he died.

"There is no mistake, madam. Master Charles is very precise in his orders. I'm afraid this is all that is available to you."

"Why, that's not possible! There are half a dozen rooms up here! What of my own room?"

"Orders are orders, miss. I am sorry," he said, lowering his gaze. For a moment she was sure she had seen some flicker of emotion in those cool dark eyes. Yet he maintained his stance by the door until she succumbed, bending to his will.

Had she expected to find the stench of a sick room, she did not. Nor were there stains of blood and death on the carpet or bedding. But the walls were the same pale blue, just as the furnishings had remained unaltered. It was a confining room, bursting with such painful echoes from the past that she was no longer able to dissuade the tears that had burned from the onset.

As Higgens had gone, there was no one to see. She could no longer erase the horrors from her mind that had begun with the freezing chills and skull-splitting headaches she herself had experienced. Her fever had risen, soaring to great heights, while her limbs weakened, limp as a rag dolls. Yet even as she floundered in recovery, her father had taken ill, matching her ability to return to health with his own controversial dilapidation.

"Oh, papa, why did you die? Why did it have to take you?" she moaned, still hearing the rambling bouts of his delirium coupled with the laborious sounds squeezed from the fluids of his lungs. Her eyes fell closed against the vision she recreated – the jaundiced skin and oozing gums that would forever haunt her dreams.

"It'll do you no good, cryin' like a babe," an impudent female voice came from behind. Hillery whirled just as a young quadroon of about twenty sailed into the room, uninvited. "I knocked, but you didn't hear," she remarked, her large mouth twisted in a taunting smile. "Anyway,

I only wanted to look at you," her fine nostrils flared. "You ain't so beautiful!"

"Who...who are you?"

"I'm Georgia," the slanted black eyes seemed to mock her. "I'm Master Charles' special servant. A sort of maid, you might say," she snickered, drifting out the door, her malevolent laughter floating after her.

Trembling, Hillery washed her tear-streaked face, applying a comb and brush to her snarled curls. Within a quarter hour she was in the dining room, freshly changed from her travel-stained garments and wearing a fetching gown with ruby trim. Her hair was piled in a becoming coiffure set off by a complexion as rosy as a cherub. Silently she vowed, Georgia would never catch her in such a state again!

By the second day Charles had still not arrived. Indeed, no one even made reference to him. Higgens steadfastly refused to discuss his employer, while Georgia, thankfully, kept to herself. Hillery vaguely wondered at the nature of the man. She had never met him, and even her father had known little about his wife's step-brother. Mariette had been a young bride when her father, Henry Couvent Betaud, remarried. Sara Thompson brought to this union a grown son of her own. That son was Charles. But Henri had much preferred his own natural daughter over his newly acquired step-son and in his will left all his properties and estates specifically in her name. When Mariette died in child bed fever, Charles disappeared. He never looked upon the tiny female infant, but left unknowing of her survival. Now Hillery pondered the sensitivity of such a man. Was he kind then? Loving his step-sister so intensely that he could not deal with her loss? Did he not realize the torment festering within these walls?

The nightmares came that night, the first in a long while. She used to have them frequently that first year in France, always dreaming of her father's corpse, cold and still. She would see his macabre stare, paired with the kind of propelling fear that kept one ever running from some unseen foe. This time there was more: The whisper of footsteps, the hair-raising tingle of being watched. She jerked awake just as the door fell softly closed, leaving her alone in the darkness once again. Bare feet padding across the floor, she shoved a small chair beneath the knob to secure it and decided that tomorrow she would have Higgens affix a bolt. It was a request Higgens would be forced to decline.

The next morning while Hillery was in the garden cutting fresh flowers for a vase, a middle aged man in gentleman's attire strolled casually into view. He cut a dashing figure in his close fitting gray coat, largely knotted bow tie, and fashionable plaid pants. His face was adorned with mutton chops linked to a sweeping mustache that was meant to enhance the sandy locks that curled about his face and neck. Peering into Hillery's startled countenance, he announced with a grin, "Come child, a hug! I'm your Uncle Charles!"

She had expected someone much older with a paunch and balding pate. This man seemed too young to call "Uncle", yet she could not properly call him by his given name. Her cheeks warmed in confusion as he moved nearer, raising her hand to meet his lips. Lingering over the kiss a trifle too long for convention, he allowed his gaze to boldly rake her figure, fastening greedily upon the snow-white breasts only partially concealed by the bodice of her yellow day dress.

"You may call me Charles, if you like," his voice sounded thick as though he had been drinking, "and I'll call you Hillery. Actually, I am only your uncle by marriage, not in fact...and I think I shall prefer it that way. You are truly quite beautiful!"

"Thank you," she stammered, feeling awkward with this meeting. His full lips softened into a wide smile that didn't quite reach the penetrating gray of his eyes, leaving her with the impression he was weighing her for her worth.

"Do you like your room, my dear?" he broke into her thoughts.

"It was my father's," she responded.

"But of course! I felt you would prefer it," he said with icy calm. "If it upsets you, I'll arrange for your possessions to be removed immediately."

"No, it is fine," she said archly, wondering at the game he played. "I've grown accustomed to it. It was a shock at first, that's all. The memories…," she gave a helpless shrug.

"Of course, how thoughtless of me," Charles moaned. But he didn't look concerned, his manner giving no indication of true remorse.

"They put leeches on my father," Hillery's voice shook. "He was so thin…so lifeless! I pleaded with the doctor to try something else. Anything! Finally, I ordered him to take his medical inadequacies and leave my home. Two days later, papa died. The doctor said his blood was on my hands," she sighed audibly, her huge violet eyes shining like liquid pools.

"I'm sorry. If you'd like to change rooms…"

"No, I…I don't even know why I told you that. I'm fine, really." But she wasn't fine. And she was well aware of why she had said what she did. She wanted to gauge his reaction to what had happened, to see how or if, her words had any effect on him. As she looked into his wide gray eyes, she saw no emotion. There was no trace of a conscience that she could see. The very thought was chilling and she prayed she was wrong.

"Huh-hum, Dinner is prepared, sir," Higgens cleared his throat quite audibly before he popped into view, standing in the archway of the flower-strewn gate. "Miss Fisher will serve at your convenience."

"Ah, good, Thank you, Higgens," Charles nodded, taking Hillery's arm in dismissal. "It's been a while since I've sampled one of her delectable meals. Do you not think her a gourmet, my dear?"

"Yes, she's wonderful," Hillery commented absently, for though her cooking was indeed delicious, it was the woman herself Hillery questioned.

Miss Fisher was small with hard, lean lines. She might once have been considered pretty with her petite build and chestnut hair, but one could not overlook the dour lines that framed her mouth nor the furrowed brow that refused to clear. She wore her hair high in a tight knot atop her head, exposing a cheek permanently marred by an ugly white scar running full length from one corner of her eye to the curve of her rigid jaw. Speaking in monosyllables, she spoke only when addressed.

Dinner, however, was a sumptuous affair, after which Charles escorted Hillery to the library where they sat over coffee. Questions of the estates kept popping into her mind, but Charles was quick to assure her that he would handle the matters just as her father had intended. He would suffer no arguments, he said, for a young lady of quality had no business taxing her pretty head with legalities. And so, for the time being, her questions were postponed. He would manage the details of the will, and then as promised, The Plantation and the townhouse would soon be hers.

In the weeks that followed they toured the city together. Hillery kept to herself the kaleidoscope-like visions that haunted her every step. She didn't comment on her increasing anxiety and the distant pounding of the drums that only she seemed to hear. She hid her nausea when they visited the New St. Charles Theater where she and her father had gone to see Lola Montez that final spring in '53. While they strolled the avenues of the Vieux Carré, they passed the fabulous homes lining Royal Street and she tried to show some enthusiasm for the sights. There, they searched out the initials left by clever architects in those intricate works of iron.

"I remember that house!" Hillery exclaimed while she paused before a large, wooden structure with a unique cornstalk fence. "They built that fence a couple of years before I left. Oh, how I loved those majestic butterflies! It's amazing what can be done with iron, isn't it?" she insisted as he led her on their way.

At the French market, they shared hot café au lait and spicy grillades. Hillery saddened as she watched the sun slip glibly down its arch where it would sink below the western horizon. It was time she visited her father's grave, something she needed to do alone. Charles was kind enough to politely lend his escort up Canal Street where he waited at the corner tavern. Hillery ventured into the cemeteries on foot, walking a great distance beyond the ramparts to where the fever victims had been confined. She had been fortunate, long ago, to secure this white-washed stucco tomb, its miniature galleries perched atop the peaked roof. In the nicer areas, some had three, four, and even five tiers with iron chairs and benches grouped about. But here in the fever section, it was too crowded for such frills, allowing only inches between graves.

Lord! There were so many deaths that year! Cannons boomed on every street corner, invading the nostrils with the stench of hot tar. Still more died with each new week. Plumed horses drove in stately procession for some. Many were smeared with lamp black then transported on foot in unstained boxes. Still others were even less fortunate – those who were left to watch their loved ones covered with lime in a common grave with only a thin sheet to separate them in their final offering to the lord.

Hillery shuddered at these gruesome memories as she knelt beside her father's tomb. Laying aside a freshly picked bouquet of blossoms, she spoke to him in prayer, bowing her head as her tears fell softly upon the earth. "I miss you so, papa," she voiced quietly. The earth beneath her shifted slightly. A moan arose softly from the ground and the winds moaned loudly in return. Hillery shivered in spite of herself. "I love you," she added in a whisper, "and don't worry. I will see to your wishes. Please don't worry."

Hillery couldn't help but notice that with each outing in the city the sounds of the drums grew louder, just as the visions of the mamaloi danced before her. Though she pondered the meaning of the visions, she quietly and wisely kept them to herself.

At dinner that evening she again made reference of her inheritance to Charles. She was eighteen after all and entitled to her rights! His response was one of immediate irritation as he rounded on her with a string of vile oaths. Why didn't she trust him, he raged? He knew what was best! If she would just keep out of it, he would handle every detail with the most infinite of care. A woman had no place in a man's world!

That night while she sat at the vanity combing her loosened hair, a knock sounded upon her door. "May I come in?" Charles asked through the closed panel. "I'm sorry for the things I said."

"All right," she whispered, drawing the sash of her dressing gown closed.

Behind closed doors Charles grinned most devilishly. When he entered the room he mouthed a string of poetic apologies. Confused by the almost schizophrenic change in him, Hillery was not quick to accept this truce.

"You needn't worry about such things," he shrugged. "I guess… what I am trying to say…is that I have come to care for you. I would be most honored if you would agree to become my wife." He preened before her, proud of this incredulous show of affection.

"But, you are my uncle!" she gasped.

"Your guardian, my dear," he corrected, "And as I have said, we are not related by blood." He had anticipated her response. In one fluid motion he drew her to him. His fleshy lips fell slack against hers as his thick fingers stroked the column of her throat. She was shocked, thoroughly and completely shocked. She pushed away from him and watched in horror as his features hardened into a cruel smile. "I always get what I want, dear girl. And I want you," he leered at her, allowing his eyes to roam freely over her bosom. In a flash his hands replaced his eyes and he squeezed hard.

All at once, her hand flew out catching the side of his face in a sharp slap. The sound of it echoed in the air between them. He stood frozen in a state of pure fury. His eyes looked deadly. Before turning away, he slapped her so hard her jaw ached and her ears rang. She fell to her knees and he spoke to her in a nasty snarl, "I will have you, my dear Hillery. And on my own terms," he vowed. "You have but two choices. You can make it easy for us both, or very, very hard on yourself!"

He stormed from the room. The door slammed behind him, setting off a tinkle of familiar laughter from somewhere down the hall.

# CHAPTER FIVE

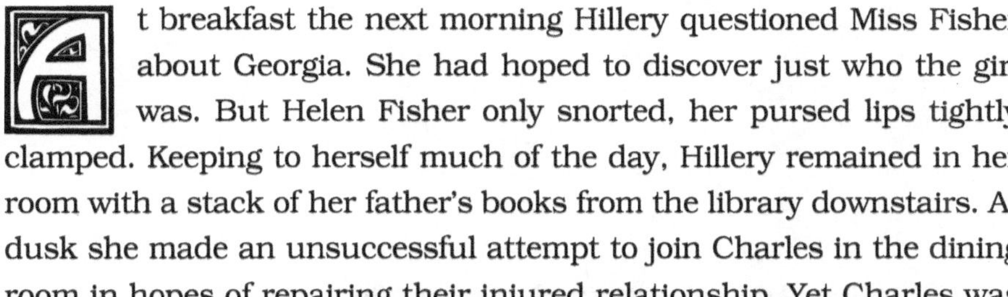t breakfast the next morning Hillery questioned Miss Fisher about Georgia. She had hoped to discover just who the girl was. But Helen Fisher only snorted, her pursed lips tightly clamped. Keeping to herself much of the day, Hillery remained in her room with a stack of her father's books from the library downstairs. At dusk she made an unsuccessful attempt to join Charles in the dining room in hopes of repairing their injured relationship. Yet Charles was pensive, still obviously annoyed, leaving her to take the meal alone.

The night was warm. After dinner she strolled sluggishly out to the courtyard in back. The air was a heavy veil filled with the exotic fragrance of autumn. Caught in her nostalgic recollections she curled upon a small bench intoxicated by the hypnotic aroma. She was completely unaware of the hungry eyes upon her.

That night, the sound of angry voices awakened her. Crawling from her snug bed, she padded softly down the hall until the words became clear enough to understand.

"Come to me again, will you," Georgia's voice spat venomously, "after you've spied on *her* all evening?"

"Ah, come, my love," Charles crooned soothingly. "Let me make it up to you."

"Oh, no, you don't," the rejoinder was hostile; "you get out of here! You been dyin' to crawl between her slick thighs ever since the first night you stood over her bed! Did you think I hadn't noticed?"

"Shut up! You sound just like a jealous wife." A sharp crack sliced the night causing Hillery to retreat to her room. Muffled sobs followed.

Unable to sleep, plus assuming Charles had left Georgia alone, Hillery ventured to check on the girl in the hopes of arranging a friendship of sorts. Though she had no great love for her, she was compassionate enough to recognize jealousy. Knowing the hurt it could cause, it was in her mind to convey to the other that she wanted no part of Charles, especially not now.

Her fingers had barely brushed against the oak panel when the door gave slightly of its own accord. In the filtered light of the room she could see their nude bodies thrashing violently upon the massive bed. Yet this was no display of love as she knew it! Her violet eyes widened at their form of pleasure. Never before had she been aware of such perversity!

After that Hillery remained clearly aloof to Charles and his attentions. No longer fooled by his show of gentlemanly manners, she spurned his every advance and barred his every proposal. Soon tiring of the game, he began to demand a reason for her firm refusal. "Why will you not give me a chance?" he fumed, swearing beneath his breath. "Is there someone else?"

"Why have you not managed my father's will?" she countered with a touch of spunk he had not known she possessed. "My inheritance is long past due!"

"A trivial thing," he dismissed gruffly, "a minor legality."

"Is it?" she returned. "Or is it that you wish to inherit all?"

"Why not enjoy the icing with the cake?" he snorted. "I plan to have you in any case. And as you have so cleverly pointed out, I also intend to retain my holdings."

"Your holdings?" she blurted, her face aflame with color. "How can you be so arrogant? I demand to see the will and get this mess straightened out. With which attorney is it filed? Mr. Pratt? Or have you a copy of your own?"

"No attorney," he roared with laughter. "Mr. Pratt's been dead for years! Sorry if I failed to inform you, but it would have made no difference in any case. You'd have still had to wait until we reached The Plantation…that's where it's filed."

"Well," she huffed, turning away from him, "then I shall see an attorney in town and ask that he return with us."

"Oh, no, you won't," he growled, forcing her back against him. "I'll have no damned attorney on my back, and you will do as you are told! Understand?" he grated, his voice menacing. His thumbs traced the smooth flesh of her throat. They tightened at the base where her pulse fluttered. There, he applied a sickening pressure. A soft burring sound had begun in her brain and she stumbled in the near darkness. She attempted to strike out at him, but he only chuckled cruelly and increased the pressure on her throat. She was gasping for air now, filled with fear. His voice whispered in her ear, "I will have you either way. And I will keep you as long as I wish. If you continue to oppose me, I will crush you. With you dead, I stand to inherit. Do you understand?"

She attempted a weak nod before the darkness consumed her. She awoke sometime later to the play of shadows on her bedroom walls. Though daylight still filtered in through the blinds, she sensed the hour had grown late. She put a hand to her head, feeling ill. Slowly, she moved to the door. But the door was locked! He meant to hold her hostage! Already her eyes were searching for a means of escape. She was terrified.

Her glance suddenly fell upon the window. It just might prove to be the only solution. She must free herself and then get in touch with Stuart. He would know what to do! She approached the tall, narrow glass. Unfortunately her room was located on the second floor. She calmed herself as she gazed outside. Not far from reach stood a tall oak. She gauged it to be roughly within her range. She snatched up her reticule which held enough coin for her to get help. She fussed with her gown until she had successfully removed her petticoats beneath, feeling fairly naked with only her long underwear. She hiked her skirts up about her thighs then crouched on the sill.

Looking down, it was a goodly jump and one that could be damning. Yet she flexed her arms, stretching her fingers in preparation for that costly leap. Why couldn't the tree have been just a little closer? She thought. Silently, she called to Saint Michael. Then she swung free of the sill.

There was a single harrowing moment when she floundered in thin air. Then in a show of great faith her fingers caught and curled around the bark of the nearest branch. Nails biting into wood, muscles straining, her legs swung up and over in a flurry of sprigged-lawn undergarments.

Her feet stung when they touched the earth. On trembling limbs she ran across the yard, keeping well hidden behind the screen of evergreen shrubbery. "Bravo, my dear!" Charles stepped from behind the bushes, giving a hearty round of applause. "An interesting show, I must say. I couldn't have planned it better myself!" She felt the blood drain from her face as her body suddenly went limp.

He steered her in the direction of the house. She went along peaceably enough until all at once, in one single burst of adrenalin, she bolted free, taking flight across the yard. He was seconds in pursuit of her so surprised was he by her actions. But he was faster and far more muscular than she. And he was livid. He grasped her tangled flow of hair and hauled her up against him, literally dragging her into the house. And for the first time since her arrival, Hillery noted the house was silent as a tomb. It was as if no one dared move, yet alone draw a breath of air.

He was breathing hard when he shoved her into her room. She fell, sprawling in a tangle of limbs and skirts. He was beyond caring if he hurt her; his movements were rough and forceful as he pulled her to her feet. Her arms were surely bruised where he gripped her, and he lashed out with one beefy fist. It caught her just below the eye. She heard the sickening sound of skin splitting even as she registered the sound of bone on bone. She had never been so terrified in her life. The house quivered a silent salute. The drums hummed in the distance and in that moment Hillery could have sworn she heard her mother's soft voice whispering to her. "Be patient," came the quiet command. "His time will come."

As Higgens hovered nearby, Charles sent him on a mission. A moment later, he returned with the items Charles had ordered. He had a strong male servant in tow. The muscular young man walked to the window and installed the boards as ordered. For Hillery, there was no escape. In her fear, she backed away from Charles. Why had she ever come here alone? She had been so naïve!

He stalked her like an animal, and closing the small distance between them, his thick spatula-like fingers easily laced in the neckline of her gown. The material gave beneath his touch exposing the firm round breasts that rose and fell against the sheerness of her chemise. He noted the discarded petticoats from her earlier action, and snarled still more.

"I will leave nothing to chance!" he thundered. "Be grateful that I am too angry to take you now, for if I did, I would surely kill you!" he swore. "But do not mistake me: you will go nowhere!"

With the window nailed shut, Charles was feeling mighty secure about his prize. His fleshy lips pursed in a low whistle as he circled Hillery with an avid eye for her lithe form. It was with great restraint that he stalked from the room. A muscle ticked in his jaw.

Hillery cowered in her bedroom, nursing a headache and the throb that had begun in her cheek. She was mortified by her fear of Charles. Never before had she been so afraid of any one person. The night passed slowly as in her Mallard bed she listened to the sounds of angry lust that drifted to her down the hall. Closing her weary eyes, she thanked God and Saint Michael that Charles had chosen to ease his passion with Georgia.

At dawn Miss Fisher arrived with a steaming breakfast tray of ham and eggs and hot buttered rolls. The food went down with forced realization of the strength it would offer, but the thick hot café au lait was a balm to her nerves, a sedative to be thankfully sipped while gingerly contemplating her situation.

Though she had not given up all hope of escape, the guard was constant, the door always locked. Yet fate brought luck in the guise of Higgens when he came to retrieve her empty tray. Higgens was considered a trusted member of the staff, but the two had shared a certain friendship when the others weren't about. Now he shifted in the doorway, his liquid eyes engrossed in the floral surface of the Kirman carpet. He did not wish to embarrass the young lady any further.

"Does madam require anything more?" he asked respectfully as though this were any normal circumstance.

Hillery startled, almost laughing at the absurdity of the question.

Though she knew there was precious little Higgens could do, she doubted not his sincerity. "No, thank you," a sigh escaped her. "I think not."

"As you wish, madam…"

"Wait! Just a moment!" she called when he would have gone. "A paper and pen, if…" she hesitated, "you could post a letter for me? Charles has stopped all my mail. There is someone I need to contact," she whispered. "It could be risky," she warned. "I do not wish to put you in jeopardy."

For a moment a light sheen glazed his forehead, but he stiffened his already too stiff back. He walked authoritatively from the room. Securing the required tools would be no problem at all, and as he was stationed on guard by her door, the transaction would pass so smoothly as to fool even the most perceptive onlookers. Yet this house had eyes of its own. Freeing the girl was an impossibility that might well cost him his life. Posting the letters, he reasoned, would be a feat easily attainable.

He was standing confidently at his post when Miss Fisher huffed her way up to the second floor, burdened with a bundle of petticoats and a freshly pressed gown for Hillery. She stopped in puzzled suspicion with a shrewd glance at a sharp corner in his vest pocket. She shrieked in such cold-blooded furor it brought the bile boiling to his throat. Higgens was dumbstruck, paralyzed by the possible consequences that might await him should Miss Fisher deem it necessary to put him on report.

Her thin lips curled in an ugly snarl as she scanned the message meant for the desk of a Counselor of Law. "You fool!" she cried, flying at Hillery. "Do you wish to see him punished? He could lose his skin for this!" she spat, crushing the letter in a balled fist. "I'll show you what happens when you risk the master's wrath," her bony fingers shook as she traced the length of her own disfigured cheek. "Look at it well! *He* laid it open with a long-blade knife…for disobeying orders!"

"Oh! No!" Hillery sobbed, nervously fingering the rose pendant that had been a gift from Rose O'Neal Greenhow. "What have I done?"

"You nearly sentenced a man to hell! A good man!" the dour little woman rounded on her. "Aye, your folly could easily have cost his life."

"Then you won't tell?" came Hillery's response. She was badly shaken.

"Nae, of course not," Helen shuddered angrily while twisting the lid off a jar of rice powder which she intended for her charge's bruised face. "But we 'ad best get you ready an' oot of here before there is any real trouble! The master wishes your company. He is preparing to take you on to The Plantation," she rambled, her highland brogue more heavily pronounced in her fury. One had to wonder just whom Helen Fisher was furious with: herself, her charge, or the master?

Meanwhile, as Charles was preparing to leave with Hillery, Higgens slipped off to town to post a second letter, one that Miss Fisher had not managed to confiscate. He held it steadfastly; a slight grin twitching at the corners of his mouth, for the address on the starched white envelope was none other than the Mr. Stuart Michaels he had heard so much about! Miss Hillery had spoken of him often, always with a certain warmth tingeing her sweet voice. Basically a romantic character, Higgens was pleased with his part in his young friend's escapade, especially since it involved a man – and a probable love affair! So engrossed was he with his thoughts, that it came as a complete shock when he looked up to spy his master's carriage pulling in along the curb.

Before him a small Creole boy whizzed by on bare feet. Thrusting the letter into surprised dirty hands, he tossed the child a coin then hurried him along. His only reply was a wide toothless grin, as jamming the note into his back pocket the boy scampered off down the street still fingering the coin.

"Little beggars," sniffed Higgens as he stooped to dust his boot with a disdainful air, all the while praying Charles had not caught the exchange.

"You're too kind to those kids," the other nodded knowingly, dismissing the episode with little interest. "They're a pack of spoiled brats, the lot of them!"

"Yes, sir," Higgens agreed, "always under foot."

"Yes, well, I am on my way now. As usual while gone, I expect you to keep things in order. Be sure not to disappoint me."

"No, sir, you can rest easy on that account. Have a safe trip, sir!" His eyes twinkled as he turned to face Hillery, "Safe journey, miss." He hid a smile as the carriage rumbled off once again, turning around near the wharf where Hillery saw the little Creole boy scurrying down the walk.

Tripping on some rubbish in his path he took a nasty spill. He jumped rapidly to his feet brushing dust from his ragged breeches. The child never noticed anything amiss, but continued on his way leaving Hillery a wide-eyed witness to the fate of the second letter. With a sinking feeling of despair, she watched as the flurry of white parchment became trampled among the cluttered debris of the city's dockside streets.

# CHAPTER SIX

hey traveled the back roads of Ashford land, passing immense fields of cotton and tidy aisles of cane. A golden sun was setting in a rainbow sky, silhouetting the field hands as they lumbered tiredly to their quarters. Dark faces beaded with sweat turned to watch as the carriage road into view, their sad melodious music melting like hot wax beneath the sinking sun. Yet the strains of anguish still carried on the empty wind, reflecting a lifetime of despair on their ravished features.

Appalled by the near-skeletal condition of many of the people, Hillery blinked at the same betraying moisture she saw mirrored in the dark orbs of a tall, reedy youth. His ebony skin flashed through the fields as he ran to greet her. "Miss Hillery's home! Miss Hillery's home!" the boy called with enthusiasm, coming to a halt a polite distance away where he stood idly shuffling his bare feet in the loosened, black soil. "Lo Miss Hillery," his voice was winded. "I sure is glad you're back!"

"Tom? Is that you?" she cried, clattering from the carriage without due assistance. "Why, you were just a boy when I left!" her eyes caressed the wide, flat features. "Just look at you! My, but you've grown so tall!"

"I was thirteen same as you," Tom grinned, pleased if a little embarrassed by her tender scrutiny.

"How's your mother, Tom? Does her back still trouble her when it rains?"

"Aw, she's just fine," the youth laughed. "She's still a cookin' at the big house and just as fat as ever!"

"Oh, how I've missed her wonderful corn pones! And the way only she can bake custard!"

"Well, I 'spect she'll be makin' plenty of them now that you is home!" he laughed.

"I expect so too," Hillery agreed with a merry shake of her head.

"Ma mignonne agneaue, Ma mignonne agneaue!" an ageless woman wearing a starched white turban dashed across the muddied fields straight into Hillery's willowy arms. "Ah, ma d'or perle, it is too good to see you!" she wept even as she laughed. "Stand back and let me look at you! The drums, they have said you would come! But, it has been such a long time! I have feared for you, ma joli agneaue."

Ma joli agneaue; my pretty lamb, Hillery smiled, cradling the maple syrup cheeks in her trimly tapered hands. "Oh, Isis, I've missed you too," she whispered, thinking how untouched by time her beautiful nurse appeared. Isis was youthful and attractive, maintaining her sleek good looks in spite of the two children she had borne. There were no lines or wrinkles to mar the smooth skin, no sign of hardness to tint the tiger-gold eyes. Shaking her turbaned head, the large golden hoops that adorned her smallish apricot ears jangled a merry tune. "Tom, go tell your mama your missy's back, and be sure to call on Cynie too! She is still at the laundry!"

"Yes 'um," the boy replied, taking flight in the direction of the house as Isis again returned her attention to Hillery.

"You're a woman now, ma agneaue," she approved the slim, graceful figure of her charge. "But what is this," her golden eyes flashed fire as her roughened fingers gently traced the carefully concealed bruise that tinged the other's cheek? "Did *he* do this?"

"No! No, I had a fall," Hillery lied, afraid for Isis should she intervene.

"All right, break it up!" Charles shouted, leaping from the buggy with something of a snarl. "That's about enough prattle for now. You folks get on home and leave my niece to me!"

"Charles, I haven't seen these people in five years," she said with quiet dignity. "I certainly did not mean to offend you."

"But you did," he growled harshly, "they're only darkies!"

"Well," she snapped her face red as she turned and climbed back into the carriage. "They are better than some white folk I know."

As the darkness enclosed the sprawling landscape, they drove in an arc to the front of the house where her memory was captured by the large white expanse shining silver-gray in the moonlight. Built in the 1830's by Henri Couvet Betaud, it stood on the charred ruins of the original foundation established by his forefather in 1753. A burst of pride surged through her as her gaze feasted upon this Grecian creation. Located at the heart of the plantation, it faced the river and boasted a tier of double porticos on all four sides, each supported by a row of massive twenty-foot columns decked with a crown of flower-strewn ionic capitols. Standing before this glimmering moon-struck mansion, she was happy indeed to be home again! She would soon turn Charles around. After all, The Plantation was rightfully hers!

Just then, an old man hobbled from the direction of the barn. For a just a fraction of a second Hillery could have sworn she saw old Rags, her father's favorite hound tagging along behind and then her vision cleared and she realized Rags had died in the same time frame as her father. There were so many deaths, how could she have forgotten? Those were sad times. Now recognizing old Jacob from her girlhood days, Hillery flashed him a bright smile. "How are you, Jacob?" she asked, laying a timid, pink-nailed hand upon his brown arm. "You look tired."

"I is fine, little miss," he beamed at her sympathetic attention. "Now that you is back, I 'spect I is even better than fine!"

Charles grimaced at this exchange and would have spoken but for the slight figure in calico that darted past, nearly unbalancing him where he stood by the porch. "Cynie," Hillery squealed, flying straight into her old friend's arms, who though only two years her junior still looked very much a child. Cyn was of a tiny build with small breasts only beginning to bud and snapping black eyes that were huge in a fragile face, nearly dominating the cream-toned triangle.

Returning the hug, she wiped away tears of joy. "Hello, Miss Hillery," her soft voice whispered. "Welcome home!"

"Miss, is it?" Hillery arched a brow, "Oh, come now Cyn! We've never held to convention, you and me!"

"No," the girl broke into a wide, white smile, shyly ducking her tightly-curled woolen head, "we never did. But I was afraid you would be different," she confided, "that all those years away might have changed you. It's so good to have you back, Hilly," she dimpled, reverting to the other's childhood nickname. "We have a lot of catching up to do!"

After personally greeting all the servants, Hillery and Cynie ventured off to the large, earthy kitchen to chat. Sukie joined them even as she waddled busily about, all the while smiling her wide-toothed smile. The fat cook had always had something special for the pair, and this time proved to be no different. So involved had they become in reminiscing, it was easy not to notice Charles' tight-lipped fury. It wasn't until much later that Hillery felt the sharp edge of his wrath when he crept into her room unseen.

Absorbed in the detailed miniature of her mother which sat on the Empire bureau, she remained unaware of her audience. Her violet shards reflected all too clearly the vivid memories the room invoked. Sighing audibly, she gazed upon the equally curving height of both the head and foot boards of the petite mahogany sleigh bed. Then seeking out the delicate escritoire she had used as a child, she sat down on the accompanying painted and grained side chair and began to braid her hair.

"I see I shall have to teach you your place," Charles boomed from behind, breaking the silence, thus shattering any sense of false security she might have had.

"What are you doing in here?" she gasped.

"I wanted to speak with you," his tone was superior. "There will come a time when you will no longer associate with these 'people'. You will become my pretty puppet, and I will use and manipulate you at will."

"Get out!" she cried, her hand itching to slap his smug face. She could see the blood visibly pounding at his temples. "You would do well to use your head, Charles. The people do not like your presence here. The Plantation does not like your presence here. Have you not felt the threat? Do you not hear the drums?"

He looked confused for a fraction of a second. He was angry and wanted to offer further threat, but at her words, he was shocked to realize he did hear the distant tattoo of drums. Momentarily at a loss, he turned on his heel and stalked out wondering if the others heard them too.

Hillery smiled to herself. She was home, and her people and The Plantation would look after her.

Sleeping late the following morning, Hillery awoke to the hearty aroma of sizzling sweet bacon, cracked-wheat bread, and the richest hot chocolate she had ever tasted! After she had eaten, she dressed in her burgundy riding habit then sauntered to the kitchen in search of Cynie, whom she found perspiring over a hot stove of bubbling jam.

"Oh, hello Hilly!" the girl's pink bow-shaped mouth formed a happy smile. "I'm nearly finished as I promised I would be. Sukie says she can spare me for a while, and I don't have to report to laundry duty until much later in the day."

"You catch a little of it all, don't you?" Hillery's smile was sad. "I suppose that's better than being in the fields like your mother," she tossed her head at her friend's suddenly shuddered expression. "But I would like to know what truly happened. Why is Isis out there when she should be running the house? She always did an excellent job."

"I got to get this jam finished," Cynie snorted, furrowing her smooth brow. "It wouldn't do to let it thicken too much."

"Let Sukie take over. We can go for a ride together like in the old days. Remember?"

"Yeah, I 'member," the young slave muttered, deliberately allowing her language to suffer. Cynie was very well cultured. In spite of the law, she had received an exceptionally fine education. "Things have changed 'round here."

"Not with me," Hillery stood her ground, accepting nothing but honesty.

"I know," the girl sighed in way of apology, "but Master Charles won't allow any of us to ride. He says it's dangerous and could lead to rebellion."

"Oh, nonsense!" frowned Hillery. "He couldn't have me out riding all by myself, now could he? And anyway, there are no neighbors we could depend on for help. Two women traveling alone couldn't get very far along the river. You'll see," Hillery concluded, not nearly as positive as she pretended, "I'll convince him."

It came as a surprise to both girls when Charles gave an affirmative reply. Galloping happily on their way they rode to the back of the plantation, walking their mounts on the sandy banks of the lake bordering Ashford land. As children, they had played there often – drawing pictures in the sand, splashing and swimming in the clear, cool water. It was much cleaner and safer than the treacherously muddy waters of the Mississippi, and although autumn, the day was warm and sunny easily convincing them to do as they had in days long past.

Quickly shucking her thin cotton dress, Cynie stood uninhibited wearing only her thin chemise. She watched as her friend disrobed from a more elaborate toilet. "Lord Hillery, you're beautiful!" she exclaimed when Hillery stood proudly in her chemise and pantaloons upon the dry sand. "You have a figure that would make any man proud."

Hillery blushed a bright cherub pink as she ran and plunged head-long into the water. They swam as mermaids, drifting and gliding. Their lithe bodies arched up and under in a movement as graceful as any cotillion and when they emerged, their faint laughter tinkled, echoing on the breeze like the ploy of an elusive sea nymph. Their sweet-sad melody could easily have lured the man who lay hidden in the brushes.

When the waters had chilled their newly revived flesh, they struck out for shore to dry in the warmth of the midday sun. "Why didn't you write?" Hillery made a pretense of sifting the fine sand through her sun-bronzed fingers. "Your writing is as accomplished as my own."

"Yes, it was kind of your father to grant me an education. But I did write, or at least I tried," Cynie shrugged helplessly. "Master Charles wouldn't allow any correspondence between us. He wanted to shut you out completely," she cocked her fox-like pointed chin, "and if you didn't make it on your own, so much the better for him! He hates you, Hilly, for your claim on The Plantation and all the people that go with it."

"Yes, I gathered that," the eighteen-year-old heiress nodded wisely. "He is a selfish man. Were you not able to receive any of my mail?"

"Only once, and mama managed to secure that," Cynie pulled a wry face. "Things changed a lot when he came."

"Is that why she was sent to the fields?" Hillery was stunned, "Because of me?"

"Only partly," the black eyes blazed like hot coals, "She rebuked him in other ways. He would never leave her alone."

"He antagonized her sexually?"

"He antagonizes everyone sexually," Cynie spat. "And you'd better be warned, Hilly, because he has his eye on you. I've seen the way he looks at you. The man is hardly human."

*The man is hardly human! The man is hardly human!* A voice screamed in her head as she found herself crouching at the foot of the great winding staircase, sweat pouring from her brow. Her palms cool and sticky covered her face. She wiped away all lingering traces of perspiration. Suddenly, a loud crash sounded from behind. Her slippered feet took flight up the stairs. She could feel the prickly sense of terror rising in the wispy hairs along the nape of her neck. The dampness of her skin altered from cool to warm. She touched a hand to her throbbing head and it came away wet with blood. All at once the breath burst in her lungs! She sat up in bed stifling a scream. It was only a nightmare, she shook herself awake. Oh, dear God, it was only a nightmare. But sometimes in Hillery's perception it was difficult to discern the difference between dream and prediction.

# CHAPTER SEVEN

he dreams were often repeated after that night, keeping her hollow-eyed and restless. To busy herself, she spent a great deal of time attending to some of the many household tasks. Charles had taken to working in the fields overseeing the cotton and rarely returned to the house until late at night. Consequently, the regular overseer was able to put most of his time and energy into the cane fields, allowing for an increase in production. Though Matt Henderson was not an easy man to work for, the hands soon came to prefer him over Charles who was extremely quick with the whip.

One day, after sorting the linens and discarded household blankets, Hillery set off to distribute them throughout the quarters. On the footpath between the huts, she was shocked to see Eliza, Cynie's sister, slipping off into the woods with Matt. Eliza was twenty-one and the oldest girl in the quarters to remain single. Her skin was as pale as an iridescent pearl and without close inspection she could easily pass for white. Holding her people in contempt, she dreamed of a life in an all-white world. She chose her men by the pigment of their skin, the better to attain that which she sought. Now near the woodland with Matt, Eliza swayed her generously proportioned hips, tossing her thick main of midnight curls as she cupped each enormous breast in restless anticipation.

With a response as hungry as the given invitation, Matt's hand dove down the front of her dress. He pulled her into a nearby thicket where the two of them thrashed in heated abandon. Eliza had always been a wanton – even at a very early age, but listening to the sounds of their wet lust sent Hillery speedily on her way.

Again that night the nightmares came. The air was thick and warm at the bottom of the stairs where Hillery found herself scaling their escalated curve in a horror of calculated slow motion. Legs frantically climbing, her breath escaped in quick, sharp spurts. She knew a great pain as a spattering of red turned the steps to slime. When she slipped and fell, her cries were muffled, drowned by the roar of an explosion from behind.

Hopping out of bed, she padded down the hall to peer along the curve of the cherry handrail that credited the polished spiral of hardwood. So peaceful was its deception, the house was encased in a restful silence. But Hillery shivered, her arms covered in goose flesh. She knew the peace was feigned. Evil had come to The Plantation.

At the stables that morning, Cynie awaited Hillery with an expression of disapproval creasing her young face. She had seen Eliza exchanging vulgar flirtations with a boy from a neighboring plantation. Upon Hillery's arrival, she rolled her dark eyes heavenward, groaning in disgust. "Ugh!" her scowl was emphatic, "She'd crawl into bed with a snake if it were white! That boy, Abe Clermont, is younger than I am!"

"I know," her friend sighed, wrinkling her aristocratic nose. "He's at least eight years behind her. Why, I know for a fact that he's only fourteen. But come, let's forget about her and go for a ride. We could go to the pond again. It's going to be simply scorching today!"

A tingle of their old excitement accompanied the suggestion. Spurring their mounts on, they raced through the woods. At the edge of the blue-green pool, their bare toes curled in the loose, warm sand. The cool tongue of the waves lapped at their feet. It was intoxicating. It lapped and swirled about their hips until they sank beneath its surface.

It was late by the time they returned to the barn to cool and curry their lathered horses. "Ah, you're such a good darling, my Angel," Hillery crooned as she brushed away the sudsy white foam that flecked the ginger and white coat. Angel snorted then nudged her mistress.

"What's the matter, girl?" the mare was stamping nervously, her velvet ears pricked at a sensitive angle. "What is it?"

"It's me," a familiar voice purred from the doorway, "I want to talk to you."

"What do you want?" both girls startled defensively.

"Just a favor," Charles countered with a sly grin. "Why don't you be a good girl, Cynie, and run along now?"

"I'll stay with my mistress if you don't mind," the girl's black eyes defied him.

"You insolent little bitch, I'll have you whipped for your disobedience."

"No!" Hillery raised a slender arm as if to restrain him, a gesture that would have made little difference had he chosen to pursue his sport. If Hillery had learned one thing about Charles, it was that he was a very cruel man, capable of just about anything. "I'll be all right, Cyn. Go on. Do as he says." For the millionth time Hillery wished Stuart was here with her.

"You're smart," sneered Charles, swatting at the narrow buttocks of the younger girl when she made her reluctant escape. "Now, you keep on being smart, and the two of us will get on just fine," he winked conspiratorially while dabbing at the saliva that drooled from the corners of his slack mouth.

"You're drunk," she said with contempt.

"Maybe I am, maybe I ain't," he chortled gleefully, rubbing the swollen crotch of his too-tight breeches. "But I saw you at the pond, twice now," his slate-gray eyes glazed over. "Your body was meant for a man to..."

"No-o-o!" she shrieked, backing suddenly from him. She brandished a pitchfork left abandoned in the stall. "If you dare touch me, I'll run this thing all the way through you," she hissed.

"You would, wouldn't you?" he eyed her suspiciously. "Given the proper opportunity," he edged toward her, "you would probably derive great pleasure from doing just that! But I," he chuckled, "am too clever...too quick for the likes of you!" Thus saying, he lunged for the fork, sending its lethal prongs deep into the hay.

Already his tone was triumphant, his belt unfastened. When he rushed her, Hillery went down with a gasp. He laughed when she struggled beneath his weight. He held her pinned to the floor of the barn. From somewhere nearby she heard the outraged sound of Angel's whinny. It echoed off the walls. All at once the great beast reared. Her white forelegs streaked the air thundering down upon the earth beside them.

Angel screamed and reared a second, then third time! She had the bearing of a supernatural beast, and Charles staggered to his feet in fear. The sight of her was such as he had never witnessed before. He shook his head at the vision he'd seen, but anger won out as he reached for the abandoned pitchfork. His fingers curled around the handle. His tone was menacing, his expression furious. "That crazy horse tried to kill me," he grated.

"No! Please!" Hillery screamed, grappling for the instrument which Charles held aimed at the animal's heart. The mare's eyes rolled wildly. She parried each new attack, hooves thrashing. Finally the pitchfork fell to the ground. Angel's clear voice carried proudly.

"Whoa, girl, Whoa," Angel calmed at the soothing words from her mistress. Her sides heaved heavily beneath the loving hands that stroked her. "That's enough. It's okay now," she whispered, leading her into her stall with no more than a perfunctory glance in Charles' direction. She did not want him to see how shook up she really was.

So Charles survived the stampede with little more than a few minor bruises. It was only his male pride that was injured. And though Hillery dubbed him fortunate to be alive, going so far as to chide him for his drunken behavior, he knew that she was covering her concern for the welfare of her mare. But Charles held no interest in the horse. In truth, he was beginning to fear the animal, but told himself that the image of the warrior he had seen in the barn was nothing more than an illusion. He spent his time moving quietly about the house, his pensive gaze reflecting the callousness of his mood. The girl was proving to be a bigger problem than he would have believed.

"Are you afraid to be alone with me?" he queried with a smirk of satisfaction. Only a few days had gone by and he watched her every move. His mind was at work on a new plan of action. He would not be put off.

"Why should I be? I am safe here. Though you have proven you have no honor, you would be a fool to try and harm me," her response was stiff. She was well aware of the way his eyes followed her. It made her feel cheap, threatened, but she did not allow her feelings to show.

He snorted in anger, at a loss for words. He did not like losing his edge.

She glanced at him slyly, only partially convinced of her safety.

"You, my pet, must learn some manners," his hand gruffly cupped her chin. "You are still my ward. That is the law. And if you care about that horse of yours..." he let the sentence drop meaningfully.

"I demand to see an attorney," she put on a brave face, blinking back the tears that threatened to spill, "I shall manage it somehow – with, or without, your approval. You cannot hold me prisoner forever."

"No? You think not?" his face became as hard and still as an alabaster mask, "Very well. It shall be arranged. I shall dispatch a letter to New Orleans immediately. You will have your attorney. We are going to settle this dispute between us."

"Good," she swallowed, thinking it must be a trick. "But wait," she held his attention a moment longer. "The attorney..."

"Yes?" he raised a thick brow inquiringly.

"I want someone who will be fair....not someone you pay to lie."

"But of course," his smile was sarcastic. "And whom would you suggest?"

"Mr. Pratt had a partner, a Mr. Saunders, I believe. He should prove unbiased."

"So be it," Charles eyed her smugly leaving her to wonder at what new game he played.

The days and nights passed slowly. Waiting to see the attorney proved a difficult task for Hillery who had written to Stuart many times, only to wonder if any of her letters had gotten through. She didn't think so as there was no return mail. Meanwhile, she spent many hours at a time sewing winter garments for the children here on the plantation. The past five years had left their wardrobes sadly depleted. Although the Louisiana temperatures would not drop severely, many of the people had no shoes nor even a jacket to ward off the chill. Accepting her responsibility, Hillery would not rest until she had completed an entire stack of clothing for each family.

She made the rounds visiting one cabin after another. Some of the workers were still in the fields, and for them she left a basket inside the door, or a stack of items where they would see them upon returning home.

When she came to Isis's cabin, she grinned to herself. For her beloved nurse she brought something special, a feather-soft shawl made of hand-twilled cashmere. The unlatched door seemed an open invitation. She bounced happily inside planning to greet her friend upon her arrival home.

The bed across the room groaned from the weight upon it. Startled, Hillery tossed a glance in its direction. Eliza's curvaceous form hovered slightly over Charles where he lay stretched on his back, his nakedness hidden only by the position Eliza had taken. She drew away, damp and sticky, and wiped her mouth with a grin. Her climax was made all the better by a perverse desire to be caught fornicating upon her mother's cot.

Hillery was appalled. She was ashamed of Eliza for the actions she took, and taken aback by the lack of respect she showed her mother and herself. Hillery spun about ducking out the door.

"Hey, come back!" the over-ripe octoroon giggled. She found the situation extremely hilarious.

"Yeah, come back! Charles joined, "I can handle the two of you! And maybe Eliza here can teach you a few tricks!" His catcalls followed Hillery long after she had disappeared from sight.

Later that day when she met with Cynie for a ride through the quiet of the forest, Hillery considered relating the episode to her. But Cyn shared enough of her sister's disgrace. She needed no further weight to overburden her slim shoulders.

"Can you keep a secret?" she asked of a sudden, making Hillery grateful she had held her peace.

"Of course," Hillery dimpled, enraptured by this new turn of events.

"I have a beau!" Cyn's voice escaped with a fanciful whoosh. "He's one of the new boys…name's David. He works in the cotton fields," her young face flushed, "Comes to see me every eve."

"That's wonderful!" Hillery beamed with delight. "Do you love him?"

"Oh, yes!" the quick smile faded.

"But....?"

"He wants me to run with him, Hilly. He says he can't wait."

"Oh, Cynie, no, he must wait...just for a while! I'm eighteen now. Soon you'll all be free. There's no need to risk the danger of running." While her words were honest, Hillery was thinking of Stuart. He would know what to do, and how to do it. He was very politically active.

"I don't know if he'll listen," Cynie shrugged doubtfully, wrinkling her little snip of a nose. "And I know Master Charles far better than you! He won't be giving up so easily, even if he did promise you that fancy attorney. I'll wager you ten-to-one he's got another ace up his sleeve!"

"Maybe not," Hillery tossed her head, looking back over her shoulder. She was remembering the quiet conversations she and Stuart had shared. There were things she could not tell anyone lest she put him and the family at risk. Unfortunately, she did not possess the knowledge he had. "Will you at least give it a try?" she asked.

"Well, I'm not promising anything...but I'll see what I can do."

"That's all I ask," Hillery concluded, spurring Angel swiftly toward home. "We're being followed again!" she shouted, her hair whipping out behind her like a banner on the wind. "Come on!"

Kicking the flanks of her agreeable mare, poor Cynie lagged sadly in the distance even as Hillery reined in at the barn. She watched as her friend slid nimbly from the saddle, handing the reins to Old Jacob as Charles gained speed, galloping in some ten feet behind.

"You've been spying on us again!" Hillery challenged, her voice filled with fury. "You have no right!"

"No?" the villain smirked, invigorated by the race. "We'll see about that."

"Yes, we certainly will," she fumed. "You'll be packing your bags soon enough!"

"Don't be so damned sure," his voice grated from between clenched teeth. "It just may be the other way around!"

# CHAPTER EIGHT

he next day at last, Mr. Oliver P. Saunders arrived upstream on the Louisiana Starlette, an independent steamer that traveled the river at will. Huffing and puffing, while mopping his forehead with tremendous effort, the rotund little man followed the footpath to the house. He smiled at the beautiful young woman who sat on the porch, blinking his beady blue eyes in sincere admiration as he thrust forth one chubby little hand.

"Miss Ashford, I presume?" his neck-less head bobbed of its own accord. "I am Oliver P. Saunders, Attorney of Law. My, but you are a lovely thing," he sighed, pressing her fingers to his dry lips. "I knew your daddy years ago. Fine man, your daddy!"

"How do you do," Hillery nodded somberly in an attempt to suppress her excitement, "Oh, but where are my manners?" she caught herself up. "I'm sure you must be very tired. Do come in and rest a spell."

"Yes, I am a trifle weary," the little man nodded affably, stepping into the front foyer where his hat and cane were whisked away by a set of practiced hands.

"Tate?" the young woman called as she directed her guest to the gentleman's chair in the parlor across the hall. "Would you please ask Sukie to prepare some refreshment? And see to it that Marta makes up a spare room?"

"Of course, madam," Tate bowed stiffly, his voice and manner oozing hostility. Accustomed as he was to the more superior position of manservant, he made his humiliation at having to follow the orders of a woman known.

In the kitchen, Sukie worked at an amazing speed, carrying the bulk of her wide girth with the ease of several years of practice. Piling an ornate Sheffield salver with a variety of cream-filled cakes, she winced at her young daughter's efforts to brew a fresh pot of tea. "Lord, Chile! Give me that 'fore you burns yourself!" she scolded, snatching the steaming black kettle from similarly black fingers. "Awe...all right, Muffin," she relented at the child's obvious pout of disappointment. "You can put some of them cookies on that plate, but mind you, don't you go a slippin' any back!"

With that said, she returned her attention to her own duties of setting out the crystal decanter alongside an accompaniment of smoked cheeses and fine white bread. Pausing to inspect Muffin's latest efforts, she was pleased to find the cookies neatly stacked. "Good girl, Muffin," Sukie smiled broadly as the girl bounced up and down, grinning ear to ear. "I'm gonna give you this one right off the top! You sure done earned your keep today."

In the French parlor Mr. Oliver P. Saunders was thoroughly enjoying the repast, displaying his appreciation with an act of vivid gusto. Accustomed to the flavorful dishes of New Orleans, he smacked his lips and bobbed his head, reminding Hillery very much of a bespectacled snapping turtle. "My compliments to the cook!" he cried, slurping his pudgy fingers as he reached for another cake. "These are excellent!" he crowed between each sugary mouthful, "Simply excellent!"

Holding her breath out of irritation, Hillery wished for nothing more than to get down to the matter at hand. But as Southern gentility and good manners dictated, she was forced to sit mutely by, nibbling, what for her, was but a tasteless morsel. At length Mr. Saunders set down his empty cup and patted his rounded paunch, the buttons of his waistcoat nearly stretched to the popping! Although it nearly choked her to ask, Hillery could see that his heavy blue eyes were quite lined with fatigue. "Would you care for a nap before we attend to business?"

she drawled in her best delta accent, hoping against hope that he would decline. "I am certain you must be exhausted."

"Um," he cleared his throat, "why, yes! Yes I would," the little man's triple chins wagged. "That would be very welcome, dear lady. I thank you kindly."

"Of course," a smile flickered. She inclined her head. "Marta will show you to your room...Marta?"

"Yes, ma'am...if you will follow me, sir," the small pixie-like girl appeared as if by the wave of a magic wand. Leading him up and beyond the stairs, she paused by the door of a tidy, pleasant room done in shades of gray and green. "Will that be all, sir?" she asked, shyly hiding behind the thick screen of her lashes.

"Hmm? Oh, yes....fine," Oliver P. Saunders mumbled absently, immediately removing his pair of thick glasses as he tested the softness of the bed. Though he had intended to indulge in only a short nap, our Mr. Saunders was apparently the worse for wear, for it was well past dusk when finally he did stir! Recognizing the lateness of the hour, he shrugged as he yawned, rolling over in bed with the assurance that the matter of a five-year-old will could await the break of a new day.

Hillery, however, was entertaining an entirely different opinion. She scowled as she paced the polished floors of her room, wishing wholeheartedly that the silly little man down the hall would awaken before the night were through! Surrendering at last to her own body's needs, she curled up beneath the satin comforter, consoling herself with the promise of a meeting first thing in the morning.

With that resolution firm in mind, she waltzed into the smoke-filled library right after breakfast, finding Mr. Saunders closeted with his coffee and cigars. Charles was nowhere to be seen. "I trust you slept well, sir?" she asked politely, continuing at his nod. "I wish to speak with you, sir. The matter is urgent," she said, coming quickly to the point. "It is my desire to claim my inheritance. That is why you are here," she stated, making eye contact with the little man. "My father, you see, clearly emphasized in his will that I was to inherit at the age of eighteen. I am that now, sir. And with all due respect," she qualified, "my uncle would have me wait until the age of the twenty-one, if indeed at all, sir."

"I see," the queer little man shook his head thoughtfully. "There should be no great problem in that."

"Splendid! I knew I could count on you, sir – being Mr. Pratt's associate and all!"

"Yes, well, everything will be in good order…just as soon as I take a look at the will." One bushy brow, as thick as a caterpillar, gave an instant lurch. "You do have a copy, do you not?"

"Why, no," she articulated lamely. "I was made to understand that Charles kept it here. But surely Mr. Pratt kept a copy at the office? In spite of what my uncle said, I was certain…" she trailed off.

"No, no, I'm afraid not. That was a dreadful summer after all! Many documents of all descriptions were lost in the general dishabille of the city."

"Yes, I understand, but…"

"Good! Because there is nothing else for it! I must have a look at the will before any legal decisions can possibly be made," he nodded as if to punctuate the point.

Into the dense forest Hillery plunged, a pack of fervid emotion roiling her mind. She burst upon the near-harvested fields, shielding her sensitive eyes from the blistering glare of the noonday sun. Charles, whom she sought, was riding among the people in that declining field of white, his whip slashing across the backs of any who dared to slow or stumble.

A young girl of café au lait skin fell to her knees in its path. "Please Master! I's sick!" she screamed, her narrow back striped with blood. "I's sick with chile, sir!"

"Get up!" he bellowed, descending upon her savagely. "Get up! Or I swear I will kill you!" The earth heaved beneath his feet, accompanied by a rumbling sound. The movement was slight, but menacing nonetheless. He wondered if the others felt it. He saw the sea of faces staring at him and shuddered.

"I cain't!" the girl whimpered, clutching her abdomen as the whip redirected its razor-sharp tongue, this time aiming at the slightly rounded curve of her belly. It snapped then crackled, whining through the air. The girl's screams were magnified by a hushed silence. Again the master's arm drew back. Again the coil flicked. She cringed as it whistled its skin-splitting song, her face pressed damp against the earth. Again the earth heaved. This time the winds bellowed through the trees breaking the stillness. Charles broke out in a cold chill. Somewhere in the distance the drums beat a harsh tattoo.

Through a haze of emotion, a tall man of color swooped before her writhing form. His fist seized the lash creating a river of gushing blood which seeped from between his curled fingers. It streamed down the muscle-corded forearm where it splattered aimlessly into the dirt.

"Stand aside!" Charles shouted his face livid with rage. He must not lose face. "I'll have you whipped for your insolence!"

"No, sir!" came the reply. "That girl is with child!"

"No? You dare to correct me?" roared Charles, ripping the coil free. "I shall kill you!" He had forgotten his own fear, he was that angry.

"Stop," Hillery found her voice, giving Angel a harsh kick in the flanks as she charged full speed ahead. "Stop this butchery at once! Is this how you've been treating the people?"

"If this is what it takes," the acidity of his mood was betrayed in the way his gloved hand played at his side. It flinched on the handle of the whip in ill-concealed desire. The unrest of the workers had drawn a tense stillness at the scene before them.

"In the future," her reply was tart, "I will see that you have no such authority!"

"In the future, if you do not care to witness bloodshed, you will stay away from the fields!"

Staring hard at one another, they clashed in a final silent battle of wills, "Mr. Saunders has need of you in the library," she said through stiff lips. "That is what I came to tell you."

"Very well," a muscle twitched in his jaw," I shall let the matter rest for now. See that you do not interfere again."

She fought to remain silent as he turned his mount. She watched him leave before nimbly dismounting and then hurried to the girl on the ground. Hardly more than a child herself, the girl lay panting. Tears coursed down her cheeks and the blood that seeped from between her thighs was not the blood of the whip.

"I can help you move her, miss," the man she had saved from further abuse spoke softly.

"No, there isn't time. We have to save the baby," her face was ashen. "Take my horse," her voice held no hesitation. "Bring back plenty of clean towels and water, and don't forget the medicine chest! Isis keeps it by the door of her cabin. If anyone questions you, tell them you are acting on my orders. That, they will understand."

"Yes, ma'am," the man uttered swinging his powerful body atop the mare. He was grateful that his mistress did not ride sidesaddle. But he had no intention of being seen. That would be suicidal.

"Isis?" Hillery swallowed a sob, her eyes searching for the nurse among the frightened workers.

"I am here, ma d' or perle, you are not alone."

"Is she going to make it?" Hillery used a swath of torn petticoat to sponge the delirious girl.

"I believe so," the quadroon nodded soberly as she reached for the small trunk of herbs the man had hurriedly delivered. They exchanged a look between them, each acknowledging the risk he had taken. Leaning low against the silken neck of the animal, he hugged the ginger and white coat possessively before dropping to the ground.

The day wore on. Sweat trickled down the faces of the women while they labored to save both the injured girl and the infant she carried. With all the skills and wizardry from a lifetime of herbal magic, Isis, with the aid of Hillery's additional set of hands, managed to regulate the exigencies of the girl's loss of breath and blood.

Later when she awoke, the girl found herself in her mother's cabin with the old woman weeping quietly at her side. From somewhere in a far-off corner she could hear the scratchy feet of a field mouse scampering haphazardly across the plank floor. The reassuring sound of her mistress's voice curled around her like a tendril of fragrant smoke, warning her that she must remain still.

"Don't try to move," a pair of cool hands trailed across her fevered flesh. "You have been very ill. You must save your strength."

"But," the girl murmured, "my baby?"

"The baby is safe for the time being," the voice held a hint of tears. "Isis believes the child will live."

Glory moaned, her breathing ragged.

"Hush now, daughter," the old woman crooned. She clenched and unclenched her fists, then turned to Hillery. "He raped my little girl… and now he done this."

"Charles?" Hillery paled, her hands methodically applying the herbal poultice in the deep gashes of the whip. The flesh beneath her hands jumped with each new stroke, eventually falling slack in exhausted slumber. "It's his child?" she gasped. Hillery was aware that some masters and overseers took advantage of the female slaves, but her mind could not entirely wrap itself around the sordid truth. Somehow she thought her people were safe from such behavior. They were, after all, destined for freedom.

"Hilly? How are you?" Cynie opened the door of her mother's cabin to her late-night visitor. "Is Glory all right?"

"She will be, thanks to your mother."

"And to you," Isis chimed, "she wouldn't have stood a chance if not for you." Isis clearly and carefully examined her own charge noting Hillery's state of mind. "You need to get some rest," she pronounced. "I was about to come and relieve you. It has been a long hard day."

"No need. You saw me through the worst of it," Hillery replied. "She is sleeping now. I left some medicine with her mother and instructions on how to use it. Besides," she reasoned, "you had your own patient. How is he?"

"Oh, he'll be all right," Cynie broke into the conversation. "He's a feisty one."

"What do you mean?" wondered Hillery, a look of confusion stealing across her tired features.

"I mean, I'm grateful you were there to intervene on his behalf. Thank you," Cynie's face softened. "That was David. And thanks to you, he is no worse for wear. His hand will mend."

"I am so relieved," Hillery confessed. "In my concern for Glory, I put your David at risk. I'm afraid my judgment was impaired."

"No harm done," Isis stepped in. "David would have acted on his own regardless. You did what you had to."

# CHAPTER NINE

t was early when Hillery returned to the house, the sun just beginning to peep over the colorful ridge of the horizon in a streaking canvas of yellow, pink, and gold, set off by an enhancing dash of cochineal. Weary to the extreme that she feared she could not sleep, she sank into the plush cushions of a feather-filled Queen Anne wing back where she relaxed in the library over a steaming cup of chamomile. As the house was beginning to stir for the events of a new day, she decided to bask in the quiet of her newfound Elysium while awaiting the audience of her house guest to whom she had scribbled an urgent breakfast invitation.

Appearing somewhat disgruntled at having been disturbed so early in the day, Mr. Saunders waved a sausage-like finger in a mild display of temper. "My dear good lady, There was no need to hurry me so! I would have come down presently."

"I apologize, sir, I truly do," she replied sincerely, "but I was up tending the ill all night, I fear, and have not yet closed my eyes. As it has come to my attention that we can no longer procrastinate with the business at hand, Sukie has orders to bring us a tray. You will feel much improved once you have eaten, and I couldn't possibly rest until I have. In the meantime you must bear with me. Were you able last night to dissolve the legal dispute which stands between my uncle and me?"

"Well," he sputtered, deliberately avoiding the issue.

"You did view and discuss the contents of the will, did you not?"

"Well…yes…"

"And?" she prompted.

"There is one problem, you see?" he stammered.

"No, I don't see," she retorted, arching a delicate brow. "Surely sir, it isn't all that bad?"

"Oh, but it is," Charles yawned from the doorway. "It is one sorry problem indeed. And as I can see that our good Mr. Saunders here is having a distressingly difficult time, It looks as though I shall have to enlighten you."

"I am sure you will find that a pleasure," she snapped more crossly than she'd intended.

"Now see here, Miss Ashford!" Mr. Saunders exclaimed, annoyed with her tone of disrespect.

"No, no, it's all right," Charles stepped in. "I am perfectly aware of how my niece's feelings run, which makes it all the harder to tell her…"

"Tell me what?" she tensed.

"That the will was destroyed in a fire years ago. It was quite soon after your father's death, actually, and with all of New Orleans in such a state of turmoil…"

"I should have known you would try something like this," Hillery could not hide her rage.

"Really, young lady!" the usually amiable Mr. Saunders was aggravated. "That was a terrible year! Many such incidents occurred!"

"That's why I sent for you in the first place," Charles purred complacently, "I knew how she would respond." Mr. Saunders did not note the false sincerity in the other's voice.

"I understand completely," the little man nodded animatedly. "This matter will take some professional sorting, I'm afraid. I am curious, Mr. Thompson, as to just what you had in mind?"

"With all due respect to my niece, and in regard to her gender, I had proposed to hold and keep her land until she came of age. Since her father is not here to say otherwise, I had thought to choose the more commonly known age of twenty-one," Charles answered slyly, "or until she married, of course."

"Hmm…sounds reasonable."

"Yes, unfortunately, Miss Ashford's is the only word I have on the contents of the will, yet I wouldn't want to do her daddy wrong. She has this peculiar notion, you know, about freeing all the slaves."

"Free the slaves!" gasped the stout little attorney. "That is a foolish notion! However would you survive," he peered at Hillery over the rims of his oval wire glasses, "without any servants at all?"

"It's what my father wanted. I'd find a way to pay them, or work something out."

"It is, hmm? I see…"

"Well then, what are you going to do about it?" she demanded.

"I can see only one thing to do! I have no authority to grant you your land, miss, under those circumstances. You will simply have to abide by your uncle's wishes until you reach the age of twenty-one, or until you are married."

"You would let him continue after what he did last night? Did you not hear what happened?" she gesticulated wildly.

"Calm yourself! Calm yourself, my dear young lady! What occurred was a shame, of course," he cleared his throat discreetly, "but it is of the utmost importance to snuff out any possible rebellion. Why, you just do not realize!"

"Rebellion," Hillery scoffed. "What kind of lies has he been feeding you, sir? Can you not see for yourself that he beat those people in cold perversity?"

"Hillery, do calm down. You must not over excite yourself," Charles pretended to console her. "You know what the doctor said."

"Yes, please, do calm down. Your uncle warned me about you," the little man sputtered. "You're a headstrong young woman who needs a firm hand, and as far as I am concerned, the matter is closed. There is nothing more I can do."

"Then you did nothing at all!" she seethed. In that moment, a huge burst of sound came from the upper floor of the house. It sounded as if every door on the second level slammed shut in unison. Later, when they climbed the steps, they did indeed find that each and every door was soundly closed. The house itself was angry.

Early the next morning, Hillery and Cynie set off for a walk in the woods to gather herbs for Isis. As Mr. Saunders had left a short time before, the girls were candidly discussing the previous night's defeat when they stumbled upon a couple in the bushes. A series of spasms wracked Cynie's small frame. The couple was Eliza and Charles.

"How could you?" Cynie accused. "You're depraved!"

"Depraved, am I?" the octoroon licked her carnal lips quite deliberately as she lowered her head, "I'll show you depraved!"

Cynie turned and bolted in the opposite direction. After following her through the woods, Hillery's demand was soft when they knelt on the banks of a clear sparkling brook. "There's more to it, isn't there – than just Eliza with the master?"

"Yes," the other splashed ice cold water on her face, filling her mouth and soaking the curly locks that framed her fox-like features. "It began when your mother and father first came here. Mama says that Charles was always chasing after Mariette. It made no difference that she was his step-sister, or that she was a married lady. He lusted after her," the girl sighed, "yet mama always stayed near, protecting her with a vengeance."

"Then one night in anger and spite, he decided that if he couldn't have your mother, he'd take her maid instead. That was far safer, he reasoned, and legal." Cynie wiped her tear-stained face with trembling hands. "Your mother never knew what happened; it would have hurt her so. Mama covered the bruises, later blaming some no good worker from a neighboring plantation for the child. There weren't many questions."

"Are you saying," Hillery cringed in disgust, for the first time comparing Eliza's slate gray eyes with Charles' own, "that Charles is Eliza's father?"

"Yes, and she's known all along," came the horrified whisper. "She has always known!"

In Washington, Stuart was worried. He hadn't heard a thing from Hillery, not a single response to any of his letters. He had a variation of the same dream every night. In it Hillery was always lost, hurt, or in danger. But he didn't know what kind of danger, or even for sure where she was. He was not in a position to be able to leave anytime soon, nor did he have anyone to turn to. He couldn't afford to draw any unwanted attention to his home and family. At the same time he could not abandon those he was helping. They not only depended on him for food and shelter, their very lives depended on him getting them safely to their next destination. There was no one to replace him. He must finish what he had started before making other plans. Yet he could find no peace. His dreams were prophetic, and these in particular, were extremely dire.

After Hillery had cooled off, she took some time to think. If Charles had led Mr. Saunders to believe that any of her people were planning a rebellion, he had pretty well sealed their fates. David would definitely run. Some of the others might as well. She had to find a way to return to New Orleans in order to get word to Stuart. Only then could she be free of Charles, and ultimately save her people, as well. She decided to play coy, as though she had given up all hope. Charles would believe that because he believed all women to be weak.

And so it was that Hillery chose a docile act. She spent most of her time sewing for the children, occasionally helping Sukie in the kitchen. But she stayed clear of the cabins, only visiting with Isis and Cynie briefly. She did not interact with David at all. That would draw Charles' unwanted attention as well as his suspicions. After all, she had not visited with David prior to that day in the fields.

Time went on and Hillery kept up the pretense of defeat, only mentioning a trip to the city occasionally, and only then in a manner of suggestion. She said it would be pleasant to have a change of scenery. She never mentioned any particular event, or any desire to be away from The Plantation, other than just a change of scenery. She could almost see the wheels of his brain turning, as if he were musing as to whether this would make her more compliant.

As she calmly drifted through the days, she became aware of a subtle change in the people around her. It frightened her. If the others believed her act as Charles seemed to, it could be dangerous. She had a discreet conversation with Isis on the subject, suggesting she speak for her. Isis must give them hope. She must warn them to have faith in her. They must wait for changes to come.

It seemed a good plan, and helped for a short while. Then one day Isis quietly whispered that David was making plans. Hillery worried she was out of time. She knew that if he ran, Cynie would go with him. Hillery was aware of the love they shared, and she knew that if anyone could keep Cyn safe, it was David. David knew the woodlands and the swamps. He was well educated on living off the land. He knew to follow the North Star by night. He also knew that the soft moss always grew on the north side of the trees. There was no question he could find his way, no way he would get them lost. But it was still a huge risk.

The following morning she discovered her fear had become their reality. Because she could not alter the facts she assisted Sukie in the kitchen, and with the aid of a few others, a small bundle of food and provisions were removed from the house. But Hillery did not sleep that night. She lay awake in dread. When Charles learned David was gone he would be enraged. A pall was cast over The Plantation. It was as if everyone moved in slow motion, afraid to speak or think or act.

And then it happened. Word spread. In less than twenty-four hours Charles returned home. He was furious. He had hired bounty hunters. A search had been organized. Charles seethed with something far worse than anyone had imagined. And what fueled the fire most was that Cynie was gone as well.

# CHAPTER TEN

ost in the race for time, the runaways foraged the hard barren ground. Grasping a handful of roots, David laid them in Cynie's lap. "Chew on these," he said, sitting cross-legged beside her. "They will help sustain your strength. We'll have something more substantial later."

"Couldn't we sleep for a couple of hours?" she pleaded. "It's been two nights now. I'm not sure how much longer I can keep up."

"You'll have to," he spoke curtly, steeling himself against the pathetic picture she made, her frail little body leaning against the trunk of an elm. "The dogs could still pick up our scent," he explained more patiently. "Chances are, they're not far behind."

"All right," she sighed determinedly. "Let's go."

"That's my girl," he gave her a hand up. "You know," he teased, a grin spreading across his tired features, "for such a puny little thing, I think you're gonna make it!" David was a quick learner in anything he set out to do. He spoke almost as well as Cynie, falling back only occasionally on old speech habits.

"Of course I'm going to make it," she tossed at him. "You didn't think I'd let you go alone, did you?"

"No way," he laughed, slowing a bit to match his long stride to her smaller one. They had already started to run. They ran at an even pace covering miles of dense pine forest before reaching swampland, where the moss-draped, feather-like foliage of the cypress emerged from cloudy waters on out-flaring bases. Soon the beauty of the place faded.

Forks of salt water flicked greedily out destroying the loveliness that once prevailed, leaving nothing but a haunting effect in the towering valley of dead trees. There was an echo of voodoo rites and ritual in the air. Cynie felt goose flesh rise on her arms.

"Can't we go another way?" Cynie asked, trembling a little. "I don't like the idea of a ghost forest."

"Awe, come on! You don't believe all that stuff that your mama told you, do you?"

"Mama doesn't lie," she said adamantly. "Look! What's that in the water?" she cried. A multitude of large ripples appeared accompanied by a loud swishing sound. Just then a pointed nose popped out exposing two bright beady eyes. "Oh! It's only a muskrat!" Cyn wailed in relief, scowling at David's unrestrained laughter. "It could have been an alligator," she added indignantly.

"Or a ghost?" he teased, chuckling still. "Seriously, babe, alligators seldom visit salt water. And Ah promise t' protect you from any ghost and ghouls!"

"My, but you are brave," she giggled, squealing playfully when he would have drawn her into his arms. "Sir, what are your intentions?" she mocked at the slight pressure of his lips touching hers.

"My intentions are nothing but honorable, I assure you," he smiled, pulling her down with him onto a bed of moss. For the first time in days she felt at peace with David's strong fingers gently stroking her hair. "Sleep a while, my love," he whispered to her. "We'll be together soon... and free of our chains."

There was no reply. He glanced at the small oval of her face. Her lips were slightly parted, her large eyes softly closed. A fringe of sooty lashes fanned her creamy cheeks as she sighed in her sleep, content in his arms.

"Aww, my girl, what have I done? You should be home with your mama, not running scared in the woods. I'm sorry, my love, but I promise you this: I'll see you to safety and treat you like a queen."

A startling crash of dead timber sounded in the distance. They had been asleep less than an hour, but it seemed like only seconds when the growling of hungry dogs awakened them. David grabbed Cynie's wrist pulling her with him into the swamps unmindful of any other inhabitants or the branches that tore at their skin and clothing.

Suddenly there was a fierce throaty growl from behind. Without further warning, a huge canine beast attacked knocking David to the ground. Thirsting for the tangy taste of blood, it lunged for his throat. He locked his fists together, hammering at the head of the great beast. The dog lay temporarily stunned, yet before David could move, another joined the fray. Its sharp white teeth sank into his muscular forearms gouging out great hunks of skin. With the smell of warm blood in its nostrils, the first of the two attackers rejoined the battle.

Cynie's screams pierced the still forest followed by the sharp crack of rifle fire. "Zanzibar! Sebastian! Heel!" a man shouted. The dogs immediately sat back on their haunches gnashing their teeth as they awaited further command. From out of the woods came three bounty hunters. "Good boy, good boy," one of them said.

"Help him! Please!" Cyn cried, horrified by the sight of David's mutilated flesh.

"Ain't no use. He ain't gonna die...not yet anyways," the man shrugged. "Tie him up, Tom."

"Yes siree!" Tom chirped. "We'll get us a mighty fine re-ward for this 'un!" he pulled the ropes taut on the unconscious form wrapping a dirty kerchief around both damaged limbs in order to staunch the flow of blood. "What about her, Jack?" he asked while he worked, giving a sideways glance at the man who was obviously in charge. He looked Cynie slowly up and down.

"I'll tend to her," Jack tilted a whiskey bottle to his lips wiping his mouth with the back of his hand. "You two just worry about getting him over a horse. One of you will have to double up. She's goin' with me."

"Horny bastard ain't you?" the third man chortled around the wad of tobacco in his mouth.

"I reckon we'll all get a piece once we set up camp," Jack grinned. "Let's move while it's still light. I don't wanna camp in these swamps. It's damned eerie."

"Yep," the others chorused. "It sure is!"

They camped a few miles back near a clear running spring. They would have liked to have camped further afield. As the couple hadn't dared light a fire themselves, the beans and strong coffee tasted like a feast. Cyn fed David, spooning the fare between parted lips. Even though he was badly injured, Jack wouldn't hear of untying him. "The man's desperate, after all, and desperate men take desperate measures," he said. When David was finished, Cynie gratefully ate her own meal, trying to ignore the eyes of the watchful men. They hadn't shared a woman in a long time. It showed in the disgusting way they looked at her.

When she had finished eating, prolonging each bite as long as possible, Jack stood quietly and walked over to her. Unbuckling his belt, he grinned almost sheepishly at the tears that streaked her soiled face; the other men sat leering by the campfire. She could feel the anticipation in their pent up bodies just as she could smell her own fear in the air. Jack reached out, ripping her dress from neck to waist, instilling in her again the fear of the hunted. David strained murderously against the ropes that bound him while Jack cupped her small breasts in large calloused palms. He groaned as he did so, rubbing his body against hers while attempting to force a kiss. The winds moaned in the trees. David intoned unintelligible words, an intense look on his face. He was fueled by something Jack did not understand. The winds moaned more loudly. The trees visibly swayed. And in the air, Jack and the others would later swear they had heard distant voices softly chanting.

"What are you doin'?" he demanded of David who completely ignored him. His frightened eyes raked over Cynie whose face was suddenly aglow. She looked at him with triumph in those large curious eyes of hers. He shoved her aside, mumbled to the others to tie her up, too. They grumbled but did as they were bid. They were afraid.

Hillery was returning from the barn when she spied riders in the distance. Paling visibly upon recognition of the two bound figures, she hurried to meet them. "How dare you? What have you done?"

"Now see here, miss, we just done our job," replied the man in the lead, "Mr. Thompson requested the capture of these two, and for a goodly sum at that. Now all we want is to collect our pay and return the merchandise."

"You had no right to abuse them!"

"Don't see that it matters much," he shrugged. "They'll be dead soon anyhow."

"What? No, even Charles wouldn't..." her voice trailed off as her purple eyes grew round. The taste of fear was bitter in her mouth.

"Aw, now you're beginning to see," the man chuckled.

"Damn you," she whispered.

At that, Jack's own temper flared. Jerking her chin within inches of his own, he grated, "Now you listen here! You'd best be mindin' your own business before I forget you're a lady, if'n you are one. After all, how do I know whose blood flows in your veins?"

"What are you implying?" she gasped.

"Well, you two have the same likeness of face," he smirked, hitching his chin toward Cynie, "same features, same pointed chin. Well, hell! Even your skin is near enough the same shade," he let the sentence hang.

Thoroughly shocked, she sucked in her breath. It was as if a missing piece of the puzzle just fell into place. She took a step away from him, one hand covering her heart.

His lips twitched slightly. "Your daddy must have liked the cabin wenches," he said crudely.

Her palm swung out smacking the side of his face with all the energy she could muster. Before Jack could respond, Charles approached with a shake of his head. "Bad habit of hers," he allowed with all calm. "She's a little spit fire."

"Somebody needs to teach her a lesson," Jack swore softly, touching a hand to his reddened cheek.

Charles only shrugged, dismissing Hillery without further notice. "I believe I'm the man you came to see," he said, not offering his hand. "I'm Mr. Thompson and these are my people. I expect you're after your reward?"

"That's right."

"Don't see any problem there," he looked up, shaking his head at Hillery's attempts to aid the returned fugitives. "That's a waste of time," he mumbled.

In her cabin Isis bent busily over David's inert form, cleansing his pitifully mangled arms with an alcohol solution. Putrefaction was setting in fast, resulting in the need to remove more flesh. Cutting away the rotting substance she doused his arms again with alcohol, glad he could no longer feel her brutal fingers. She had treated many serious wounds in her time, but for the first time doubted her own abilities. Praying that she might save the limbs, she wrapped them carefully in clean, soft bandages after first applying a thick plaster of herbs.

On the far side of the room, Hillery sought to calm Cynie, "He'll be all right, you'll see," she crooned. "Your mother knows what she's doing." She set about treating the numerous cuts and abrasions. When finished, she pressed a kiss to Cyn's cheek. "Sister, my beloved sister," she said in awe, "I have loved you all my life, yet it took a complete stranger to point it out to me. Why did you never tell me?"

Cynie stilled momentarily, her big eyes huge in her small face. "We thought it best to spare you," she said sorrowfully. "There has been too much hurt over the years."

Behind them, Isis silently approached. "It is true," she quietly acknowledged. "Cynie loves you, child, just as she loved your father. He was kind to her...and he would have acknowledged her too! But we couldn't have done that to him. He would have paid dearly, you understand?"

Hillery nodded in assent even as tears streamed down her face.

"Your daddy was a good man," Isis intoned. "He just needed someone after your mama died, that's all."

"I know. I understand," Hillery laced her fingers together. "He must have cared for you very much. I am grateful you were there when he needed you," she added as she looked directly into Isis' shining eyes. "You loved him, didn't you?" The question required no answer. "Yes, I think you loved him very much. And he loved you as well." The stiffness seemed to leave Hillery's spine as if in just that second she matured far beyond her years.

Knowing they were in no condition to escape, Charles fully intended his prisoners to squirm in those final moments of justice. Standing tall with arms akimbo, he condemned David to a blazing hell – death by fire, to be burned at dawn. Cynie was sentenced to be sold to a certain shady bordello when he no longer required her services himself. He had long since been looking her over, and he had decided to sample her before removing her from the property.

Strapped to a beam in the center of a pile of timber, David watched in helpless torment as Cynie was led mutely away. Except for the trembling of her lower lip, there was no indication of the panic she felt. She held David's gaze bravely, her large brown eyes were unblinking. She gave no opposition. Silently she prayed to her gods and in return she became aware of the shifting of the winds. Hillery stood erect, never removing her gaze from her beloved half-sister. She, too, prayed silently. Soon, all the people of The Plantation stood perfectly erect. They each in turn appeared to focus their gazes on something only they could see. The winds picked up carrying an odd vibration. Those in the house spoke in quiet whispers. The house itself seemed to hold its breath. Charles became aware of the shifting winds, the eerie sounds of the night. Suddenly, everyone in unison turned their gazes upon him, even those who were terrified only moments before. Each and every one of them held his stare. A single howl erupted in the night, joined by another and another after that. Charles felt the hairs on the back of his neck rise. He felt chill bumps sweep down his spine. Casting his eyes toward the crowd, his apprehension grew. His gaze swung to Cynie whom he was about to pillage and he felt his manhood shrivel. Fear swept through him. He loosed his grip on Cynie whose eyes were bright, then flung her to the ground. She made no sound, only stared at him until he stumbled away. In his rush to escape the sudden madness, he forgot to secure her bonds. Charles did not look back.

In the North Stuart was growing more and more concerned for Hillery's safety. Once he got this final group of families to the next station, he would return home and pack. It was past time for him to travel south, to see for himself what was going on. He was nearly at the end of the journey where he would deposit the people into the capable hands of a conductor known only as Moses. He had worked with this particular member of the Railroad before and knew very little about her except that she was both kind and reliable. It was best that way, safer. The less one knew about the other, the less one had to fear. No one could give you away if they knew nothing of you.

The infants always worried him most. It was difficult enough to railroad adults and children. But babies! Babies were scary. Babies cried, sometimes could not be stilled. They had been fortunate thus far this trip. He would be grateful to complete this run.

Now at the last leg of the journey, everyone hunkered down in both fear and hope. He had tried to instill confidence without allowing any frivolity, just as he had attempted to feed and nourish them to the best of his ability. Still, they were a wet, cold, shivering lot forced to follow rivers in sake of woodland trails. It was far safer that way.

One of the babies fussed a bit; his mama stilled him quickly. He was impressed with her skill, her intuition. It was as though the infant understood her quiet crooning. His lips puckered, but his eyes closed as he drifted back to sleep. Up ahead, he spied a slight rustling in the brush. Everyone ceased to breathe. Then he let out a breath as he recognized the lumbering gait of the approaching female. She was both stealthy and smart. Some, who did not know her, thought she was addled in the mind, but he knew that was not the case. He had the quiet suspicion that she, herself, had been a slave who had found her way to freedom. She always approached by way of Canada before meeting a new group of desperate people. Now, with one index finger to her lips, she beckoned them. He watched in mute awareness as she turned and led the way.

# CHAPTER ELEVEN

ong after midnight, with Charles in a drunken stupor, Hillery crept stealthily across the yard. She met her friends as planned earlier that night. Seeing no sign of the overseer who had disappeared along with Charles, she boldly drew a hunting knife from her coat, handing it to David. "A precaution only," she warned. "Run until you come to the first spring. Wait for me there. I'll be riding. No...Shh," she signaled silence. "We cannot afford to waste time. Just because Charles is a coward, we can't assume he won't send others after you. They might kill you on sight. Just go! And don't try to cover your tracks; I want them to be found!"

The couple fled into the woods. "Why isn't she coming?" Cynie worried, crouched on the bank of the first inlet.

"She'll be here," David said firmly.

"What is she planning? How can she hide us? How can she possibly get us safely away?"

"The way I see it," David said thoughtfully, "she's trying to place a false trail. Throw off the dogs. Miss Hillery is a smart lady. She won't let us down."

"There she is! Upstream!" Cynie stepped carefully into the water. She moved without sound, waving her hands in Hillery's direction.

"Thank God you made it," Hillery breathed, slipping from the ginger and white back of her mare, Angel. "Now, run over to the other side of the water, Cyn. That's it... there, a little farther. Leave a shred of your dress on a bush or tree. Good. Now come back the same way and mount Angel. You, too, David, you're both exhausted. I can walk. It's not far. We'll have to go back the same way we came."

"Go back? I don't understand," Cynie looked frightened.

"Remember when we were children," Hillery sought to calm her friend, "and I told you I had discovered a secret room? It was just before I left on that last trip to the city with papa."

"Secret room," Cynie scoffed incredulously. "Oh, but it was make-believe. You were playing at some new game!"

"No. No game. It was part of a wine cellar really, built in the old part of the house. Mama's grandfather must have feared an insurrection at one time. I don't know. Come on, we'll talk once we are safely inside," Hillery instructed, leading Angel toward home.

Entering the basement from an outside door, the trio slipped soundlessly past the kitchen to the wine cellar beyond. Though small it proved quite efficient with all four walls lined in shelving from floor to ceiling, even above and around the door. Moving to the far right corner, Hillery pressed hard against what appeared to be an ordinary shelf, but was in fact the latch of an ingeniously constructed panel. Once inside, the room was comparable to the wine cellar in space – a rectangle of perhaps eight by ten feet. There were no openings with the exception of a few cleverly installed ventilation slits, protected on the other side by a natural overhang.

"It all happened so fast," Hillery explained in hushed tones. "Papa's death, my being sent away, I never had the opportunity to show you," her voice trailed off. "I've brought everything you'll need," she continued, pointing to a large bundle of supplies in one corner. "You mustn't leave this room for anything," she warned. "I will tend to your needs – your food, water, even your chamber pot. You do understand? You cannot risk stepping outside this door, not even for a second."

The impact of their confinement startled them at first. But after a moment Cyn shook her head, sinking to the floor in acceptance of the situation. "What about mama?" she wondered aloud. "Does she know where we are?"

"No. Isis will be the first suspect. We need to protect her by keeping her innocent of your whereabouts."

"Then what?" she muttered. "How long do we stay here?"

"A week... maybe two," Hillery sighed. "Look, I know it will be cramped and uncomfortable, but we can't make a move until the search dies down."

"She's right," David said. "They will eventually conclude we got away. That's the best protection we can get."

"Okay," Cyn agreed as they each looked at the other. They were in this thing together, after all.

In New Orleans Higgens was concerned for his young friend. He knew that she had not received any mail at the townhouse, just as he was aware there had been no change in her situation at The Plantation. Word spread in these parts. Therefore, he must assume that Hillery had been unsuccessful in posting her letters. And Charles had thwarted her every attempt by snaring any missives that arrived in her name. It was past time for Higgens to take action.

Standing straight as befit his position, Higgens climbed the stairs to the servants' quarters entering his own small chamber. He took a seat at a rickety pine table and scrawled a letter to the address in Washington that Hillery had given him. He only hoped he had not waited too long. Although his penmanship was not as accomplished as his speech, he managed to portray the situation adequately enough with an earnest request for immediate aid.

Charles' hatred and jealousy of the young mistress knew no bounds. His intense longing for The Plantation held roots back as far as his youth when his mother, Sara, first planned to marry Mr. Henri Couvent Betaud. However Henri much preferred his adored daughter, Mariette, who completely overshadowed Charles as possible heir. Devon Ashford married Mariette the same day that Henri took Sara as wife – with the stipulation that through this union, The Plantation would become Ashford land upon Henri's death.

Charles' ire knew no relief until one stormy night when Henri was needed at a neighboring plantation. The weather was extreme, and Charles had overheard him ordering Sara to remain at home. Little did he know as the carriage rolled away that she had coyly arranged to accompany her husband, arguing that it was her duty as a proper Southern lady.

When the axletree of the front wheels snapped, it appeared an accident to all. The horses bolted, screaming in fright, while the carriage plummeted into the river resulting in the deaths of both Sara and Henri. Charles had mistakenly destroyed his own mother! Charles would never admit it to another human being, but he tasted true fear when he discovered what he had done. He had not needed to be told about the accident, for it was as if something dark and ugly reached up and took hold of him, letting the disaster sink in of its own accord. In that instant, Charles had become something less than human, and he knew beyond a shadow of doubt that he was doomed to hell when the time of reckoning came. As he did not see a way around this, he chose to pretend his fear did not exist.

With Devon's death in 1853, Charles returned to claim the land he now felt he deserved. He would not admit his fear even to himself. He chose to swallow it in his hatred of all else. Hillery's presence in the scheme of things incensed him, until looking upon her that first night in New Orleans when he promptly decided to claim both the land, and the lady! Stuart Michaels – a nemesis he had discovered by reading Hillery's mail – did not fit into his plans at all.

Two weeks passed. The night was dark as the couple in the tiny room behind the wine cellar waited in tense silence for Hillery to return. Had it been a lighter time, they might have laughed at each other's costumes. Instead their faces were solemn, their stomachs knotted in apprehension. While they nervously paced their cramped quarters, Hillery edged her way around the east pasture taking care to leave the gate slightly ajar. She made certain that Angel was safely locked in the other pasture. Then she led two choice mounts into the woods tying them out of sight before erasing her tracks. When she finally returned to the wine cellar and released the pair, she gave them each a warm hug. Provisions had already been attended. They were anxious to be on their way.

"Go with God," Hillery breathed in farewell.

"Thank you, my dear, dear sister," Cynie's voice held a husky quality as they clasped hands one last time. They embraced briefly. It was a moment of raw emotion.

Hillery drew back, sadly brushing away the tears that glistened on Cyn's pale cheeks. "Don't forget your voices must suit your roles if you are questioned," she advised. She was wishing she could see them to safety herself. She sighed into the darkness as they rode out of sight, the muffled sound of their horses echoing in her ears.

No one would suspect, nor challenge, the very young planter's son traveling with his respectable manservant in attendance. Riding steadily on the deserted back roads by night, they would fade into the shadows by day finding sleep where they could. Their food supply was generous, their arms heavy, yet discreet. Cynie's woolly hair had been cropped short beneath the constant company of her panama slouch hat. Her small breasts were tightly bound beneath the too large shirt and jacket. Her narrow feet were encased in a pair of men's riding boots which were stuffed with cloth at the toe to give them extra length. Hillery had even thought to contribute a packet of rice powder to further pale the cream-toned complexion. From a distance, Cynie cut a very fine boyish figure!

While Cynie and David were making their way north, Stuart was boarding the B and O Depot located on the corner of New Jersey Avenue and C Street. When the letter from Higgens arrived at the home of the Michaels' family, the entire clan gathered in anticipation certain that the news was of Hillery.

"Go on, open it!" Gran insisted.

Stuart quickly tore at the seal. Rapidly scanning the contents, he handed the parchment to his mother then brusquely excused himself. In less than an hour he was sitting in a private car listening to the shrill singing of the steel rails beneath him. Lines of worry creased his high forehead.

# CHAPTER TWELVE

harles was so furious that David and Cynie made good their escape that he decided a trip to the city was now necessary. He intended to send out an extensive search party, and he also intended to force Hillery into marriage. If she did not agree to his terms, he would find a means to eliminate her. To this end, he made arrangements to leave on the morning packet. Higgens was there to meet them at the wharf. He gave a stiff bow before assisting Hillery into the carriage, but his eyes showed his pleasure at seeing her again. "Good afternoon, miss," he gave a nod.

Hillery caught the gleam in her friend's eyes and felt a surge of hope. "Good day, Higgens," she returned softly. They dined that evening on Charles' favorite dish – filet de truite amandine. Charles seemed preoccupied so Hillery enjoyed a quiet meal then escaped to her room where she soaked in a warm hip bath lathering generously with a cake of lavender soap. She held the sudsy bar close breathing in its delicate scent before rinsing a final time. When she had completed her toilet she relaxed with a book for a peaceful night. As before in the city, Hillery felt off kilter with the distant echo of voodoo drums resounding in her head. Her fears were closing in on her! Before retiring, Higgens had managed a private word with her, quietly informing her that she would no longer be disturbed by Georgia's company. The woman had been dismissed, he said. Hillery was wise enough to leave well enough alone.

With Charles away on business, the following days were peaceful.

Even Helen Fisher was behaving kindly. Yet Hillery sensed something was afoot. Charles had been acting strange of late. It was perplexing. In an effort to restore her peace of mind, she had spent the morning in the gardens. She looked radiant in a moss green gown with long puffed sleeves gathered with ribbons at the wrists and a matching pair of kid slippers. Her honeyed hair was swept high on her head and fell in long curls down her back with loose tendrils escaping to frame her face. Higgens burst through the garden gate wearing a smile reminiscent to the Cheshire cat. "Excuse me, miss, you have a visitor," he beamed, but he needn't have said a word for already another figure had stepped behind him through the gate. Hillery's heart nearly failed at the sight of the dear, familiar face and tall lean form. "Stuart," she breathed rising slowly from her stance, suddenly rushing into his arms. He crushed her to him raining kisses over her hair, brow, and lids before coming to rest on her beautifully full lips. "Oh, Stuart, thank God you are here! But we must hurry!" she began to panic, "Charles…!"

"I have taken care of Charles," Stuart's demeanor had instantly changed, and she saw without a shadow of a doubt that he had things in hand. "He will bother you no further. I will brook no interference from the likes of him! And I have already spoken to your attorney and set things to rights there. I also have a special marriage license so that we might wed without delay. Charles would be a fool to take me on. He has no leg to stand on."

Earlier that day Charles had stood before Mr. Saunders, a sneer in his voice. He was so angry a muscle ticked at the corner of his mouth. Mr. Saunders' pale complexion had paled even further, but he was no fool. He had called ahead for back up before setting this meeting into motion. There was comfort to be taken in the attendance of the official law man he had attained. Comfort too, in the audience of one, Stuart Michaels. Mr. Michaels was no fop! He was by far more frightening than Charles ever could be, and Oliver P. Saunders was grateful to have him on his side!

Charles, himself, had been a fool to presume Mr. Michaels easy prey due to his profession. He saw that now in the scornful mask of the stranger. The love letters meant for his niece had been deceiving, as had Charles' own opinion of the other man's profession. Surely a man who made his living by dabbling in paint could be no great threat? Or so he had thought. He had always believed that a womanly occupation. Now he stood corrected. As the two men locked gazes Charles had known his mistake. He had shuffled uncertainly. To retreat at this point would brand him a coward, to stay – a fool! Yet retreat he must for already he read death in the eyes of his opponent, and opponent he was!

"It may be you have won this time," he had snarled in a pretense of bravado, "yet I assure you we shall meet again."

"A daring comment for such an idle threat," Stuart had flung, his gaze hooded, "for if I should ever find you near my wife again," here he had clearly emphasized the word *wife* – "I've no doubt you would be hard put to escape with your life." This last had been spoken with a deadly calm that truly filled Charles with fear.

Charles had made a low growling sound deep in his throat, but his pallor had gone from mottled red to white as he had beaten a quick retreat.

Now in the garden as Stuart took in the abject fear in Hillery's eyes, he recalled every word that was spoken between Charles and himself. And because he now suspected that she had been physically harmed by this man, he knew an anger so raw and intense that if Charles ever so much as looked her way again, he knew without a doubt he would kill him and gladly. It troubled him deeply to see that fear in her eyes and he knew he would spend a lifetime protecting her.

The Michaels' women arrived on the morning of October first. The wedding was to take place on the third. Gran was as excited as a child. She had made the long journey without complaint, and brought along a passel of gifts, many of which had been made by her own hand. Among these were various jars of jams and preserves to stock the kitchens. Each included its own unique recipe. Added to these were several bottles of Stuart's favorite wines from the family cellars as she knew the couple would spend time at each location and didn't want her grandson to go without. She had for Hillery a dainty gift set of scented soaps, perfumes and candles all made from the labors of Rachael,

Natalie and herself. As Hillery opened each in turn she sighed, "Oh, everything is wonderful! Thank you all so very much!"

"You are quite welcome," it was Rachael's warm voice that answered with both Natalie and Gran nodding along.

Stuart gave a knowing look, "Your gifts are much appreciated, ladies, as is your company. We will make a point of visiting soon." He had a slightly haunted look about him that only Hillery noted. She would inquire about this later when they were alone.

"We will have plenty of time to visit," Hillery echoed. "It will be such fun." She sensed a bit of what Stuart had seen and was a trifle shaken. Gran was special to each of them, and from what Hillery had just glimpsed, her health was in peril.

Gran's head swiveled in the couple's direction. "Don't over analyze," she cautioned quietly, "I will be fine." Natalie looked truly taken aback while Rachael nodded thoughtfully. She had obviously been aware of some health issue, but had known not to dwell on it. "I am a tough old bird," Gran assured them, her manner bold. It was clear she would brook no argument.

"Well said," Stuart nodded knowingly. He was looking at his grandmother in a very different manner. Hillery literally witnessed a transformation in the old girl right before her eyes! Whatever ailed Gran, she was fully aware of, and apparently had it in hand.

"There is one more gift, and it happens to be a very special one," Rachael declared, shifting the subject back to safer ground. She did not want to antagonize Gran. She was fully aware that when Gran was dealing with controversy, it was best to allow her to do just that.

"Yes," Natalie blurted excitedly, "we hope you do not mind that we took the liberty?"

"We do hope we did not misstep, dear, as we did nose into your affairs," Rachael apologized as she handed Hillery a delicately wrapped gift that she had not yet seen. It weighed next to nothing but was a fair bundle in size. Hillery did not realize she had been holding her breath. She quickly untied the package and stared in awe as yards and yards of beautifully worked Venetian lace spilled out. It was the perfect veil. And it was worth a small fortune!

"I don't know what to say!" Hillery exclaimed. "It's gorgeous! It's the most beautiful lace I have ever seen! I am so deeply touched."

Rachael nodded her appreciation. She had been correct in thinking Hillery would not have been so extravagant on herself. She, like her son, knew that Hillery would guard her finances so that she could better care for her lands and her people. She took her responsibilities seriously.

Natalie beamed at her friend. "Gran insisted you have the best, and we all concurred. We hope that you wear it proudly."

"Oh, I shall! Thank you! Thank you all so very much!" Hillery hugged them each in turn.

The wedding was a small, but beautiful affair that took place in an ancient chapel Hillery had always admired. She was among family and close friends for the service and wore a fresh white cambric gown. The only colors to alter the purely white bridal illusion were the tiny golden jewels encrusted in the delicately embroidered sleeves and the band of yellow rosebuds that held the bridal veil in place.

Their vows were exchanged in hushed whispers. Hillery's rosy lips trembled when she repeated the words that would forever bind her to the tall man by her side. A single tear slipped down her soft cheek when he withdrew a golden wedding band from the recesses of his vest pocket, then slid it over her small, pink-nailed finger.

"It belonged to Gran," he offered simply. "She wanted very much for you to have it."

"I am honored," she answered gravely as she studied the delicate hearts and flowers etched into the precious metal.

Rachael and Natalie sniffed softly while Gran looked on with a broad smile. If her eyes were a trifle misty, she would never acknowledge it.

The minister then resumed his duties, clarifying the pledges they must keep. They gazed in wonder at each other for both of them had been afraid this day might never come.

At the townhouse, Helen Fisher and staff were busily preparing the reception. Earlier, Helen had dabbed her swollen eyes and wailed, nearly begging Hillery's forgiveness. Hillery had smiled kindly, reassuring the indentured servant that there was nothing to forgive. "I understand your fear of Charles. He had everyone frightened near to death," she assured. "Moreover, you are free to make your own choices. I do however hope you will decide to stay with us and consider this your home, as well." From that moment on, Helen had been devoted to Hillery, and therefore held the staff in hand in order to turn out the best wedding reception that could be had!

Higgens had been in charge of the guest list, a giant task in itself. His first duty had been to check with the new master of the house in the event that Stuart might have friends or family in the city as well as those back in Washington he would like to invite. Then of course there had been a trip to the office of Mr. Oliver P. Saunders in the event of any currently residing citizens of New Orleans who may have been in close companionship with the deceased Mr. Devon Ashford. Manners would dictate an invitation to each. And finally, as this was to be a formal reception, perhaps he could stir the interest of society's upper-crust with this special opportunity to make the acquaintance of The Plantation's recently returned heiress and her new groom, the renowned Washington Artist, Stuart Michaels.

Higgens had also been charged to bring additional hands to help with the cooking and other household chores. All these things had been accomplished within a few short weeks. Now with everything underway, Helen stood over a pot of some four dozen crawfish, breaking each one in half before peeling and chopping the tails to combine with a cup of well-soaked breadcrumbs. To this she added a dash of salt, pepper, garlic, diced onion and several sprigs of fresh green parsley. She then scooped the contents of the heads into another pan adding water to simmer for bouillon. The empty shells were quickly stuffed with the breadcrumb mixture then rolled in flour. These were then butter-fried until crisp and dropped into the hot soup.

A plump immigrant girl of sixteen popped a rich rice pudding laced with wine and aromatic spices into the oven wiping her sticky fingers on her apron before turning to Helen Fisher for that opinionated woman's verdict. "You did fine," Helen praised, again almost startling the help with the change in her disposition. Helen was indeed a different person these days! "Tis a job well done," Helen declared. "I must now go check the guests. 'Tis nearly time to serve."

Surprise was clearly etched on the thin scarred face as Helen gazed at the picture of success before her. The cream of New Orleans society strolled elegantly about the expanded double parlor after being personally greeted by the young bride herself. Helen's withered old cheeks crinkled in a proud smile at the vision Hillery created. Swathed in a heavily-flounced, honeyed gown with highlights as mysterious as those in her own natural halo – further graced by the deep plunging valley of creamy white cleavage – she reflected the image of glorious womanhood.

When the last guests were seated around the extended claw-foot table enjoying an entrée of sweetmeats, Helen proudly presented her famous crawfish bisque. She ladled the rice into the setting of Old Paris soup plates, adding the bisque with the steaming hot soup last. The second course was Poulet Chanticlair, a marvelous chicken dish basted in claret, flavored with bits of bacon then smothered in mushrooms. There were side dishes of candied yams, buttered turnips and tiny sweet peas. When the table had been cleared, the expert combination of strong coffee with hot milk was served as the traditional café au lait followed by a spicy rice pudding and a golden-brown, deep-dish cobbler.

After-dinner conversation filled the parlor where the ladies sat with sparkling goblets of mild white anisette, while as hostess Hillery mingled among the tittering females, careful to speak to each. Though many seemed silly, if not a bit too stuffy, there were two in particular whom Hillery favored.

Edie Timberland was a lovely blonde, short in stature yet very petite. She possessed an uncanny smile and the greenest eyes imaginable! Her wit matched her charm, clearly expressing an intelligently open mind. She confided in Hillery that her dark-haired husband, Richard, was also an artist and had spent two years of travel with Stuart studying and painting the European landscapes. It was a rough profession to pursue, but as the third son of a wealthy planter he had had the good fortune to inherit a small, but richly productive farm just outside the city. Edie confided for her ears alone that they also owned a home in

Washington D.C.

Jenny Harlan was the other guest of interest to Hillery. She was a shy redhead, short and buxom with an impishly freckled face whose kind, gentle manners won her the friendship of most. Mistress of Moon Shadow, a fine plantation twenty miles north of The Plantation, she and her husband, Robert, were visiting their house in the city which enabled them to attend on such short notice. The Harlan's were the proud parents of two bouncing infant sons, Jason and Jonathan. Jenny loved to discuss her boys, timidly regaling the ladies with stories of their latest antics. While Jenny talked, Hillery became aware of the echo of voodoo drums and realized she was watching Jenny through a veil of smoke. Flames danced between them. Hillery shook herself slightly. She understood that no one else heard or saw what she was witnessing. But she wondered at the meaning of it all.

There was one other lady, a guest of honor actually, who demanded Hillery's full attention. Rose O'Neal Greenhow had caught wind of the union between these two young people, and had of course accepted her invitation straight away. She had swept into the room with an air of wealth and position. Hillery was honored she had made time to come, and had of course, told her so. Rose nodded graciously at the compliment. She wore her sleek black hair in a chignon as usual, but crowning it was a pert creation of gauze and flowers which tied with a large bow beneath the chin lent the charming effect of youth. Thus was the setting when the gentlemen entered after a congratulatory toast to the groom.

"Everything was perfect," Hillery whispered to Stuart after the last guest had departed. "Thank you."

"You are worth far more to me than you can imagine," he returned. "I would have gladly granted your dream wedding had we but more time."

"It was my dream wedding. I am wed to you," she said, "and we no longer have to fear being apart. We have our entire future."

"And we have this night," he whispered into her mouth as he kissed her yet again, this time demonstrating a new urgency. Her senses heightened in expectation. They stood alone in the doorway of the newly made-over master bedroom knowing that everything was as it should be. Flames danced in the hearth to be reflected in each other's gaze. The sheets had been turned down in invitation. There was a beautiful, sheer French gown draped across the fluffy pillows. "Shall I give you a moment?" he asked quietly.

"Please," she returned his bold gaze, "I shall only be a moment." Isis stood inside the room, the better to assist as soon as Stuart departed. He stared at his bride a moment longer and she blushed, a gloriously shy blush that was filled with both innocence and invitation. He felt himself becoming too aroused and quickly ducked through the doorway leaving her alone with her maid.

She was true to her word. Isis stepped out only minutes later, and ducked her head in a polite bow. Stuart re-entered. He stood inside the room staring at Hillery where she stood by the hearth. She looked mythical with her unbound honeyed locks spilling down around her hips and thighs. The sheer gown hid nothing from him. Stuart stood spellbound for a moment, and then he tenderly traced the delicate features of her face. His sensitive fingers stroked the slender column of her throat as he kissed her yet again. It was a deep, all consuming kiss. She returned the kiss and spread her small hands against his chest, reveling in the manly display of muscles beneath her fingertips. He sucked in his breath and allowed his own hands to roam as he discovered her curves and valleys. Before she knew what he was about, he swung her into his arms and strode to the bed. That night Hillery became a woman in every sense of the word. They explored each other's body again and again, coming together many times before they finally slept.

# CHAPTER THIRTEEN

n that year of 1858 many great things had come to pass. First Stuart and Hillery had met and married, taking care of each other while making their home at The Plantation. They would, of course, travel and spend time at his Washington home as well which would allow lengthy visits with his family. Rachael, Natalie and Gran had long since returned home to Washington. But before Stuart and Hillery felt free to make other plans, they both felt honor bound to carry out Devon Ashford's wishes. Hillery's father had believed that by freeing the slaves, the curse against all those on The Plantation would be broken. Hillery hated slavery and wasted no time in freeing her people. Stuart stood proudly at her side. As it turned out many of the former slaves opted to remain with them. They provided jobs for everyone and paid them fairly. In truth, they needed them as much as the former slaves needed jobs. Freedom was a great thing, but without work they would have starved. And without workers, The Plantation would have failed. They formed a new beginning, one they all had faith in. And they took the time to celebrate the lifting of the curse.

No one lived in fear, and visitors began to come to The Plantation for the company alone. Some came to see for themselves how it operated since the people were now free. There were a few spoilsports, but for the most part, it was a happy time. The Timberland's and the Harlan's were regular guests who visited often. The three couples became great friends, and during the private visits they shared, the business of the Railroad bloomed anew.

"I met Richard in England while under the tutelage of the same instructor," Stuart explained as Hillery was the only one who did not know all the facts. "His family had only recently moved to the South, and though his father understood his compassion for the plight of the slaves, he thought it best that Richard go away for awhile. Thus he sent him to England to further his studies of the arts. To be fair," Stuart shifted his gaze to his friend, "Richard is a very fine artist having benefited from our European tours as much as I. But when we returned to the states our shared empathy for the institution of slavery was still there, and that's when our work began."

"I see," Hillery nodded, "and Edie? How did you enter into it?"

"That's fair," Edie dipped her head in acknowledgment. "Richard and I met three years ago," she began just as Richard picked up the story.

"Edie and her father were sympathetic to the cause," Richard qualified, "allowing us to hide a sick young woman who was with child in her cellar. The girl lost the baby, but thanks to Edie, she came through alive."

"Where is she now?" asked Hillery.

"Rebecca? She lives with us still, in the townhouse up North," Richard answered, giving his wife an appreciative grin. "She is our only servant – and a free one at that."

"What about you?" it was Edie who spoke the thought aloud gazing at Hillery with the same curiosity she knew the Harlan's possessed. "Surely it wasn't Stuart alone who aroused your sympathy?"

"Well, no," Hillery admitted, "but it was great to have him on my side as if he understood me so well."

"It was the curse of The Plantation, wasn't it?" Jenny piped up, her red curls bouncing.

"In part, yes," Hillery confided, "but I have always believed it wrong to hold humankind in bondage. Many of these people are family to me, all are my friends. And then, I discovered that Cynie, my best friend growing up was in fact my half sister. That definitely defined what I must do. My father's wishes would have been honored in any event. But I do believe we, as a whole, need to take greater responsibility for our part in all this."

"Well said," Stuart approved a sparkle in his eye.

"What about you two?" Hillery inquired of the Harlan's. "How long have you been involved? I mean, I know you have been together the longest, so might one assume you have been on the same page all along?"

"Absolutely," Robert announced. "Plus we are safer than most. Moon Shadow is a well-respected plantation with many generations of family behind it."

"Yes," Jenny agreed, "we wouldn't feel right if we didn't take our part seriously in all of this."

"Jenny and Robert should be commended," Edie dimpled at her friends. "They have carried the load for all of us from time to time."

"Well, now that we are up to speed," Stuart suggested, "we should speak of it no more. All we have to do is play our parts when needed and guard each other's backs."

"Exactly," Richard echoed. And with those simple words a pact was sealed. The friendships forged that evening were to be honor bound.

The Plantation had been quiet thus far, but that night the winds howled and the people shifted slightly, each looking at the other as if to ascertain each other's views on their safety. There came a slight mumbling among them. Winter was fast approaching. Yule Tide was upon them, and with that a new year would come. Were they as safe as they had assumed? Were they truly free of the curse?

The following morning the Harlan's departed for Moon Shadow on the Louisiana Starlette. The Timberland's set out cross-country as the distance to their farm was not so great. The couple's first Christmas came and went along with mail from Rachael, Natalie and Gran. Gran was thriving just as she had predicted. Hillery wished she would hear from Cynie as she missed her sister sorely. Thank the Lord they had received word that she and David had arrived safely in Canada! The close of this year of 1858 arrived along with the New Year and the sad tidings that another child, the first born baby girl, had been stolen from her mother. In the small cabin she shared with her mother, Glory sobbed piteously.

Fear spread like wild fire across The Plantation. Stuart and Hillery worked hard to regain the trust of the people, many of whom fled all the same. In this time of unrest it was not a safe move to make. Even those who stuck around long enough to receive and carry their papers were not necessarily safe on the roads. Many of them were found dead; others were taken hostage and never heard from again. After all, the nation was in a time of turmoil and people of color were not, in general, trusted. Those who remained lived in fear, but they also knew that Hillery would do anything she could to protect them, and that Stuart was equally trustworthy. So the days marched on and the people gossiped among themselves as to what else could be keeping the curse alive. The old master, Devon Ashford, had firmly believed that with their freedom the curse would lift. They had come to believe this too.

Stuart and Hillery spent many an hour closeted with Isis and a few of the most trusted among them trying to understand why this was happening and what actions they could take. The Plantation was finally running smoothly and the workers had known their first increase in wages. Isis shook her head setting the large hoops she wore in her ears to jingling, and said, "I hate to say it, but there are tales of the mamaloi's powers, beliefs that she cultivates a new baby girl each year, preserving the infant's heartbeat so that if she so needs, she may cross and return to life in a healthy new body. Those who say this also reason that she has worked out all the details, including the services of all those beings that are now in her employ, therefore in her power."

"I don't understand," Hillery stated, truly baffled. "What beings? Is she so powerful as to control others to do her bidding for generations upon generations?"

"It is so believed," Isis nodded. "After all, the mamaloi is ancient, and she is widely feared. It has been said that she has ruled this land for over one hundred years and would not lose her position here."

"And you believe that?" Stuart interjected.

"I believe it plausible," Isis acquiesced. "Voodoo is something we don't fully understand, yet we know to be true. Many of us have seen the effects of what can happen to regular, trustworthy people when someone powerful enough is in charge. The mamaloi is the ancient daughter of a dark goddess. I have seen some frightening things with my own eyes. And doubt it not, she can and does surround herself with those she has turned into slaves."

"But what are these beings, these slaves, you refer to except for people that she has cast a spell upon?" It was Hillery that dared to voice the question.

"They are exactly that," Isis breathed. "Many call these beings zombies because they believe them to be the walking dead. I do not believe that. Rather, I believe that she sees and knows the ones she can easily control. Perhaps they are weaklings, easily led by their earthly pleasures."

"That does make more sense," Hillery supplied. "After all, it is known that many people feed addictions. And many are weak in general."

"Okay," Stuart had difficulty believing all this. "Then how is all this done? What does she do to overcome them?"

"Many can be brought under control by food, for the people are hungry," Isis stated with candor. "Others crave alcohol as it is new to them and they enjoy the feel of it. There are many addictions such as tobacco that will gain their obedience. Ultimately, she will get them, and keep them, on narcotics. Opium would be my guess. And doubt it you may, but she is powerful and knows the ways of magic. She has only to snag them. Once in her power, she will enslave them."

"And once enslaved, once on opiates?"

"They will do her bidding. Though they are flesh and blood, they may not seem so," Isis breathed. "And it is this that terrifies the people. This and the power she wields."

"How do you propose she kidnaps the babies?" Stuart interjected. "How are they stolen in the night?"

"Yes," Hillery chimed in. "No one has ever heard or seen a thing. And the people always bolt their doors at night. So how do they disappear without a trace?"

Isis said but one word, "Voodoo."

A hush came over the room. There was much to consider. How does one stop something one does not understand, something more frightening than logic? Voodoo was to be feared. It was real to the people of the South. It was prominent in New Orleans. Even Hillery had seen such things. She did not to take it lightly. If Stuart didn't quite accept it, neither did he know how to combat it.

The year of 1859 brought more turmoil to the South and more political unrest to the nation. The new year of 1860 blew in with another child stolen. The Plantation was feared by all in the South. Gossip spread throughout the country. The workers lived in abject fear. Several decided to risk their future and set out for the North. All were found dead in unnatural ways. Few attempted to stray after that. As summer faded into fall the people grew more and more uneasy. All dreaded the New Year; they mumbled among themselves.

November arrived and in the turbulent currents of the political storm that swept the nation Abraham Lincoln won a sectional triumph for the Republican Party. But with that victory fell the defeat of the Union when on December 20th the South Carolina Legislature met in Charleston pronouncing it dissolved.

With secession a unanimous vote, South Carolina was quickly followed by Mississippi, Florida, Alabama, Georgia, Louisiana and Texas. The North was stunned when even their last minute compromise attempts failed, for on February 4th, 1861, the South formed the Confederate States of America. Their concession to world opinion terminated any slave trade with Africa, but otherwise left them isolated in many of their political views. It was in the middle of this family-torn struggle of brother against brother that the Michaels' found themselves. And in this state of contradiction they stood when Lincoln took his rightful seat to the presidency, March 4th, 1861.

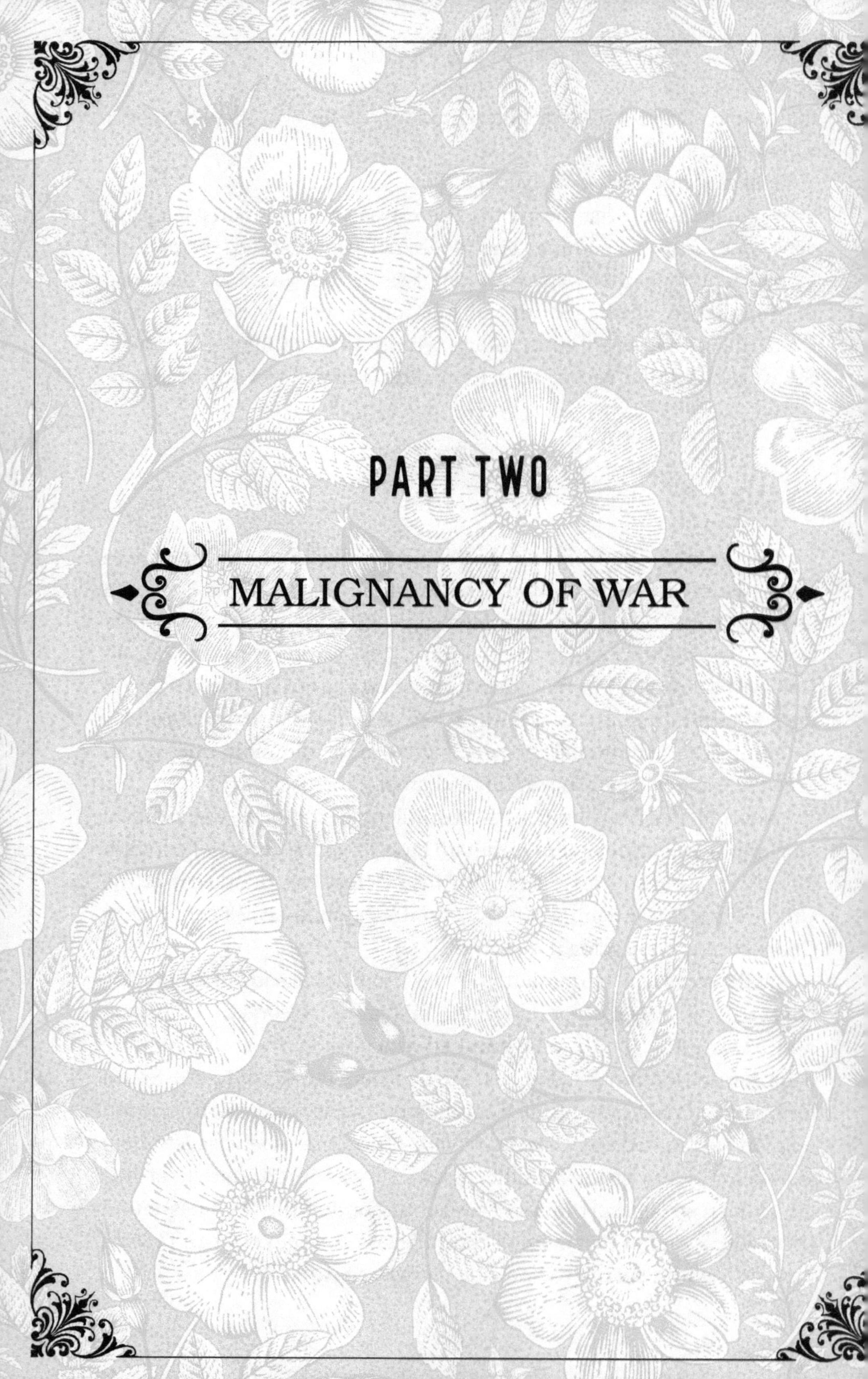

PART TWO

MALIGNANCY OF WAR

# CHAPTER FOURTEEN

t the break of dawn April 12, 1861, Edmund Ruffin fired the first shot of Civil War over Fort Sumter in the Charleston Harbor. In spite of dwindling food supplies as well as a tremendous shortage of men and ammunition, Major Anderson of the Union Army fought a brave, if initially, weakened defense in the red-hot artillery engagement that raged throughout some thirty-four hours and virtually thousands of shrapnel-filled shells. The tiny, battered garrison within the seven foot walls had forcibly surrendered to General Beauregard by mid-afternoon April 13th. Thus was the beginning reality of a war-torn nation.

Hillery tossed, tangled in the sheets of the massive mahogany bed, swept away in the phantom world of nightmares where the air about her literally rained blood. She climbed the curving staircase, footfalls sounding close behind. Whirling to face her unknown foe, she drew in her breath at the image in military blue. "Charles," she gasped, bolting upright in bed. "It is Charles who seeks to haunt me!"

"Shh," Stuart soothed beside her, but his skin prickled from a similar dream. His dreams were more developed, possibly because he had been experiencing them far longer. Their minds were much alike and worked on a level. "You are safe with me," he insisted, but he wrapped his strong arms tightly around her.

There came a rapping on the bedroom door, "War's broke out!" one of the housemaids called out, "We just got word from the packet that a place in Charleston harbor has been fired upon!"

"Oh, Stuart," Hillery wept quietly in her husband's arms, "what will become of us?" She realized, of course, that the dream meant far more than Charles coming back into her life. It ultimately spoke of the war that only now was beginning, and made it clear that Stuart could not remain safely at her side.

"I don't know, my love," he spoke softly as he caught her face between his large hands and peered deeply into her huge, frightened eyes. "We both have known it would come to this sooner or later."

"You'll go with the North, of course," she stated as calmly as possible. "Whatever will I do without you?"

"You will manage because you have no choice. We will both manage," he nodded sadly. "It is my homeland, my constitution," he slanted a look in her direction.

"I know," she sighed, kissing his weathered cheek.

"You could stay with my mother while I am away," he ventured. "I wish you would consider it."

"We have discussed that possibility before, my darling," she whispered. "But don't you see? Even though my heart is with you and my politics with the North, the South is still my home. I must stand by my people, Stuart. I couldn't possibly desert them now, nor would it be wise to do so."

They fell silent then, each accepting what the other must do. For them it would be a bittersweet parting. Their bodies joined as if for the last time for they knew well the hour of separation was upon them.

The news of war spread throughout the land like a blazing inferno. This was accepted with elation by most in the South as an end to the tension long since building. As each gallant soldier prepared for duty, every state in the nation struggled to equip its own. Still much of the toil fell to the local seamstresses. Genteel ladies sewed day and night while neighborhood artisans contributed what they could. Every Southern household donated blankets, quilts, and buggy robes. Even oilcloth piano covers were magically transformed into waterproofs for field use. While the exalted youths of the Confederacy marched off to the tune of Dixie tempered by the recruiting speeches of old campaigners from the Mexican War, their wives and mothers were left behind with tear-stained faces and nagging fears.

That year of 1861 grew increasingly difficult for those scratching out an existence on the impoverished plantations back home. Perhaps more difficult still was the lot of the self-confident youths who were fast becoming tough, grumbling soldiers. The damp rainy weather coupled with a severe shortage in food took its toll on the men. But the South held her head high with pride with the July victory of the First Bull Run – sometimes termed "Lincoln's crucifixion Day."

The Union Army was forced to return to Washington in a pouring rain. Though Lincoln's despair was great, he maintained the Federal blockade calling General McClellan – a superbly able organizer – to take charge of the Washington troops. Little Mac, as he was called, applied himself vigorously to the drills and military procedures eventually building a force of one-hundred and sixty-eight thousand men. However his extreme caution often proved his undoing, as did his explicit faith in Alan Pinkerton whose position in military intelligence frequently deterred his purposes. Pinkerton badly miscalculated the Confederate's number and strength, many times plunging the North into unexpected, as well as, misleading circumstances.

Early that autumn Hillery received the sobering news of Rose Greenhow's arrest. Accused of both spying and treason by the forementioned Alan Pinkerton, Rose became a prisoner in her own home. Her devoted servant, Lily Machall, remained by her side of her own volition. Rumors rippled heavily of the belle's dreadful misuse. While her house was drastically demolished, her chambers altered into cells for several other female prisoners, it was reputed that her honor had been seriously soiled.

"Poor Rose," Hillery sighed, allowing the letter she had been reading from Natalie to flutter silently to the floor where her little dog, Ariel, lay fast asleep. Stuart had given her the small blond pup as a gift when they had parted, saying that he would grow to be a protector for her as well as a companion. She shuffled slowly to the velvet-draped windows, her thoughts drifting to Stuart as they so often did these days. She was tired and her back ached from laboring alongside the field hands.

Harvest time had come and gone. With the mountains of white fiber piled high in the warehouses, she decided it was time for a trip to the city. She was lonely. Perhaps she could enjoy a visit or two with Edie while attending business. She had noted a shortage of supplies that could be better bargained for in the city than purchased from some high-priced salesman on the packet. It was with good resolve that she made the decision to travel.

It was a nice change to visit the townhouse in New Orleans. Helen was happy to see the young mistress and turned out a fine dinner. As Glory had never recovered from the kidnapping of her child, Hillery had asked her to be her companion while in the city, giving the girl a change of scenery. Helen took to Glory at once, and Hillery smiled at the unlikely pair.

"'Tis true, I tell you! I just needed a wee bit of a friend!" Helen assured the girl. "'Tis lonely, I am!" Glory smiled shyly and ducked her head at the show of affection and Hillery knew she had made the right decision.

Now on the plank sidewalks of New Orleans, Hillery became aware of the frantic froufrou of nearby skirts. She had walked this city a million times and had always felt safely at home here. She cringed, suddenly aware of an angry mob of raging women. A viper-like voice hissed in her ear, "Slut! You shouldn't be allowed on the streets!"

"Why aren't you in the North where you belong?" another voice joined.

"Yes!" someone else agreed. "Are you here as a spy?"

Hillery squared her shoulders, recognizing the angry voices of women she had known her whole life. Lifting her chin, she held her ground. "I am a Southerner just like the rest of you. Now please, let me pass."

Though they did, the mob followed her to her destination. As the bell above the door of the seamstress's shop tinkled, she watched as Thelma, the proprietress stepped timidly forward. The woman's cheeks had turned quite pink and it was obvious she was made nervous by the commotion. "Hello, Thelma," she stated calmly. "I came to purchase some flannel and thread."

"Ask her what color?" one of the women spat, and the crowd roared its approval.

"I say she ought to be tarred and feathered!" another chimed.

Thelma looked nervously about, unsure how to handle the situation, but Hillery smiled kindly and said, "This will do nicely," as she laid her selection on the counter.

Thelma, who had always liked Hillery, took her coin, worrying her lip with her teeth when Hillery bid her fair well. She was afraid for the young lady. People had a way of doing bad deeds in times of hardship. Before she could offer up anything more, Hillery had thanked her sweetly and stepped outside.

The crowd followed in a temper and Thelma felt herself pulled along as if by an invisible cord to watch from the safety of the window. Hillery saw her there and felt sorry for the woman. Thelma was a kind soul and to Hillery's knowledge had never harmed another. Their eyes met. As Hillery turned away, the crowd turned on her! In that moment came a fierce growl, low at first, then more loudly. The women paused. They stared as a ravenous beast hunkered low, approaching in a very deadly manner. The dog was wild. He appeared to be near starving and he was ready to take on the crowd. The women slowly backed away in abject terror. The dog bared his teeth, growling low in his throat. Hillery was the first to break the trance that had come over the crowd. She smiled sweetly. "Why, Rags," she crooned, "have you come to save me then, you poor, sweet boy?" And to the astonishment of all, she stepped fearlessly up to the beast patting his head in a loving gesture. The dog followed her down the walkway unharmed. She remembered him from many years ago for Rags was her father's dog, a great beast of a thing whose loyalty was for father and daughter alone. She had been told he died when she was away to the convent in France. She hid her surprise well under the circumstances. As they rounded the corner, Hillery became aware of a change in energy. Beside her Rags was fast fading away!

Once back at the townhouse, Hillery was met by the puppy, Ariel. Ariel's eyes held a sheen she had never seen before. And for a fraction of a second, he seemed larger than life as she bent to pet him. His little face looked both older and wiser as if he knew what had just transpired. She spoke to him kindly, loving him up before heading off to the kitchen in search of a treat. Ariel showed a lop-sided grin, and then followed in her wake.

The following morn, Edie came to visit. She and Hillery took tea in the cozy parlor with Ariel sleepy-eyed in the corner from which he watched. Edie was indignant as to the treatment Hillery had endured while in town. She had heard the story from the locals and came at once to offer assistance. Hillery thanked her friend, assuring her that all was well. Glossing over the part about the beast, she warned, "We must be careful. It wouldn't do to draw any unwanted attention to ourselves. And I do not wish to compromise your reputation."

"Oh, fiddle! I am in good social standing, and well this city knows it! While you are here, I shall accompany you wherever you go. And you must come join my sewing circle. It will put you back in good standing as well."

"You are such a loyal friend," Hillery confided. "With our husbands away, we have only each other."

"Then we shall guard each other's backs," Edie returned steadily. Edie did not miss the fact that Hillery had not chosen to explain the presence of some strange beast that vanished into thin air. She knew the reputation of The Plantation and assumed it was a part of it, whatever *it* was! She also knew that Hillery had a great deal of psychic awareness. As Edie had known Stuart for several years, and he was her husband's best friend, she was both open-minded and compassionate for those with heightened abilities. To Edie's mind, it would be a heavy burden to shoulder! Because they were such good friends with shared interests and concerns, Edie promised to visit The Plantation after the New Year.

And so it was Hillery came to join Edie's sewing circle. She arrived at the Timberland's modest home at precisely eight o'clock that evening, the first of many such evenings. The steady chiming of the mantel clock met her as Rebecca opened the door.

"Hello Rebecca," Hillery greeted, handing the servant her garment, "How nice to see you again."

"Good evening, Miss Hillery," Rebecca smiled fondly. Most of the ladies were pleasant to Hillery and genuinely did seem to have missed her company. The few who attempted to snub her wound up being the minority. They left the circle earlier than usual making only themselves look bad. No one mentioned the incident of the day before.

Hillery thrived during her visits with Edie. When left alone they spoke candidly about the war and how badly they missed their husbands. Having someone to confide in gave them both a boost. Hillery enjoyed viewing Richard's paintings as much as Edie loved showing them. They were all very good yet so different from Stuart's! Though they had studied under many of the same great masters, each put his own personal slant on his work. It amazed Hillery who was not particularly artistic. And in an odd way, it made her pine for Stuart all the more.

Hillery remained through December, sharing the Christmas holiday with her friends in the city. There had been letters from Stuart updating her on the war and his personal whereabouts. He missed her deeply and advised her with regards to her own safety and well being. She missed him and held the letters close, finally tucking them away. There was also news of Rachael, Natalie and Gran. The threesome was sharing a quiet holiday. Hillery returned to The Plantation the following afternoon. She had with her the pup, Ariel, as companion for Glory had opted to remain with Helen for the time being. "Do tell mama not to worry," Glory repeated yet again as Hillery made to leave.

"I will, Love, "Hillery smiled. "Have no fear, your mama will understand, and Helen will delight in your company."

January blew in with scads of public news sheets circulating the streets of every Southern city. Higgens forwarded the lot to Hillery. Depicted was the plight of Fort Greenhow as well as the sorrowful death of Lily Machall. There was a second, more inflammatory article which arrived on the heels of the first. It had been written by the widow herself, and then somehow smuggled into the South.

Rose Greenhow was a born and bred Southerner. Like most Southern ladies, she had no understanding of the North – or sympathies for the slaves. She was an otherwise good person who was generous to those she loved, and loyal to her country. Rose was both widow and mother, but the times had turned her into a spy. As Hillery continued to read, she grew more and more subdued. Rose Greenhow had been transferred to the Old Capitol Prison which was known to be an infiltration of lice and disease. The South was only beginning to see just how cruel war could be.

Edie arrived in the middle of the month as planned. The energy of the place was scary. Hillery was more subdued than usual and the workers were obviously terrified. There was a dark cloud over The Plantation that was visible to all, and it hovered low over the fields. There had been no babies stolen as of yet, which seemed odd as there had been three births so far this month. One was a boy which gave the parents of the male child a small measure of peace, but the other two infants were females. While this would normally be construed as good news, everyone wondered what lay afoot. The dark cloud above them bode only evil. The air fairly screamed with anger and hostility. Even Edie felt a chill ripple her spine. Something terrible was pending. The people feared they had angered the mamaloi.

Hillery put on a brave front as she went about her duties, but in the evenings after everyone else had settled down for the night, she and Edie sat in the small parlor speaking openly between them. This evening Hillery listened to the distant drums that only she could hear. They were growing louder and this, in and of itself, disturbed her. It was different than all the other times as there was a foul odor in the air that turned her stomach. Edie noticed the change in her demeanor and inquired about it. Hillery paled, but explained what she was experiencing.

Time seemed to creep by making everyone's nerves and tempers short. Gradually she noticed as some of the others became aware of the odor. A few began to hear distant drums, yet for Hillery the drums were now pounding a reckless tattoo. Louder and louder they rapped out their evil message. This signaled something foreboding was on the horizon. The women of the house slept in pairs that night. Those in cabins threw their bolts and took turns guarding their families and friends.

And then it happened. A shrill scream pierced the night air. The people gathered in small groups to investigate. At first it seemed everyone was accounted for. Even the newborn babes were present and well. But then an old woman shuffled forth, her eyes swollen from crying, her face contorted with shock. She shook with fear. She was known only as Grandmother and she lived with her daughter and granddaughter, both of whom she claimed were missing. They were the last of her known family. One moment they were right before her eyes, she said. The next thing she knew she had awakened from a deep sleep that was entirely unnatural. Grandmother felt as though she had been drugged. When she finally pulled herself back from some deep, dark place, she saw that the cabin was still tightly locked, but she was the only remaining occupant!

"Grandmother was alone in that cabin," Hillery reminded, when Isis and Edie joined her in the parlor, "and the door was bolted from within."

"Do you think she could have done something to her family when she claimed she was drugged?" Edie questioned. It seemed like a fair question, a logical one, but both Isis and Hillery nodded against this.

"No," Isis brooked no argument, "Grandmother was in a state of deep shock, but she loved her family and would have died for them. Besides, she was not truly drugged, not with any known opiate, that is. Rather, I think, she was under a spell. But I do not believe she would have harmed them in any case. Those under spells who act out in aggression only do that if that aggression is a deeply rooted part of them," she qualified. "Grandmother held no such temperament."

"Plus," Hillery supplied, "some of the men found a brush trail deep in the woods."

Edie paused then said, "What if..."

"No," Hillery shook her head. "The brush trail was a rough one. Not one an older woman could have easily traveled. And it left off in the woods. Besides," she shivered, "there were inexplicable marks on the outside of the cabin door. The people claim it was a sigil of evil. It has been scrubbed off."

"And don't forget," Isis intoned slowly, "Grandmother is devastated. She won't eat or drink, and if that is not proof enough, have you not noticed? The cloud is gone. The stench is gone. The prophecy, however changed, was fulfilled."

"That's true," Hillery agreed, "Even the God-awful drums have stopped."

The women looked at each other knowing the crisis at hand had ended. But a new horror had visited The Plantation that left the people strangely silent. Hillery crossed herself. "Saint Michael, protect us," she murmured. In his small bed at her side, Ariel whimpered.

# CHAPTER FIFTEEN

arly in 1862 Major General Henry Halleck ordered General Ulysses S. Grant to move on Fort Henry on the Tennessee River. Grant took 15,000 men and a squadron of new ironclad gunboats commanded by Flag Officer Andrew Foote and launched an attack. Fort Henry proved to be unexpectedly weak. The fort was built on low ground and was partly under water, the Tennessee being almost at flood stage. Foote's gunboats pounded it into surrender before infantry could get into position. Grant then turned east marching his men cross country to attack Fort Donelson on the Cumberland. He sent Foote around to join him by the water. One week after Fort Henry had surrendered the Federals launched an attack on Fort Donelson.

In smoke so thick it was difficult to see, Stuart fought alongside his men. He would later remember the dreams he had been having of Hillery as the smoke was thick in them as well. He was concerned for his wife whom he had not seen in such a very long time. Now his mind was occupied with warfare. God, how he wished this war over and done with. Next to him he heard a man call out in shock, "Hey, lookie there! That boy over there in butternut was gut shot, and he just got up and walked away!" Stuart nodded blindly, understanding only too well what the other had seen.

Fort Donelson proved a great deal stronger than what Fort Henry had been. General Grant got vast reinforcements and shelled the place into submission. It took three full days to take it down. Fort

Donelson surrendered on February 16th. Grant suddenly found himself famous – not only had he captured 15,000 Confederates, but the note demanding capitulation had struck a strong chord with the North: "No terms except an immediate and unconditional surrender can be accepted."

With General Johnston's necessary retreat, Nashville could not be held and it was evacuated with substantial loss to the Confederacy. Even the fortress at Columbus had to be given up. General Johnston had understood that the Federals would bring staggering numbers against him. He had no other course of action.

Life at The Plantation had settled in peaceably enough. Edie had long since returned home after first issuing Hillery an invitation to come visit once the weather had cleared. Hillery had eagerly accepted knowing that a break from plantation life would do her good. The earth was nice and rich, the crops were ready to be sewn. The people had for the most part worked past their newest fear, still not understanding the new twist in the curse that was upon them. Everyone, it seemed, made an effort to move on with their lives seeking contentment where they could find it.

Along with the bloom of spring the city of New Orleans was left to stagnate under the Union blockade. Prices soared. Products that had been scarce before became even more so now. The docks and warehouses were deserted while the only existing industries were those producing war materials. Yet still the crescent city of New Orleans felt she dealt a tremendous hand of security with her two stone and masonry forts built well armed and manned on the river below.

Hillery gleaned most of her news from the city as she and Edie were in constant touch. Higgens forwarded all mail and newspapers while Natalie wrote regularly with news of family and war. Stuart wrote whenever possible.

Grant had put his army on the western bank of the Tennessee at Pittsburgh Landing, and Stuart was camped near a country meeting house known as Shiloh Church. Hillery followed what became known as the Bloody Battle of Shiloh as well as she could. It sent terror into her soul. General Grant was caught off guard. On the first day of the fight, his army was nearly pushed into the Tennessee River, she read. Hillery feared for her husband's life. She was a woman torn, and the Bloody Battle of Shiloh which began on the 6th of April, ended on the 7th.

Southern General Johnston was killed in action. The Union lost 13,000 men. The Confederacy lost 10,000. The battle had been poorly handled, especially by the Federals. The terrible casualty list and the fact that Grant allowed himself to be taken unawares stirred violent criticism in the North. It was not until Hillery received word of her husband's well being that she was able to relax. She sighed as she wiped tears from her eyes.

Word spread like wild fire among the people who always seemed abreast of the activities in the area. Scandalous stories poured in of a Union fleet stationed just outside the city in the very mouth of the river. In the beginning it was wagered they would turn tail and run, for although Southern defense relied solely on a small flotilla, was not the stern Fort St. Philips on the other side of the river, and the star-shaped Fort Jackson nearby, a formidable sight? Union strategy was completely lost on the frivolous belles of the South. Had they known the naval background of Union David Farragut as well as his services and commands since the early age of nine, they would have rightly feared the sixty-year-old commander whose stolid determination was to invade this Confederate stronghold. Once it became clear that the North had no intention of retreat, fear began to prickle the spines of those in the audience of sound. Twenty mortar schooners had opened fire on the Rebel forts pounding away for five days straight.

Edie shook her head at all the commotion. She and Rebecca were all alone on the small farm she shared with Richard during happier times. She had only a couple of hands from nearby farms to help her with the heavier chores. They had their own families and their own burdens to shoulder, but would come by once a week or so. For all that she was of a tiny build Edie was strong of mind and body. Unlike most women of her time, she understood the threat the Union posed. However, Edie was secretly affiliated with the North. Even so, this did not in any way make her safe. Rather it was another complication with which she must cope.

By April 24th, as neither side had willingly surrendered, Farragut decided to send his ships up river by cover of night to take New Orleans. Two Yankee vessels had previously sliced a successful cut through the boom allowing for the passage of the Northern fleet. Three columns of Union fleets steamed upriver smashing their way through Confederate lines within a matter of seventy minutes. They were silhouetted by Rebel bonfires. Pandemonium had preceded Farragut's arrival in the city the following day. Though nearly all the Rebel fleet had been sunk in action by the more powerful Union rams and ironclads, the city still refused to surrender. Confederate flags waved to the tunes of Southern patriotism while soft-spoken ladies spat on tired Yankee soldiers as they trudged through town. It took the firm hand of legendary "Beast Butler" to line these people out, but line them out he did.

Through it all, Hillery had been busily tending the crops. She worked alongside the others without qualms, and now a healthy harvest was on the horizon. She smiled with contentment as she rode along toward the city accompanied by her groomsman. She had hired the assistance of an extra man as well who rode alongside them. These were, after all, times of war. Both Edward, the groomsman, and the additional hand, Thomas, were armed. In the back of the buggy was a passenger.

When they reached the city, Higgens expressed his disapproval. He was concerned for the young mistress and did not think her safe in the city. "The mob in town grows worse each day," he stated as he helped her alight. Ariel popped his sleepy head out of the blanket in which he slept. "You need to have a care."

"Yes, dear Higgens," she dimpled, then quickly sobered when he scowled, scratching Ariel behind the ear. "Seriously, I will take care, Higgens, but I need to check on Edie and Rebecca. They may have need of us. If it becomes too difficult for them, I want them to know they are welcome here. They are two women alone."

"You are alone as well."

"I have many hands at The Plantation, and I have armed them well. Besides, I need to pick up supplies in the city. With things as bad as they are, I fear they will grow worse and we will be left with little or nothing." What Hillery did not say was that she had been having visions of the Harlan's plantation, Moon Shadow, and it was on fire.

She now understood why she had seen flames the day she met Jenny. She needed to warn her. Jenny was virtually alone with her two young sons and Hillery's concern was growing in leaps and bounds. Word was that most of the Harlan's people had fled, leaving Jenny without protection.

Higgens nodded with proud bearing. "Prices are terrible," he conceded, "and you should purchase what you can. It will only get worse. Next time, if you will write, I shall make your purchases for you. I can have them sent directly."

"I am sure you are right, my dear friend," Hillery smiled only slightly, not wanting to offend him. "I shall consider that next time. The other reason I chose to come in person," she hesitated only briefly when she espied Glory's round face in the window peering out at her, "was to oversee the transportation of a fellow passenger. It has come to my attention that while Glory is happy here with Helen, her mother has become quite lonesome." Hillery paused to open the door of the buggy allowing a very old woman to alight. "Therefore, as she is a free woman, I suggested she might also like to live here in the city."

"Oh, Missy Hillery," Glory came bounding out of the house her broad features alight with excitement, "Thank you! Thank you for bringin' mama!" Glory and her mother hugged.

"Oh! Ma'am! Please excuse me!" Helen Fisher burst out the door. "I just got wind o' the news!" she cried. "There 'as been a hanging in town! Some poor stupid fool who was daft enough to destroy an American flag! He may have been drunk, but now he is dead! They thought t' make an example o' him, they did!"

"Dear God," Hillery whispered, "what is to become of us?"

Edie was walking the streets of New Orleans with Rebecca in tow. The women were gathering a few necessities before returning to the small farm, though Edie was trying to decide whether to swing by the house on Chartres Street in the Vieux Carré in the event that Hillery was home at last. She knew that Hillery would welcome the intrusion as the two did not stand on ceremony. Still she had a great deal to accomplish this day and decided to get her errands finished before making any further plans. She knew her friend would inform her of her whereabouts as soon as she was free and able. With her mind crowded with so many thoughts, she did not at first notice Rebecca's quick intake of breath or her small hand on her arm. Edie looked up in surprise to see the sidewalk before her blocked. Men in Union blue milled about with no apparent mind to step aside.

"Whoopee! What have we here?" one man crowed while another joined the fray. Edie's large green eyes widened while poor Rebecca edged behind her.

"Pretty little filly, ain't she?" the second man chortled in a nasal voice, his narrowed eyes meeting hers.

"I'll say!" another man roughly cupped her chin and Edie automatically swatted him away. "Aw, how about a smile, honey?" he quipped.

Behind her Rebecca trembled. She had been sorely used in the past and this knowledge gave Edie the will power to stand up to these bullies. "Unhand us!" she exclaimed, slapping the men away.

"What's the trouble over here?" a loud voice boomed from behind.

"Sir, Major! Sir!" the men saluted smartly.

"What's the trouble?" the major repeated his eyes hard and formidable.

"This woman made a direct reproach of Order Number Twenty-Eight!" the first man had regained his composure and was now bent on revenge.

"Is this true, ma'am?" the major barked. "Do you realize the severity of the charge?"

"I...I committed no violation," Edie stammered. She was frightened in the midst of so many soldiers and though her husband, Richard, was a spy for the Union she could hardly make a fact of that on the streets of New Orleans. For all intents and purposes, the people of this fine city accepted her on the basis that she and her husband were true Southerners. Only Hillery knew her secret.

The more offensive of the soldiers snickered in the background. Edie shifted from one foot to the other, her expression troubled. The major drew himself up to his full height. He did not like this duty of arresting women. "Ma'am," he said, "I am afraid I must ask you to come with me for questioning. I will require the services of your slave here as well."

"Rebecca is a free woman. Is it necessary to include her in this?" Edie asked stiffly. She was aware of her servant's discomfiture.

Rebecca, in turn, straightened her narrow shoulders. "I would not abandon you, mistress," she stated with quiet dignity, her liquid eyes solemn.

The major glanced from one to the other with growing admiration, "Ladies, I do apologize," he cleared his throat, "but with all these men on the street, it would be best for both of you to come with me." He brooked no argument as he proceeded to escort them down the street.

"What is this about?" Hillery's soft voice broke through the sounds of male laughter. "Surely you big, strong men can't be causing my friends any trouble, can you?" she said in her sweet Southern accent. As she looked about at all the faces, keeping her own free of any fear or intimidation, the men began to back down a bit. They scuffed their boots nervously.

"This is a Federal offense, ma'am," the major stated, eyeing this new arrival. "It would be best to stay out of it." He then ordered the lingering crowd to disperse and be on their way.

"May I accompany you, major? I promise not to get in the way," she replied.

With a stiff nod from the major, the small group set off down the walk. Edie eyed her nervously but held her silence. Rebecca looked straight ahead. Hillery was fully aware that the other women were grateful for her presence. There was safety in numbers, wasn't there?

Hillery inclined her head toward Higgens where he stood respectfully waiting near the buggy. "Please, Major…"

"Carter," the major responded.

"Major Carter, this is my manservant, Higgens. Higgens, it would seem that Miss Edie and Miss Rebecca have need of our council. Oh, but I have forgotten my manners, sir. I am Mrs. Stuart Michaels. My husband is a captain in your army. Perhaps you have heard of him?"

Major Carter raised one thick gray brow as bushy as a caterpillar. His mouth opened in a surprised O. "Captain Michaels," he frowned. "Captain Stuart Michaels! Of course!" he exclaimed. "I heard he had a wife down here. Well, I'll be…" he chuckled pleasantly, running a calloused palm through his silver locks. "I attended West Point with your father-in-law, young woman! I was mighty sorry to hear of his demise. Thomas was a true friend." As the man tiredly closed his eyes pinching the bridge of his nose between his thumb and forefinger Edie flashed Hillery a look of pure admiration. Rebecca swallowed audibly and Higgens hid a tell-tale grin, thinking how easily Hillery could turn a situation around. The matter was dropped and before they departed, Major Carter had accepted a dinner invitation for the following evening.

Hillery had dreamed of fire all night. She had virtually watched Jenny's home ignite. Union soldiers were looting the area. Morals and social graces had literally gone up in smoke. She hopped out of bed, her eyes wide with fear. Ariel whined in his sleep, his bed next to hers. He stretched and opened his eyes giving her a look as if he already understood she was leaving him behind again. Jenny had been standing outside in the front yard, a plump baby boy on her hip. She had somehow managed to escape the men but there was something terribly wrong with the image she had seen. Oh, dear God! Where was the other child? Hillery dressed quickly and flew out the door. She had called out to Higgens upon rising, asking him to have Edward ready the horses. Then she had sent Thomas over to the Timberland farm to warn both Edie and Rebecca. She just might need their help. Edie and Jenny had known each other the entirety of their lives. Edie would want to be there for her friend.

As they neared Moon Shadow, Edie and Rebecca alighted in unison. Hillery was ahead of the rest. She was already looking for a way inside, following what little she could from the dream. The men worked to sooth the horses who were terrified of the flames. Jenny was nowhere to be seen. Rebecca was first to speak, "We've got to find Jenny and the children!" She had to shout to be heard over the roar of flames and the groaning of the house as its structure had begun to crumble. The smoke was so thick tears filled their eyes making it difficult to breathe.

"The soldiers haven't been gone long," one of the men qualified. "Probably didn't think anyone was home."

"We'd best keep watch," the other added. "They could come back. I'll take a look around; see if I can find Miss Jenny and the boys. You stand guard."

"Okay, holler if you need me!"

A door slammed and Jenny stumbled outside. Sparks showered down upon her and she swatted them away. She had a deep gash on her forehead. She was hysterical as her eyes frantically swept the yard searching for her child. She had a baby on her hip that she jiggled without conscious thought. The boy screamed; his little face terrified. Rebecca was immediately at her side. She took the infant in one arm and cradled Jenny with the other. Edie joined them. She took charge of Jenny when the frantic mother would have reentered the flaming house. "I'll go!" Rebecca yelled above the roaring flames and crackling timber, placing the baby safely in Edie's arms. Burning wood and shattered glass exploded nearby. Part of the house sagged and crumpled to the ground.

Inside, Hillery was lost. She did not know the layout of the house and had somehow taken a wrong turn. The smoke was so thick she could not see which way she had entered. Her head swam. She heard Rebecca shouting for her, but could not tell from which direction. She had torn off a part of her skirt and used it to cover her face. Suddenly, she heard a very clear and extremely familiar voice. Without knowing how she knew, she recognized it as her mother's. "Go straight to the back of the house. You will find the child there," the voice said urgently.

Hillery blinked and did as she was told. The little boy was curled up in a ball in the corner of the kitchen. He was sucking his thumb. His eyes which had been tightly screwed shut, opened when she entered. He held out his chubby little arms and she swept him up. Together they stumbled out the back door.

When she rounded the house with the child in tow, Jenny broke free of the others and ran to meet them. She sobbed as she gathered her child in her arms, alternately kissing him and wiping his tears. The little fellow did the same for her, mimicking her gestures with great care. It was this sight that met Rebecca's field of vision when she stumbled out the front door, tears streaming down her cheeks. She had feared that in her failure all was lost. Seeing that the other women and both children were safe brought a radiant smile to her face. The small group moved out of range of the house, the women making over each other and the babies. Jenny let them lead her away. She didn't care about the house and her belongings. Those things could be replaced.

# CHAPTER SIXTEEN

 ajor Carter sent a small detail of soldiers to accompany Hillery to The Plantation. Though she had both Edward and Thomas with her, he ordered his men to see her safely home. She was flattered by the major's concern and attention and was happy to have the additional company and protection. The countryside was rife with mischief. A woman couldn't be too careful.

Ariel slept in a cushioned basket at her side. He was a small dog but extremely loyal. Every so often his blonde head would pop up and he would give Hillery a knowing look. He was a wise little fellow and was making it clear that he knew what was going on. Ariel had long since decided he was in charge.

They stopped only briefly during the trip so that Hillery might stretch her legs and see to her needs while the men tended the horses. She spoke to them kindly and was pleased to find that many of them knew Stuart personally. She smiled as she pleaded for any stories they might pass her way, and they in turn were only too happy to oblige. It was obvious they liked and respected Captain Michaels.

Hillery joined in caring for the horses although she had been instructed not to. It didn't take the men long to see that she was good with animals and eager to help. Young Lieutenant Markham drew her attention with his black hair and deep-set, blue eyes. He was quite young, no more than twenty-two, but he reminded her of Stuart. He had the same coloring and a similar build although he was lean and lanky lacking the more defined muscle of Stuart's taller frame. They found common ground in conversation. With him she felt easily compelled to speak of her feelings for her husband. He smiled shyly in return, telling her that her husband was a lucky man. "I have a girl back home," he spoke quietly. "Her name is Elizabeth. Would you like to see her likeness?"

"Of course," she responded, eyeing the crossed sabers on the uniform so much like Stuart's own while he produced a daguerreotype from an inside pocket. He opened it with great care and gingerly handed it to Hillery. "She's lovely," Hillery smiled. "I'm sure she misses you very much."

"Sometimes I wonder if this war will ever get over," he confided. "I admit I am anxious to make her my wife, and when it seems so far away," he swallowed, "like the time will never come, I open this case and stare at her likeness. It makes me whole again." He glanced at Hillery as if to gauge her reaction.

"I understand," she whispered. "I miss Stuart too. Sometimes I fear something will happen to him, or to me. I wonder then if I'll ever see him again. The feeling is so powerful, it's overwhelming."

They gazed at each other in silence for a moment, grateful to share their thoughts and feelings. War was frightening as was the unknown. Thereafter the journey continued.

Hillery was, as usual, excited to be home. She waved as the soldiers turned and rode away. They were honorable young men who had paused only briefly to rest their horses, gratefully accepting the food Sukie quickly packed for them. Hillery had missed Isis sorely. It was always good to be home in spite of all the hardships. That night she slept soundly.

Somewhere, outside city limits, a small band of men lay in wait in the bushes. They were a rough bunch, each in contrast with the other. But they had a single-minded purpose that showed in their quiet actions. Their patience was rewarded when in the distance they heard horses approaching. It was the very detail of soldiers whom they were awaiting. When the soldiers drew abreast of them, they signaled each other according to plan. In a matter of minutes it was over, for the soldiers lay dead. The attackers quickly corralled the horses, tying them nearby. They then stripped the bodies of both uniforms and weapons before burying them in the bushes. It would be easy from here on out. Garbed in Union uniform, they could roam the countryside freely.

Towards morning Hillery's dreams had become fitful and she awoke to find Ariel prancing alongside her bed. In that instant she realized she smelled smoke. She and Isis nearly collided in the hallway.

As the women poured from the house with Ariel at their heels, one of the hands called out loudly, "Fire, Fire!" A bucket brigade was quickly formed.

"It's the warehouses!" Hillery cried. Already the flames were growing. Hillery's eyes were round with shock. She saw the same expression on every face she passed. The people worked quickly but the fire was spreading to the other outbuildings. Their harvest was at stake, their horses and homes were also at risk. They broke into small groups, each going a different direction. Ariel never left Hillery's side. She issued orders, but remained with the warehouses until the fire was out. They had lost a good deal of food. Still they had managed to save some as well.

Next, Hillery checked the stables, making sure Angel was in good hands. Her orders had been carefully followed and Angel was safely away. The other horses were secured as well. She heaved a sigh of relief as she lovingly hugged her mare, pressing her face against Angel's own. Ariel cocked his head as he watched her. His tail formed a question mark.

It wasn't until she left Angel in the pasture that she realized something was still amiss. There was an eerie vibe in the air that crackled and popped. And then it dawned on her: had someone set the fires? How did they start? Just because no one was seen did not dismiss the possibility. As she grasped the idea that this was no accident, she felt a chill course down her spine. Ariel shook his little body and met her gaze.

Some of the women were fast approaching with Isis in the lead. They had come to the same frightening conclusion. Who could have done this, and why? For that matter, if this had been arson, where was the perpetrator? Had he or she left the grounds? Quite honestly it didn't make sense.

By the time the people gathered to discuss the issue at hand, an argument had erupted. There was a difference of opinion. Some of the men folk felt it was more than possible the winds had shifted in the night, sparking fire to dry kindling. The women, however, were listening to their intuition. They sensed something dark at hand. After all, were they not on cursed ground? Finally, to gain control and hold the peace, Hillery took charge.

"It has been a difficult morning," she qualified, "and we are all tired and hungry. Let us break the fast. Surely then, our minds will be more clear."

"There was no sign of intruders," one of the men spoke up.

"We don't really know that," Hillery reasoned. "We were too busy putting out the fires to look for anything more. We shall meet back here in an hour." With that she headed toward the house with Ariel, Sukie, and Isis behind her.

Sukie immediately separated from the others and went the back way to the kitchen where Muffin had already headed. Isis went with her, thinking she best lend a hand. Hillery walked up the front steps leaving Ariel outside on the porch. Ariel tried to push his way inside. He didn't like it when she made his decisions for him. But Hillery turned and said to him, "It's been a long morning. Go do your job. I'll fetch you in a bit."

When she closed the door against him, Ariel whimpered. It was clear he thought she made the wrong choice. He tried to nose the door aside but it wouldn't budge. He whined again and he heard her laugh, "Silly boy! I'll get you in a bit!"

Hillery stepped inside the house, her mind in turmoil. The events of the morning had left everyone exhausted. Still there was much to do. The grounds would need to be cleaned up, and some of the buildings rebuilt. The animals needed tending, while the contents of the warehouses must be accounted for. But first, she would wash up and enjoy a belated breakfast. She was making a mental list when she realized that something was off in the house as well. From somewhere behind her, she heard the clinking of a wine glass, the rustling of material. She turned, and froze. A gasp escaped her.

"Charles!" she cried, her eyes wide with horror. One hand flew to her mouth as if to quiet herself. She unconsciously took a step backward.

"Hello, my dear," he leered at her. "Miss me?"

Her eyes missed nothing as she stared at him. He wore Union blue; the crossed sabers on his uniform identified him as cavalry. Fear clutched her heart. "What...what are you doing here?" her voice cracked.

"Why, I came for you! Isn't it obvious?" he mouthed. "You and I have unfinished business."

"You set the fires," she breathed the accusation. "It was you. You sought to burn us out," she said.

"How very astute," he approached, circling her, letting his eyes drink their fill. "I find I have missed you very much."

"Stuart..." she began.

"Is not here," he finished for her. "There is no one here to help you."

"He'll find out, and come after you."

Charles made a mocking sound with his tongue. "I am not afraid of a dead man." He laughed as she paled. "Ah, now I have your attention, do I not? It is all part of my plan. Did you honestly think that I wouldn't seek revenge?" She stared into the glassy gray eyes realizing that Charles was quite mad.

Just then another man entered the house. Hillery looked up to see a dusky, familiar face. "Tate," Charles spoke curtly, never taking his eyes off Hillery, "what is it? Can you not see we are in the middle of something? The lady and I have a score to settle."

"I figured you'd want to know the cabins are aflame," Tate boasted while Hillery gasped aloud, already tearing herself away from Charles. Charles scowled but allowed her to escape.

"There is nothing you can do for any of them!" he called after her. "You would do well to look after yourself!" To Tate he said, "Let her go, but keep an eye on her. I want her returned to me in one piece. I have looked forward to this for a very long time."

Hillery was already long gone. Her slippered feet flew down the old familiar path to the quarters where the white-washed cabins were aflame. It took only a second to see that most were empty. There was one cabin, however, that was imprisoned by a raging blaze of red-orange flame. From the depths of the inferno came the most horrifying screams.

"Who is in there?" Hillery screamed.

One of the women spoke up and told her, "Two of the women folk were hidin' under the beds!"

Hillery glanced around at the men standing guard. It infuriated her to see that they were doing absolutely nothing to help those inside. Their screams were pitiful. They tore at her heart. Without conscious thought, Hillery cast about for a means with which to help. There on the ground beside her was a bucketful of water and a wet blanket that someone had abandoned when the soldiers took charge. She was aware they were watching, but she didn't care. In one swift movement, she lifted the bucket above her head letting go the contents. The water cascaded over her like a waterfall. She gasped as the cold water made contact and snatched up the blanket.

The man nearest her made as if to grab her, but she eluded him easily. Sparks flew and sizzled in a creaking dance of groaning timber. In that one millisecond since she escaped the pair of groping hands, Hillery disappeared. The man cursed knowing Charles would hold him to blame if any harm came to her. For the briefest moment he considered going after her but stepped back just as a scorching red tongue licked across the thatched roof. Charles would have his head he thought glumly, but at least he was alive.

Once inside Hillery went to the aid of the two women, only one of which was still breathing. She drew her with her into the water-protected cloth and fled back through the flames. They fell together on the earth. In spite of the watching soldiers who obviously did not intend to get involved, hands immediately reached out to help them. Someone thrust a cup of water into Hillery's palms and she took a deep drink before passing it to the other woman. It was then she realized her mistake for the woman beside her did not look relieved to be alive. Instead her shoulders shook with sobs and she coughed when she spoke. "Charlotte Ann," she cried, "Charlotte Ann is in there!"

As Hillery's face drained of color, she gasped in dismay. "No, Molly," she shook her head, "that can't be! I...I would have seen her!"

"In the cupboard," Molly choked, "she was hidin' in the cupboard!" The woman's eyes rolled to the back of her head as strange noises erupted from her throat. She whimpered even as she lost consciousness.

"Oh, dear God," Hillery clamped a hand to her mouth, remembering the plain pine cupboard with doors just large enough for a child to climb inside. She felt sick to her stomach. "I'll get her," she promised fiercely even though the woman could no longer hear her. "I've got to get her! See to Molly!" she called to the others before snatching up the drenched coverlet again.

Hillery scrambled to her feet, racing to the now collapsing cabin. Through a space in the wall where the logs had caved, she caught sight of a little girl sitting in the center of the smoke-blackened room. The cupboard door still swung on its hinges giving evidence to recent abandonment. "Charlotte!" Hillery screamed as she fought to gain entrance. "Charlotte!" she called again but the child did not respond. Instead she sat in a state of shock, her bare legs crossed, her doll-like face smudged with soot. Charlotte's long black hair fell straight down her back, sweeping the floor where it mingled with the darkness that seemed to be everywhere.

More sparks flew. More timber crashed. The fire roared with a life of its own. While Hillery fought valiantly for a way in, Charlotte Ann sat perfectly still. And this time when Hillery would have made her move, strong arms reached out to stop her flight. She struggled against them, but it was useless. In the end she watched along with the others as the cabin burned to the ground. She looked around at the people, and felt tears prick the backs of her eyelids. The few remaining men were dead on the ground. Thomas, who would have fought to the death, was among them. Even Edward, the groomsman, lay sprawled just a few feet away.

Against her will she was returned to the house where Charles awaited. She was escorted by Tate and one of the other men. She made an attempt to reclaim her dignity. It was all that was left to her now. She had heard the cries of the women and knew what fate had in store for them. Her own future looked bleak as well. Poor little Ariel was shut outdoors.

"Well, my dear," Charles appraised her, "I have taken the liberty to have a bath drawn for you. After which, I have ordered a fine meal for the two of us. Our room is being prepared even as we speak. I have taken every precaution to make this night special." He chuckled at her expression, knowing she desperately sought to conceal her fear of him. It made him swell with pride. At that, she allowed her gaze to sweep over him regaining a measure of scorn.

"I should have thought you'd have joined the Confederacy," she stated clearly. "Instead you wear Union blue. You have no honor."

He did not deign to answer her directly. Instead he glanced down at his uniform and said, "Fools seek honor, wise men seek fortunes."

"Of course," she replied, her voice laced with a mockery of its own. "I should have known. Only a fortune would appeal to you."

"Not true," his lips curved slightly. "I'm here, aren't I? I came for you, not your money." The way he looked her up and down made her uneasy. He saw her tremble and grew bold. "If you agree to come with me, I could be persuaded to behave more honorably toward you. I am not completely without scruples, and I don't like to share."

She raised her chin in answer, her expression haughty. He frowned. "You would be wise to please me," he stated then nodded for one of the women to assist her with her bath. The girl's name was Tanya. She was young and frightened and obeyed only out of fear. She cast Hillery an apologetic look that was lost on Charles, but Hillery knew there was nothing either of them could do. "I am a winner," he clarified gesturing at the blue uniform he wore. "The Union holds the trump card. They have twice the population, nearly all the nation's wealth, most the farms and factories as well as a much larger network of railroads. That makes me a conqueror and you a fool if you do not reconsider my offer. Think on it. You would have much to gain." Before she could respond, he glanced at Tanya and said, "See to her bath. We shall dine in one hour. And I want her properly gowned. I have made my selection."

With that Hillery was dismissed. Throughout the hour her anxieties grew. As she was escorted to the dining room, lit and set for two, she strove to hide her fear. Charles had always been able to frighten her and this time was no different. In fact she couldn't have felt more vulnerable, more alone. God, if only Stuart were here!

Charles stood when she entered. His shrewd gray eyes landed on her cleavage that was showcased in the ruby gown he had chosen. The dress was an intimate one that she had selected for her husband. It was meant for a special, but very private reunion and she seethed at having to wear it for Charles. "You look stunning, my dear," he said softly, the look in his eyes frightening her still more. Fear was a terrible thing, she decided. She would strive to keep it in control. She sat when Charles pulled her chair out for her. Tanya was dismissed but ordered to remain nearby. She did as bid, her eyes wide. Hillery felt numb.

As Charles watched his manners throughout the meal, it was clear he wished to impress her. Unfortunately that did not dim his appetite for her. It showed in his every look. Occasionally their hands brushed and his eyes glittered dangerously. When they had finished with dinner, they retired to the parlor where he poured them both a drink. Hillery only sipped at hers while Charles eagerly replenished his own. He eyed her slowly up and down. The ruby gown clung to her every curve, so much so it was as if he could see straight through it. She blushed. His eyes narrowed when he whispered hoarsely, "You may call it what you like. But I call it the spoils of war. You are mine and you'd best remember it." He let his fingers trace the firm line of her jaw. They trailed the column of her throat before sliding lower still. When Hillery cringed, his jaw tightened.

She felt rather than saw his ardor grow. Tension hummed in the room. Hillery glanced about, busily scanning for a weapon. Had Charles peered more closely into the depths of her smoldering purple eyes, he might have been forewarned of her dangerous thoughts. Hillery was listening intently to a higher vibration. Charles was intent on the heaving flesh of her bosom. He grew bolder still as he plunged his hand into the low cleavage, pleased with the fullness there. She gasped when he rubbed his thumb across her nipple and it peaked. He sighed with satisfaction when it hardened to his touch. Hillery stiffened in his arms when he egotistically misconstrued the mild reaction of her body. She was angry. He was aroused.

She suddenly noted the ill fit of his shirt. It was a bit too snug across the belly. From an inside jacket pocket she noted the corner of a case of some sort and it struck a familiar chord with her. In dreaded fascination she recognized it as the case of a daguerreotype. "You're no officer," she accused even as she snatched the case free. Her eyes widened as reality set in. "Why, this is Elizabeth," she stated as she stared at the likeness. "What did you do to Lieutenant Markham?"

He chuckled in answer. Her face whitened. But he was not to be thwarted. He went too far and too fast when he cupped one breast fully in his meaty palm at the same time pressing his swelling groin against the fitted gown. The ruby dress was so well tailored that it took no margin of imagination to aim for and hit the perfect juncture between her thighs. When she moved he thought he had managed to seduce her. Instead, she shot for the staircase at full speed, making good her escape.

Furious, he charged after her. There was no way he would let her go now. His manhood was throbbing and he had ached for her since the first time he had laid eyes on her. He reached for and grabbed the fabric of her gown swinging her around to face him. She fought him and he was forced to hurt her in his need to tame her. He did not want to break her spirit, but he fully intended to bed her.

He struck her too hard; he could see that now. Her lip was swollen and blood dripped from the cut he had inflicted. It was bold against her skin. She grew hysterical and managed to break free, tearing her gown in the process. Charles knew only full animal lust as he chased after her. She fled up the curve of the stairs and in that moment she recognized this as the nightmare that had plagued her for years. She heard him following close behind and knew she was nearly out of time. She could not bear the idea of him taking her. She called out to her mother who had guided her so many times in her young life.

It was then Mariette appeared at the top of the stairs. Hillery's eyes grew round, but she hurried past. Charles gaped at the ghost of Mariette who in that split second gained solidity. She reached out and shoved him hard, a deafening scream tearing from her ruby lips. Charles froze, the sound chilling him to the very marrow of his bones. He teetered on the edge of the steps, shocked by the actions of the apparition before his body toppled backward down the stairs. He landed with a sickening thud on the marble floor below, his body twisted at an odd angle. His vacant stare gazed directly into the angry visage as she faded into thin air. The villain, Charles Thompson, was dead.

# CHAPTER SEVENTEEN

ate stood on the verandah with one of the other men. "Secure her," he said calmly. "Go ahead and enjoy yourself. I'll join you in a minute."

"Sure," Clem spat, nodding eagerly. Clem was an unkempt man and a very ugly one at that. He had a black heart and evil soul. His features clearly reflected his personality. Even the other men found him grotesque. Tate didn't care. He felt it a fit punishment for Hillery to endure. Tate had always been jealous of Hillery's fancy home and secure life style. And he greatly resented her status as mistress. He wanted to bring her down a notch and what better way than letting Clem have at her? Then once she was broken, he would take his pleasure. The mistress of The Plantation was not so grand after all.

Indoors Hillery stared at Charles' dead body. She tiptoed down the staircase, unsure of what to do. In some corner of her mind she was already making plans. She must find Isis and see for herself that her friend was well and safe. Together they would find a way to help the others and reclaim control over the situation at hand. From behind, a floor board creaked. She turned to find a monster of a man leering at her. He was only a hair's breath away with a gaze so filthy she knew what he was about. She tried to dart away from him, but for all his size, he moved with great speed. She screamed when he caught her in his giant paws.

His breath was fetid in her face. She cringed away from him but he immediately tore away the bodice of her gown. She was completely exposed and tried to cover her naked breasts. He would not allow that. In his greed to have her, he did not hear the front door slam open.

Simultaneously, Isis heard Hillery scream and stood poised in the connective door to the parlor. Her eyes grew wide as she watched Stuart enter sight unseen. For a fraction of a second their eyes met. Isis gave a nearly imperceptible nod. In that instant Stuart drew a baby dragoon from an inside pocket and fired. The conical bullet hit its target. The giant crumpled with a look of pure shock on his ugly face even as Isis swept Hillery away from the gore of the scene. Stuart reached them in three long strides and gathered Hillery in his arms. He held her while she cried. She didn't even know why she was crying. It was just suddenly all too much for her: The ordeal with Charles, the fire, the loss of Charlotte Ann, the attempted rape, all came rushing back in full force. To find she was cradled in the arms of her husband was more than she could have asked for. But she was never as grateful as she was in that moment.

Isis slipped quietly away only to find the others outside receiving aid from a Union troop Stuart had encountered on the journey home. He had been given a short leave of absence and the men, having seen the smoke, were heading in the same direction. It was fortuitous for them all. The small group of soldiers had corralled the remaining perpetrators all of whom would be facing charges. Only then did Isis notice Tate was not among them.

Riding against the wind, Tate grinned to himself. He wasn't as foolish as the others, for he had known when to leave.

A muscle ticked in his jaw when Stuart thought of how close Hillery had come to being raped. God only knew what else would have befallen her. When his dreams had clearly shown his wife in mortal danger he had requested a leave of absence. He had long ago assessed when to act on his dreams, and how to interpret the visions was a skill he had honed. He was well liked and respected by his men as well as his superiors and had had no difficulty obtaining the request.

He sighed with relief as he gazed upon Hillery's beautiful face, now peaceful in sleep. How terrified she must have been! How brave she was! He frowned when a tear escaped and rolled down her cheek. She hadn't made a sound. As he gently wiped away the single tear he thought of the man he had killed only a few short hours ago. His fingers had itched to pull the trigger. Never before had he felt a longing to kill. It had always been a duty to his country, an act of necessity or self-defense. It shocked him a little to realize how good it had felt to pull that trigger. He only regretted that he had not been the one to kill his nemesis, Charles Thompson. And that made him wonder what this war had done to him, or if he had done it to himself.

The next few days were busy ones with Stuart working alongside Old Jacob, who was the only remaining male resident on The Plantation. Old Jacob had received a serious head wound in the barn where he had been left for dead. He was grateful to be alive, and equally grateful to find Stuart here as well. The pair labored long and hard to rebuild the needed cabins and repair damages to the warehouses. Though some of the crops were lost to them, they found they were fortunate to have salvaged as much as they did. New cabins went up rather quickly. There were not so many people left after all that had transpired.

Hillery and Isis tended the injured. Molly, who Hillery had fought so hard to save, perished after all. Isis confided that she believed the woman died of a broken heart. Her wounds were superficial, though she did inhale a lot of smoke. While her lungs had labored to breathe, a wicked cough racked her body. Nevertheless Isis was convinced it was the loss of her daughter that had cost her life. The women had searched in vain for the child they all mourned. Ariel followed Hillery about.

Sukie, with the aid of young Muffin who was fast becoming a good little cook herself, managed to feed everyone as they went about their chores. Marta and Tanya, though shaky and sore from the abuse they had suffered, managed to put the house to rights. They were young, Isis reasoned. They would mend, though she was troubled by the trauma that had been inflicted upon them. Marta's mother had been killed in the skirmish Charles had led. The girl had yet to mourn and Isis confided to Hillery that she feared Marta was in a very deep state of shock.

At night Stuart and Hillery treasured the hours they had together. Their time was limited as Stuart would soon return to his post. It was not something they wished to discuss overmuch. They made love in the quiet of the night, sometimes desperate and heated, other times slow and leisurely. Hillery loved the taste of him. She would never tire of his scent. They lived only in the moment.

Ariel whined outside the bedroom door before settling into his basket. He was used to sleeping in the room near Hillery. But he was a good little guy and he adjusted to his new surroundings bravely.

On the morning of Stuart's departure Hillery could not keep from crying. She fought hard to control her tears, but in the end allowed them to flow unchecked. They did not know when they would meet again or how long it would be before they could be together. Ariel, hearing Hillery's sobs, whimpered when Stuart rode away. Apollo's whinny carried on the wind.

With the downfall of New Orleans, the South not only lost its wealthiest city but its prime seaport as well. Seizure of the Mississippi was of enormous import to the North. Farragut soon began his way upriver capturing Baton Rouge, then Natchez in turn. Hillery walked sadly through the nearly barren fields. There were so few of them left to work the land, they could only plant a portion of the rich black soil that stretched for miles. She stumbled wearily along the footpath to the isolated hills beyond where the people had held their burials for generations.

Hillery had just come from the kitchen where Sukie was busy taking inventory of the remainder of their food supply. Young Muffin followed solemnly in her mother's footsteps, her round tummy growling with hunger. Ariel trotted protectively at Hillery's side. Many of the men were dead upon the hill. Some of the women too, had died in the fire or from abuse.

Marta sat alone in the graveyard humming soft hymns to family and friends beneath the sod. Hot moisture pricked against her heavy lids as she mourned her mother. She had endured much Hillery knew, but she was stronger than she looked. She would heal. As Hillery approached, Marta steeled herself against the pity she read in the other's eyes. Though she lifted her chin, her own eyes glittered with unshed tears. She could hide nothing from Hillery, she loved her too well. Each registered the other's pain. The silence was broken only by an occasional cry of a wild creature. A huge bird flapping its great wingspread squawked in a nearby tree.

Marta moaned softly, her dark eyes ringed with shadows. She could not help but blame herself for her mother's death. If she had not tried to drag her mother into the woodland to hide, she may have been spared. The man who had caught them was not interested in the old woman. He had wanted Marta. His bold look had said as much. She had seen his lust and she had panicked! Marta feared men. Like many women Marta had been ill used, and she was of a tiny build and easily injured. Her bare feet took flight when he came after her! She had taken up her mother's withered hand pulling her along with her through the thicket. But the man was fast, his senses heightened. He tore Marta's dress away at the same time shoving the old woman to the ground. While Marta fought, her mother attempted to rise to her defense. The man was hardened. He didn't hesitate to thrust the bayonet on the muzzle-end of his rifle deeply into the old woman's belly. An eerie sound issued from the aged lips even as her eyes glazed over in a milky film. As his body pounded away at hers, Marta watched while her mother's soul left the earth.

Someone was nudging her. Marta opened her eyes to find Hillery standing over her. She had forgotten her presence there on the hill, so caught up in her grief was she. Her fingers stilled on the string of wild flowers she had been shaping into a funeral wreath. Hillery gently took them from her, promising to complete the task for her. "Get some rest," she coaxed the melodic voice both sad and tired. Marta peered at her, blinking rapidly. Hillery had lost loved ones as well, she realized. The people were family to her. She had risked her life to save Molly. Molly had been dear to them all, but Molly lay just over there where Hillery had been standing. Her epitaph included little Charlotte Ann's name. Marta knew that Hillery blamed herself for the child's death. Hastily she climbed to her feet.

While Marta made her way back to the house, Hillery walked among the graves upon the hill. She paused beside each rustic marker to deliver a silent prayer. So many of her friends were laid to rest here; she felt responsible for them all. Her thoughts trailed off as she realized she had come full circle. She was back at the place where Marta's mother was buried. Her cheeks were damp as she bent to the earth to lift the wreath from the white-washed stone. She didn't know how long she sat there, her fingers rhythmically braiding the flowers into a ring. It didn't matter.

# CHAPTER EIGHTEEN

irds squawked in a nearby tree. Ariel growled low in his throat. Hillery tried to shush him, but he refused to behave.

"Miss!" a voice seemed to carry on the wind. "Miss!" it came again.

Ariel cocked his head, his growl gaining volume. Hillery looked up cautiously. "Who is it?" she called out uncertainly, her somber gaze screening the graveyard for any sign of life. "Where are you?" her voice was hesitant.

"Over here...I need help," the voice came again accompanied by a shower of tell-tale pebbles. Hillery stared into the trees beyond. The sun was glaring in her eyes. She raised a slim hand to her forehead, shading them so that she might see. At first she was frightened by the scarecrow figure in butternut that blended so well into the woodland. It looked like death itself! But the figure spoke so pleadingly, begging for help. He pointed a bony finger at a lump on the ground beside him. "My partner is dyin'," the man croaked, "Took a bullet in the leg. I think it's infected. Got a head wound as well. He couldn't have fended for himself. He's sufferin' somethin' awful. You got to help him, ma'am. He's just a kid."

"Yes, of course," Hillery nodded. She was shocked to see that the shapeless form that blended so well with the ground was actually a wounded man. The boy's breeches were stained a putrid color. His head was wrapped with a bandage soaked through with caked blood. "Where is the rest of your unit?"

"Don't know," he looked away. "It's too late for that now. We've got to find a doctor, one who'll keep him hid away."

"There are no doctors here," Hillery shook her head, "Only Isis. But you can trust Isis."

The man didn't wait for further information but turned to his friend on the ground. "You'll have to help lift him," he managed to say as he staggered from the shelter of the trees. It was then she noticed that he leaned upon the upended barrel of a breech-loading rifle.

Hillery caught her breath but hurried to lend a hand. He caught her look and said, "We're all of us hurtin', ma'am." He seemed oblivious of his own pain. "I reckon it's a clean break. I'll be walkin' near to normal soon enough." He paused to draw breath. "Here, you take him under the arm…that's good," he instructed, approving the way she handled herself. "You have much trouble with blue coats round here?"

The question caught her off guard. "No," she shook her head. "They came around a while back. There's not much left to take."

The man nodded his understanding. "Be smart to keep a guard on duty just in case."

"Yes," she agreed, "we've been taking turns. I have a safe place for you both."

It took some time to near the house. By the time the others spotted them, both Hillery and the man were winded. "Good Lord, Missy!" Sukie scolded using her pet name for Hillery. She made no further comment but hurried to assist as fast as her girth would allow.

"Thank you, Sukie," Hillery murmured when the large cook had taken charge of her burden. "This is Will," she added by way of introduction. Her shoulders ached from the long walk down the hill. Muffin, never far from her mother, joined them. Hillery sent her to fetch Old Jacob. "Have a bed made up for him," she murmured. "I'll fetch Isis."

"You have faithful servants," Will offered.

"They are free people," Hillery corrected.

"I had heard that," he replied. "I wondered if it was true. I might as well ask," he paused to look at her, "Is it as haunted here as they say?"

She smiled slightly. "You have nothing to fear," she said, then as an afterthought, "It's only those who seek to harm me or the others who need to tread softly." She wasn't sure why she added the last, but there was something about the man that made her wary.

Will nodded and Hillery steered him toward a chair in the nearest available cabin. She didn't feel safe offering him a room at the house and she never ignored her intuition. "I'll have Isis examine that leg as soon as she has time," she spoke quietly as she turned to leave. "She will tend to your friend first, of course. What is his name?"

"Tommy," he supplied. "He's only eighteen."

"I understand your concern," she said kindly, only there was something about Will that felt off. "I'll have Sukie fix you a bite to eat. She is an excellent cook."

Will had eaten his fill and was dozing in his chair by the time Isis arrived. The hour had grown late and it was the dark of night, leaving the quadroon weary. She had tended Tommy without pause keeping him well drugged. By and large he had been unconscious and unaware most of the time. Every so often he would cry out. His leg had been badly infected. She worked hard to drain it and then pack it with a poultice she had made from dried herbs. The boy had a concussion as well which meant they needed to keep him as quiet as possible. Hillery had assisted. She had been trained well. The dressing on the injured limb would need to be changed on a regular basis. Now that the fever had broken, the boy stood a good chance of surviving. Isis said as much to Will, though he seemed preoccupied, mumbling that he was relieved about his young friend. Even so, Isis didn't care much for the man. Hillery joined them briefly when she came to clear away the dishes. A look passed between the two women before Isis hurried her on her way. Will's lips turned down in a slight frown.

The days flew by. Young Tommy grew stronger with each new day. He was easy to like and brought a smile to the faces of those around him. He spoke of his home and his family, and from his stories emerged an image of a fine family with little money but a great love for each other. His mother and sister were frightened for him when he followed his father into war. But Tommy had done all he could for them, teaching his sister, Ellie, how to hunt and fish so they could fend for themselves. He was honor bound to follow his father who, though growing old, felt a need to fight for his country. Tommy could do no less.

Will kept to himself much of the time; he walked the aged garden path on a daily basis. His strength was fast returning and he showed a kind of restlessness he was unable to hide. It was clear he had a desire to move on, yet he did not speak of it. The women couldn't help but notice that despite Tommy's physical pain, he was always eager to lend a hand. This was not true of Will who seldom offered to help with the chores, using his broken leg as an excuse to beg off. The women who were on their own now, with only Old Jacob to guard and protect them, disliked this. They muttered among themselves.

"Your leg is mending well," Hillery commented one evening.

"Yes, I am a lucky man," he replied. "I owe you and your people a great deal. I can't thank you enough."

"You are quite welcome. We could have done no less."

"You are a gracious lady," he observed. "How is it you have managed to keep your livestock? I would have expected the Union to have confiscated them."

She noticed that when he looked at her something had changed in his manner. His eyes held an unnatural glitter. It made her nervous, ill at ease. "My husband is a captain in the Union army," she stated quietly.

He looked into her eyes for a few seconds then stated in a firm voice, "I have need of a good horse."

"Do you?" she replied. "We have none to spare."

As she stepped away from him, he advanced. His earlier manners fell away as did his concern for Tommy. The boy had been an easy ticket home. He explained how he had used the boy to gain her attentions. Will was a deserter who had stumbled upon the injured boy. He had told Tommy he would get him safely to a doctor and Tommy had been grateful. "How could you do such a thing?" she demanded, angry now.

"They rolled right over us," he grated. "I would have been killed if had I fought."

Hillery who knew both honor and courage responded with scorn. "So you ran. Just like that," she spat.

"Don't be so smug," he wanted to slap her. "I did what I had to in order to survive. And Tommy would be dead right now if not for me. I could have left him there. I could have let him die."

"You believed he would anyway, didn't you? And that would have been okay so long as you got help first. Am I correct?"

"So what?" he growled. "He made it, didn't he? Now... you are going with me to the horse pasture, and you are going to act all friendly like. I want that horse of yours. You know the one."

"You'll never get away with it," she warned in a cold voice. "You'll never get off this land alive."

He had the good grace to look ill for a moment. He actually turned green. It was then he heard a growl from behind. Hillery had glanced that way a couple of times, but it had been so imperceptible that he thought it a ploy. Now he knew his mistake. The growl came again and this time he spotted Ariel. He should have known, the dog was never far from his mistress. Funny thing, Ariel appeared far bigger than before. He had a mean look about him too. Will drew his sidearm, cocking the gun as he took aim. Before he could fire, a ball whistled past barely missing him. It was so close he felt a current of air. He stared in disbelief when Tommy stepped out from behind Ariel who wickedly gnashed his teeth. Will couldn't help but notice the dog looked much like a wolf in that moment. He couldn't fathom that. Tommy confronted him. It was clear that the boy was prepared to fire again, and he knew by his look Tommy would not miss a second time.

"I heard everything," Tommy confirmed in a quiet voice. Sometimes when a man spoke in such a voice it was more alarming than not; this was one of those times. "Don't move. I won't hesitate to shoot you." Tommy's gaze never left his own. The boy was far more seasoned than he had realized. "Throw down your gun. That's good," he breathed when Will let the side arm fall to the ground. "Now, open your coat and turn your pockets out, nice and slow." When Tommy was sure Will had been stripped of all weapons he told Hillery to get the others. They would need a plan.

Hillery was grateful to Tommy for saving Ariel, who once again looked like himself, and for coming to her aid. She intended to make sure Tommy would remain a free man. Prison was not an option. She would see him to safety herself if need be. Tommy had proven himself to be an honorable young man.

They met in the kitchen to discuss his future. It was agreed that Tommy was well enough to move on. They found fresh clothing for him, and Hillery gave him a list of addresses where he could safely stop for food and a good night's sleep. He would be treated like family at the house on Chartres Street, she told him, as she had written Higgens and suggested he have a room prepared. All in all, Tommy would have care along the way.

Before his departure, Tommy helped Old Jacob secure a cell where they could safely lock Will away until help arrived. Again Hillery had picked up her pen, this time addressing Major Carter whom she prayed was still in New Orleans. In the event that he may have moved on, she had also addressed the issue with Higgens knowing she could trust his judgment.

Will was furious to find himself behind bars. He cursed Hillery and the others for locking him away, but his curses fell on deaf ears. The Plantation was already truly cursed. Why worry about the ramblings of an angry man?

Then one day Ariel set off an alarm. The people of The Plantation gathered to see what all the commotion was about. Ariel was not a barker. He put up a fuss only when something was afoot. Hillery and the others stared off in the distance noting a cloud of dust. They were about to have company. Ariel stood proudly next to Hillery. He cocked his head as if to say he was in charge.

Hillery's breath caught when she noted a Union flag riding high. The others followed suit. As it happened, it was a small detail of soldiers who approached. The balding officer in charge dismounted, introducing himself as Lieutenant Bernard. He had a pudgy round face, but a strong meaty build. His manner was forthright, wasting little time on amenities. "Mrs. Michaels," he addressed, "I have orders from Major Carter to remove a prisoner from your land. If you'll show me the way," he gestured, "we'll take this responsibility from your shoulders."

Hillery thanked him and did as she was bid. She was grateful to see the last of Will. Everyone slept better that night knowing that Will was no longer a threat to them. They would miss Tommy, but knew he was safe and that they had been instrumental in his recovery.

That night Hillery dreamed of a mansion on a hill. It was enormous. It beckoned her. Nearby was a bleak building that sent shivers down her spine. There was something so ominous about the place that it terrified her. There was something very personal about it as well. Instinctively, Hillery knew the mansion was somehow involved, somehow important. She awoke with a start, and with the full comprehension all this was in Virginia. She was deeply compelled to go there.

"What the devil? Who's been a thievin' from this here garden?" Sukie huffed under her breath. Produce had been going missing for some time now it seemed. As soon as the kitchen garden had started bearing its rewards, the fat cook had been plagued with a thief. Knowing that none of them was doing the dirty deed, Sukie had a theory of her own. She suspected a ghost.

Hillery heard the complaint and laughed softly. Isis was pleased at the sound of the tinkling music she so rarely heard these days. "Sounds like Sukie's phantom has struck again," Hillery said. "She is simply positive we have a hungry ghost!"

Isis hid a smile when Sukie scolded, "It's not funny, Missy Hillery!" The rebuke set her many chins wagging. "Something's been a gobblin' up our food just as quick as it pops through the ground! How can you just stand there and laugh?" Sukie gave one of her famous scowls.

"I'm sorry, Sukie," Hillery hid a giggle. "I'll tell you what," she added soberly, "I'll help you keep watch. We'll put an end to this mystery together."

"Well, I surely hope so!" the fat cook huffed. "That spook gonna eat us outta house and home!"

It was decided there was a good possibility they were once again dealing with a deserter. This being the case he would likely strike at night. Thus, whoever took the night guard need beware. Yet night after night the grounds were quiet, only to make a new discovery of a plundered garden in the early mornings. And with each night Ariel took off on a quest of his own. Hillery watched him slip away at dusk, only to return an hour or so later. What did this mean, she wondered?

By now, everyone was taking the raids seriously as a good deal of their food was quickly disappearing. There was, indeed, a phantom. As the hour grew late, Hillery took her turn on guard. She was stealthily armed with a Navy Colt of her own. The 1851 percussion revolver had seen her through many a target practice and she took her duty to heart. Night cast its shadows in a mantle of mystery black. Hillery felt more keyed up than usual. She knew for a certainty the riddle was about to be solved.

Her eyes remained wide open throughout the night. She kept a silent vigil until the sun came to replace the moon. It was then that she became aware of a faint stirring sound as if someone was moving very stealthily toward the garden. Hillery remained perfectly still. She was well hidden behind the giant base of an ancient oak when a miniature figure of scarecrow proportions darted swiftly across the yard! "Oh, my Lord and Saint Michael!" she gasped to herself. "It's a child!"

She watched in pained silence as the pitiful little thing clawed at the earth with broken nails. It scooped the nourishing treasures into the tattered ruins of a skirt at the same time sucking on the muddied food. As Hillery's awareness echoed in her head, she glanced down through a sheen of unshed tears to find Ariel watching avidly. He was bravely trying to champion the child, gently urging Hillery forward. Bless her heart, Hillery thought. The poor little thing is starving! She crept silently forward. The child's head was skeletal in structure and it jerked in sudden awareness of Hillery's presence, staring with the vacant eyes and hollowed cheeks of one who'd known starvation.

"Charlotte!" Hillery choked in disbelief, hot tears scalding her cheeks. "Charlotte Ann!" she cried quietly. She approached Charlotte Ann like she would a frightened foal, her own shock and anguish mirrored in the haunted eyes. Without a word she took the small hand in her own, stroked the delicate cheek ever so lightly, and led the child into the friendly kitchen where all the children loved to come.

# CHAPTER NINETEEN

he train ride to New Orleans north to Memphis, then east through Tennessee was a colorful, if tiresome, journey. There was an air of restlessness blanketing this city of rolling hills, a political outbreak of harried anxiety. Hillery and Charlotte Ann had set out on this new adventure after much thought and consideration. Ariel, of course, accompanied them. Hillery had sat with Isis well into the wee hours discussing the probable benefits of taking Charlotte on this trip. Under the guidance of the others the little girl thrived. After a healthy trim, her long straight black hair had regained its natural luster. The creamy pliant cheeks filled out with a color born of vibrancy. The thin pale lips transformed into a shade of dusky red. But Charlotte Ann did not utter a sound. Her thin, corded throat became frustrated with the effort. It seemed that Charlotte might never speak again.

The women discussed this behind closed doors. It was possible, of course, that Charlotte's vocal cords had been damaged in the fire. Still, they had not seen any evidence of this, and it was equally possible that Charlotte had lost her speech due to shock and trauma. Thus it was agreed a diversion might be of some worth. Hillery had determined it was past time for a visit with Stuart's family, and in so doing, a stop in Richmond might be valuable as well. Hillery's dreams were pulling her in that direction. It was time to face her fears and the mansion on the hill. Whatever was drawing her to that hill was of the utmost importance.

In spite of her love for her homeland, Hillery now knew beyond a shadow of a doubt her heart and beliefs were with the Union. It was also logical to conclude that Charlotte may very well benefit being placed in a home brimming with love and support. Thereby, Hillery decided to take her North. Her common sense and loyalty to her beliefs guided her to pass through Richmond on the way. She wasn't sure what she might learn, nor how she might use any given information. She just knew she must follow her instincts. And even though in many ways they were on opposite sides, she truly did want to visit Rose and see how she was.

Hillery acknowledged a keen sense of discomfort when she and Charlotte left the security of the depot to go in search of the nearby residence of Rose O'Neal Greenhow. Ariel strutted alongside them acting as protector. The widow herself greeted them in the foyer of her very charming Victorian home with its ornament of bric-a-brac and sweeping wide staircase. Though her features were a bit strained, her glowing olive complexion a shade too pale, Rose remained a vibrant beauty. "Welcome, my dear," she smiled gaily as she held wide the door. "Why on earth didn't you send a message? Someone would have picked you up! We weren't sure which day to expect you."

"No bother," Hillery dimpled, relieved to find her friend in good health and spirits. "It was a pleasant walk. Only a couple of blocks! We did, however, leave our trunks at the station if someone could pick them up after while?"

"Of course, consider it done," Rose ushered her guest into the parlor. "You must be exhausted. I shall ring for refreshments. And this must be the child you spoke of? She'll make an excellent companion for little Rose!" Rose's gaze swept over the quadroon girl with little interest, then landed briefly on Ariel. "You did know my daughter and I were reunited here in Richmond? And what a brave little girl she has been, too! She stayed with me as much as allowed."

"Of course, you mentioned her in your letters. I'm so happy for you, Rose, and most anxious to make her acquaintance, as well." Ariel let out a soft whimper.

"And so you shall," Rose beamed. "Come along, Charlotte," she directed, attempting to pry the small fingers away from Hillery's gloved hand. A slight frown marred her countenance when she quickly turned the assignment over to a servant.

"I'm afraid she's rather shy," Hillery defended.

"Yes, so you mentioned," Rose mused.

"So, do tell what's happening here," Hillery said a trifle too brightly in an attempt to quit worrying about Charlotte. Charlotte was an able child, and in spite of Rose's brusque demeanor, she knew her to have a kind heart. "Tongues are wagging all over the city. Are the Federals so very close then?"

"Indeed, they are," Rose replied over a steaming cup of tea. Her words were candid as she continued, "McClellan has his men camped on the very banks of the Chickahominy. They have been there nearly a month, crouching, ever watching."

"Oh," Hillery's hand flew to her mouth. Ariel sat up straight.

"No cause for concern," Rose continued shrewdly. "McClellan's not about to make that leap! No, he'll just sit there and ponder, biding his time with miscalculations and extravagant worries."

"How do you know?" Hillery ventured. "How can you be so sure?" She wondered at the other's studied calm.

"That's my secret," laughed Rose, an expression she used frequently. "I am a spy, am I not?" She gave Hillery a sly look. "Besides, I know his tactics quite well, just as I know how he admires that idiot Pinkerton."

Hillery didn't like to admit, even to herself, how Allen Pinkerton had botched so many of his endeavors. It was, however, the truth. "And what do you think will happen?" she inquired.

"Lee will come to our rescue, of course! You must have faith in our Confederacy, my dear," Rose admonished. "Mr. Davis will not let us down."

"Of course," Hillery was honest enough to admit to herself that the conversation was making her a bit uncomfortable. Still she forged ahead, "I heard he paid you a formal call. That must have been quite rewarding?"

"Yes," Rose sighed proudly, tears gleaming in the depths of her rich dark eyes as she squared her shoulders, "It made it all worthwhile…that whole terrible year in that dirty, vermin-infested cell." She shuddered slightly, but lifted her chin, her face alight. Both women knew the game they played. They were friends, true, but even friends knew a price. "He made rich mention of my efforts for Bull Run and Manassas. General Beauregard was extremely complimentary on that score." Her eyes glittered in challenge. Hillery didn't utter a sound.

A young maid entered with a silent curtsy. When addressed, she whispered that the children would be out on the terrace. Hillery watched in silence as the girls filed past. It was uncanny how much mother and daughter looked alike! Despite herself, Hillery couldn't help but notice the differential treatment the white girl received. Hillery blushed slightly when she felt Rose's gaze upon her. She was wise enough to keep her own counsel.

"How is Captain Michaels?" Rose asked softly. "He hasn't managed to change your allegiance, has he?"

"How can you ask such a thing? I was born and raised in the South," Hillery felt her heart flutter.

"Ah, yes," Rose agreed, "I sensed your love of the South from the very first. It is a vital part of your charisma. Yet," she paused, "You also possess a dynamic strength that could either rival my own…or back it. I would prefer you as an ally. You have much to offer, and you are certainly in a position to gather vital information. What say you?"

Hillery was completely taken aback. She was stunned at how close Rose had come to the truth. After all, she was already an active member of the Underground Railroad. A spy was very close to the surface. Hillery was aware she was walking a fine line. "I could never forsake my husband so completely," she answered evenly.

"Yet you remained in Louisiana when you could just as easily have stayed in Washington."

"My husband understands that," she murmured. "He would never forgive the other."

"I see," Rose replied briskly as she rose from her seat. "We dine at eight."

"Rose, please," Hillery regretted the conversation. She hated to offend a friend. "I have long valued your friendship," she offered in all honesty. "If you prefer, I can take a hotel while I'm in the city."

"No," the older woman paused to wonder at the attraction she felt for the other. "We are still friends," she said at length, "and I would not put a friend out. What do you say we call a truce?"

"Yes," Hillery swallowed, "a truce."

Hillery had come full circle. She had no choice but to face her own convictions. As much as she loved the South, she would never agree with its politics. Nor would she ever do anything that would jeopardize her husband's safety. It was difficult to admit, but in reality her heart was no longer with the South. She was a steadfast Union sympathizer. And even though she held Rose in high regard as a friend, she was very much aware that she was on the opposing side of the well renowned Southern spy.

Rose disappeared frequently during those rainy days in mid-June often returning with a spirit of triumph. While Hillery and the children remained close to the house, the threatening sounds of war carried to them on the wind from behind a screen of distant campfire. Beyond the tall spiked spires of the city, McClellan's men huddled in the damp protection of their shelter halves. Wrapped in rubber blankets, the rains continued to pour down upon them until the river swelled then flooded, adding to their misery. And though the Yanks bore silent witness to the regular striking of the hour, they were doomed to suffer the malarial atmosphere of their camp. In the distance church bells tolled.

With Lee in command of the Army of the North Virginia – supported by Stonewall Jackson as well as A. P. Hill – McClellan felt he was facing an overwhelming opponent. He gave the command for Porter to move to the designated ground east of Gaines' Mill. This was an easily accomplished maneuver which enabled the Union to protect their right and left wings as well as the bridges on the railroad. Porter soon dispatched a request for additional troops. It was a plea that never reached General McClellan.

On the fateful day of June twenty-seventh the Battle of Gaines' Mill was fought. Although Porter exerted an extreme effort repelling a force twice his size, defeat was sure to come. McClellan had again overestimated the force and size of the Confederate troops. While he sat pondering his defense situation, Lee and Jackson assaulted the Union lines capturing many cannons before finally driving the Federal troops back into the woods.

With the masses of wounded from the battle thus engaged, Hillery went on temporary assignment at the military hospital only recently established on East Broad Street. Ariel was left behind to watch over the children. The hospital already stretched between the streets of Thirty-Second and Thirty-Fifth overlooking the wharves. Little did she know as she stood speaking to the head doctor that this growing collection of buildings and tents would soon become the largest military hospital in the world!

"Welcome aboard," the weary doctor shook her hand then thanked her for her time.

"I'm happy to help while in the city," she responded, feeling slightly like a traitor. She told herself as she turned away that she would have nursed either side. It was a truth that helped only a little for if she were being completely honest with herself, she would be forced to admit that the many Union prisoners who haunted the sidewalks drew her sympathy far more!

After the fight at Savage Station coupled with the heated Battle at Frayser's Farm, the Union army retreated to the advantageous height of Malvern Hill with the Rebs in swift pursuit. Malvern Hill was a high, flat plateau which loomed above Harrison's Landing. The Union's position of defense was ideal. Below them lay a wealth of swamp land which forced the enemy to concentrate in a single area of attack. The battle fought was bold and bloody. Brigade after brigade of Confederate riflemen charged up the hill into a blanket of shrapnel, grape, and canister. Those who survived these powerful odds were cut down by musket fire from the 14th New York. Though the Confederates were easily mowed down by the hilltop artillery, the greatest victory remained in their hands for the City of Richmond was safe.

McClellan retreated to Harrison's Landing while Lee withdrew to Richmond. Now that the Federals were no longer camped just outside city gates, the people were caught up in the explosive aftermath of the so named Seven Days Battle. Accusations were running wild. There was no compassion for anyone even slightly connected with the Union. Hillery knew her days in the city were fast coming to an end.

Hillery accompanied her hostess to the Hollywood Cemetery located on Albemarle Street where the bluff overlooked the James. Sliced in hollow breath-taking ravines, the cemetery earned its name from the dense forest of holly trees. It was so immense; it seemed to roll on for miles. Rose wanted to visit the cemetery for many reasons. She wanted to visit the graves, of course, but more than that, she wanted to see and be seen by the Confederate elite. And because of Hillery's affiliation with the Union, she wanted her seen there as well. Hillery sighed as she walked with Rose among the graves. It seemed death greeted her wherever she went.

When at length they prepared to depart the cemetery, Rose had a sparkle in her eye. The women had met and spoken with many of the city's most prominent citizens and they walked away with a long list of invitations to every tea or social of any worth. Rose was extremely satisfied with the events of the day as they made their way home in the carriage, but Hillery watched with mournful eyes all the Union prisoners upon the street. She ducked her head at the sight of their shackled, miserable forms. She did not allow Rose to witness her grief, but sent up a silent prayer for her husband so far away.

The ride home seemed an eternity. To lighten her mood, Hillery soon began to take note of the many beautiful homes and mansions scattered about the area. As she gazed up at the three and one-half story mansion that graced Church Hill, she felt a shiver penetrate to her bones. This was the mansion she had seen in her dreams. And this was the hill that tormented her very soul. Before her rose another vision. It wavered momentarily. It was the frightening building from her dreams. And she sensed it was nearby.

# CHAPTER TWENTY

n the days that followed, the city was caught up in a whirlwind of galas. Rose considered it a particular honor when the arrival of a formal invitation to the governor's mansion was delivered directly to her door. She and her house guest were invited to a victory ball celebrating the retreat of the Union Army. It was a personal invitation from Governor Letcher himself. Excitement was brewing on the day of this grand event. Every lady in the city who was planning to attend was busily repairing her finest – if slightly threadbare – attire.

Hillery patted her loosely flowing curls into place then bent to smooth the flounces of her best velvet gown. It was a charming creation the exact hue of the moss that draped the magnificent live oaks of the South. Carefully, she opened an aged ivory fan that had belonged to her mother. It was studded with tiny emeralds and laced with moss green ribbon. Pirouetting before the mirror, she discovered little Charlotte's reflection in the glass. "Hello," Hillery said gently. "I didn't hear you come in. How are you today?"

Charlotte raised her well trained fingers in the fashion that she had been taught to indicate that she was all right.

"That's good," Hillery grinned continuing in a tender voice, "because I have been worried about you."

Charlotte moved her fingers rapidly, concerned with Hillery's dismay. "You don't know why, do you?" asked Hillery in response to the child's ready hand signals as well as the slight frown that marred her face. "It is only that you have looked a little sad lately. It bothers me to see you unhappy. Has little Rose been treating you fairly?"

Charlotte dimpled, signaling that she had.

"Ah, but you are still lonely, are you not?" Hillery asked. "It's okay, I get lonely too. My mama died when I was born, you know, and I miss my husband so much it hurts. But I have to believe it will all be okay someday. Maybe you can believe that too?"

Charlotte nodded solemnly and Hillery took her small hand in hers weaving their fingers together. "We are going on another adventure when we leave here," she promised. "But at any time, if you are unhappy, I will take you home. Do we have a deal?"

Charlotte nodded in agreement and then wrapped her slender arms around Hillery's tiny waist. She carefully laid her braided head against the velvet of the other's gown. "Don't worry, you won't muss me," Hillery giggled as she crushed the child closer still. "Do you like my gown?" she asked at the girl's wide-eyed admiration.

Charlotte nodded vigorously, her tiny fingers knitting a soundless exclamation. "Beautiful?" Hillery laughed. "I'll show you beautiful! Come look in the mirror, Char. You have the face of a princess!" Charlotte stood shyly before the delicately fluted Federal looking glass while Hillery pointed out each charming feature. The child stared at the huge, heavily fringed black eyes peering back at her then glanced at the small straight snub of a nose and dark-red mouth. She fingered her thick black hair and grinned when Hillery squealed, "And such hair!" Hillery praised openly, admiring the glossy black braids. "You know, I just happen to have the perfect length of bright red ribbon to dress your lovely head! Here, see?" Hillery produced the proffered ribbon from a nearby drawer. "Now we'll just fasten it like so...there! Doesn't that look pretty? You shall outshine all the other little girls at the party."

"I do hope I'm not intruding?" Rose stepped regally into the room. "Little Rose is awaiting you, Charlotte. If you are to attend her needs, you must be prompt. Hurry along now!" the widow snapped, her glowing olive complexion expressing a bit of annoyance. Charlotte had already scurried out through the bedroom door when Rose called after her. "And remember, you girls are to stay out of sight! You may watch through the balustrades if you must."

"She is such a darling," Hillery sighed then just as quickly added,

"I hope you and little Rose are both satisfied with her?" Though Hillery was slightly irritated at the way Rose ordered Charlotte about, she said nothing to indicate this.

"You pamper her overmuch," Rose sniffed in return.

"Let us not quarrel, Rose dear," Hillery was quick to change the subject. "What is it you have brought me?"

"You always find a way around me, don't you?" the older woman scowled. "I have not been close to many women in my life. It baffles me at times. But," she handed Hillery the silken pouch that had not gone unnoticed, "I haven't time to ponder it now. Well, go on! Open it!"

"Real silk stockings," Hillery breathed, fingering the generous gift with open pleasure. "I haven't seen real silk stockings for...well, I don't know how long!"

"Well, yes," Rose's full lips curved in a genuine smile. "I thought the occasion deserved better than lisle."

"Where on earth did you find them?" Hillery simply could not suppress her curiosity.

"Ah, ah, ah," Rose wagged her finger to indicate she would not reveal her source. "That is my secret!" she laughed aloud. "Well, what are you waiting for? Try them on!"

Hurriedly, Hillery stripped off her worn pair of lisle stockings, happily replacing them with the new silk ones. It was a luxury to feel their softness against her skin. There was a time when she had known nothing but silk, but that seemed an eternity ago. Since the beginning of the war there had been many things she had learned to do without.

Completing their toilets with a quick flourish, the ladies elected to leave early for the ball in order to tour the sculptured slopes of Capitol Square. Bound by an immense wall of brick, the Square contained twelve acres of rolling hills heavily canopied by a natural forest of shade trees. The recently unveiled sixty-foot Washington Monument stood in the northwest corner, a bronzed equestrian statue of that famous president flanked by a group of other important political figures. The State Capitol boasted an effect something akin to the famous Greek temples, its mammoth columns circling all around with a lofty portico attached by a pilaster treatment to the main part of the stuccoed building.

Strolling up the walkway to the governor's mansion, the party gazed up at the two-story Federal home crowned with four chimneys on its wide deck roof. Charlotte and little Rose stood nervously in the background waiting for someone to whisk them away to their hidden corner of the gala.

"Follow me, girls," a woman with coal black skin smiled broadly as she urged the children indoors by way of a side entrance. "I'll show you where to go."

"Have fun," Hillery whispered encouragement into Charlotte's shell-like ear, "and don't look so frightened! You'll have a wonderful time!"

"That's right," the woman grinned displaying a healthy set of large white teeth. "You is gonna have a fine time! I have a special table set just for you young-ins, with special dishes and all!"

Soon little Rose was chattering gaily while Charlotte looked on with an eager smile. They followed obediently after the friendly maid.

The ladies were announced with great aplomb then swept away in the tide of meticulously groomed cavaliers. Rescued for the time being from the drudgeries of war, they were immersed in the pleasure of this magical evening.

Rose openly enjoyed the flattery of her male companions while she and Hillery drifted apart in the arms of their partners. Hillery, too, derived pleasure from the breezy dances and charming conversations, but in her heart she felt a wealth of emptiness as she dreamed of another pair of strong muscular arms...in another place...another time. Her amethyst eyes fluttered shut as she envisioned Stuart's finely chiseled features. When at length she opened her eyes it was to meet the bold stare of her partner.

"Come now, am I that poor of a dancer?" he teased. "Or do I bore you so completely?"

"You know you do not," Hillery smiled impishly at the man's contagious grin. "I am having a fine time." She kept to herself how his boyish good looks did nothing to compare with Stuart's more sensual physique, or that his broad grin only left her aching for the flashing white smile of a husband far away. Oh, how she longed for the familiar twin dimples that creased the corners of Stuart's firm lips! How she hungered to touch the deep cleft of his chin, and to run her fingers through his thick raven hair! She averted her gaze as if in shyness and when she lifted her head it was to reveal a dazzling smile.

He took it as a compliment and asked attentively at the end of the dance, "Would you care for some refreshment, a glass of punch perhaps?"

"That would be very nice," she acquiesced. Her partner bowed briefly, returning only a moment later with the cooling drink. She thanked him kindly and did not allow her relief to show when manners dictate that he allow another to take his place. She danced for only a moment more before making her excuses.

The young men watched her retreating figure as she made her way across the ballroom. "Are you not enjoying yourself?" Rose asked as she intercepted Hillery's flight.

"Of course," she answered, "I only need some air."

"You are a complete success. All the young gallants are totally enamored with you! Any one of them would have been flattered to take you for a stroll."

Hillery laughed lightly and said, "I find it a bit vexing to play the coquette. Marriage certainly does change one. I believe I will get some air."

"Of course," Rose agreed, but her shrewd eyes followed Hillery until she disappeared from sight.

Her time in Richmond was quickly coming to a close. Hillery had already purchased her train fare and was packing the last of her bags when Rose came to say good bye. The women hugged, promising to stay in touch. Rose, herself, was about to embark upon a journey, Hillery thought. She knew better than to ask any questions or to let on that she was aware of this. She went about her day as planned and long before nightfall Rose had vanished on one of her mysterious missions.

Hillery took Charlotte's hand, and with Ariel at her side, set off in the direction of Church Hill. Without conscious thought, she found herself standing quietly before the building that haunted her dreams. Those dreams were more frequent now. Somehow, she knew this building was connected to the mansion on the hill. Terror gripped her insides when she realized what she was seeing. This was the infamous Libby Prison! Visions of the many Union prisoners she had witnessed on the sidewalks danced before her eyes. She had not heard from Stuart in a long while, and she was very much afraid he was here. Why else would she be so haunted by this place that it stole her sleep at night? Libby's reputation was notorious. Many wound up here. Few walked away. It was reputed that as many as one thousand officers were housed here.

As she stood staring wide-eyed, both Charlotte and Ariel felt the tension course through her. It was as palpable as a living thing. The child and the dog appeared to communicate silently, leaving Hillery, who knew the history of the prison, to her thoughts. It had gotten its name from the ship chandler who had owned it at the break of war. Captain Luther Libby had been given only forty-eight hours to vacate. Now evil erupted from this place and horror stories were told about it. The prison was located on the James River with Belle Isle nearby. It stood a full four-stories tall with barred windows that let in the chill of the river as well as the weather. Hillery would later swear she could smell the mold and mildew even from a distance. As she breathed in the rotting flesh of its residents, a chill swept through her. Goose flesh rose on her arms. She choked back a gag and then sent up a prayer asking that her husband be spared this. When at length she walked away, she had paled considerably.

Since her destination to meet with Elizabeth Van Lew was a private one, she had made the arrangements accordingly. Yet as she stood before the bewitching mansion, she was unable to shake the horror of the prison. Perhaps she would come to some understanding of her own personal nightmares this day. For everyone's discretion, she had agreed to meet at a side door. Richmond was a city alive with gossip.

Just as she raised her hand to knock, a large colored woman cracked the door. She took in the small group with a nod and then held the door wide. "You are Mrs. Michaels?" the woman spoke quietly. She didn't wait for a reply, but led them into the house where Elizabeth was expecting them. She greeted Hillery politely, giving both Charlotte and Ariel a brief smile. Before seating herself Elizabeth asked her servant to bring refreshments. They appeared to be quite close and Hillery liked the kindness Elizabeth bestowed upon the other. The servant woman whose name was Martha took a shine to Charlotte. She engaged her in a one-sided conversation taking it in stride when the child answered with gestures in place of words.

Charlotte asked if she could help Martha in the kitchen, and Hillery grinned, giving her assent. Elizabeth seated herself, indicating that Hillery do the same. Seconds ticked by as each woman measured the other. Elizabeth was petite; her movements were somewhat spastic giving the impression of a tiny bird. Her features were sharp, her eyes bright. Those eyes were guarded now, but there was a graciousness about her that was indicative of a keen intellect. Hillery had heard all the rumors, of course, but she was fairly certain the woman was in full possession of her wits.

For her part, Elizabeth saw before her a beautiful young woman with Southern roots laced with Northern influences. She was well aware that her visitor had been a house guest of Rose Greenhow's, but somehow this did not trouble her. Hillery looked deeply into the slightly faded complexion opposite her. Elizabeth had a rather angular face that spoke of previous beauty. Hillery was aware of all the local gossip, and knew Elizabeth went about muttering to herself, just as she knew that she generally wore mismatched clothing. Most of the local folks thought her daft. Hillery did not agree. She believed Elizabeth knew exactly what she was about.

"To be quite honest," Hillery broke the silence, "I am not entirely sure why I am here except to say that I have been drawn to you. I simply needed to meet you. I believe we have a great deal in common. My husband is a captain in the Union army," Hillery watched Elizabeth closely as she spoke, saw the vague blue eyes flicker with new emotion, "and like you, I am a Union sympathizer."

"What can I do for you?" Elizabeth's eyes grew bright. There was a brilliance in their intensity that had not been there before.

"I am worried about my husband, Captain Stuart Michaels. I can't explain why, but I wondered if you had any word of him?"

Slowly Elizabeth sank back in her seat. It was perfectly obvious to Hillery that Elizabeth was mentally competent in spite of the dull facade she chose to present. In that moment Elizabeth shed that facade, and with a knowing look asked Hillery where she was from. It wasn't lost on Hillery that Elizabeth had not chosen to answer her question, but had asked one of her own. A tremor shook her.

Hillery answered levelly in spite of the keen suspicion that Elizabeth was already privy to this information. "My home is in Louisiana. Since my father's death a few years ago, I am the owner of The Plantation. Perhaps you've heard of it?"

"Indeed," Elizabeth smiled at her for the first time. "And you, like me, freed your people, did you not?"

"That I did," Hillery nodded. "It needed to be done. They deserved their freedom."

As if testing the waters, Elizabeth then said, "Your loyalties are divided." It was not a question.

"No, they are not," Hillery assured her. "I love my homeland, however I cannot abide slavery, nor do I believe in the politics of this war. The Union must prevail."

"I concur," Elizabeth stated the obvious. "And in so far, I can assure you I have not made your husband's acquaintance."

"But if you do...?"

"If I do," Elizabeth paused in thought, and for a moment Hillery thought she might refuse to help her. Instead Elizabeth changed the subject. "You have taken a great risk in coming here today," she observed. From a nearby crystal carafe Elizabeth poured two glasses and handed one to Hillery. Hillery took this as some sort of truce. "Try it," Elizabeth advised. "It is the finest homemade rose-petal wine," she insisted. "Martha is a wizard in the kitchen."

"Thank you," Hillery replied succinctly. "It is quite good," she said after an initial sip.

"If you are truly against this war, you are honor bound to help put an end to it. If you are against human suffering and bondage, you must help abolish slavery. And if you seek my aid in any way...you must pay the price." Elizabeth's eyes truly gleamed and in that moment Hillery did nearly question the woman's sanity. However, Hillery was wise enough to realize that Elizabeth was only protecting herself.

"What do you want of me?" she asked. "I am playing an active part in this war. I have led many people to safety and will continue to do so. What more do you ask of me?"

"I, too, have led many to safety," Elizabeth disclosed, "although very few Southerners know that. I am cautious and have trustworthy contacts. Our nation cannot remain as it is. Though I am a devout Virginian, our people of the South cannot always abide within the rules of the Confederacy. I would welcome the Union troops within our dear city, just as I have furbished a room in my own home for General McClellan's personal comfort. Now I will ask a boon of you."

Hillery sat still, barely breathing. Elizabeth was a very intense woman. Part of her already knew what was coming, yet she didn't want to fully acknowledge it. As she waited, she counted the quiet ticking of the clock. And then Elizabeth spoke.

"I want to know any and everything you learned while staying with Rose Greenhouse."

Hillery's breath escaped her. Did she not admit before her arrival that she was unsure of what she would find? Or how she would use it? Hillery realized she was on a precipice right now, and there was no turning back. Although she had always considered Rose a friend, wouldn't Rose betray Stuart if she could? Of course she would. And Hillery could do no less then to assist the Union in any way she could. Even as she related what she knew of Rose's missions, she felt a traitor. But she straightened her spine, and realizing that Rose would do the same in her position, she forged on.

"Thank you, my dear," Elizabeth said warmly. "And now to answer your question, when and if I hear any news of your husband, I will pass it on to you immediately. It would be my honor to aid such a strong woman. May I shake your hand in friendship?"

Without pause Hillery extended her hand and Elizabeth took it. She had a quiet respect for this woman. After all, Hillery herself had been relatively able to keep her adventures secret. Elizabeth, on the other hand, was hated by many in the South. She had made it a habit to speak openly about her Union sympathies. As a result she was frequently harassed. And Hillery knew instinctively that there had been times when Elizabeth had feared for her life.

# CHAPTER TWENTY ONE

ow good to set eyes upon the warm, pale yellow house that belonged to the Michaels' family in Washington! It had been a long time. Yet even as she stood soaking in the treasured memories that the home aroused, Hillery wondered at the proof of gaiety – the tinkling laughter and harmonious song that sifted through the billowing curtains of the large airy windows. No one knew of her arrival. She had not written as there had been little assurance of getting through. Now as she peeped into the door of the front room, she chuckled aloud at the startled faces that swung in her direction.

"Hillery," Natalie squealed, running to greet her, "what a wonderful surprise!" The deep blue eyes sparkled with genuine tears of pleasure as she drew her sister-in-law close in something of a bear hug.

"Darling," Rachael beamed, shining like a golden star in a brilliant yellow gown as she glided across the room.

Gran tripped along behind as fast as her inevitable twist of ebony would allow, then touched a withered hand to the downy-soft cheek of the young woman her grandson had married. "It's good to see you, child," she crooned. "Have you a hug for an old lady?"

"Of course," Hillery bent to give Gran a hug, then stooped to plant a kiss on the withered cheek. "I'm so glad to be here! Surely those aren't tears, are they, Gran?"

"Of course not," the old woman blustered, her hooded gaze sweeping the floor. "I've a cold, that's all."

"Come join the celebration, darling," Rachael insisted. "We've just witnessed a wedding!"

"Who got married?" Hillery's amethyst gaze flew to Natalie's shining complexion.

"Not me!" the other girl laughed. "I'm not ready for nuptial bliss! There's our bride," Natalie pointed to a blushing Annie who was happily sharing a wedding toast with her new husband, Cecil.

"Congratulations, Annie. You look radiant," Hillery whispered sincerely to the aging mulatto woman who did indeed look decidedly attractive in her gold-tone bridal gown. In one hand she carried a basket filled with an abundance of deliciously scented blossoms. A fresh wreath of glorious yellow rosebuds crowned her silver locks transforming the tired face into a mask of renewed vitality.

"Thank you, Miss," Annie accepted the compliment with a show of strong, white teeth. "Come, join the festivities!"

Hillery grinned outrageously but did not budge an inch. Her musical laughter spilled throughout the room in answer to the curious stares. "I will," she agreed pleasantly, forcing a sober expression, "but first, there is someone waiting outside I would like you all to meet."

"You've brought someone with you?" Rachael looked taken aback.

"Yes, a child," explained Hillery. "I hope it's all right? She has no parents. She recently lost her mother in a fire, and it seems she lost her voice as well." Hillery glanced around the room until her gaze met Cecil's. She could feel the electrifying sensation of compassion mixed with pity and knew without words she had brought Charlotte to the right place. "If you'll excuse me," she announced, "I'll go get her." Hillery then slipped quietly out the door then back again. When she re-entered Hillery carried Ariel who wagged his tail in excitement. Charlotte clung to her side. All eyes fastened upon the frail, beautiful child with skin the color of sand and hair as black as midnight. Charlotte peered warily up at them through a pair of deep-set dark eyes heavily fringed with sooty lashes. Her sleek raven tresses cascaded over her shoulders in a thick cape that reached her waist. The small dusky mouth remained tightly clamped while the girl's nimble fingers held fast to the hand of the one person in the room she knew she could trust.

"It's all right, Char," Hillery soothed, "these people are family. Come, I'll introduce you. You remember Mrs. Michaels, my husband's mother? I believe you met her a long time ago. It's all right if you don't, you were very small," Hillery inclined her head, proud of the exquisite figure her mother-in-law cut, "and this is Stuart's Grandmother, but everyone calls her Gran."

Charlotte carefully scanned each face in turn then directed her gaze toward Natalie. "Natalie is my dearest friend as well as my sister by marriage," Hillery explained, noting the child's curious stare. "She's very pretty, isn't she?" Charlotte nodded in agreement, a soft smile curving her ripe red lips. She might like it here after all, she thought to herself. Hillery's family seemed very nice, but there were two others in the room who had not yet been introduced. As the child turned to inspect Annie's well groomed appearance, Cecil flashed a conspiratorial wink. Charlotte's face creased in a smile as she signaled Hillery to continue the introductions.

"Ah yes! The happy couple," Hillery smiled broadly. "This is Annie and Cecil. They were just married. So you see...we arrived in the nick of time! They have invited us to join the party!" Hillery laughed at Charlotte's pleased expression, then whispered in her ear, "Cecil has a hardship as well. He can't speak either. Perhaps the two of you can help each other out? I don't think Annie would mind. What do you think?"

Charlotte struck a pose somewhere between newfound revelation and a deep rooted sympathy that should have been too mature for her tender years. While Hillery digested the realization that Charlotte hadn't known there were others with her affliction, Charlotte ambled over to the grizzled old man taking his gnarled hand in hers. Looking sideways at Annie through sober dark eyes, Charlotte silently bargained for the old man's welfare.

"Looks like you have competition, Annie," Rachael teased, a smile playing at the corners of her mouth.

"Well, I can sure use the help!" exclaimed Annie in her guttural English. "It's gonna take an awful lot t' turn this old bachelor round. Sides...he eats like a bird! I'm gonna need somebody t' gobble up all them cookies an' gingerbreads I'm prone t' bake! It'll save my waistline an' keep me busy at the same time!" she laughed, placing a protective arm around Charlotte's shoulders. Charlotte paused, her shapely brows furrowed in thought. She surrendered to the temptation she felt building and returned the gesture with one of her own. As her slim arms coiled around Annie's thick waist, Charlotte was suddenly giddy with the knowledge that this was where she wanted to be! She felt a certain kind of peace wash over her. She smiled at Hillery who smiled in return.

In the days that followed, Charlotte was often found chasing after Annie, performing as many household chores as her slight frame would allow. Each evening she spent an hour or more with Cecil – sometimes assuming the role of a miniature mother figure. They made a handsome threesome.

While Charlotte bloomed anew beneath the wistful parental tutelage of both Annie and Cecil, Hillery thrived on her own solid friendship with Natalie. The pair was constantly seen together. Mornings were spent in familiar cafes or touring the city's many sights. Afternoons were usually reserved for visits with Natalie's friends or attending a special tea. Evenings were family time in which the women frequently sat sewing while discussing politics and fretting over Stuart's whereabouts.

Sometimes Hillery disappeared on missions of her own as her work with the Railroad had grown. This, she kept to herself. She did not wish to compromise the family any more than Stuart would have. But Gran's sharp eyes missed little. The old girl was well aware of the odd hours Hillery was prone to keep. And while she worried about her grandson's wife, she also had a great deal of faith in her.

But clearly the girls' favorite respite occurred when they could temporarily escape the social pressures in favor of a brisk ride in the well sculpted parks of Washington. Mounted on their favorite steeds, they rode until their long hair billowed out behind them like banners on the wind. They slowed their pace only when they reached the site of the Union battalions who were feverishly practicing their wartime maneuvers. With a wicked smile curving her lips, Natalie gave a rakish salute, her deep blue eyes searching out one soldier in particular.

Hillery did not miss the gleam in her friend's eyes, nor the flushed hungry look that answered the bold invitation. Hillery smiled inwardly. So...Natalie was indeed interested in one specific swain! With a nod befitting a woman of her marital status, Hillery dug her heels into her mare's flanks. The vibrant white beauty automatically answered her desire. As her front hooves proudly pawed the air, horse and rider disappeared as one.

Hillery was oblivious of the admiring eyes that followed her frenzied flight, but Natalie caught the yearning glances of many of the meticulously uniformed men. She followed her sister-in-law at a sedate pace knowing that Hillery's thoughts would have only room enough for Stuart. It was not the first time Natalie had seen that well guarded expression, nor was it the first reckless escape Hillery had made from a battalion of men – any battalion of men. Therefore, Natalie concluded that Hillery did not wish to come into contact with any uniformed man…unless of course that man was Stuart! Dear God, where was that brother of hers?

Alone in her chambers Hillery sank into a state of dissimulation. Ariel whined and settled next to her. It was a private hell every time she entered the master bedroom that was her sole right to occupy. As Stuart's wife she no longer retired to the feminine room across from Natalie's, but had come instead to recognize every regnant line of the bold red and black master bedroom. From the griffin-winged armchair that graced the French Empire dressing table – ornate with bronze mounts and lyre legs – to the pane glass bookcase reflected in its beveled mirror, Hillery allowed her amethyst eyes to roam the silver embossment of the black silk walls. She stretched across the plush magnificence of the heavily swathed Empire bed secure beneath its canopy of deep red velvet.

Quickly she scanned the coordinating hue of velvet that draped the full length windows while admiring the massive collection of Napoleonic prints. It was at the hearth her gaze came to a crashing halt, for there above the mantel hung the majestic portrait of she, herself. Before their wedding Stuart had lain across this very bed absorbed in the empyrean vision he had created. Hillery now stared at the painting that was an emblem of their love; what was it Stuart had called her…the goddess of the moon and stars…a creature of unearthly beauty?

They had been here only twice since they were wed, the war having taken so much from them. But in those visits she had been radiantly happy. The room had felt masculine, yes, but she had thrived here in his presence. Now she felt lost and alone. Dear God in Heaven, please keep him safe!

A knock sounded upon the door shattering her daydreams into fragments. Ariel woofed low in his throat while Hillery dashed the tears from her eyes before she called, "Come in!" The door creaked softly open. A timid face peered at her through a pair of heavily fringed dark eyes. "Charlotte!" Hillery's voice caught in her throat. "Come in, child."

Charlotte nodded then scampered into the room seating her slender figure cozily next to Hillery on the bed. Ariel nudged her with his nose, craving attention. She dimpled slightly though the smile did not quite reach her eyes. "What is it, Charlotte? Is something wrong?" Hillery asked as she slipped a comforting arm about the girl's shoulders.

Charlotte's face crumpled. Her liquid eyes streamed tears. Releasing a soundless sigh she began to tell her story by way of her nimble fingers. Hillery soon came to understand the child's erratic emotions. "I see," she inclined her golden head allowing her riotous curls to blend with Charlotte's smooth ebony tresses. "Annie and Cecil wish to adopt you." It was a statement, not a question. "I had expected as much," Hillery admitted as she began to dry the child's tears. Sometimes her ability to see into the future plagued her, for she had become very attached to Charlotte. It would be painful to let her go. Aloud, she said, "I have only one question for you, Charlotte dear. Do you wish to live with them, for that is what matters most?"

Charlotte's gaze fell to the floor. Her lower lip quivered violently. With both hands Hillery gently cupped the girl's trembling chin. "You must be honest with me, Char. This is an opportunity of a lifetime! Are you afraid you will hurt my feelings if you accept their offer?"

Charlotte's response was quick as lightening. Her slight arms flew to encompass Hillery's slender curves. Ariel's ears rose as if in question. A series of silent shudders rippled through the delicate frame. "I shall always love you, Char. You are as precious to me as any child could be," Hillery murmured against the tousled tresses. Again she lifted the girl's chin tenderly brushing the tear-streaked face. "But you have brought Annie and Cecil tremendous joy! And between you and me, I happen to know they are not likely to ever have a child of their own. I have seen the love in their eyes when they look upon you! If that weren't true, I would tell you so. As for me," Hillery felt her own heart breaking but soldiered on, "I will visit often for this is my family too! And if you ever need me, you have only to write. I am never far. Go to them freely. You will be so treasured. Be happy, Char!"

Charlotte planted an eager kiss upon Hillery's rosy cheek feeling as though a huge weight had been lifted from her narrow shoulders. Ariel wagged his tail in response. At last she would have a family of her own with a mother and father both! Charlotte felt so blessed. She would always have a special bond with Hillery. That would never change.

The papers were drawn, the adoption final. As free people of color, papers were important. Charlotte moved into the small cottage behind the main house feeling complete for the first time since the tragedy that had taken her mother's life – in every respect save one. Now in the privacy of the enchanting room that Annie had created especially for her, Charlotte stood before the small oval mirror centered above the painted child's vanity. The room bespoke its love and affection from the frilly pink curtains that hung in the small square windows to the handsome quilt that covered the bed. This last had been a gift from Hillery and it was comprised of all her favorite colors.

The perfectly turned spool bed was made from the finest cherry. Charlotte's eyes scanned the entire room before returning to the mirror. Annie had even thought to produce a variety of children's prints to adorn the freshly painted walls. Yet with all this newfound happiness Charlotte continued to stare into the mirror, stroking the smooth café au lait column of her malfunctioning throat. Though the physical scars had quickly faded, the straining cords produced no sound. Angrily she dashed the tears from her eyes. If Cecil could manage, so could she!

Mail arrived the following morning. With it came a swarm of letters from Stuart, the bulk of which were badly worn. Hillery was quickly summoned. She and Rachael opened them together. Natalie and Gran sat on the edges of their seats. The mail had obviously been held up.

Stuart declared he had written to Hillery on numerous occasions, and was concerned that he had not heard back. He asked his mother to inquire after her and had said he would continue to write. He sounded worried. The women drew a collective sigh of relief in which Hillery did not attempt to hide her tears. She held the pages he had written about her to her chest and slipped quietly from the room. Thank you, God, she breathed. Thank you, God and Saint Michael!

# CHAPTER TWENTY TWO

he days passed peaceably enough for Hillery. Each dawn she tucked the grief of her enforced separation from Stuart away in the cloudy recesses of her subconscious, only to bring it forth again when darkness engulfed the world. "Thank God he is alive," she breathed softly into her pillow. But the dreams of Libby persisted, and in them she witnessed its yawning depths as if in person. After each episode she chilled and curled into a tiny ball beneath the covers. By day, she began anew as she drew herself up, straightening her spine as she did so.

"What's the matter, dear?" Rachel's voice broke into her troubled thoughts as Hillery sat buttering a thick slab of bread. Until then she had been alone in the quiet of the morning room. Rachel's step had been so light that Hillery had missed her entrance.

"Good morning, Rachel," Hillery forced a wan smile.

"There is something troubling you," Rachel insisted as she took a seat across from her daughter-in-law. "I can see it in your eyes. It is more than just this dreadful war. There is something else," she said with strong conviction. "Won't you tell me about it? Sometimes just sharing a worry can be of great value."

There was a moment of silence so complete that one could hear the whisper of telltale leaves brushing the house from handles of outstretched bark. After a thorough examination of the altruistic woman before her, Hillery was surprised how easily she could divulge her innermost fears. She told Rachel about Charles' death at the hands of her mother, the attempted rape which Stuart had thankfully aborted, Tate's disappearance and the disquiet of Richmond. Although Rachel knew about the curse on The Plantation, Hillery had never discussed her premonitions with her. In an effort to put her mind at ease, Stuart had once explained his family's acceptance of his unique gifts. This allowed Hillery to draw on her own courage and forge ahead, describing the dreams and visions that were rapidly growing in intensity. And then she looked her mother-in-law in the eye, and said succinctly, "I am worried about Stuart."

That said, there was no going back. Hillery explained what she was seeing and what she feared it might mean, ending her commentary with a vow of her own. "I swear, Rachel, I will not allow this. I am watching and waiting. I believe I will know when to return to Richmond, and I am making contacts in case Stuart needs aid."

"Oh, dear God," Rachel sighed, one delicate hand over her mouth as if to hold back a sob, "You poor child. I do not share these visions you have, but I know Stuart has always been very psychically aware. It bothered him greatly when he was small, but he came to accept it more easily as he grew older. He's also quite accurate. That's a very deep bond between you, I expect?"

"Oh, yes ma'am," Hillery reached for and grasped Rachel's hand. "I love your son very much. If I am right, and I believe I am, then I must follow the dictates of my dreams. That is how Stuart managed to show up in time to save me," here Hillery shuddered violently. The memory of Clem's monstrous paws on her still made her physically ill.

"You have a rare gift. You and my son both," Rachel conceded. "You will tell me if you learn more?"

"Of course," Hillery agreed easily, pleased to have this connection with Rachel. It was important they could talk, important they could share on such a very high level.

"Good, then it is settled," Rachel nodded absently. "We will work together on this." At Hillery's questioning look she continued, "I do not have your abilities, but I do have a great deal of contacts in the government as well as in the military. I will see that introductions of the highest order are made while you are in Washington, and I can keep you abreast as to Union movements. That way you will have ready assistance."

Hillery's heart swelled with pride and admiration. Her mother-in-law was an extraordinary woman! Ariel, who was curled up nearby, yipped in his sleep.

Hillery and Natalie sat alone in the library matching wits over an afternoon game of chess. They sat in a matching pair of gondola chairs that were graced with ram's heads at the corners of the seats. The feet were hooves. Nat stole a furtive glance at the board then drew a sip from the ice cold lemonade by her side. "I had forgotten how good you are," she lamented with an exaggerated sigh. "You know, I am really glad you are here. It was dreadfully dull before you came – but then we always did have fun together." Before Hillery could respond, Nat looked up with a rakish grin. Her lean fingers stretched easily across the board. "Check!" her voice rang out triumphantly as she made her move, the blue eyes so like Stuart's sparkling with mischief.

"Very good!" came the heedful compliment, sounding not a bit like defeat. "Checkmate!" It was Hillery's turn to lean across the board.

"Bravo!" applauded a dainty figure at the far end of the room. "Bravo!" the lady clapped her hands in mock delight as she stood in the open doorway.

"Crystal," Natalie scoffed rudely as she turned her back on the intruder. "Haven't you the manners to knock?"

"Natalie Michaels! You have always been unfair to me," Crystal simpered in reply. Hillery rolled her eyes under the canopy of her hand. Nat giggled even as Ariel yapped. Ariel gave the blonde intruder a cross look making it clear he did not like the woman. "I didn't come here today to start trouble. I came to call a truce with Stuart's wife! Mrs. Michaels?" Crystal addressed Hillery almost timidly. "May I call you Hillery?"

"Don't trust her," Nat broke in with a whisper.

"It's all right," Hillery soothed. "Of course you may call me by my given name," Hillery turned to face Crystal squarely. "What is it you have come to say?"

"Only that I am truly sorry for my past behavior," Crystal spread her hands before her. "I hope you will excuse it as a young girl's foolish jealousy and accept my apology? I fear it is long overdue!"

"Of course," Hillery replied graciously, further irritating Natalie when she proceeded. "Would you care to stay for tea? We were just about to bother Cook."

"We were?" Nat snorted in a most unladylike fashion.

"Yes, that would be nice," Crystal seized the opportunity, ignoring Natalie's jibe with practiced nonchalance. Ariel growled softly when she took a seat.

"I'll go help Cook," Hillery skittered across the floor with a wicked grin in Natalie's direction. "Why don't the two of you enjoy yourselves? And you, Ariel, be good." Natalie frowned at Crystal's brilliant smile. Ariel shook his head vigorously before settling it back onto his paws.

"Thanks a lot," Natalie mumbled beneath her breath, choosing to ignore the other's presence. She made no exceptions when it came to Crystal. The woman was up to something.

"Here we go, ladies!" Hillery stepped into the room balancing a silver tea service. "Cook will be along in a moment with some of her fabulous little fudge cakes. Shall I go ahead and pour?" She tripped delicately across the Savonnerie carpet placing the tea service near Crystal where she sat perched on the edge of a small Empire sofa with its eagle and cornucopia carvings.

The visit was brief, though it seemed quite lengthy to Natalie who fumed silently, not even bothering to hide her displeasure. Crystal appeared delighted by the discomfort she caused. She looked proud of herself for fooling the little fop Stuart had married. When at last she took her leave, Natalie gave Hillery a cross look. Her expression spoke volumes. Ariel seemed to agree with her as he scrunched up his little face. He looked absolutely crabby! Hillery sighed then gave a small smile. She decided to out wait Natalie whose patience always ran on the thin side. Patience was not her best attribute. And that's when Natalie erupted, "What the heck was that? Have you lost your mind?"

Hillery chuckled, smoothed her skirts, and said, "That was a performance, Nat; not bad, huh?" At Natalie's lack of comprehension Hillery set down the fudge cake she was about to attack and explained in a neutral tone, "It is always best to keep one's friends close, and one's enemies closer. That way I gain the advantage, not the other way around." As Natalie's mouth dropped open, Hillery popped a piece of the coveted fudge cake into her own rosy mouth.

The Sherwood mansion was a regal delight. Broad and sprawling, it was an architectural heaven. Located on the outskirts of the city, the mansion was surrounded by acres of intricately cultivated gardens. Some of the most pretentious horticulturists in the nation had attended galas on these very premises for the sole purpose of observing the blooming wonder of its exquisite blossoms and petals.

"I am delighted you could make it, my dears," Colonel Sherwood greeted the Michaels' women with a broad smile accompanied by a tug at the curling end of his silver mustache. "I do not believe I have had the pleasure," he turned to Hillery openly eyeing the swell of bosom above the lace edged curve of her coral tinted ball gown. "You must be Stuart's beautiful bride," the man bowed low in a chivalrous fashion. "I am your host, Colonel Sherwood, but you must call me Edward! It is entirely proper. The Michaels' have been in long standing with the Sherwood's. Isn't that so, Rachael?" he cast a solicitous glance in Rachael's direction awaiting her nod of agreement. "I hope you and I shall become close friends," he squeezed Hillery small hand in his own large, clammy one.

"It is an honor to meet you," murmured Hillery with a slight blush as she purposefully withdrew her hand. The colonel chuckled at her obvious discomfort. Ah, an innocent, he thought wickedly to himself. What matter that she was already wed? An unwanted husband was not so very difficult to deal with. After all, he was an expert on such matters!

"I told you he was an old lecher," Natalie whispered sometime later. "His wife is sweet enough, but you must never allow yourself to be left alone with him."

"I should say not," Hillery's response was dry. "I did not care for him overmuch."

"It is rumored he has seduced over half the ladies in Washington," Natalie continued, her eyes round. "Mother would not have brought you here at all, had she not believed there were people worth meeting. Many of the elite are in attendance this evening," Natalie tossed a worried glance in Rachel's direction. Rachael was sitting with a subdued Gran in a quiet corner. Natalie knew it was because Gran disliked Colonel Sherwood and did not like putting Hillery in his company.

"I understand that, Nat," Hillery soothed. "Please do not worry about me. I shall steer clear of the colonel." Natalie still wondered at her mother's reasons for submitting Hillery to that despicable man. After all, she did not know of the conversation between the two of them, nor did she know of Hillery's underground activities. Gran was the most enlightened among them, for she alone shared Stuart's gift, and was therefore aware of Hillery's. Hillery was becoming aware of all of this as there had always been a certain light in Gran's eye. It was there now. Even as she acknowledged this, Hillery knew she would keep her activities to herself. Barring the part about Stuart, even Rachael didn't need to know any more than she already did. Hillery was protective of her husband's family. She loved them far too much to put them in harm's way.

Across the way, the girls noticed Crystal in the crowd. She was beautiful in peacock blue. She laughed at something her partner said then threw them a pointed look. Hillery inclined her head in acknowledgment while Natalie remained aloof. Crystal's dance partner looked Hillery carefully up and down as though Crystal had just shared some privileged information. Natalie did not like the looks of him. If Hillery felt the same, she did not let on. Crystal's laughter carried across the room.

"Mark my words," Natalie spoke softly, "Crystal is up to something."

"Yes," Hillery nodded in agreement, "I believe so. Do you know the man she is with? I don't like the feel of him."

"No, I've never seen him before," Natalie looked at Hillery in open curiosity. "What do you mean by the "feel" of him?"

"I mean there is something about him that smacks of mischief. I don't trust him, and I certainly don't trust Crystal. They are in cahoots."

"How about I circulate?" Natalie chewed her bottom lip in worry. "Maybe I can discover something about the man. You be careful. And stay near mother and Gran."

"Oh, I shall," Hillery assured her.

Natalie disappeared into the crowd. Hillery watched until she lost sight of her. She cast a glance in Rachael's direction and saw Gran mouth something to the other. Gran looked directly at Hillery, and it was as if she sent a very clear telepathic message, "Be careful. Something is afoot."

Hillery gave a perceptive nod. She was about to join them when Crystal approached with her dance partner in tow. Gran's eyes flared wide. She looked terrified as if she was watching an awful episode unfold. She sat bolt upright in her chair, clutching at Rachael who had stiffened beside her.

Crystal introduced the fellow as Jeremy Slater. He had dark hair and even darker eyes that did not light up when he smiled at her. The smile itself seemed vacant, more like the stretching of muscle. It sent shivers down her spine. It was clear the couple wished to engage her in further conversation, but as luck would have it she was saved by another man who had apparently been watching the whole event.

"Excuse me," he spoke quietly but firmly, "I was speaking to your sister-in-law, and Miss Natalie gave me permission to make your acquaintance." Hillery quickly scanned the crowd and did indeed see Natalie nodding at her. She looked back up at the man, feeling relief steal over her. "Please allow me to introduce myself. I am Benjamin Courtley, Captain Benjamin Courtley," he sketched a bow.

"Nice to make your acquaintance," Hillery breathed more easily now. "How is it you know my sister-in-law?" She felt rather then saw Gran and Rachael relax.

Crystal gave a tight smile, looking momentarily defeated. She looped her arm through her partners, made an excuse and walked away.

Hillery vowed to keep her eyes open. The man beside her was speaking, clearly answering her question. "Miss Natalie and I share mutual friends. She was concerned about you and asked that I intervene. I didn't mind," he assured her with a smile that crinkled the corners of his brown eyes. He had puppy-dog eyes that made her think of Ariel.

She laughed at his admission finding him charming. "Your husband is a very lucky man," he said. "I hope he won't mind sharing you for the evening? I thought you might enjoy a dance?" He dared a rakish grin causing Hillery to laugh out loud.

"That would be nice," she grinned up into the sun-bronzed face that loomed above her. Benjamin responded in kind and offered his arm. His dark eyes twinkled. His blonde hair was shorn too close to his head. It tumbled in reckless curls nonetheless. He was a handsome man in a rugged sort of fashion, yet his manners belied the untamed look that was so much a part of him. Benjamin was a perfect gentleman. Yet even as Hillery thought this, she found herself wishing it was Stuart who held her in his arms.

Watching from a distance Crystal strode petulantly over to where the colonel stood conversing with some of his guests. She slipped an arm around him, easily drawing him away from the small crowd. She cocked her head, licked her lips, and managed to show off a bit more cleavage. The colonel had been chasing her for such a long time, she nearly had him panting. She moved closer than was socially acceptable, let her hand splay between their bodies, and gripped him sexually. He groaned as she smiled. She said, "We have to act soon before she gets suspicious."

"Not to worry, my dear," the colonel indulged her. It was obvious he was already picturing her in his bed. That mouth, he thought to himself, what he could do with that mouth! He suppressed another groan as Crystal's smile widened. "Everything and everyone is set. Just don't forget what you promised me."

"I won't forget. It will be fun," she gave a wicked laugh. "Only I do want to watch first."

"As an act of revenge, or foreplay?" he countered watching her closely.

"Hmm, both," she giggled, "I find it arousing to watch such activities."

He gave her such a smoldering look; she thought he might try to take her right there. "Your wife is watching, Edward dear."

"My wife," he grinned insolently, "is used to my little indiscretions. I have taught her well. She sits and watches obediently while I smile upon other women." He flashed his most charismatic smile as if to demonstrate his words. "She even holds her tongue when she sees me publicly stroking them," he ran his fingers along the bare swell of her bosom, and then caressed her cheek after which he spun on his heels and walked away. He could be an insufferable boor at times, but he would serve his purpose well and she was even looking forward to their assignation. She smiled evilly as she watched him pause, speaking briefly to a man she knew only by reputation. The scene was set.

Having finished her dance with Benjamin, Hillery graciously excused herself. She was indebted to him for his chivalry and told him so. He told her it had been an honor and watched her walk away. She was headed in the direction where Gran was still seated. He felt she would be safe now and was truly relieved. Hillery Michaels was an exceptional woman!

The dance floor was crowded. Just before Hillery reached her destination, she was accosted by a stranger who told her to accompany him. He spoke precisely even as she felt the snub nose of a pocket derringer in her side. She had little choice but to do as he said, though she kept hoping for someone to notice them and come to her aid. No one did. They had reached the terrace door leading into the gardens when she suddenly realized they weren't alone. She gasped when she recognized Jeremy Slater. He was standing directly in front of her, a cruel look on his sharp features. Behind him another figure loomed. Dear God it was Tate! How had he found her? As she backed away, they closed in. She cast a glance back toward the terrace and was shocked to see Crystal and the colonel standing there. Crystal wore a diabolical expression.

Hillery fought for all she was worth. The men were toying with her. She was running out of time. Slater made the comment to Tate that she would bring a good price in their bordello. She gasped aloud. They laughed, elaborating still more on their business and their intentions for her. She had no idea how the colonel fit in but she was pretty sure it involved Crystal.

Her gown was torn and the tide of emotion turned dangerously serious. Things were getting ugly when all at once Crystal joined the mix. She had a cruel glint in her eye when she said she wanted in on the fun. She stared at Hillery like a hungry cat who was captivated by the scene about to unfold. She started hurrying the men, wanting Hillery's clothing off. She licked her lips. And in her excitement got in Slater's way, knocking his gun to the ground. Hillery lunged for it. The gun roared. The men froze causing them to act quickly, disappearing in the blink of an eye. Hillery watched as Crystal teetered unsteadily before her. It took a full moment for her mind to accept what was happening. Crystal gaped at her, her hands splayed over her abdomen. She opened her mouth to speak then dropped to the ground. Crystal Fleece was dead.

# CHAPTER TWENTY THREE

n March of 1863 General Ulysses S. Grant strode quietly from his headquarters aboard the steamboat, Magnolia, to stand in contemplative thought by the softly swaying ship's rail. Below, not many miles away, sat the Confederate 'Rock of Gibraltar' – that sought after city of the Western Campaign, Vicksburg! While he stood soberly puffing his cigar which was sheltered by the wide brim of his hat, the rain continued to fall in torrents around him streaking his overcoat with hundreds of winding rivulets.

Lincoln viewed Vicksburg as the Union key to the war. It not only divided the great Mississippi River, but it was a main stem of supplies for the Confederate troops as well. Indeed, it supplied the entire Confederate Army! From the connective flow of the Red River, the Rebels were gifted with cattle and corn. From the magnanimous lengths of the Arkansas and White Rivers came hogs and cattle by the thousands to be generously distributed by rail all over the South. Weapons and munitions were imported from Mexico and Europe via Texas. These, too, passed through Vicksburg before falling into Rebel hands.

Staring up at this unassailable stronghold two hundred feet above the high-water mark, Grant pondered his failures of the past two months. On a trial and error basis, he and his men had struggled to reach the high ground of the east bank in spite of the outbreak of malarial fever. Rampant cases of smallpox peppered the area as well. The winter had been bleak – heavy with showers. Even now in the bud of springtime the river continued to rise, swamping the shores, sponging any and all ground that chanced to escape its thirsty tongue. Thus there was little comfort for a camp of weary men, many of whom were deprived of tents. Shifting to a dryer location, Grant sent his cigar butt speeding through the air to bob among the collective debris in the sluggish brown waters. It was in his mind to surge forward to a positive victory, a weighty decision for one man to perceive. Yet even as the red tip of his cigar was snuffed by the gentling pelts of raindrops and tossed upon the rocking purple waves, he knew in his heart that he must defy Sherman's more conservative advice. He must push ahead for the conquest of Vicksburg! There was still the possibility that it could be taken from the rear.

On the twenty-third day of March, Grant ordered his command to Milliken's Bend. One week later found them marching a single unpracticed road for the goal of New Carthage. They were a motley crew, yet they held the highest of spirits coupled with a natural aura of confidence. Though there were some who remembered their general from Shiloh, most put forth their ability with an enthusiasm to move their ammunition while spurring the progress of the bulky artillery.

An ungainly youth of perhaps sixteen cocked his bandaged head in a stoical manner before speaking, "How much farther you reckon we'll go, captain?" he asked around the wad of prized tobacco in his mouth. He had won the tobacco in a card game. Although he was unaccustomed to the bitter taste, he felt compelled to chew it just the same. It gave him a sense of security – or perhaps it was maturity for which he was groping. "Do those on the barges plan to take Grand Gulf?"

"They hope to," the captain nodded thoughtfully in friendly companionship with the boy, "but it is my guess they will wind up disembarking before that. They will probably have to join us on foot. Still the possibility exists."

"Yeah, the possibility exists," the boy echoed. "Do you reckon we'll make it? Takin' Vicksburg, I mean?"

"We'll make it," the captain nodded decisively. "Look around you. Most of the men are more than certain. If I know Grant as well as I think I do, he'll not let us down."

"Yeah, as long as he don't touch the bottle," the boy surprised him with his retort.

"That's impudence, boy!" the thirty-four-year-old captain snapped defensively. It never failed to surprise him how one so young could be so quick to judge. "General Grant is a man to be trusted and held in respect," he explained more patiently. "There are those among us who would aid him conquer his weakness for the bottle. He is under a great deal of stress. His job is not an easy one. Yet we rely heavily on the capaciousness of his brilliant mind and powerful leadership."

"I meant no disrespect, sir," the boy mumbled, displeased with the turn in conversation.

"Then show none," came the quick reply. "The general is as clear of eye as any other you will find, and he is a good deal more capable than most."

"Yes, sir," came another mumble.

The captain recognized his own gruffness by the sulky tone the boy released. "Get some rest, man," he made an attempt to soften his words before seating his long frame on a fallen log. In a weary gesture he raked his sun-bronzed fingers through the tangled mass of blue-black curls. His deep-set blue eyes closed in a single moment of respite.

"Captain?" someone called. "Captain Michaels?" his head jerked up at the sound of his name. A one-eyed sergeant stood before him.

"Yes?" he was used to others asking questions…used to others depending on him.

"It's nearly nightfall, sir. Do you expect the rations to arrive this evening?"

"It's hard to tell, sergeant. Keep a detachment posted just in case," Stuart sighed in dismissal. The soldier shuffled his feet but did not leave. "Is there something else?"

"The rations, sir," the sergeant appeared uncomfortable. "They are running extremely low."

"They will be replenished," Stuart assured gravely as if speaking to a small child. "In the meantime you will have to divide them once again. It is best to cut them down continuously, rather than to run completely out."

"Yes, sir," the sergeant scurried away across the littered ground of rubber blankets and butchered oil cloths, which if unable to provide comfortable bedding, at least supplied a dry section of otherwise soggy earth.

It was several hours before the band of Union gunboats were able to run the batteries successfully enough to land the badly needed supplies. This success, however, was a happy one delivering twelve barges filled to the brim with rations. They drifted past the city by camouflage of night. Still the problem of how to reach the highland remained. The corps in motion on the river would have continued their journey south had they been able to break through the fortifications of Grand Gulf, but that staid fort held her head high beneath the constant shower of gunfire. Before long, the Federal troops had no choice but to disengage at Hard Times where they were united with the marching army, then ferried across at Bruinsburg.

The bayous were treacherous. Through swampland and ravine the fallen timber formed a density of scrambled undergrowth, yet if the men found fault with nature's veritable battleground they were equally in awe of the abrupt acclivities that were often followed by fields of growing corn. Somewhere in the green trees of unfolding blossoms they drew nostalgic memories of pretty maids with honeyed voices and smiles that sparkled like the very sunshine they craved.

Early morning found the troops in the thick of battle. Their dreams of yesterday vanished as they crouched low in the thickets, the whistling of rifle shells overhead. They were deep in enemy territory. Men were loading and reloading. Stuart watched with a detached calm. He had seen it all before. His participation in this was not unlike any other such battle. Nearby a youngster was busily reloading his weapon even as Stuart fired his. Even in the thick rise of smoke he could tell it was a boy by the awkward movement of his limbs. They were unsure, jerky movements not stiff and swift like those of an older man, nor strong and fluid like those of a man in his prime. Stuart felt an almost paternal softening as he watched the youth tear a paper cartridge from an inside pocket ripping it open with his teeth before pouring the contents down the barrel of his sturdy Springfield rifle. He shoved the bullet quickly inside then drew the ramrod out.

Before the boy had time to pull the hammer back, a mini ball came skidding through the air. It smashed into him with a force that took his life. The boy's corpse twitched a macabre dance as it crumpled to the ground. Stuart flinched at the sight. Grimly he reached into the pockets of the lifeless trunk to withdraw any personal effects. It was the sixteen-year-old who had questioned him earlier about Grant's courage and ability. He recalled the conversation with a deep shadow of remorse. He had been brusque in his irritation with the ever-ready jibes about alcoholism. He realized now that the cause of those criticisms had been nothing less than fear itself. Tears stung his eyes, prickling at his lids. The gun fire continued. Dully he reloaded, aiming at the enemy.

Dusk fell. The mortars thundered on. Bullets rained in thick conglomerates. It was difficult to see beyond the smoke – beyond the darkness. A footfall fell in hushed silence from behind. Stuart whirled automatically, his bayonet thrust forward to spike the unknown assailant. "I could have killed you," he growled at the tall, lean figure standing lazily beside a stunted oak tree.

"Is that a greeting?" the other chuckled, a deep rumbling in his chest. As he ducked into the brush beside Stuart his teeth gleamed white in contrast to the night.

"Ah, Richard, you know I am glad to see you!" Stuart clasped his friend on the shoulder, the harshness of the moment already forgotten.

"It has been a long time," Richard sighed, flicking the soiled cloth of his Confederate grays. "I am tired of wearing the cloth of a traitor."

"You have served the Union well, my friend," consoled Stuart, "perhaps far better than if you displayed the fancy bars of a Federal officer. Your contributions to the cause have been priceless."

"It is kind of you to say so," Richard cracked a ghost of a smile, "yet I do grow weary of the charade. But alas!" he brightened visibly as he quickly produced a cipher from an interior pocket. "I have a message for your general."

"I'll see that he gets it immediately," Stuart sobered, knowing their moment of shared solitude had passed.

Richard gave an affirmative nod. "I must be off before I get shot by one of my own men! Keep the faith," he whispered. The sound of his voice lingered in the damp night air where Stuart stood, no longer able to distinguish his friend from the surrounding brush.

Richard's words now held only serious import. "Your path is clear. Port Gibson is about to fold, and Lord knows Grand Gulf will follow soon after!"

"Take care," Stuart mouthed a reply in the sudden commencement of rifle fire.

"You bet," he thought he heard the words correctly, but felt unsure of Richard's safety until a scrambling in the nearby underbrush reassured him on that score. As a matter of record Richard's words did prove accurate. With the dawning of a new day Port Gibson sat securely beneath Union flagpoles, while the Confederates beat a swift retreat with the evacuation of Grand Gulf.

Though Stuart's division fortified their rations of hardtack and coffee at the fort, they truly thrived upon the country. They foraged for meat in the thick of the wilderness, confiscated molasses, bacon, and poultry from the homes of Southern citizens, and cooked their food over the burning timber of trees and fence posts. The rains continued to pour down upon them as they marched day and night through the mud and mire. Yet with each new city they conquered, Stuart felt the reproachful glare of accusing violet eyes. Hillery! It had been such an incredibly long time since he had held her in his arms, longer still since he had witnessed the soft tinkle of her laughter floating on the magic carpet of her sweet lavender cologne. All the joy had gone from her eyes when he had left that last time – those beautifully haunting violet eyes, flecked with gold when happy, smoldering to a dusky purple when in rage or in passion. He thought only of those eyes...of that sweet triangular face when his troops swept through the cities. The soft weeping of maidens carried on the air. He knew what was taking place behind many a shuttered door. His thoughts swept again to Hillery and to his fellow soldiers in her vicinity. How he wished she were safe in Washington! He should have been more persuasive, more forceful in his decision concerning her safety and well being. War was a horribly repulsive thing, and so many times a war of politics merged into a battle of lust and courage as well. It was for her safety he prayed.

A rude voice broke his concentration. "Gad! Wouldn't ya like to get a hold of one of them broads?" someone shouted from behind the ranks. A muscle in Stuart's cheek tightened convulsively. The comment darkened his already black mood.

"It's been a long time since you had a furlough, ain't it, captain?" a small voice piped. Stuart sent a swift sidelong glance to the youth next to him. The boy muttered a quick defense. "I didn't mean no jest, sir. It's just that I heard you have a pretty wife down in New Orleans. The men gossip about all the officers, sir. I hope you don't take offense."

"No, I am not offended," Stuart softened at the youth's nervous tone. In his mind he was hearing the voice of another boy whose conversation had been reckless, impetuous. "It has been a long time since I have seen my wife," he resumed speaking. "I worry about her alone on the plantation."

"Is it true the plantation is haunted? They say it's The Plantation we all hear about. Is it true?"

"Yes, it's true," Stuart nodded. He heard this all the time, rumors were always flying about. But the men needed things to talk about other than war. "My wife is very strong," he said. "She isn't afraid of the curse." He hid a grin when he saw the boy's jaw drop.

"I see," the boy puffed out his chest importantly, feeling as if he rated high in his captain's personal confidence. "I have women folk back in Tennessee...my mother and girlfriend," he explained shyly. "It bothers me they have no men folk around to protect them."

"Then we share the same concerns," Stuart nodded thoughtfully as though speaking to a man of his own caliber. He deftly lit his pipe and sat back to enjoy a rare smoke. The boy seemed to grow before his very eyes. He, too, relaxed in quiet company with his captain.

The city of Jackson was quickly captured leaving the flag of the United States flying high above the Capitol building. Orders were given to destroy the machine shops, foundries, and arsenals as well as the many warehouses that were in existence. Despite the quantity of waste, the Union troops sustained themselves, capturing many cannon and field pieces. An enormous amount of inefficient Union arms were replaced by an improved make of European muskets. These were gladly taken.

The battles were many. The men continued to push ahead. The measured tread of marching boots lent a cadence of sound to the atmospheric quiet of the forest. At last the goal of Vicksburg was met! Grant and Sherman investigated closely, each keeping a superb watch to the rear. Sherman was verbally enthusiastic during the constant vigil of the warily milling city. Grant sat pensively smoking a cigar while mentally sketching his final steps of conquest. The men behind them on the slopes could easily view the citizens below. They watched the young Negresses, their breasts left unbound, as they balanced heavy laundry atop their plated heads. Old men could be seen sitting idly about on the front steps of many a store. They were obviously too weak, too tired to play an effective part in military life. Hospitals were widely spread and roofed with canvas. Even from the distance, one could make out the presence of the cots that supported the critically wounded, the feet of which were placed in water jugs in an effort to spare the occupants the further annoyance of the bayou's lizards.

Nearly two months passed. In the fuming cloud of raging mosquitoes the spirited high morale of the soldiers began to wilt. Added to this burden was the startling episode of searches that began early one morning and did not cease until every man and his bedroll had been checked for even a clue of alcohol. Rumor had it that General Grant had succumbed to his genuine, if misguided fondness for the bottle. Every bottle found in camp was smashed by the merciless hands of his supporters. Yet if Grant had truly sought relief as believed, it was a single short-lived surrender to his former weakness. Soon after this incident Grant's efforts redoubled in the slow, heavy procedure of siege. Each day the shelling of the town persisted. With the increased support of the Federal fleet, the beleaguered people of the city began to fret for their lives. Cave homes became immensely popular. They provided an adequate substitute for the houses recently evacuated. Most of these had gone up in flames. In the caves the people merely built a false sense of security.

With Vicksburg in mind the Yankees held a firm stance all around the bluff to the edge of the river's shore. Stuart's division trudged to the left where they were to hold their position beside the water. They did not see the well-concealed Rebels in the muck of the river's bend where they lay in wait, biding their time for their plan to unfold. Prior to the arrival of the Yankee troops, the Rebs had just completed hanging a pair of powder-filled kegs below the surface of the water. The Union troops were now stationed at that precise point. Because this particular type of explosive was set off by percussion caps, the Rebels crawled silently away. They were fully aware of the guarding Federal vessel that would wander in close enough to cause the desired reaction. From the river, the steamer signaled the Union men on shore. It was an advance command for the division to proceed with their climb up the hill. The boat moved in, its white lights flashing. The waves of murky water rolled to and fro. The soldiers of the Fifteenth division turned in eager pursuit of the enemy. Their captain remained at the rear, seeing to it that all orders were carried out. Suddenly a violent shaking seemed to grasp the earth! A deafening sound wrenched the shore line. At the exact same moment Stuart shoved the man ahead of him into the brush. The air rang with an ear-splitting explosion followed by the splintering of wood and a gigantic blast of gun powder.

When the man in the brush rolled out from under the protection of his captain's body, he stared in horror at the blood bath that surrounded him. Men were groaning, gasping for breath in every direction he dared look. Panic gripped him. He turned the captain's still form over as gingerly as possible. What met his gaze brought a terrified scream from his painfully tightened lungs. Guilt consumed him. The captain had saved his life by sheltering him with his own body. Now Captain Stuart Michaels wore a death mask! It was impossible to tell if he were whole, yet alone alive! Carefully the man took hold of the captain's feet and dragged him into the shelter of the trees away from the water's edge. After hiding the body he turned and walked away, hoping to join up with another unit. Hopefully he could send help back for the captain and the others who were injured. He was stopped in his tracks by a mini ball that tore savagely through him. He would not live to tell of the explosion by the river.

With warfare at this savage extreme the Union troops steadily squeezed the life out of the city. With grim determination they closed in. They must end the deplorable siege in order to gain the coveted base of supplies with its unobstructed communication with the North. During the course of the past few months Pemberton's men had grown weak in resistance as well as low in rations and physically fatigued. Due to these circumstances, with his back against the wall, the Confederate leader surrendered.

At ten-thirty a.m. on July fourth General Grant telegraphed Lincoln of his success. This news coincided with the equally significant triumph at Gettysburg. Victory resounded throughout the White House walls. Among those missing in action, Captain Stuart Michaels was listed.

# CHAPTER TWENTY FOUR

n those final weeks in Washington, Hillery quietly recovered from the events that had unfolded at the Sherwood mansion. Colonel Sherwood was not held accountable for Hillery's near assault, nor the death of Crystal Fleece. He claimed he had nothing to do with the tragedy that occurred and there was no proof that he was lying. Perhaps his wealth and position bought him some security. Hillery learned from Gran that Crystal had indeed been quite mad just as Stuart had explained such a long time ago. While she knew that Crystal's instability ran in the family, she had not known that her mother had ended her life when Crystal was a small child. Hillery had never liked Crystal, but she did feel a genuine remorse for her part in her death. The family tried to put her mind at ease. It would have happened regardless, they said, because Crystal never learned, never ceased interfering in the lives and relationships of others. The woman had no female friends. Even the men in her life held her in contempt.

Benjamin visited occasionally. He had recently stopped in to bid the family farewell as he was returning to duty on the Mississippi. Hillery and Natalie watched sadly as he rode away. All the young men and many of the older ones as well, were off to war. The Mississippi Campaign was Stuart's location. And God knows they were all concerned for him! Benjamin thought a great deal of Natalie. But Rachael suspected, and Gran knew, that he thought an awful lot of Hillery too. Hillery did not appear to be aware of the way his eyes followed her, so neither of them ever mentioned it. It was clear Hillery saw Benjamin only as a friend.

Stuart was the one who held her heart.

Charlotte had made every attempt to bring joy to the family. She thrived under the love and care Annie and Cecil heaped upon her. And she would always love and adore Hillery who seemed so sad these days. Throughout the long winter, Charlotte had been secretly working her vocal cords. Yet she was as shocked as anyone to hear the sound of her own voice! She had never truly believed it would return, so she was elated when she heard the first whisper of sound. She coaxed it along gently, working in small intervals, afraid of straining it still more. Then one day her voice poured out of her as beautifully as water from a fountain! When she first spoke to Annie and Cecil, tears streamed down their faces. They were so excited they hurried to share the good news. And at once, Charlotte found herself the center of attention. The girl possessed a brilliant voice, a high clear lilting sound that lifted naturally in song and won her an appreciative audience wherever she went.

Hillery made a captive audience indeed when Charlotte sang to her. She was so proud of the girl, she told her so. "Then why do you look so sad?" Charlotte sank gracefully to the floor next to Hillery's seat where she sat with Ariel, wrapping her slender arms tightly around Hillery in the process. Her chin rested at an angle atop the flounces of Hillery's skirts. Ariel angled his chin as well.

Hillery sobered, unable to form a reply. With new insight she realized Charlotte was trying to draw her out...to force her to speak about what was troubling her. "I believe you know the answer to that," she said softly.

"Yes, I do," Charlotte wrinkled her high forehead speaking in a tone too wise for her years. "I understand why you're hurting, and I know I'm not supposed to know all about it, but I hear things. I pay attention," she admitted archly. "When I lost my mama in the fire, and I lost my voice, it took me a long time to figure it out. I couldn't talk because I couldn't let go of the hurt. Now you have to let go of the hurt, Missy Hillery." Hillery shot a startled glance at the ageless features beside her. Charlotte was an enigma! "Those things that happened at the Sherwood's were truly awful, but you survived them and you have to let them go. Miss Crystal was pure evil. You aren't to blame for what happened to her. Likely, she set you up to begin with, and if she were alive today…she'd do it again!"

"Charlotte Ann, you never cease to amaze me!" Hillery whispered. "I believe you have grown up too fast!"

"We colored children have to grow up fast, Missy Hillery," the child's response was matter-of-fact. "Mama warned me about life when I was way little," she measured with her hand to indicate an early age.

Hillery closed her eyes in a weary gesture. "Thank you," she spoke the words sincerely. Charlotte stood to kiss her cheek. She then trailed a hand down Ariel's back and the little dog wagged his tail furiously. Charlotte winked at him before turning away. Before all that's holy, it surely did appear that Ariel winked back!

One week later as Hillery was readying herself for bed the sheriff came to the door. She heard his bold knock followed by the sound of the door scraping open as Rachael answered softly. Hillery was instantly alert, her stomach knotting in fear. Something was dreadfully wrong, she thought as she crept to the edge of the staircase where she listened to the conversation below. "I'm sorry to disturb you this late, Mrs. Michaels," Sheriff Wright said. "Unfortunately, I have come with a warrant. I need to take young Able in for questioning."

Rachael gasped audibly as she digested his words, her eyes scanning the night. The deputy shifted his weight where he stood silently beside the other man, and she realized both law enforcement officers were uncomfortable with the notion of disturbing such a prominent family at so late an hour. "I don't understand," she voiced softly, her back straight as she opened the door wider. "Do come in and explain."

The pair gratefully removed their hats as they stepped inside. Sheriff Wright cleared his throat then began anew. "I'm afraid Able was seen on the night of the Sherwood ball," he stated.

"That's right," Rachael replied archly, "He filled in for his father as he often does these days. There's nothing unusual about that. Able is the coachman's son, and Old Ben was feeling poorly that night."

"I'm afraid he was seen in the company of Miss Fleece," Sheriff

Wright looked uncomfortable. "We have a witness who claims it was Able who pulled the trigger. He's being accused of murder, Rachael."

At the use of her given name, Rachael wavered. She had known Sheriff Wright all of her life. He was not a bad man. He was only doing his job. But Ben, the coachman, was getting up in years. Able was his only surviving son. He was a good man with a young wife and bright future. "I'm afraid that's not possible. I know for a fact that Able never left his post."

Hillery paled where she stood in the shadows at the top of the stairs. Ariel whimpered softly and she silently hushed him. She was wondering whether to go downstairs and set things right or stay still and see how serious the situation became. It seemed full blown. As if sensing her predicament, Rachael offered, "Miss Hillery is in bed asleep. She is the only one who can clear this matter up. I think you should return tomorrow and allow her the opportunity to do so."

"I can't do that, Rachael. You know that." The sheriff looked uncomfortable. He swallowed nervously. "I'm afraid our witness is a prominent citizen who swears he saw Able pull the trigger in Miss Hillery's defense."

"That is not what happened," Rachael stood her ground. "My daughter-in-law already gave her statement. She and Miss Crystal were alone. At any rate, you are wasting your time. Able is away for the night. He took Ben's place tonight as well, and will not return until tomorrow morning. There is nothing more to be done this night."

"This doesn't change a thing, Rachael. I'm sorry," the sheriff said sternly. Clearly he was not backing down.

"You are accusing an innocent man, Matt," she made use of his given name to appeal to his softer side. The two of them were friends once.

"I have to ask you where he has gone," the sheriff persisted.

"He is with family. Old Ben's sister had need of him. Able went to her aid."

"I will return first thing in the morning, Rachael. Be sure he is expecting me. This is serious," he reminded.

Rachael felt faint when she closed the door. Hillery hurried to her side. Ariel hopped along beside them as the pair stepped into the parlor. "We have no time to waste," Rachael offered. Her voice was steady, but her hands trembled.

Hillery packed a bag while Rachael gathered some necessary provisions. Gran met them at the door. The old girl wore a sad expression, but she drew Hillery in for a tight hug, kissed her cheek, then said, "I know you will be careful, but listen to me: you will travel farther than you plan this time. The trail will be rough. So when you round a bend in a stream that forks abruptly, get down and hide in the brush. Do not move until you are certain the path is clear. This is vitally important. I cannot stress it enough." Gran took hold of her hand and her grip tightened in warning. Hillery paled, and then nodded knowingly. She bent to kiss Gran's withered cheek.

"Thank you, Gran. I will do as you say," Hillery breathed.

Gran nodded. Her blue eyes twinkled with tears. "Do you have a weapon on you?"

"Yes, of course," Hillery smiled a small smile. "Rachael gave me her husband's derringer. It is better than the one I had."

"That is good. Thomas was an excellent judge of weaponry," she said with an additional squeeze. "There is one more thing. I cannot see who it is, but you will meet with someone important to you. Just remember to take the extra precaution."

"Thank you, Gran. I love you," Hillery whispered before disappearing into the night.

The trip north was incredibly difficult. This one was personal. This couple was a part of Stuart's family. And the woman, Ellie, was heavy with child. Hillery was concerned about this. The young man, Able, had not set out for trouble. Rather, trouble had found him when a white man accused him of murder, forcing Able to flee. There was no choice, no going back. His skin governed this decision. Hillery had sent word to a conductor with whom Stuart had worked. She felt she could trust her instincts. She had brought along an adequate supply of herbals, and once again sent a silent prayer of thanks to Isis for all the years of training. She never could have done this without her friend and former nurse. Isis had instilled in her a strong sense of confidence as well as the priceless knowledge for living off the land and healing by the same means.

They laid low during daylight hours, choosing to sleep under cover of brush, and only then after she had carefully erased their trail. She and Able took turns on watch, sleeping in small doses. She counseled the couple carefully on what to do, and what not to do. She had a code that allowed certain sounds, but no words. They nodded in solemn agreement while she breathed a sigh of relief.

They made slow progress following the rivers and streams to eliminate any possible trail. She led the way, studiously placing Able at the rear where he could keep watch overall. There was no permitted conversation. She thought of Charlotte, wisely advising that children of color had to grow up quickly. This, she saw, was completely true. Most had seen nightmares they would never shake.

They had traveled farther than she had expected. Still the conductor did not show. They were nearing Canada where the winds blew far colder, and the waters grew icy. She was grateful for the warm clothing she had worn. She wrapped a woolen shawl around Ellie's chilled form. It was then she noticed the abrupt fork in the stream. They had only just rounded the bend and her senses were on high alert. She motioned them to an abrupt halt and stealthily led them into the brush. She then backtracked, silently erasing anything they might have disturbed, keeping an eye out for cloth or any other synthetic material that might have snagged the bushes. When she rejoined them, she heard the sound of approaching horses. There was a full patrol of men, ostensibly guarding the border into Canada. Hillery did not know how many there were, but she did know they must remain completely still. No one dared move. They held their position in the brush, their already taut muscles strained still further.

Once the troops had passed, Hillery sensed rather than heard the unspoken question: *"Is it safe to move now?"* She gave an imperceptible nod, shaking her head to the negative. She looked within, a trick she had been cultivating, and what she saw chilled her to the bone. There was another smaller patrol heading their way. If they were seen, they would be caught between the two patrols with nowhere to run. She held her breath. The others did likewise.

Finally the last of the men had passed. Hillery waited still longer, and then looked within a second time. This time she saw that all was clear. She moved silently from the brush, motioning the others to stay put until she could take a look around. After a short time that seemed like an eternity to them all, Hillery returned. She motioned them to remain silent then slipped into the icy waters. The others followed without question. It was clear they had experienced a very close call.

It was with great relief that Hillery became aware of another soul approaching. She paused, forcing the others to again crouch low. She watched raptly until she heard the sound of a bird whistle, only it was a sound she had been awaiting. She rose slowly, leaving the others in hiding, and met the candid gaze of the conductor who put a finger to her lips, never making a sound. Hillery motioned the couple on. They filed past with looks of gratitude. Hillery knew she would never forget them, and likely they felt much the same. Quietly, she watched them go.

It was then she realized she was aware of another presence. Gran's words came back to her, "*I cannot see who it is, but you will meet with someone important to you.*"

Hillery's wary gaze swept the small clearing. She was startled to spy the conductor standing rooted to the spot, the others having gone on ahead of her. Moses never made a sound, yet the look that passed between them spoke volumes. There was a twinkle in her eyes that had not been there before. Hillery watched as she silently disappeared. Expecting to be alone in the clearing, she was truly startled when a figure stepped from behind the trees. He stood with a smile teasing the corners of his mouth. Hillery gasped, slapping a hand to her mouth to stifle any sound. She mouthed the word "David!" And as she did so, he stepped aside to allow Cynie to come into view. On Cynie's hip she carried a bright-eyed babe. Another child, slightly older, tugged at her skirt. Cynie smiled broadly, unable to contain her joy. Tears spilled from her luminous eyes and within seconds the women were exchanging hugs. They spoke in quiet whispers as David led them deeper into the forest until Hillery found herself in a crude shelter where they sat to share a meal and some long overdue conversation.

"This is Caleb," Cynie said, gesturing to the little boy who had been so solemnly tugging at her skirt, "We named him after David's father. I think he would like that. And this," she paused briefly as she held up the baby for Hillery to hold, "is Louise."

"Hello Louise," Hillery smiled even as she swallowed a sob at the use of her own middle name. Cynie brightened visibly. "That's so sweet of you!" Hillery exclaimed, enraptured with these tiny replicas of their parents. "Thank you."

"It was the only way I could think of to keep you with me," Cynie whispered.

"Oh, dear Lord, it's good to see you!" Hillery could not take her gaze from Cynie's own. David had risen silently, taking charge of the children to give the women some time to themselves. They knew the visit would be clipped short. Each intended to treasure every moment. "You have beautiful children," Hillery said for the tenth time. "You seem so happy! You are, aren't you?"

"Oh, yes," Cynie sighed, knowing how badly Hillery missed Stuart. "This war won't last forever," she proclaimed. "When it's over, you and Stuart will come to visit. We have a fine house…just across the border. We would have taken you there, but…"

"You're right, I know," Hillery provided. "I can't stay. Rachael and the family would worry. I have been gone over long as it is."

As they stood they hugged one last time, not knowing how long it would be until they would meet again. Hillery saw the sparkle of tears in Cyn's eyes and took the Initiative. "I love you, my sweet sister," she cupped the other's face, "and the main thing is that you are safe…and you are free. We made that, together. And you are right, the war will end."

David returned and with a nod, pressed additional provisions into Hillery's hands. "You take care, little sister," he said with sincerity. "I would see you part way home…"

"But you are needed here," Hillery interrupted, "and I will find my way. God and Saint Michael are good to me," she smiled.

Cynie turned her face into her husband's chest, and in the blink of an eye, Hillery was gone.

The long journey back was brutal. Hillery was beyond exhaustion. After settling things with the sheriff, she slept for twelve hours straight. He knew only that Able had taken flight, and Miss Hillery had taken ill. She awoke to the intense heat of the nation's independence. Word of Vicksburg had reached Washington.

Hillery dressed quickly, then stood before the gilt mirror that hung above the walnut Regency bombe' commode gaining a quick assessment of her toilet. Unmindful of the prismatic array of rainbow spectrum reflected from the flanking bronze Dore' and crystal girandoles, she hastily tied the bow of her pink floral bonnet before flying from the house. She climbed into the carriage without assistance, calling to Natalie as she did so. Nat hurriedly caught up with her and they set off at a brisk pace. The ladies were too tense to discuss their fears. They were each one lost in an eerie silence. Hillery felt a now familiar lurch in her belly. She glanced at Gran who stared somberly back at her. It was not always a joy to know the unknown, to see what others did not see. She bit her lip to stifle a sob. Gran reached over and took her hand. Witnessing this exchange, Rachael stiffened her spine. Even Natalie was somber. She, too, bit her lip.

Upon arrival they pressed through the crowd. They had reached an agreement before setting out. So it was Gran sat alone in the carriage knowing she would slow the pace of the others. She took the time to steal herself for what lay ahead. In her mind's eye, she watched as the list wavered before them. And felt the blow like a physical force. She saw Hillery's face pale, felt her knees buckle, and wondered how the young woman managed to stay erect.

PART THREE

THE TUNNEL

# CHAPTER TWENTY FIVE

he march to the Confederate camp that housed a Federal prison was not a lengthy one. The camp was an overcrowded, crumbling parapet of out-stretched tents that supported an overwhelming number of men. The prison offered no comforts...no bedding or blankets, or even a flap of canvas. If a prisoner owned a tent or shelter half he could keep it for a price. And as they would soon learn, there was a price for everything! Even their canteens and cooking utensils had to be bargained for. The officers were quickly singled out. Their days at this particular site were numbered, for within a fortnight they were transferred by rail to a far more formidable place.

A four-story brick building, Libby was reputed to be the most feared prison in Richmond. Located on the corner of Twentieth and Cary, it was as well guarded in front as it was backed by the heavy flow of the James River. The austere building had originally been the place of business for Libby and Son Ship Chandlers. Now, with no sign of the former trade, the empty shell held more than a thousand men between its grim walls.

Stuart and the others were led to the basement where nearly every section of floor was occupied. The area was completely overcrowded. Creatures that had once been men now crouched on their haunches watching listlessly as new prisoners were shoved down the wooden stairs. Some had lost their grip on reality. A few no longer knew the meaning of sanity. All were sick and starving knowing very little hope for the future. The entire place smelled of human vomit and excrement.

Mold climbed the damp walls covering large areas of the floor as well. The door above them slammed shut. The bolt fell heavily into place. A sick feeling of despair washed over each man in turn. They were utterly lost down here away from the wild comfort of the woodland. Here there were no fences to be climbed or cut, no possibility of overtaking the guards. Here they had little or no hope of escape. It was as if they had been devoured by the thickness of the walls.

Stuart soon collapsed on the floor as inmates grudgingly made room. It was good to sit, to cradle his aching head in the palms of his hands. He longed to stretch out, but nearly every foot of space was accounted for. At some point he had fashioned a sort of bandage, but the wound throbbed and in spite of his best efforts it had started to bleed again. He was surrounded by fellow officers most of whom were wounded as well. Some spoke. Many kept to themselves. A quiet keening filled the room.

"Your head looks bad," one of the men offered. "You need a doctor."

"You'll never see a doctor here," a scarecrow figure in rags cut in. "Best not to ask."

Stuart was grateful for the insight. He hadn't expected much. He knew what type of place this was. Everyone had heard tales of Libby. He knew he was pretty much on his own. But at least among officers there was some honor to be found.

"I'll take a look at it," another man offered. He was among the new men, and wore the bars of a captain. Stuart recognized him as one of his fellow comrades, captured at, or near, Vicksburg. They had previously been allowed no conversation between them. As he leaned forward Stuart took in his blonde hair. His brown eyes crinkled at the corners when he said, "I was a veterinarian before the war. So if you don't mind that I'm better with animals," he shrugged, "I can still clean a wound."

"I don't mind," Stuart replied with a shrug of his own. "I'd be obliged."

"How were you injured?"

"I was caught in an explosion, at the water's edge."

The man looked taken aback. "Good God, man," he laughed, "you have the devil's own luck to have survived that!"

"Guess so," Stuart agreed. Because the conversation kept his mind off the throbbing in his skull, he didn't notice when the other man stiffened. He was simply grateful when he finished, having pronounced it clean of infection.

"But," he added, "It'll need checking from time to time."

"Thanks, Ben." Benjamin Courtley ducked his head. They had made the introductions while Benjamin worked and were surprised to find they knew each other's families. Benjamin felt a twinge of jealousy whenever Hillery's name was mentioned. He admired her greatly and had entertained ideas of someday taking this man's place beside her. It was a bitter brew to swallow to find he actually liked her husband. Liked, tolerated, but did not accept.

In the days that followed, the two men became well acquainted. Stuart accepted Ben's friendship with an ease that left Benjamin feeling guilty about his private thoughts. But Ben couldn't help but admire the other's stoical temperament. When he found his patience ebbing to the point he felt he could endure no more, he would look upon Stuart with a feeling of envy and determination. Stuart was the very symbol of perseverance.

"How the hell are we going to get out of here?" Ben staged a whisper. It was a hot, muggy night and he was having difficulty falling asleep. All around them men shifted positions. The vast room was full of moaning, snoring men.

"I don't know," Stuart replied somberly, "but if there's a way, I intend to find it."

"Perhaps we shall be granted cartel exchange?" Ben said hopefully.

"Don't kid yourself," Stuart snorted, running a set of lean fingers through his tangled mane. Though his wound was healing nicely, it still ached like a son of a bitch. "Look around you! All of these men are officers! All waiting endlessly for parole! You've got to wake up to the world, Ben," Stuart's voice softened with compassion. "There are three floors above this one – each crowded with men just like us. You won't get your parole, and I won't get mine. The days of exchange are past."

"You're a pessimist," Ben claimed bitterly.

"I'm a realist, Ben," Stuart corrected.

Nearby another voice joined the conversation. "I been here long enough to watch the flesh fall off me bones," the new comer vowed. "You're a dreamer, maun! No one gets out of Libby, least ways not alive!"

Stuart grunted then turned on his side. Benjamin stilled. He was something of a dreamer, he knew, but he was losing hope and he knew he could not allow that. He was quiet the remainder of the night.

Benjamin continued to keep to himself while Stuart made friends with many of the men. Stuart watched soberly as Benjamin withdrew into himself with every passing day. He wished he could ease the other man's tension. It was like watching a caged animal that could not deal with his cage. They were all in the same predicament, only some of them could handle it while others could not. He was silently contemplating the matter when one of the men addressed him. It was the same man who had joined the conversation the other night.

"How 'bout a fine game of checkers?" the man said. He waved Stuart over as he pointed out the game board. He was surrounded by men each cheering the next on. He appeared well liked. Stuart sat opposite him for the first time noting the fellow was missing a leg. It didn't deter him from making the most of any given opportunity. "Ye'd best hurry if ye want t' play," he cackled. "We hae t' take turns, ye know."

"Sure," Stuart smiled appreciatively at the crude wooden board the men had made. His gaze slid to the colored rocks that served as chips. "My name is Michaels, what's yours?" he asked as he extended a firm hand.

"Me friends call me Cricket," the one-legged man grinned a toothless grin, "on account of I hop like one! Get it? I hop like one!" A chorus of laughter greeted this claim. In spite of the situation these men seemed determined to keep their spirits high.

Stuart chuckled as he seated himself on the floor opposite Cricket. Within a few minutes they were all laughing. After a couple of rounds Stuart glanced over to where Benjamin still sat with his head on bent knees. He knew an overwhelming sense of pity. "Come on over, Ben," he coaxed. "You can take my place. A round of checkers might heal your morale."

"No thanks," grumbled Ben. "I don't want any favors from you."

Stuart regarded him for only a moment, "Then don't consider it a favor...just a game among friends."

Again Benjamin muttered, this time incoherently. Stuart wondered at his action. "Oh, leave him be!" Cricket chortled, gleefully unaffected.

"The maun's got a chip on his shoulder, that's fer damn sure! 'E don't want t' be bothered by the likes o' us! Let's play, maun! Taint nothing' else we kin do."

So Stuart played. He played checkers. He played cards. He played anything the men could come up with. One of the men had a deck of real playing cards with naked women on each one! They were garbed in ribboned undergarments such as those worn in cheap bordellos. Stuart chuckled with good humor. He was biding his time as they were biding theirs. He wondered at Benjamin's surliness. It felt personal. He resolved to ask him about it at a more convenient time, either when his mood lifted, or perhaps when it didn't.

The moment presented itself soon enough. He had won at yet another round of cards and he heard Ben mutter something about his wife. He knew it was his wife because he heard her name clearly enough to wake the dead. This time his own temper flared and before he knew what he was about he had his fist raised. It was Cricket who quickly broke up the dispute. "You'll hae the guards upon us," he growled low and Stuart dropped his fist. He saw the truth in this. Benjamin could grumble all he wanted. Sooner or later he would find out what was eating at him.

Meantime, Benjamin glowered and Stuart planned. Always in the back of his mind was the thought of escape. It was a thought that grew beyond measure. There had to be a way, he mused, and he had to find it! It would be dangerous, even deadly, but it must never be considered impossible. If he accepted defeat he had little doubt that he would perish along with all the others in this God forsaken place.

In the weeks that followed Stuart became friends with many of the men. He talked to them, swapped tales with them and in moments of despair, he shared his hopes and dreams with them. Many of them looked up to him. All trusted and admired his courage and ability. But perhaps the most important friendship forged was between himself and Thomas Rose. Rose was a dark-haired colonel whose hooded gaze recognized in Stuart a complaisant intelligence as well as an extraordinary strong will to survive. Soon the two were secretly planning a means of escape. Thomas seemed to know his business, even venturing so far as to admit that this was not his first escape. He had connections all over the South, many of which he had relied on heavily in the past.

Cricket soon became the third member of the crew. Though of an unconventional background, his backwoods education had taught him much in the art of survival. If somewhat unconditioned, his brilliant mind set him apart from his fellow backwoodsmen quickly earning him the rank of Lieutenant. The trio spent many hours quietly plotting in the dark of night. Theirs was a secret that must be kept, for in the rank confines of Libby...the walls had ears. Only a handful of others were allowed to join the small band. Each was carefully selected.

Benjamin hovered behind the bitter armor of jealousy. He had not yet confided in Stuart. He had said nothing of his feelings for Hillery – the only woman he had ever loved. When he had spoken of Natalie and the family, he had been careful to ease around the mention of Stuart's wife. He still harbored hopes of someday winning her for himself. In his mind he sought to rationalize the justice of his secret, but he slept little, often lying awake for long hours at night. It was thus he became aware of the late-night rendezvous the small band kept.

One night after making sure everyone else was asleep he crept silently toward the tiny storage room in back where the group held their meetings. He could hear the low rumble of voices, but sighed impatiently when he could not make out the words. He felt certain they were laying infallible plans of escape and he wanted in on the action. It was an opportunity he could not afford to miss. Straining so he might better hear, he leaned slightly forward against the cool stone. It was damp with mold and his slight movement dislodged a few pebbles. He cringed when they showered the floor.

Within a matter of seconds Cricket's strong hands had grasped him firmly about the throat. "Spyin' on us, were ye?" his voice ground out as his hands increased their pressure. Benjamin was dizzy for lack of air. Bright lights danced before his eyes.

"Let him go," Stuart demanded in an angry tone, his voice low. His face was a formidable mask of rage.

"But 'e was spyin' on us! He could be a snitch for all we know," Cricket grumbled. "We can't afford the risk. We've been rottin' in here for too long as it is!"

"Agreed," Thomas spoke quietly, "he could be a snitch."

"There are many to be found within these walls," another voice joined. Tempers were quick, the despair in the place added to the tension.

"I said let him go." Stuart insisted with a stubborn crease to his brow. "He's no snitch. He just wants out of here like the rest of us. Anyway, if he heard, he heard. There's damned little we can do about it."

"There's plenty we can do about it," Cricket growled low in his throat. He had no qualms about another course of action. "We can put 'im in 'is place...teach 'im a lesson he'd ne'er soon forget. I'm not looking for some bully boy to wreck our chances to shed this place!"

"Look..." Ben swallowed hard, "I only wanted in on your plans."

"It's true," it was Stuart's firm voice again. "He can't handle the confinement." The mumbling stilled, all gazes locked on Stuart's own. "If I'm wrong, I'll take full responsibility."

"You sure, Michaels?" Thomas' gaze missed nothing; his eyes were piercing coals in a shrewd face. They caught every detail...every fleeting expression.

"I'm sure," Stuart sighed. His features had not altered. "He helped me out once," he answered in way of explanation.

"All right, he's in," Thomas spoke quietly "The plan is this..."

"Only a fool would put 'is faith in a maun what would sneak and spy," muttered Cricket. His voice was angry but controlled.

"Well, that makes me only half a fool," Thomas grinned, "for I do not intend to jeopardize our safety in any way." Benjamin glared at this announcement. Cricket and the others chortled. Stuart simply wanted to hear more. Thomas continued in a smooth tone, "I only meant to advise him that we are still in the waiting stage. Plans...good plans... take a long while, Benjamin. First everything must be prepared...down to the very last detail. By then we will know you better. It will give us time to evaluate your trust."

"That's it? You know nothing further?" Benjamin snorted in a derisive fashion. "You expect me to believe that?"

"You have very little choice," Thomas stated flatly, "and a good deal to prove." His level gaze remained cool. Benjamin muttered beneath his breath. Thomas was correct, of course. He had no choice but to wait…to be patient until the others came to trust him. In the sweltering heat of the prison, surrounded by death and disease, Benjamin had to admit his temper had been vile. He had done nothing to endear himself to the others. He had never sought their companionship. Instead, he had shut them out ignoring their existence. It was only natural they would choose to steer clear of him! Now with startling clarity he realized the impact of his hatred. It had been a small thing, kindled by a tiny spark of emotion. His jealousy had known no bounds. Instead it had burst into flame with an all consuming fire because of the love he felt for another man's wife.

Sadly Benjamin shook his head. His fingers swept through the soiled mane of blonde hair. Gravely he reflected on his actions and contempt for Stuart Michaels. To be fair, Stuart was an agreeable sort, sticking his neck out for him on more than one occasion. Once when Benjamin had been ill with an acute case of dysentery, Stuart had freely given him his entire day's ration thinking nothing of his own hunger. Benjamin's recovery had been slow. He had eaten the cornbread and sweet potatoes with little thought. It had helped sustain him. It had been a vital part of his recovery, yet Benjamin had failed to thank him.

There had been other occasions as well when Stuart had stood beside him against the better judgment of his friends. Thinking back, Benjamin knew the bitter gnawing of guilt. Shaking away the future promise of attaining Hillery as his wife, he forced himself to admit that he had been cultivating a dream these many months. Hillery had never even known of his feelings for her. She was totally committed to her husband. And that would never change. "Only a dream," he mumbled aloud, then looked up to find Stuart watching him. "Michaels? Could I speak with you in private?"

"Sure," Stuart replied easily in spite of the disapproving glares he received from the others. "What's up?"

"Let's sit on the stairs…away from your friends," Benjamin's voice faltered. He could not meet the honest blue eyes across from him.

"You're a friend, too, Ben," Stuart assured him. "You're just suffering from the confinement. It's more difficult for some."

"You had better reserve your judgment for later," Benjamin swore. "I have something to confess." The two sat. Silence ensued. Ben spoke up, "I have been no friend to you. I have betrayed your trust."

"How so?" Stuart's expression hardened even as his posture stiffened. He sat erect, no longer sitting in a casual stance.

"I was honest when I told you I am a friend of your sister's. I have known Natalie for quite some time. We have many mutual friends." Here, Benjamin's voice roughened. "What I did not tell you is that through Natalie, I met your wife." Stuart stiffened still more. Benjamin took a deep breath before continuing. He mopped his brow with the back of his hand. "Your wife, Hillery, is a perfect lady. She is ever true to you. But I...I had hoped to capture her heart. I fell in love with her." A mask had slipped carefully over Stuart's features. Benjamin was so guilt-ridden he did not take notice. A lump had formed in his throat and he swallowed. "I coveted that love. I had this dream of returning to her...of making her mine."

Before he could say another word, before he realized what was happening, his head jerked backward and his face exploded in a world of pain. He heard the crunch of bone and knew his nose was broken, felt the spurt of blood even as his eye swelled closed. He hadn't even seen Stuart's fist coming! He hung his head as the other man walked away. The entire basement had stilled.

# CHAPTER TWENTY SIX

illery spent the winter of 1863 at The Plantation. She worked long hours, fussed over the people, and dreamed of Stuart. In each dream he was being held captive but the prisons often varied. One was an encampment, a crumbling parapet of outstretched tents while the other was nothing other than Libby itself. Though she knew in her heart that he was in trouble, she had no way of knowing where he was in the now. Was he already a prisoner of war? Or was it his future she was seeing? And if he was indeed a prisoner, which prison was he in? She yearned to write Elizabeth, but knew her newfound friend and ally would contact her if she had any news. Liz had contacts all over the South. She had many influential friends who were ready to help wherever they could. So Hillery attempted to put her fears on hold and assist the people with the problems at hand.

Food was scarce and the men folk few. It had been a plantation of women for quite some time after the massacre prompted by Charles Thompson. Only Old Jacob was still about, unharmed and helpful as ever. Though Charles was dead, Tate lived on as a potential threat to the people. With Christmas upon them, both Marta and Tanya had recently borne infants as a result of the assault. A few of the others had gradually met men from neighboring plantations. All was quiet for a time. Some of the women were with child, or like Marta and Tanya were new mothers themselves. But they were still in the thick of war. And war meant hardships.

Hillery had just completed reading the paper along with an update from Higgens. Rachael had written with information as well. Hillery sighed when Isis swept soundlessly into the room. She carried a tea tray and handed Hillery a steaming cup. "Yellow Yarrow," she said, referring to the tea. "It will fortify and protect you." Her eyes were wise.

Hillery looked up and arched a brow. Ariel whimpered beside her. Yarrow was scarce this year, Hillery knew, which meant Isis was fussing over her. "What worries you?" she asked softly. She caught the scent of zinnias, and realized a dash of the flora had been added to the tea. "Zinnia as well?" she inquired.

"A little playfulness would do you good," the other acknowledged with a nod of her turbaned head. Golden hoops jangled at her ears like music to the soul. "I am worried for you, ma d'or perle. You never laugh anymore."

"There is little to laugh about," Hillery's curls tumbled over her shoulders. Beside her, Ariel mewed like a kitten. "I have been having more dreams of late," she offered, "but I am unsure what they mean."

"Do you wish to discuss these dreams?" Isis asked gently, always careful not to pry. "Perhaps I could be of help?"

Hillery nodded sagely. "Besides the dreams of Stuart, I keep seeing my mother… only not my mother," she admitted hesitantly. "She is saying something to me I cannot understand."

"How do you mean your mother, only not your mother? Do you believe these dreams to be coming from Mariette?"

"I'm not sure," Hillery's young face showed confusion. "I mean, I recognize my mother. But it is like there is a second version of her, as if at an older age. It does not make sense!" She shrugged her shoulders delicately. Ariel stretched as if mimicking the action. "My mother died in childbirth."

As one, Hillery's eyes rounded while Isis sucked in a breath. Ariel woofed as Isis muttered. "Marietta!" she stated, "Your grand mére!"

"My grand mére," Hillery reiterated. She was astounded; shocked that she hadn't recognized this on her own. "Of course!" she exclaimed softly. "Whatever this is, it has to do with my mother and her mother before her!"

"It would seem so," Isis intoned calmly. The women looked at each other in awe, each wondering at the riddle at hand.

In Richmond, the inhabitants of Libby Prison watched as a petite blonde bustled in through the prison gates. Her movements were jerky as if ruled by nerves. Those who were long-time residents knew her by name. Newcomers like Stuart merely watched with interest. There had been other visitors as well. All had been inspected, some had been turned away. But he had seen her before in his dreams. When the woman was allowed entrance, she made her way as if she belonged. In truth she appeared almost as ragged as they! She wore mismatched clothing that clashed in color alone, and she picked at her skirts as if something disturbed her comfort. The guards laughed as she passed among them. Stuart heard one of them clearly state that she was harmless as a fly. His interest was piqued when she paused at the top of the wooden stairs. She behaved as if she had a specific purpose, yet her gaze roamed the rancid crowd without expression, and her unkempt head of hair was tangled beyond belief. The woman carried a chafing dish which he knew the guards would have inspected. They always inspected everything. Nothing got passed their notice.

The woman opened the chafing dish to the man she had chosen. They were silent as he took a few hungry bites of marinated beef. The smell was heavenly and Stuart's mouth watered. He hadn't tasted beef in a very long time! They spoke in hushed whispers, saying little before she passed the dish to another. The second man took only a bite or two while the lady waited in silence. Stuart knew she was a lady by her very correct stance even though all else made her look rather vulgar. The beef fed several men, at last reaching Thomas Rose who ate the last delightful bite. He took his time chewing as if his life depended upon it. Stuart marveled at his control.

When the lady turned to leave she swept close by him. He, in turn, acted on impulse, and beckoned her to him. She was the lady of his dreams. He didn't know much about her, but he knew her contact was important. Her hem brushed his boots, it was that crowded, and he watched in fascination as her blue eyes widened then retained their blank stare. Her features were vague, but as an artist he realized it was her expression that made them seem so. She was really quite fine, if one chose to look. "Miss?" he queried then waited for her response. Beneath the heavy growth of beard she saw a handsome face of nobility. It was clear the man was attractive, but it was his eyes that drew and held her attention. They were passionate eyes, caring eyes. She could read so much in them! He had a quality one seldom saw: it was as if he looked into her very soul! "Miss, I wonder, would you write a letter to my wife? Just to let her know where I am? She must be worried."

"Of course," she answered kindly. "What's your name?" The man had affected her deeply. There was something about him she could not name. Elizabeth loved all her boys as she fondly referred to them. But this one stood out in a way she did not understand, and she found herself thinking of Hillery Michaels. Her mouth formed an O of surprise when he said, "Michaels. Stuart Michaels."

As the bells tolled he gave the address. The lady smiled a genuine smile that reached her eyes. "I'll see that she gets word," she promised. She touched his hand in a gesture of farewell as she whispered, "Your wife looked well when last I saw her."

After she had gone Stuart exchanged a look with Thomas Rose. He would get the scoop later in the still of night.

When he questioned Thomas as to her identity, the colonel replied with a grin, "That was Elizabeth Van Lew. She's the contact that I spoke of. The guards have a nickname for her," he added. "They call her 'Crazy Bet' because they believe her to be stark raving mad and therefore no threat to security."

"Nothing could be further from the truth," Stuart surmised correctly. "Yet how would she know Hillery?"

"I couldn't say," Thomas shrugged, "but I would take comfort in the fact. She is an agent for our side and a valuable one at that. Perhaps your wife is in league with her?"

"Perhaps," Stuart mumbled a response. Elizabeth's words rang in his ears. "*Your wife looked well when I last saw her.*" Her statement was indicative that the two women not only knew each other, but had more than likely interacted in the recent past. It warmed his heart to hear that she was well, but disturbed him greatly to think of her taking such chances and in Richmond at that. And to hear Thomas tell it, Elizabeth lived and operated in and around Richmond. Her connections were wide and varied, leaving her free to remain at home.

Later that night, Stuart and Thomas took the heating apparatus from the bottom of the chafing dish. There, bobbing in the still warm liquid, were a couple of tiny chisels and a small pocket knife.

A chill set in that winter of '64. Disease in the packed quarters of Libby Prison sported a rampant outbreak. Miss Van Lew continued her visits, each time bringing a substantial amount of food and medication. Still the bouts of dysentery and scurvy lingered. New prisoners arrived, each one more ill than the next. And despite the dead of winter, flies trapped within the crowded confines laid eggs in the damp moisture of open wounds. These eggs hatched overnight leaving the flesh alive with maggots. The victims died a terrible death. Their bodies were tossed outside in a heap beyond the prison gates. Gangrene, too, took its toll leaving once solid bodies severely crippled. In the midst of all this horror the few in the confidence of Colonel Rose knew the time for planning had ceased. Now – before the onset of further madness – was the crucial moment of action.

At The Plantation, Hillery still dreamed of Stuart behind prison walls. These dreams were interwoven with scenes of her mother and her grandmother as well. She realized with great clarity that the dreams of Stuart had settled firmly in one location. She equally recognized that the dreams of Mariette had something to do with the curse. She was busy trying to cope with these images when word came that another child had gone missing. It saddened her greatly to recognize her own failure in helping her people. This time the child was a toddler – just under one year of age. It took all the women to calm the poor mother who had firmly believed her baby girl to be safe; after all, there were several younger infants to choose from. The occupants of The Plantation were, as one, horrified. They feared there would be no end to the curse. They feared they would have no future.

Hillery, along with Isis, spent the day tending the mother and working to calm the people at large. Many of them threatened to leave, taking their chances in the wild. Those who had lived there these many years told of the runaways in the past that had died horrible deaths – from freak accidents to murders that showed no mercy. Hillery, with Isis' encouragement, told of her dreams. She hoped to instill peace among them by allowing them to understand that she believed they were figuring out the reason behind the curse. "And with reason comes understanding," Hillery insisted. "What we understand," she concluded, "we can work to correct." She had their attention now, she noted, and that was the best she could offer.

That night she dreamed again of Stuart. In this scenario, Mariette pointed out the grim shadow of Libby Prison, showing her daughter the ugly brick building with Stuart among its inhabitants. While Hillery shuddered visibly, Mariette whispered thickly, "You must go to him. He has need of you."

When she awoke, her mother's scent filled the room. It was the same scent she always associated with her mother's presence. Yet this time it did not bring Hillery comfort. This time it had the opposite effect, for Mariette's message implied Stuart was in grave danger. Maybe more than what the confines of prison might typically offer. Hillery did not know what to make of it. She knew only that she must make ready to leave for Richmond. And that the matter of the curse would have to wait. This worried her immensely.

She felt positively chilled even with Ariel pressed against her side. It was as if the little dog sensed the risk as well, and she startled when she glanced on the bedside table and saw that someone had delivered her mail. There, on a silver tray, was a letter from none other than Miss Elizabeth Van Lew. Hillery's heart sank. The dream had become a reality. Oddly enough, no one on The Plantation owned up to delivering the letter. This made no sense as they were a tight little group that loved each other as family.

# CHAPTER TWENTY SEVEN

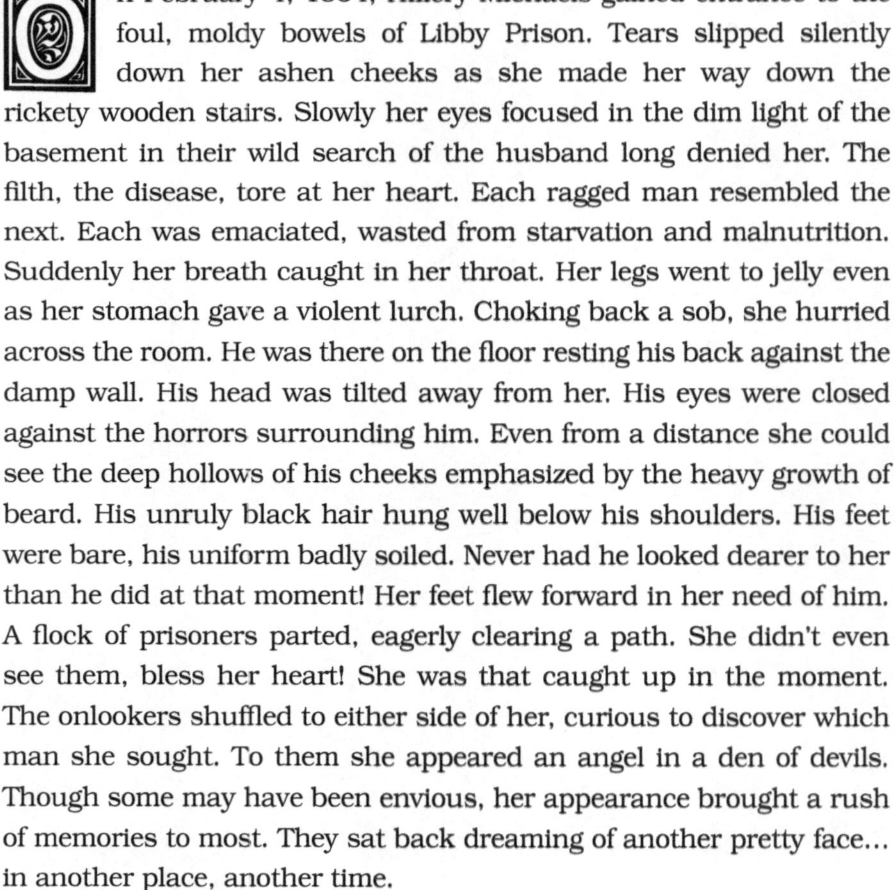

On February 4, 1864, Hillery Michaels gained entrance to the foul, moldy bowels of Libby Prison. Tears slipped silently down her ashen cheeks as she made her way down the rickety wooden stairs. Slowly her eyes focused in the dim light of the basement in their wild search of the husband long denied her. The filth, the disease, tore at her heart. Each ragged man resembled the next. Each was emaciated, wasted from starvation and malnutrition. Suddenly her breath caught in her throat. Her legs went to jelly even as her stomach gave a violent lurch. Choking back a sob, she hurried across the room. He was there on the floor resting his back against the damp wall. His head was tilted away from her. His eyes were closed against the horrors surrounding him. Even from a distance she could see the deep hollows of his cheeks emphasized by the heavy growth of beard. His unruly black hair hung well below his shoulders. His feet were bare, his uniform badly soiled. Never had he looked dearer to her than he did at that moment! Her feet flew forward in her need of him. A flock of prisoners parted, eagerly clearing a path. She didn't even see them, bless her heart! She was that caught up in the moment. The onlookers shuffled to either side of her, curious to discover which man she sought. To them she appeared an angel in a den of devils. Though some may have been envious, her appearance brought a rush of memories to most. They sat back dreaming of another pretty face... in another place, another time.

It seemed an eternity before she reached the far wall. She made no sound, but dropped swiftly to her knees. His eyes opened of their own accord. His fine head swiveled in her direction. She almost cried out as she met those eyes, but instead allowed her gaze to roam the deterioration of his slim build. It was obvious he had lost a good deal of weight, yet he was still well muscled beneath the tattered shirt. She correctly assumed he had found a means of exercise even in this mean existence. Her eyes filled with moisture as she drank in the sight of him. She witnessed the tell-tale ripples of sinewy strength through the remains of his shirt. Still she could find no words. His nostrils caught the scent of her, and he breathed in the lavender he had so often dreamed of. Now he could only stare. They drank in the sight of each other.

"Stuart," her voice broke on a sob. "Stuart!" she breathed again, this time reaching out to him. Suddenly she was in his arms. He cradled her like a fragile child as tears streaked her face. Men sniffled, and then looked away. They were unashamed. He traced her tears with gentle fingertips, tasting the sting of salt as their lips met and held. It was not a passionate kiss; it was a union of infinite need. They clung together as one. It was enough to feel the pulse of life heating their entwined limbs.

Gently Stuart cupped her chin breaking the spell that bound them. His eyes devoured her. His fingers trembled as he read the despair in her beautiful gaze. "I love you so much," she whispered shakily. "Your mother is fighting for parole."

"And I, you," he returned, "but mother is wasting her time. There is no hope in that. The time for parole has passed."

"I will not return home without you! I will not lose hope," she sucked in her breath in an attempt to control her wayward emotions.

"I am not suggesting as much," he told her, "but I want you safe. These walls have ears," he hushed her gently when she would have spoken. "Many of these men," his eyes took in those around them, "would betray us for a sum."

"What will you do?" her words were softly spoken, nearly imperceptible. She had seen the purpose in his gaze.

"I want you safe," he repeated. His words were low, barely audible. "Go to your friend, Elizabeth. She will explain." He set her at arm's length even as a guard growled from a few feet away. "Please," his gaze shifted to the guard. "See my wife to safety," he said. "She has no business here."

The guard was elderly, but not unkind. He agreed with Stuart's remark and hurried to take Hillery's arm. It paid to watch one's expressions, Stuart knew, and to know the guards by name.

"May I return later?" Hillery dared to ask. "I would come again today."

"Yes, of course," Stuart flashed a grin engaging the confidence of the guard, "only ask for this one. Old Rex has a good heart. He will look after you. Isn't that right, Rex?"

Rex was old and sick to death of war. He did not wish to see it linger as some seemed to, and he did not wish any harm to befall the ladies who came to visit. "I will keep her safe," he vowed. "You can count on that," Rex assured him, and Hillery knew Stuart had made a wise choice.

In her hotel room, Hillery washed up, changing her attire, before paying Elizabeth a discreet visit. She wondered how all this had come about. How did Stuart know Elizabeth? And how deeply was the other woman involved? It was clear Stuart would not take any unnecessary chances. For this, Hillery was grateful.

Once seated in the comfortable confines of the Van Lew mansion, Elizabeth informed her of the escape plans. What she was told caused Hillery's breath to catch in her throat. As risky as it might sound, she had to acknowledge the prisoners had no choice. They had to take action now. "John Winder, the provost marshal, has been trying to move the bulk of the prisoners to Georgia for some time now," Liz explained. "They are building a new prison in Macon. Once there, the men will have no further chance. Winder is becoming extremely vicious," she advised. "He will see his goals accomplished." This last was said in quiet warning.

"And in the meantime?" Hillery's voice was soft.

"He has increased guard rotation. And he will continue to make conditions insufferable. This is not Colonel Rose's first escape," Elizabeth continued gently, "nor is it the first attempt to be made at Libby." She paused to let the importance of her comment sink in. "Winder becomes more livid with each attempt." She had placed a supportive hand on Hillery's shoulder even as she handed her a cup of tea. "Here," she said, "have a sip. It will refresh you." Elizabeth's eyes gleamed in the late afternoon light. Hillery saw a keen intelligence in her that the local populace missed entirely, they were that certain of her madness. "Colonel Rose is a brilliant leader," she said decisively. "He will do well. I will assist in any way I can, of course, but you...you must be off and away before the escape is final lest you be placed in the thick of it all!"

"But," Hillery began only to be politely refused.

"Your husband does not need to worry about you as well, don't you see?" Elizabeth posed. "His burden is great enough. There is, however, a thing or two you can do before heading back home. Perhaps aiding the cause another way will give you comfort?"

Hillery brightened visibly. She looked to Elizabeth for guidance, listening patiently as the other spoke. "You must pay a visit to the Greenhow residence, no matter how brief. After all, you still have an open invitation, so to speak. Rose may not trust you any longer, but it is common knowledge you are friends. Why, she has even been to your home, not to mention your ties in D.C.," Elizabeth nodded, a bird-like gesture. "We need to know what she is about. Oh," she waved away any further comment, "we know she's in England, but we do not know what she plans to accomplish there. I'm certain Governor Letcher is aware of, and behind, her endeavors. But we have nothing further," here Elizabeth paused, regarding Hillery with a quizzical smile. "Perhaps you can discover her purpose?"

Hillery nodded, unsure how she could discover anything, but more than willing to try. Elizabeth nodded in satisfaction at Hillery's expression. Liz was adept at reading people's intentions, and she knew without doubt when a seed had been planted. "My informants in the Confederate White House tell me much, mark my words," here she paused again, for the door had softly opened and Mary

Bowser stood there. Hillery noted the raised brow of the newcomer, and correctly surmised Mary was uncomfortable with her presence. Mary Bowser had been with Elizabeth all of her life. Elizabeth and her mother had freed Mary as a child after Elizabeth's father's death, and seeing in the young woman a wealth of promise Elizabeth had sent an eager Mary on to college in Philadelphia to be educated same as she, herself. Later, after the onset of war, Elizabeth had carefully secured a place for Mary in the Confederate White House where few whites paid any attention to the Negroes who served them. Hillery, who had noted Mary's tense stance, stood and prepared to take her leave. She had heard Mary's story and guessed at her identity. "I'm Hillery, and I was just leaving," she said directly to the girl who had yet to move. "I believe I have been given a mission," she grinned shyly, a gesture meant to reassure.

The girl gave a stiff nod, "I'm Mary," was all she offered.

Elizabeth's demeanor warmed still more. She liked Hillery and it showed. She appreciated how quickly she took her leave upon seeing Mary's discomfiture. "Do not tire yourself, my friend," she cautioned Hillery. "You have much upon you at this time, and all is well in my household." Her look took in Mary where she stood in the doorway. Mary bobbed her head. "Please give my regards to Colonel Streight, will you? Do you know it was that Sansom girl that got him captured? Emma, I believe. Foiled his raid into Georgia, and landed him in prison. She's just a girl, really, but should you cross her path, be aware."

With a last look that took in the room at large, Hillery took her leave.

Hillery returned to the prison that evening with renewed insight. She moved among the men, introducing herself to them. She learned their names and where they were from, promising to write their families when she returned home. She dressed their wounds, changed their bandages, and more than all else, offered them hope. With Stuart beside her, she passed food and provisions among them, making them feel as comfortable as possible. They looked upon her with pride, seeing her for the angel she was, and she acknowledged them as friends and fellow countrymen.

The following morning Hillery rose early and paid a visit to the Greenhow residence. She had sent her card on ahead, giving herself no time for worry. Instead, she readied herself for the task at hand. She disliked feeling like a traitor, but she knew her duty and realized as much as Rose would despise this, she would also respect it. She, herself, would do no less.

She feigned ignorance when she was told that Rose was not at home. She had chosen her issues well, and said in way of explanation that she had hoped for a happy reunion. Still, she would welcome a visit with young Rose as she needed to return a garment Charlotte had borrowed. As she spoke she pulled a scarf from her reticule.

"But I did loan her one just like that," young Rose said, "only Charlotte returned it immediately after the ball." Her eyes showed her confusion. Young Rose had been taught well however, and as a blooming Southern bell, she directed Hillery into the formal parlor while she, in her mother's stead, rang for tea.

"Well, I'll be," Hillery murmured, "perhaps she liked it so very much that she purchased an identical one? I did mention she is living in D.C. now, did I not?"

Young Rose said she had not, but feigned interest. After a visit only long enough to cover the necessities of a good hostess, she stood and said she would have the maid show Hillery out. "I will, of course, give your regards to mother," she concluded as Hillery stood with her. Rose disappeared immediately, allowing Hillery a few brief moments to herself. She did not miss a beat. She knew exactly where Rose kept her books and slipped into the connecting library. As she leafed quickly through the contents of Rose's escritoire, she took mental notes about a possible launching of a Confederate ship, and more importantly, the mention of an acquisition of a tidy sum of Confederate gold! Good Lord and Saint Michael! Rose had found Southern sympathizers in Europe who were willing to financially support the Southern states! That's what she was doing overseas! She was overwhelmed with the extent of this information when she distinctly overheard pieces of a conversation coming from the next room. She stepped back into the parlor where a young maid soon found her and escorted her out.

In order to clear her head, Hillery opted to walk the few blocks back to her hotel room. What had the voices said? She recounted. "Rose is to bring back a fortune for the Confederate states. That is a certainty." And in gold, thought Hillery. The voices had then gone on to reference a particular ship's captain. The name of the ship was familiar to Hillery just as the information was now tattooed in her brain. This was huge! This, she would pass on to Elizabeth! Liz would know what to do. Hillery glanced back over her shoulder only to spy John Winder skulking a few steps behind. He had been following her! She smiled slyly to herself. Let him watch! It was fine that he saw her leaving the Greenhow's. Fine indeed!

Hillery was only a half block from her hotel when she bumped into a familiar figure. The sudden impact jarred both young women. Hillery was first to recover. "Jenny!" she exclaimed, excited to see her friend, Jenny Harlan. The two embraced. Tucking a stray lock of hair into place, Hillery asked, "What are you doing here?"

"The children and I have been living in Richmond," Jenny explained. "I swear I've written you! I don't know why you haven't received my letters. I have family here."

"Oh, it's so good to see you!"

"You too," Jenny sighed. She felt much like pinching herself. "I can't believe you're here! I'll always be grateful to you."

"It was a terrible fire," Hillery shuddered as she remembered every detail of the day Jenny's house caught fire. "I'm so glad everything worked out. You have family here, you say?"

"Yes," Jenny recovered her manners in time to extend an invitation. "I'm hosting a social at our house tomorrow. Why don't you come? It will give us a chance to can catch up. You can meet my cousins."

"Sounds wonderful," Hillery accepted as Jenny scribbled off the address.

"It's isn't hard to find. And it's close to your hotel," Jenny provided after Hillery told her where she was staying. "I'll look forward to seeing you!"

When she returned to her hotel room, Ariel was fit to be tied. He yapped at her for leaving him behind, kissing her in between yaps. His tail end wiggled so much when he pressed close, she knew she had been missed! Then he snuggled up to her while she took her lunch, and ultimately fed him his. She was already dreading leaving him again, poor little mite.

That afternoon Hillery returned to Libby with a large platter of beef and seasoned potatoes. It was then she first saw Benjamin and was sorry that he, too, was an occupant here. She wasn't terribly surprised as she had seen his name on the list as well, but Libby was not an enviable place, and Ben did not look as though he had fared so well. She offered him a bite of food then passed it along to as many as it would feed.

"Lord, you look beautiful," Ben complimented in a perfectly polite voice. Stuart acknowledged him as a friend, and if Benjamin's eyes roamed a bit too freely, Hillery accepted this graciously. These men had been locked away a goodly amount of time. Yet she knew Benjamin to be a gentleman. He caught the scent of her cologne in the same instant Stuart's eyes flared with a possessive look. Ben politely dismissed himself even as the guard allowed the couple a few precious moments to themselves. They sank together on the floor, Hillery completely unmindful of the dampness of the stone. Her only care was that she was snug in her husband's arms for the time being. His arms tightened around her, her head sank comfortably against his shoulder. Neither spoke.

Soon enough reality set in. The bodies around them shifted and moaned. Hillery had, by this time, met many of the men, and tended more than a few. They welcomed her help and her company. The gentle sex was greatly missed in this place, and her herbal knowledge was keen. She never failed to offer her kindnesses and always carried a thorough supply of medications with her. She laughed with them, prayed with them, and went out of her way to humor them. She watched the death toll with great anxiety, weeping openly when a comrade was lost. In short order she had fast become one of them.

At nightfall Hillery stood by her hotel window imagining the events unfolding at Libby. Now in the darkness of her room, she could almost hear the sharp prick of metal chipping away at the unrelenting earth. She stood with her arms wrapped around her slender form. Soon she would have to leave this city behind and return to The Plantation. Her husband's future was at stake as was their future together. She roused at Ariel's soft, menacing growl. Had she seen someone standing beneath the street lamp? She blinked, and if she had, the street was now quite clear. She was aware of a slight uneasiness when she climbed into bed.

# CHAPTER TWENTY EIGHT

n the night of February 5th while Hillery stood at her hotel window, Stuart was deep beneath the earth. He loosened the dirt with a pocket knife, then laboriously shoveled it free, using nothing more than a wooden spittoon. It was a grueling job – that of a human mole – but with much precise planning a tunnel was underway. He was deep beneath the grounds of Libby... some forty plus feet... under the surface. He was fighting the rats as they crawled atop him! He had to focus to keep from crying out. The rodents gnawed at him even as he knocked them off and resumed his chore. And who among the guards that walked the grounds above would suspect such a thing? That was a secret worth guarding!

Though the night air was crisp, it seemed humid to the men who labored in such cramped quarters. They worked well into the night chipping and digging, boring through the earth. The earth when gathered was hauled away in a haversack made of rope and cloth, then spread out beneath the straw of Rat Hell. Rat Hell was an abandoned portion of the basement that had, at one time, been a kitchen. The rats had long since taken over until the Confederates had sealed this portion off. Every few hours the shift changed. Thomas Rose took over with grim determination while Stuart shook off the rodents and assumed a different position. The elements were harrowing. The rats – as bad as they were in the rest of the prison – were far worse here. There was at least one man, generally two, on watch. And there was always a man secreted beneath the two-foot layer of filthy straw. It was an unenviable position as there was a great deal at stake. An additional hand was busy covering their tracks. There could be no sign of disturbance here. It was not an easy venture. Those involved did their level best to move things along as quickly as possible. All hands were efficient.

The gentle light of dawn showed all men asleep in their tattered blankets. The back room showed no trace of the previous night's work. To the average eye they were as any prisoners: worn, tired, ravaged and beaten. Their weariness washed away the hostility they felt. Their rebellious minds were tucked away until the return of night.

On the morning of the sixth Hillery entered the gates of Libby with a huge basket of loaves. The bread was passed from hand to hand for she had brought an ample supply. While the men ate she walked among them, speaking to each man she passed, checking their wounds and making small talk. There were several newcomers who were by far the worse for wear. She went to Rex asking prettily for a tub of hot water. He returned in short order, including towels and a fresh bar of soap. Hillery praised his many kindnesses earning a blush from the gentle giant. She then turned and busied herself cleaning the injured. "I'll do what I can," she soothed a young lieutenant whose earnest gaze pleaded with her. It was painfully clear that the young man had little chance of survival, but his pain was great, and she could at least keep him as comfortable as possible. To many, she was fast becoming an angel of mercy. They looked upon her with grave respect. And God bless her! She would freely relinquish all she had to aid their cause.

She left with the loud tolling of the bell only to venture back again within the hour. From her reticule she withdrew a parcel of medicine and a handful of coins. She was attempting to bribe an arbitrary guard when Rex appeared making her mission far easier. He would gladly take the medicine to the young lieutenant. She beamed at him, pressing the coin into his palm. When he declined she laid a slim hand on his stubbly cheek, saying, "Rex, you are the only one I can trust in here.

And you have a keen sense of honor. Take the coin. You have more than earned it." He looked into her wide violet gaze and murmured his thanks.

Rex, it seemed, had an ill wife at home and Hillery was more than happy to help. After inquiring into the nature of his wife's malady, she fished through the contents of her bag until she located the object of her search. "Tell Millie to make a hot tea of this herb then rub the remainder on her chest. She can mix it with anything, even water, to form a plaster. She will breathe easier on the morrow." Rex smiled his thanks and quickly delivered the medicine to the soldier in question.

Early that afternoon found Hillery at Jenny's home where she met her extended family and mingled with her guests. Some of the women were openly friendly as they had heard the story of the fire and how Hillery had saved the life of one of Jenny's children. That type of bravado was to be rewarded. Others, however, were a bit snippy. Jenny was embarrassed by their rudeness while Hillery made every attempt to shrug it away. "They're wondering where my loyalties lie," she said with conviction. "You can't fault them. I am here in Richmond to visit my husband. And I am sure it is common knowledge."

Jenny blushed to the roots of her red hair. Hillery felt a rush of compassion for her. In reality, Hillery knew Jenny's true convictions. Yet she was a Southerner with a husband ostensibly fighting for the Confederacy. But the fact was, she was a lifelong friend of Edie's as well as a dear and loyal friend of her own. And Hillery had cause to trust her. These were, however, dangerous times so Hillery chose to tread softly and thereby spare Jenny any problems here in the South. Jenny had family and friends to protect. Therefore the subject remained carefully guarded. Besides, Hillery liked and respected Jenny. Regardless of the war, they were friends.

The afternoon wore on with tea and cakes and idle conversation. Hillery liked Jenny's cousins who were loyal to Jenny and made the little things in life fun. That was sometimes difficult in times of war. Jenny, in turn, did all she could to help establish a safe haven for their combined little ones. As the conversation turned serious, children were chased outdoors to play while the ladies plied their needles to make good use of their time. Jenny slanted a look in Hillery's direction.

"I hear the Albemarle is nearly up and running," a woman named

Sue stated with matter-of-fact calm.

"I don't believe the men folk want us to know anything about that," a second woman chimed in a slow, sultry accent.

"Ha," the first laughed then applied herself to her sewing with a fury, "that's because they like to keep us uninformed, the better to keep their secrets to themselves!"

"That may well be," the other said, not to be outdone, "however I do believe you are misinformed. The Albemarle is merely underway. Our brave men are determined to clear the sound country of eastern North Carolina to open ports for blockade runners. I doubt they'll rest until they do," she laughed when the other scowled. Hillery took note of all that was said to be filed away for further use. Women everywhere had an uncanny way of picking up seemingly useless information in an effort to keep up with their husband's activities.

As the day wore on women began to take their leave, clearing away dishes and piles of sewing as they did so. They bid their farewells and headed off towards their individual destinations to prepare dinners and put children down for the night. Hillery stood, taking Jenny in her arms in a final hug. "It was so good to see you, my friend," she whispered. "Thank you for the invitation."

Jenny gave an impudent grin, a dimple on each cheek, "It was wonderful to see you as well," she said with genuine warmth, "and you're welcome." She was, as always, amazed at how Hillery managed to put those around her at ease! To a woman, everyone there had become perfectly relaxed.

Later that day Hillery returned to Libby with a fresh supply of medications. Her time in Richmond was coming to a close, and she knew an immense sorrow. As she approached the prison gate she noticed a large group of men on funeral detail. Her heart gave a painful lurch. It was not that it was an unusual sight. It was the prevailing sadness that disturbed her. These were prisoners who had lost some of their own and were in the stark duty of burying them. They were dealing with the hardship of digging a common grave. It was the only option afforded them, as well as the difficulty of bidding their friends and fellow officers farewell. She approached with solemn face and downcast eyes. As she quietly skirted the gravesite, she was rudely herded by a routine battery of guards who cruelly nudged her nearer than she would have otherwise chosen to have gone. They laughed when she nearly stumbled. One of the prisoners stepped forward, awkward in his shackles, in an attempt to right her. When she glanced up to thank him, she inadvertently had a clear view of the bodies. She gasped when she peered into the visage of the young lieutenant she had sought to ease. She later heard there were thirty dead from the basement alone. Tears stung her eyes, but she carried herself proudly, her head high. Little did she know that the audience of shackled officers would speak well of her in the future, often referencing that moment.

Her time with her husband was limited. Too soon she was heading back to the hotel to face another lonely night. Only this night was to mark the end of her journey. Tomorrow she would say her good-byes. It was time to return to The Plantation – she would leave on the morning train.

When darkness fell leaving the occupants of the basement snoring restlessly, Stuart and Benjamin crept from their beds to take their shift in the tunnel. Cricket stood guard with two others behind him. They created a human barricade against the curious. The men had labored endlessly when at last Thomas Rose and a man named Boyle came to relieve them. Cricket remained stationed at his post, eyes wide, and mind alert. He appointed replacements for the other two guards, then signaled Stuart and Benjamin to their beds. He kept a constant vigil on the mass of sleeping prisoners. It wouldn't do to rouse the others. They could not risk discovery now! His well trained eyes focused on the pair of bone weary men as they silently made their way to their blankets. Everything was going as planned. Their work ran as smoothly as a well oiled clock.

At that same moment Hillery had been awakened by a distant sound in the night. Ariel, who had been asleep at her bedside, had moved to the window. She stared at him as if in a fog. The little dog had suddenly grown! He loomed large against the curtain. But it was not only his shadow that appeared larger! He was large. And he was ominous. He was baring his teeth at something outdoors. She was reminded of Rags and the many times he had come to her aid. Ariel always seemed attuned to those visits. As she watched, the two dogs merged; they were one and the same! And this Ariel was not playing games. He was furious about whatever lay in wait. She crept from her bed, knowing that she was safe with him, and drew aside the curtain. Below, in the lamplight, she spied a man. Had he been looking up at her room? She was so sure of it she felt chill bumps break out on her arms. He was dressed in coat and hat, yet something about him was strangely familiar. Ariel growled a menacing sound. She saw the man look up over his shoulder, his face shielded by the night. She knew that figure, she thought, tasting fear. Tate chuckled as he turned away. Somehow the sound carried.

Morning dawned with its usual breakfast of gruel and chicory coffee. This was followed by the traditional rounds of card games and checkers. The repast was tainted by the tattered remnants of whatever refuge floated in their food and drink. It was the usual fair. Though sickened by this the men sought to ignore the vile bits and pieces they could see and taste. Likewise, they no longer heard the laughter of the guards who enjoyed their humility. They each made an attempt to scrub themselves clean. Most of them broke off at one point or another to launder what remnants of clothing were left them after first applying a sponge to their dirt-encrusted bodies and finger brushing their teeth. The communal tub of water was all that was provided for their cleanliness and they sought to make use of it. It, too, was brown with dirt and debris.

There was an air of subdued excitement this morning, though those involved in the escape made a show of relaxing, of fitting into just another dreary day. Stuart was at odds with the thought of Hillery leaving for The Plantation. Though he wanted her safe, he missed her already. His unusual melancholy carried over to the others. It was a wise cover. He was jittery and didn't want the others to know why. His dreams of late had been unnerving. He kept seeing a successful escape entwined with visions of despair. Shackled men haunted his dreams, and he was unable to separate one from the other. He didn't have a clue as to which category he belonged.

Hillery had made all the necessary farewells on the outside. She had packed her bag and collected her ticket. She had only to pick up Ariel before departing. Her final stop was the one that hurt most. Telling Stuart good-bye was too difficult to fathom. She hated to leave him behind, but knew she must – for his safety as well as her own. She entered the gates of Libby, easily dismissing the taunts of the guards, falling into step with Rex when he approached. His kindness was nearly her undoing. She focused on his wife, asking after Millie's health and well being. Rex regarded her with solemn eyes. He again offered his thanks before escorting her below. She made her rounds among the men, wishing them well in turn. She held her head high, fighting the tell-tale moisture that filled her eyes when she spotted Stuart. She kept to herself the knowledge that she was being watched. Her fear of Tate never left her lips, nor did her fear of the provost marshal. She allowed her husband to hold her for a long minute, then broke away fussing with his hair, righting his uniform with busy fingers. "I won't say good-bye," she whispered. "I won't. I will see you soon," she nodded, attempting a smile that wavered badly. He returned her smile.

"See you soon," he whispered then fell silent. He stared after her when she walked away noting that each man she passed saluted her in turn. The basement knew a quiet it had never before known.

# CHAPTER TWENTY NINE

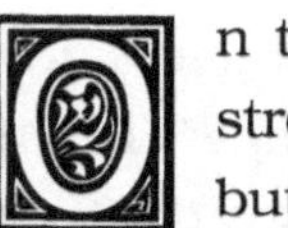n the train heading out of Richmond Hillery sighed as she stroked Ariel's rich fur. She had been fighting tears all morning, but dared not let them flow. She didn't want to invite the stares of the curious. She did not think for a single moment that she went unnoticed. All in Richmond were eager to learn her true convictions. *Was she really only visiting her confined husband? And if so, where did her loyalties lie?* She had noticed sly glances in the crowd. People were hostile in times of war, many were quick to judge. She was also aware of the bold looks of the provost marshal. John H. Winder was definitely suspicious. He had watched her with rapt attention. On more than one occasion she had spotted him near the gates of Libby just as she had seen him lurking on the streets of Richmond, always just a step behind as though he were following her. On her visit to the Greenhow residence she had deliberately allowed him to see her. She had hoped the ruse had thrown him off track, but here he was again in the crowds of the train station. Hillery was tired. She wanted desperately to sleep without fear. She wanted peace.

Only now as the train pulled away from the station did she allow her mind to settle on the dreams she had been having. They had begun a few nights ago. She had been too caught up, too overwhelmed to even attempt to unravel the mystery of them. Now with the warmth of Ariel as he snuggled his little body close, did she allow her mind to wander. In these visions, Mariette was very clearly trying to tell her something. Hillery could hear her voice as if in conversation, though it was strangely muffled. She had an occasional glimpse of Marietta – her grand mére in the background, but Marietta was too far removed for her to understand. She, too, spoke to her, though her words were mostly lost. The visions then took the form of a pictorial, showing her grand mére as she would have been in her youth.

Marietta had been a beautiful young woman, slim yet full figured. Both Hillery and her mother had inherited her large violet eyes and full red lips, but Marietta had darker tresses that spilled around her hips in coffee colored waves. She looked happy in the beginning with Henry at her side. Henry was a proud aristocrat of French descent. He, like Marietta, came from a fine family and was very well educated. He was the wealthy owner of the land now known as The Plantation. Henry was easily twenty years her senior and loved to indulge the young bride of his choice. Hillery watched the story unfold with a growing sense of foreboding. Marietta, who had appeared radiant in her wedding finery with Henry looking on with the proud gaze of a possessive groom, soon began to fade. Her joy was replaced by a sense of disturbed unhappiness, and Hillery wondered why. The picture had become cloudy... the train jarred her awake just as she had started to doze, and Hillery realized she had lost the pictorial...just like that.

On the night of the eighth, the first of the escapees were safely beyond Confederate sentries. They were fifty-some feet from the prison when the first of the men took refuge in the abandoned tobacco shack where they had surfaced. Thomas and Stuart headed the mission. They stood and stamped their feet on the packed earthen floor, grinning at each other. Their smiles looked a great deal like blackened grimaces. Their teeth shone white in the night. They brushed at their clothing absently, still troubled by rodents even as their eyes continually returned to the tunnel exit. At any moment the others would come spilling through the opening, carrying the hated rats in their wake. The damn things still squealed in their ears, nipped at their skin, hanging on to any and all appendages. They were underfoot even now in the shack. Benjamin and Boyle were close behind. Streight would follow them with Cricket bringing up the rear. He was worried about Cricket. The man had been determined to wait his turn because of the lack of a leg. He didn't want to jeopardize anyone's freedom. He was as scrappy as he was strong. But it would be a mob when the other occupants of the basement caught wind of the tunnel and Stuart wished not for the first time that he had pushed the man ahead of himself. He vowed now to wait for him, waving the others on.

Slowly they crouched, stamping their feet when they straightened again. They stretched their legs and arched their backs against the walls of the small shack. They were not fooled by the illusion of peace for they knew they were far from safe. This was the first resting place, that's all, and only for a very brief moment in time. From here they must make their way to the Van Lew mansion under cover of darkness. The men were extremely grateful that the citizens of Richmond refused to take Elizabeth seriously, seeing her instead as an idle fool. Liz proclaimed her Union sympathies to the world, and the world refused to see the tiny, bird-like woman as a threat! Well, the more good it did them, and the Union at large!

Elizabeth Van Lew was no stranger to the Northerner forces. She had multiple contacts in every avenue of the service with many good friends among them. She had accomplices throughout the South she would never betray, many of whom would do just about anything to come to her aid. She had friends in high places and she accommodated them in every possible way. In short, Elizabeth loved the Union. She abhorred slavery and had, in fact, freed all of her father's slaves upon his death in 1851. Many of them stayed with the household. Some, like Mary Bowser, even helped Elizabeth with her wartime espionage activities. Her brother, John, handled the estate for her and their mother, as well as owned and ran a profitable hardware business.

Upon learning the conditions at Libby, Elizabeth had petitioned the commandant for permission to provide humanitarian aid. Lieutenant David H. Todd, half brother to Mary Todd Lincoln, denied her request. Unwilling to give up, Elizabeth then approached the Confederate secretary, Christopher Memminger, who at length gained her access. John was able to provide Elizabeth with the funds needed to supply "her boys" with food, clothing, bedding, medicine and reading material.

Her contributions were as magnanimous then as they were now. Now she offered housing to the escapees in her very own mansion! Every man involved in the escape had the directions memorized. There was no paper trail.

Stuart looked at Thomas where he stood by the exit. He was getting ready to sprint out into the cover of winter branches on a relatively cloudless night. They could not spare another minute. They had paused only enough to ease the cramps from their limbs. Later, they would talk of their successes. Later they would welcome the others – each as they arrived at the back door of the mansion. Pray God there was a later.

Benjamin and Boyle joined them in the crowded shack. With a quick glance over his shoulder, Thomas disappeared. Silence loomed. Stuart listened to every nuance of the night: a twig snapped, from somewhere nearby a dog yapped, a sentry's voice carried on the wind, but there was no warning to it. All these little sounds were normal, yet they had Stuart on pins and needles. It was then he heard Thomas' voice, "The underground railroad to God's country is open!" It was just a quiet echo in the night, but he sensed rather than heard the effect it had on the others. He waited the agreed upon three minutes, then motioned the others on, clamping an arm around Cricket's shoulder as they, too, slipped into the shadows. Cricket grinned, patting his pocket. He had won the deck of playing cards they had all coveted!

He had already lost sight of Thomas. And he was intensely aware of the rustle of activity behind him. Streight was only slightly ahead of him. Knowing he was being pursued spurred him on, yet they slowed to a casual stroll when they reached the gates, behaving as though walking through them was the most natural thing in the world. They had agreed to separate into small groups in order to lessen the odds of capture. To spread out, to take different routes would work in their favor. The guards, when alerted, wouldn't have one single trail to follow. In a manner of speaking, each man was out for himself. Yet they each had the other's backs, and they all shared the same destination.

Stuart's dreams haunted him. When the mob broke free – and it would - he wanted to be a good distance away; that, or safely behind the walls of the mansion. Yet he had no idea how Elizabeth could shield them, only that she would. Tiny she might be, but tough she was! She was also highly intelligent and apparently without fear. He had been privy to the means in which she questioned new arrivals, gaining information with ease. He was equally aware that she had a network with which she forwarded this information. Nothing much with Elizabeth would surprise him. And like the others, he would protect her without a qualm.

Upon arrival at the mansion, Stuart found Thomas safely seated, warming himself before the fire. Boyle had arrived as well. He eased Cricket's way as others began to pile in after them. They were each given food and quickly whisked away to hidden quarters behind concealed panels.

At the prison, a stampede had formed. Men crawled rapidly through the tunnel, moving furiously to combat the rats. They exploded into the night, yet still no alarm was sounded. The majority of them remained calm enough to walk out the gates rather than risk discovery. A quick movement might draw the eye. They made it beyond the gates and into town or toward the river, seeking survival in small groups. When dawn lit the sky they were still coming! A prison guard was heard to break the quiet with a weary comment, "Hallou, Bill – there's somebody's coffee pot upset, sure!" The muffled response was lost on the escapees, who by this time, had traveled beyond hearing.

At roll call that morning, the guards were becoming agitated, but not because they knew what the prisoners were about. They seriously believed the men were tricking them, pulling pranks as they had so many times before by switching places and creating the illusion of missing men. After all, how else could one explain all of the commotion? After a lengthy morning, and an array of varying emotions, it was duly noted that over one-hundred prisoners were actually unaccounted for!

As Rat Hell was closed off, it was many hours later when the tunnel was discovered and reported. By then the entire surrounding area was crawling with militia. Troops patrolled the territory. Additional guards had been called in. Libby was surrounded, sealed off from all else. Shots were fired. The escapees were deeply concerned for the others who had found the passage, taken a chance, and were now hunted with dogs and guns.

John Winder, the provost marshal himself, was sighted patrolling the streets. He was furious. Stuart watched as his dreams became a reality. A goodly number of men were caught and returned in shackles. Two were reputed to have drowned in the James River. Those of them who were safe were lucky indeed.

Hillery was in New Orleans when she learned of the escape. She hadn't been back long due to the condition of the rails, and she was both tired and edgy. As she neared the city she became increasingly aware of the persistent tattoo of the drums. They kept time to her dreams which were now taking over her waking hours. She was grateful to both Helen and Higgens for their devotion to her. They had readied everything for her comfort. She welcomed the sight of the turned down bed and blazing hearth. She went to bed early that first night with a cup of Helen's chocolate and Ariel tucked neatly next to her. He spent exactly two minutes licking her face before succumbing to the creature comforts of sleep. She smiled tiredly, glad to be home. She had slept very little on the train and very poorly at that. She dozed off with her hand still warm from Ariel's coat.

She rose early in spite of her fatigue, probably because she was accustomed to the morning hours. Ariel's eyes inched open when she slipped from the bed. He whined in protest to the loss of her warmth and watched through sleepy eyes as she dressed. She made quick work of it, giving her hair a healthy brushing before tying it loosely to one side to fall in riotous curls over her shoulder. Deciding to take breakfast after a brisk walk to chase away the last traces of sleep, she asked Ariel if he'd like to go out. He sprang from the bed as if he had grown wings and stretched on the run. Hillery laughed at his antics as he led the way. Once outdoors, he marked his territory in as many places as he could, his small back feet scratching the earth repeatedly in hurried abandon. He nipped at the cold morning air, enjoying himself immensely, and Hillery could have sworn that as they walked, he grew in size!

She heard the familiar rhythm of the drums even as she realized that she was most likely the only one in the entire neighborhood who did. She accepted this just as she accepted all the other peculiarities that she possessed. Ariel tossed a look over his shoulder that said she wasn't alone, and for the first time she wondered if he, too, heard the drums. She decided that he did. And in her mind, that explained still more. They kept a brisk pace and in spite of herself, Hillery was laughing when they returned home. When she entered the kitchen, she was humming. Ariel's tail waved like a banner in the wind when she tossed him a treat. It was then that she spied the morning paper on the little table near the stove.

She didn't remember walking into the next room, or sinking into the small slipper chair with the colored throw that she favored. She didn't remember Helen tiptoeing past with the silver tea tray. She just found herself there with Ariel nearby, a cup of tea in one hand, a full pot on the small table at her elbow. The newspaper was spread across her lap. She stared fixated at the bold print of the headlines that featured the escape from Libby. Numbly, she realized she had read every word several times through as if afraid she might miss something. There were quotes from the Richmond Sentinel and the Richmond Examiner as well as the Charleston Mercury and the New York Times.

It was the morning of the 11th, and already rumor was rife. Women in the city of Richmond were afraid to open their doors. They kept their children locked away with them. People speculated on the outcome of this new threat. Every day more news leaked out, more details, more horrors.

On the 12th, there was a detailed description of the escape. Twenty-two prisoners were reportedly recaptured. On the 14th, there was a full account of the tunnel Colonel Rose and her husband had engineered. It was all there in black and white: the triumph of those who had gotten away – the trauma of those left behind.

On the 20th, the count of those recaptured had more than doubled! She read all about the one-hundred-and-nine men who had managed to escape, and wept for the two who had drowned. She sobbed openly for the multitude that were shackled and returned to an even worse fate. Forty-eight prisoners! Forty-eight men recaptured. And among them was Colonel Thomas E. Rose of the 77th Pennsylvania– the instigator of the whole operation!

Bile rose in her throat, and she took an absent sip of the hot brew Helen kept at the ready while willing herself to stay calm. There was no mention of Stuart – no list of names, save the many references to Colonel Rose and a hazarded guess that Colonel Streight had been captured as well. And that only because some hungry reporter had grabbed hold of the juicy tidbit that further embroiled Thomas Rose, and no doubt brought further torment his way. The capture of Colonel Streight, however, was said to have been an error. Oh, how sorry she felt for Thomas! She thought a lot of him. She thought a great deal of all the men she had come to know and respect. It was difficult to imagine their plight! Hard to picture them in such circumstances! And in all of this – where was Stuart? More importantly, *how* was he?

The nights had grown longer. Hillery slept little, caught in the throes of fear for her spouse, further tormented by the onslaught of dreams. She watched the parade of captured men, grateful only when she didn't spy Stuart among them. Knowing that held no conclusion, she was at loose ends. Add to this the pictorials of Mariette and her grand mére, Marietta. Hillery watched in silence trying to understand, working to grasp the meaning of it all. And through it all, Ariel watched her, his little head propped on his front paws. Small paws, she called them. Ariel shook his head and resumed his watch.

# CHAPTER THIRTY

lizabeth wasted no time in smuggling the men out of the city. She didn't dare keep them with her for too long a period of time, nor did she feel she could play any games with their futures. She was in constant touch with General Benjamin Butler. Early in the war, she had learned an ancient cipher using a two-digit number for each letter of the alphabet. Her messages to Butler and other Federal leaders were written in an ink that became visible only when dipped in milk. Her contribution to the Union gained her much in turn. She was given answers. Her contacts supplied the means. She had only to act on them.

Since food was scarce, it was no surprise when basket-toting servants ventured from the mansion to nearby farms and back again. Messages were often hidden in an empty egg shell. No one ever suspected a thing, and correspondence moved ahead a notch. Thomas McNiven, the owner of a local bakery, supplied wealthy and poor alike. He provided bakery goods to the Confederate White House as well as the Van Lew mansion, all the while carrying messages as he went. He provided services to Elizabeth and she returned the favor. All this helped her to provide for her boys. She fed them, clothed them, and made certain they had plenty of provisions when they took their leave. She kept contact with Samuel Ruth who was an active Union spy. He was in the Richmond office of the Richmond, Fredericksburg and Petersburg Railroad and besides carrying information gave aid to Federal fugitives. He and his assistant, Lohman, used their positions to slow down shipments of supplies to Confederate forces. They worked together well and welcomed the fugitives on board. Elizabeth breathed a sigh of relief when the last of them left her home. She would miss their company, but their safety came first and brought her peace of mind as well. In the days to follow, Elizabeth would continue her mission at Libby, all the while unsuspected by the cream of Richmond society. Richmond might scorn Elizabeth due to her choice of loyalty, but never would they fear her. Rather, she often yearned for a means of security for herself and her mother. It was an ordeal to be an object of scorn. Elizabeth shook her head, squared her shoulders, and resumed life as she knew it.

Aboard the RF & P Rail line, the fugitives remained gratefully quiet. God willing, they would wind up safely in the North where they would be reunited with family and given an opportunity to regain their health. Those who were able would return to duty. They were well aware of their good fortune.

The days in New Orleans were bittersweet. Hillery became increasingly aware of the voodoo drums even as their effect on Ariel was made glaringly apparent. The little dog seemed to grow in size with each and every walk they took until it became necessary to limit these outings to their own immediate neighborhood. She couldn't have the neighbors talking, after all. She figured there was plenty of gossip as it was. The rhythmic tattoo became more violent each day. It was nerve-racking. There were times when she very much wanted to clamp her hands over her ears. She refrained from behaving this way mainly because she knew in her heart it would do little good. The beat of the drums was in her soul. She could no more separate herself from them than she could sever any part of her own body. They were a natural part of her reality. Hillery knew that what was happening was something she needed to get in control. She had to find a way where she controlled the drums, not the other way around.

She often pondered the circumstances that brought Ariel into her life. She knew without asking that Stuart had chosen him because he had known he would be the perfect protector for her. In spite of his size, Ariel could be formidable, and he would go to any lengths to keep her safe. She never doubted his devotion, never questioned his loyalty. She was equally aware that Stuart's gift had literally taken him to Ariel and that Ariel was somehow involved in the curse of The Plantation. The little dog had been a part of it from the beginning, and though she didn't understand the workings of this, she knew enough to take it seriously.

Her dreams, as well as her waking hours, had become entangled with the drums. She would go to sleep at night listening to them only to have them take her dream state more deeply into the heart of the city. And in the heart of the city lay the soul of the bayou. Her dreams would wrap around her with the mamaloi at the fore. The voodoo priestess smiled her triumphant smile. And in it, Hillery saw pure evil.

The newspapers continued their heated assault on those who dared trespass the city of Richmond. The escapees from Libby were both feared and hated. She prayed Stuart was safely out of the South by now, but had no way of knowing. She was afraid to write Elizabeth, afraid of the danger she might cause the woman. So she waited, and read, and worried. Then one day in early March the papers announced yet another escape attempt from the basement of Libby Prison. The escape had been launched on the twenty-eighth day of February. Though this attempt failed, much like the previous three attempts prior to the successful tunnel escape, it provoked the provost marshal John H. Winder to issue a threat against all the inhabitants of the prison. On behalf of the citizens of the nation's capitol, who were considered to be under daily threat, Winder proposed to have a mine dug in the basement of the building. Upon receiving the ascent of Congress, he would then fill that mine with a quantity of some two-hundred pounds of gun powder, enough to cause the prison to blow. An explosion like that would rock the entire building, which in turn would become a death trap claiming every single life therein. This should keep the men in line, ending any future escape attempts.

Hillery feared John Winder. She saw him for what he truly was, and knew he would carry out this threat, his hatred was that great. She was uneasy for the inhabitants of Libby Prison. She discussed her qualms with Higgens who was well versed in war and the plight of humanity.

She pondered her dreams nearly every waking moment and visited with Edie who advised her to speak to Isis. Isis could guide her, she said. She had been with the family all her life, and loved Hillery like a daughter. Isis could help fill in the gaps as well as provide comfort like no one else. Hillery agreed with Edie and tried to lay aside her concerns for the remainder of her time in New Orleans. She continued to analyze her dreams along with the constant pictorial that would spring up before her very eyes during the hours of wakefulness as well as sleep.

Then one day, after making certain they were alone, Edie disclosed in some excitement that she had at long last heard from her husband, Richard. Her green cat's eyes were huge in her face when she told Hillery of the visitation she had not shared with another single soul. The women clung together as they discussed their husbands, and Edie quietly confessed that Richard had caught wind of the fugitives. "Richard was recently in Baltimore," she breathed. "He saw Stuart! He is safe, I swear it! Richard spoke to him, he says he looks well. He misses you. I am so grateful to be able to share this news with you!" She beamed at her friend as she withdrew an envelope from her reticule. "He said to tell you there are more in route. You will be hearing from him in a few days time."

Hillery stared at her friend, unaware that tears streamed down her cheeks. Stuart was safe! Richard had seen him! And Richard could be counted on for the truth. Her hands trembled as she accepted the proffered missive, but she tore open the envelope without pause. The missive was brief and quickly scrawled as though he had written it in that moment while Richard waited. He spoke of his love for her, his anguish and alarm for her well being, and then reassured her that he was well, he was safe. He promised to write again soon and consoled her with assurances that they would be together again soon. She sobbed quietly to herself, unaware she had been clenching the paper so very tightly. She was spellbound. When she looked up, tears shimmered on her tawny lashes. "God bless you, Edie! God bless you and Richard both!" she reached out to her friend, holding her tightly and the two clung together.

With spring upon them it was once again time to return to The Plantation. Hillery shopped with Higgens in tow, gathering seed and other items needed for a successful spring crop. There were many mouths to feed as well as money to be made. Fully aware of the inflated prices, she fussed over all the necessary purchases. She gathered cloth and thread, adding in a few precious staples as well. She stocked medicinal supplies, and picked up on a few small gifts for Isis and Sukie. When at last she was satisfied with her purchases, Higgens loaded the buggy while Hillery checked the Post Office. She was delighted to find a small stack of mail from D.C. She saw letters from Gran, Rachael and Natalie. And oh! So thankfully, she recognized the strong male scrawl that belonged to her husband! At last she could sit back and visualize his beautifully chiseled features while reading of his journey north. It was such a relief to know he was safe.

She secretly hoped he did not return to active duty, and then scolded herself for the coward she was. Hillery was a brave woman in most every way, but when it came to her husband's safety, she wanted only to keep him that way – out of peril, without further harm. She was no fool and knew that eventually everyone ran out of luck, and she did not want Stuart to run out of luck! If Libby Prison had not struck her with terror she did not know what had. She shivered suddenly at the memory of all the emaciated bodies, all the soldiers too ill to recover properly. She thought of the rank odor of gangrene and unwashed human flesh alive and wriggling with maggots, remembered the painful hunger of men too long deprived. No, she did not feel one tiny little bit guilty for her thoughts. She did not want her husband in the thick of battle yet again! And in her heart, she knew that when he was able, he would be among the first to re-enter the fray.

A tiny frown marred the smooth skin of her forehead. She jumped slightly when a voice spoke in her ear, and then smiled at Rebecca. Rebecca broke into a wide smile of her own, her honey-brown skin glistening in the warm sunshine. She liked Miss Hillery, knowing her to be an honest woman. More to the point, Rebecca knew that

Hillery truly loved Miss Edie and never judged anyone by the color of their skin. She dimpled when Hillery exclaimed, startled. Hillery smiled, happy to see her. Then she wavered slightly, staring at Rebecca who had suddenly faded right before her eyes! In her stead, superimposed over Rebecca's soft features, she saw the twisted face of the mamaloi! And the mamaloi's visage was harsh even as she smiled in triumph. Hillery shivered again, this time without control. Her hands automatically wrapped around her small waist. It took seconds to regain her composure. She then blinked away the apparition and saw Rebecca clearly once again. Rebecca's face looked pinched. Seeing that she had alarmed the other woman she put a hand weakly to her forehead and said, "I declare, I had such a headache for just a moment!" She smiled, and then shrugged her narrow shoulders. The women broke into conversation and the moment was forgotten.

Stuart arrived in D.C. so exhausted he slept for the better part of a week. He was grateful to see his family, grateful to be whole and incredibly grateful to be alive! He had written Hillery in his waking moments, eaten, bathed, and returned to sleep. Rachael and the others tiptoed about the house, happy to have him back alive and well. But Rachael knew her son well enough to know the visit would be short-lived. Stuart would feel it his duty to return to battle. Hence, she coveted the quiet moments and the needed rest that kept him here. In her private time she wrote to Hillery realizing how shaken her young daughter-in-law must be. Hillery had traveled when and where she had been needed. Hillery had aided him in every way she could, and with a great deal of regret, returned home without him. Rachael knew how much courage that took, and what kind of heartbreak it caused. She pined for the young lovers, wishing she could push them back together and be the glue that held them there. But Rachael was too pragmatic to believe this time had come. She reconciled herself to helping them with the *now*. And so she wrote. And in her letters she suggested a small family reunion, knowing that would have to suffice.

Hillery responded to Rachael's offer with enthusiasm. By this time she was at The Plantation where she had busily planted the vegetable garden she and Sukie had planned. Each day she worked from sunrise to sunset alongside the others in the fields, and then walked the endless miles back to the house to bathe, eat, and relax with her mail. Stuart's letters did much to cheer her, though she longed to hold him in her arms and to be held in return. Oh, how she missed him! She burned for him!

She had waited as long as she had because she didn't want to arouse suspicion. She was already under constant vigil, but the law as it stood, could not touch her. They could not prove she had done anything illegal. They simply had no charges against her. In short, as far as they knew, she had broken no laws. Therefore, they could not prevent her from journeying as she pleased. Try as they might, there was no law against a wife visiting her husband's family in the North – nor even her husband, himself, should he be safely recuperating from an injury received in the line of battle. And they had found no reason to detain her. She had known her husband was in good hands and had chosen to bide her time. Her decision afforded her the time she needed to assist the people with the spring planting while making certain she, herself, was safe.

Therefore, when Hillery responded, she offered to come straight away, knowing she had accomplished much. She left without awaiting a response, choosing not to waste any time. She had her travel pass in hand when she boarded the rail line. Before she knew it, she would see her husband! She was so excited she could scarcely contain herself. As if on cue, Ariel's tussled head popped up beside her. He had been sleeping soundly only a second before. He winked at her, and then stretched his front legs giving his whole body a vigorous shake.

Hillery laughed, ruffling his curly head before settling back. She visibly forced herself to relax. It would be a long journey! She had brought along her sewing to occupy her time, tucking a couple of her favorite books into the basket for good measure. She sighed as she picked up a worn copy of Leaves of Grass by Walt Whitman and began to read in earnest. She never tired of his collection of nature poems. She liked the man himself and had even read somewhere that he was active as a nurse throughout these troubled times.

She fell asleep alongside Ariel with the book of poetry resting undisturbed in her lap. The bookmark had fallen to the floor, the pages closed where her fingers had let loose their hold. Her dreams carried her away into another time and place where Marietta was sitting with her sewing, one hand resting on her abdomen. In the dream Hillery noted she was with child. Marietta wore a faint smile. Next to her curled up on a rug by the hearth was a small dog. Though she couldn't see him clearly, there was something familiar about that dog. Even in her dream state, Hillery wondered at the meaning of it.

She awoke when the train rumbled to a stop. She was surprised she was nearing the end of her journey! A new one was about to unfold.

# CHAPTER THIRTY ONE

tuart alone met her at the station. He stood tall and proud in civilian clothes and she was secretly happy to see him dressed so. For just a moment it erased the war from her mind. It was as if it had never happened, as if everything had remained safe and happy. Her world was temporarily put to rights. Hillery smiled a wide, saucy smile meant for her husband alone. He looked into her violet eyes and returned the favor. She glanced around seeing that they were indeed alone amid the crowd of strangers. "Where is everyone?" she queried.

"Everyone is at the house," he smiled, a twinkle in his eye. "Mother decreed we could use the space, and Gran seconded the idea."

She laughed with pure delight. "I bet Natalie is fit to be tied! She would want to be here."

"She'll understand one of these days," he agreed. "My little sister is growing up."

"She has a beau of her own," Hillery giggled, feeling like a girl again. "She tries to make it sound casual, but believe me, it's anything but!"

Stuart smiled knowingly, then said, "Let's have our own affair and keep it anything but." His lips caught hers before she could respond. She swallowed any further comment wanting only the comfort of his arms.

"Hmm, do we have to go directly home?" she sighed, then returned the kiss giving it all she had. She had missed her husband and wanted him to know it. God, it seemed like a fairy-tale world in a distant time and place! She laughed when the couple next to them gave them a look.

"No, but it might be wise before this goes any further," he crooned, twin dimples flashing.

"Agreed!" she smoothed her skirts, settling back in the landau, "I'm so glad you came alone!"

"Me too," he chuckled. "We have a lot of catching up to do." The sun shone down on her honeyed curls until they came alive, crackling like fire. "You are the most perfect woman," he breathed, his eyes tracing the features of her face.

"And you are the most perfect man," she responded.

They set off toward home, arriving at the yellow brick house with the tall pediment, Palladian front topped with a wide balustrade roof. Rachael came bustling down the front steps, her violet silk skirts fanned out around her causing her to look every bit as much a flower as those that filled the well-tended front yard. Natalie was right behind her wearing her favorite bright yellow. Gran could be heard bringing up the rear, the familiar tap-tap of her twisted ebony walking stick a comfortable sound. There was a burst of shared laughter as everyone hugged. It had been a while since they had all been together.

Dinner that night was a sumptuous affair. Annie had outdone herself with Charlotte's skilled assistance. Charlotte had proven an avid student of the culinary arts. Cecil eyed them knowingly, his dark eyes shining with pride. He was an entirely different man nowadays. He no longer kept to himself but was content to listen to the prattle of his own small family. Hillery admired the joy that radiated from him.

The ornate dining table groaned under the weight of both fried chicken and Virginia ham. There were two different kinds of potatoes along with pole beans, corn, and baby carrots. Large loaves of fluffy white bread accompanied by crocks of creamery butter completed the menu. Just as the last bite was consumed and the dishes whisked away, an array of deserts replaced the wholesome fare. Everyone groaned even as they reached for the desert of their choice while hot café was poured from a silver set teamed with servers of both cream and sugar.

There were sweet meats and apple pie, fresh fruits and homemade ice cream. The family was fully and completely content when they retired to the parlor. Later that evening, everyone enjoyed a toast from their own wine cellar. The conversation was trained on Stuart and Hillery, but also contained bits of news and events that had taken place since they had all been together. It was a fine evening. Still the young couple were flushed and pleased when they were alone at last!

Stuart stretched out across the massive Empire bed, appearing fully relaxed beneath the brilliant canopy of plush red velvet. He was anxiously biding his time while he awaited Hillery. She was nervous, he knew, as it had been a very long time since they had been together. He had turned down the coverlet, poured another round of wine, and struggled to retain his calm exterior. He had missed his wife immensely!

His gaze strayed to her portrait above the hearth. God! She was beautiful and she had not changed a bit! She was a stunning woman and he was proud of her. As his thoughts slid back over the past, he saw her in all the many ways he had come to know her: Hillery, as he had met her, young, fresh and eager, a magnificent horse woman and accomplished herbalist. Hillery laughing, her sense of humor so fantastic she had held him in thrall. Then, poised, dressed for the ball – the queen of any gathering no matter how elite! Hillery decked out in her wedding finery –the very picture of feminine beauty. And then again bravely triumphant when working with the Railroad where she was compassionate and fearless all at once. Her loyalty and sense of leadership could not be faulted. And of course Hillery in debate when others, particularly men, attempted to ensnare or belittle her. Her education spoke volumes in her own defense or in the defense of those less fortunate. And last but not least, Hillery in grief, watching as he walked away when he had no choice but to leave for duty. She was a remarkable woman. He was a lucky man.

A floor board creaked and he glanced up from his reverie to find her looking resplendent in a gown of sheer ivory. It was trimmed in black lace and clung to her curves like a second skin. For just a moment, he could find no words. His eyes narrowed and she blushed under his hot scrutiny. He reached for her hand, drawing her near, and handed her a glass of wine. She sipped, and then licked her lips catching a drop of the ruby liquid with the tip of her tongue. He watched that tongue in fascination then trailed a finger along her jaw, down her neck, and around the curve of her breast. She shivered, a shudder running through her. He watched in rapt interest as her nipples peaked. They hardened and stood erect. He bent and flicked his lips over first one then the other, barely touching. Her nerves screamed as she grew wet at the juncture of her thighs. The fabric rasped as he slid his tongue back and forth across each nipple. Then becoming aware of her heightened breath, he glanced down the length of her body. Her gown was damp at the navel and lower still. She felt a bead of sweat roll down her spine. He bent low, falling to his knees, and licked her at that very intimate place between her thighs. She stifled a sound and he encouraged her to finish her wine. She tipped her head back to do as bid, suddenly very thirsty. As she swallowed, his tongue flicked across the material again and again, wetting it – and her. His slender fingers found the hem of her gown and he lifted it slowly, letting his fingertips caress the insides of her calves, then thighs, then higher still until he had exposed the feminine bud that was begging for his attention. He indulged her gladly, rubbing it softly at first, then more rapidly. She was completely bare to his touch. She gasped when he nudged her thighs apart and she nearly stumbled, her fingers finding purchase in his thick locks. He used his tongue and fingers with expertise. She moaned, feeling faint and he lifted her off her feet, still busily exploring that private part of her.

Suddenly they were together on the bed, her gown where it had pooled at her feet on the floor. His hands took full possession of her breasts, tweaking the nipples, stretching them. She cried out softly as her own hands roamed, freeing his clothing one item at a time. He helped her until they were both completely naked upon their knees.

They rubbed against each other in utter abandon. He groaned when her tongue began its quest flicking over his flat nipples, laving the dip of his navel, trailing lower still until she came to that hard male part of him. He gasped when she rolled him between her palms working her hands from shaft to tip. Her head dipped low and he made as if to stop her. But she would not be denied. She took him into her mouth, teasing just as he had teased, tasting gently at first, flicking her tongue across the tip of him, then along the length of him before taking him more fully into her mouth. He growled low in his throat grabbing her by the hair and pulling her up to meet his kiss. Their tongues danced then sparred in a wicked game.

He forgot to be gentle when he dropped her to the mattress, straddling her. She didn't mind. He continued to make love to her with his hands and mouth. When he entered her, he raised her hips with his hands to increase her pleasure. She cried his name out loud, raining kisses on his neck and shoulders. They climaxed simultaneously. He nipped her with his teeth. They breathed heavily, content to remain entwined together until they were newly aroused. At long last they slept.

In the days that followed Hillery became reacquainted with some of the men from Libby who had traveled North with Stuart. She remembered Boyle and a man called Duffy and was surprised to learn they hailed from D.C. as well. And of course there was Benjamin, who looked much healthier nowadays. It was a relief to see he was recovering nicely. But she was especially happy to be reunited with Cricket, the one-legged Scotsman they were all so fond of. She invited him to visit them at The Plantation in a happier time in the future. "Better still," she said with a secretive smile, "You should come visit us in New Orleans. We have a beautiful home there. I believe you would like the city," she mused, thinking of Helen but keeping the thought to herself.

"I would be honored, ma'am," Cricket returned. He had excellent manners. "I've always been drawn to New Orleans. I shall look forward to the day our visit is at hand."

"Me too," she laughed, already laying plans for matchmaking. Cricket was an honorable man and he and Helen were of an age. They had both endured a hard life. She couldn't wait to get them together! And she had already glimpsed into their future. Sometimes it was a pure joy to see things others did not.

Cricket, a superstitious sort, noted her expression, but said nothing further. He, like all of the men from Libby, loved and admired Miss Hillery. Nevertheless, he knew something was afoot. He smiled to himself. The Scots were a superstitious sort, of course. But they were also more aware than others believed. What Miss Hillery did not know was that he, too, had the sight!

Natalie, who was always full of life and happiest when her social life was at a peak, was eager to be surrounded by gentlemen once again. There was one particular soldier who was home on furlough and Natalie had set her cap for him. She dimpled when she spoke of him, her complexion coloring just enough for Hillery to see what she was about. Natalie always thought she was more mysterious than she truly was. Hillery knew her to wear her heart on her sleeve and it was obvious she was doing so now. She thought back to her last visit here in D.C. and smiled to herself when she recalled a young man her sister-in-law had been taken with. Since that time Natalie had remarked on the same fellow three, maybe four times, in their correspondence.

Hillery was pleased when at last she was introduced to Randolph Wick. She recognized him as the young soldier she had glimpsed while out riding. Natalie's eyes shone with pride when he took Hillery's hand. It was apparent Stuart had already met and approved of him. Hillery was careful to express just the right sentiment toward her sister-in-law so as to set the tone. Randolph weighed his words carefully in return, a gleam in his eye that mirrored Natalie's own. Hillery smiled her secret smile, and then looked up to find Stuart watching her. His expression said it all. Wedding bells were in the near future!

If the days were a social whirl and the evenings were a time for family, the nights were reserved for the lovers alone. After their bedroom door was closed for the night, no one ever disturbed them with the exception of little Ariel who found it an insult to camp out in the hall where his bed had been placed. Even so, after his initial nightly complaint where he made himself known by whining and pawing at the door, even he settled in for the night leaving the couple to themselves. And every night they laughed quietly at his ritual before making love until they fell asleep in the wee hours of the morning.

When the day came for Stuart to return to duty, Hillery kept her promise to herself and didn't cry, at least not in public. She slipped away to the library where her tear-filled gaze fastened onto the portrait of Thomas Maurice Michaels. Stuart had done an exemplary job! The portrait seemed so lifelike. She felt she had come to know his father quite well over the years. As she stood staring into the painting she found herself unburdening herself on Thomas as she had so many times in the past. She smiled to herself when the scent of Cavendish filled the air. Stuart loved his father, and through him she had come to love him too. The strong masculine scent gave her comfort. She squared her shoulders, dried her eyes, and went to join the others.

She found them in the parlor and realized Stuart had deliberately given her time alone. He no doubt knew how tangled her emotions must be. She looked at him and smiled the way she wanted him to remember her. Then she told him how handsome he looked in his new uniform, praising him for the promotion he had earned. He wore the rank of major well. When he suggested a walk in the gardens, she looped her arm through his.

Telling him good-bye was the hardest thing she'd ever had to do, and this time she kept the biggest secret of all – one she wondered if he even suspected. She did not think so for if he did, he didn't mention it. And that didn't seem like Stuart. She assumed his mind was too crowded with other issues. War had a way of doing that to folks.

He looked at her as she stood smiling and knew he would forever hold this image of her in his heart. The way she looked now touched him deeply. He knew the pain she was struggling to hide in order to wave him off as bravely as any soldier's wife could. It was the same pain he experienced with each separation. He knew, too, that the tears would fall as soon as he was out of sight. And that she had probably already shed quite a few. The shared moments of the past weeks would have to keep them both warm. But he would remember her as she stood there with her violet skirts billowing out around her, the winds blowing her honeyed hair. The beauty of their love would see him safely home. It would get him through the duration of the Civil War between the States.

After he rode away on Apollo, her slim hand slid to rest on her flat abdomen in awe of the new life growing there.

# PART FOUR

## THE GHOST FOREST

# CHAPTER THIRTY TWO

he spent another week with the family in D.C. before striking out for home. She did not mention her condition, telling herself that she wasn't sure, after all. In reality, Hillery was aware of the dangers that lie ahead, but chose not to burden the others. Though Rachael pleaded and Natalie cried, Gran looked on knowingly. She alone understood the struggle Hillery faced. She certainly knew more than she had been told, and Hillery respected her silence and understanding. Hillery was struggling to comprehend what lay before her. The days and nights in Washington had been quiet. Now the drums resonated in the distance growing louder by the hour. They called to her, and she instinctively knew she had no choice but to follow. Yet again something had shifted. Fear threatened to chase her as she realized the peril that she and the child would be in if her suspicions were correct. Pray God they were not.

When she boarded the train with Ariel in tow, she was granted an appraising glance. It was as if the faithful little dog sought to reassure her. Hillery thought he was an amazing ally, and drew comfort from his strength. In spite of his small size, she knew Ariel to be a true hero. She grinned at him, patting his tousled curls. He woofed quietly and cocked his head in turn while she fished through her belongings. Clucking her tongue, she slipped him a morsel of cheese. She laughed and he rewarded her with an enormous yawn, turned once, and curled into a small ball. He was sound asleep in seconds.

She wished she could sleep that readily, but was troubled by her thoughts. She was truly shocked when she startled awake some time later. She had been dreaming again. And in those picturesque episodes she glimpsed Marietta with a small companion who looked identical to Ariel! Ariel, himself, was sitting by her side with such a knowing look that she was absolutely astonished. She gasped when he winked at her. They looked at each other for a full minute before she chucked his chin and whispered what a wise little guy he was. She wished she could read his mind as easily as he appeared to read hers!

After the bloody repulse of Sherman's drive on Kennesaw Mountain the Battle of Peachtree Creek flared with McPherson and Schofield striking hard against the Georgia Railroad. While the Western and Atlantic Railroad rested safely within the security of Union hands, there were other railways yet open to the South. The Georgia running east to Augusta was the initial target. The success of the Union in this particular battle would end the exchange of troops between Hood and Lee.

Hood's replacement of Johnston in the Confederate movement was a bonus for the Union. General Sherman could not have been more pleased had he arranged the exchange himself. Though Jefferson Davis was dissatisfied with Johnston's actions, Sherman knew Johnston to be a wily opponent. Hood, on the other hand, was a pugnacious leader. His judgment was often rash. Although a fierce soldier, having been seriously wounded in battle not once but twice, Hood was sure to take the offensive which gave Sherman an edge on his own maneuvers.

On July eighteenth McPherson and Schofield approached Atlanta from the northeast swinging wide to slash the Georgia Railroad while Thomas moved in from the north. The gap between the Union troops was too great a temptation for Hood to ignore. As Sherman predicted, Hood drove a smashing blow against Thomas, but Thomas held ground surprising Hood with his artillery reserve. Hood suddenly found himself sadly outnumbered. Before he realized what was happening, McPherson and Schofield pressed in upon the screening force that

Hood had left behind to protect his right. Hood had no choice but to retreat. Although he returned to his barriers in Atlanta he had lost over two thousand men.

With this the setting for their arrival, Stuart and a small number of others joined the anxious talk around the campfires. Feelings were strong that Hood would surrender Atlanta – the goal for which the Federals fought. Yet if their expectations proved too hasty, they were spared further contemplation when on July twenty-second Hood launched the Battle of Atlanta. In what was perhaps a desperate attempt to save the Southern stronghold, Hood sent Hardee on a roundabout attack on McPherson somewhere down Decatur Road past the Oakland Cemetery. Rifle fire filled the smoke-clogged air. Mini balls hurled with furious impact into their ravished targets. Stuart knelt behind the brush, his fingers methodically loading and reloading in automatic defense. His nostrils stung with the pungent mixture of smoke, human excrement, and blood. Sweat trickled freely from his forehead, painting paths through the dirt on his cheeks. Beyond, he could see the onrushing offense of gray-clad soldiers. To his rear came the answering response of his men in blue as they climbed from the trenches fighting across the enemy in reverse. General McPherson was to his left heading for the woods. The general had called upon his reserve corps. All around him was a whirling kaleidoscope of red and green. The woods in which McPherson rode were mercilessly riddled with Confederates bullets. It was then Stuart witnessed the general's horse bolting from the trees. The beast was seriously wounded. The saddle he bore was empty.

Dropping position Stuart half-ran, half-crawled through the brambles, ducking the explosions of shot that whistled in his direction. More than once he was forced to take shelter. He stared hollow-eyed as a pair of Union soldiers carried the apparently lifeless body of his general from the woods. A musket exploded at close range grazing the flesh at the nape of his neck. His body jerked spontaneously as he leveled his own gun square into the face of his assailant, quickly shattering that stunned visage by the simple motion of his thumb. Another time he would have felt remorse, another time, but not now.

A vengeful cry rang out over the littered battleground, "McPherson and revenge!" The message resounded. Suddenly there was a whirl of renewed activity, for Stuart along with the rest of the Union men knew for a fact their beloved general was dead. The fighting increased with newfound fury. Hood then planned a frontal attack concurrent with Hardee's rear attack. This frontal attack was ridiculously late. Cannons boomed while sabers flashed. At length the outnumbered Confederates were forced to stumble back in retreat. By nightfall the battle had met its conclusion. General Logan moved into McPherson's command while Sherman wept unashamedly for the officer who was perhaps his favorite general. Angrily Sherman made plans to plunge more deeply into the Southwest thereby striking a fatal blow against the Atlanta and West Point Railroad.

With less success, the Federals then strove to slash the lines of the Macon and Western Railroad, a failure that was meaningfully interrupted by the skirmishes at Ezra Church just west of the city. Yet it was the final attempts to cut the lines at Jonesboro that won the North its most vital victory, for Hood could no longer see his way clear to save the Southern city of Atlanta. Citizens were by this time huddled in cellars or hidden in caves. The Federals slowly circled the city tightening their already strangulating grip. Hood was even then contemplating the need to evacuate. Still the blasting continued and the siege guns roared. Sherman received a pair of deadly Parrott guns from Chattanooga. The forty-two hundred pound monstrosities spat forth their thirty-pound shot with fiery clarity. These functioned with an elevating screw at the rear of the mobile siege carriage. Aiming the cast-iron tube directly into Atlanta, Sherman's men blew death in the face of the Confederate city.

Retaliating in kind with a powerful weapon of their own, the Rebels wreaked havoc with the terrifying Williams machine gun. Having spent three days in positioning the gun at the end of Peachtree Street, they fed it caps and cartridges until its accuracy was impaired by the expansion of the breech. On the first eve of September, Hood evacuated the city leading his men to the safety of Lovejoy's Station. Behind them lay a road of destruction. Atlanta was in chaos. The people of the city knew total fear. They watched through streaming tears as the Confederate troops disappeared down old McDonough Road. Flames swept through the supply houses demolishing the rolling mills as well. Hood left no ammunition or freight cars for the hated Yanks.

With the sky a rolling black cloud, panic wrung the hearts of many. Their only hope was to escape the nearing threat of Yankee drums.

At The Plantation Hillery discussed all that had transpired with Isis over a steaming blend of yellow yarrow and comfrey. The yarrow was sure to lend emotional strength and protection while the comfrey would serve to repair the higher vibrations of the soul that may have been damaged over past or present lifetimes. Hillery knew most people would have no understanding of all this, but Isis had taught her well and had never misled her. "I believe there are still some of Marietta's things packed away in the attic," Isis offered with a nod that set her golden hoops to jangling. "Perhaps it is time we took a peek?"

"I think so," Hillery agreed. "Mama would have kept anything she deemed important as well as those things she chose as mementos. What do you know of my grand mére? Were there other children besides my mother? Papa never mentioned any."

Isis hesitated only briefly as she stared into her cup. The tea leafs had settled in the bottom and she read the warning in them. "We have to tread carefully," she disclosed. "The walls have ears. But to answer your question, your mother was the first of several pregnancies. She alone survived. I never saw any reason to share that with you. It is something that troubled Mariette very much."

"I see," Hillery said, and she was beginning to fear that she did. "It is all somehow connected: the curse, the dog, the other infants…even – maybe especially – if they did not survive." Her pearly white teeth bit into her ripe lower lip.

Isis stared in horror. "You are right! We must go at once. I shall fetch the keys."

They climbed the winding staircase together then conquered the attic steps in turn. When they stood before the door with the large brass ring and matching key hole they each glanced at the other. Already Hillery knew they were walking into an awakening. She felt a chill race up her spine, heard the whisper of distant voices. Isis nodded knowingly. She was accustomed to her young charge seeing and hearing things that others did not. She inserted the key, turned it until the latch hissed, and the door swung free.

They went inside together, and as one, began a thorough search through the many trunks and boxes that had belonged to Marietta. They laid aside items of antiquated clothing and pieces of the past. At length Hillery picked up a box with a fitted lid. It felt somehow different from all the rest. She opened it slowly already feeling the past reaching out to her as though it were literally stepping from the box. She laid aside a few baby garments, felt the chills wash over her, and then produced a small charcoal sketch of Marietta. In the sketch Marietta returned her look with a mysterious air, one hand snuggled into the warm fur of the little dog at her side. The dog was Ariel! There was absolutely no doubt about it. Not just a look-alike, but Ariel! As she stared at the drawing she watched as the dog grew in size and took on the form of Rags, her father's old hound. Then, in a blink, he became Ariel again. Only this time, the Ariel in the portrait looked directly at her. There was a subtle difference in the original pose. This Ariel displayed the same twinkle in his eye she often saw when his mind was working overtime. She shivered suddenly with the realization that Ariel had not chosen to come upstairs with them. He always accompanied her, but this time he lingered at the foot of the staircase. At least that's where she'd left him. She thought for a moment, rifling back through the infant clothes, her brow furrowed. When she mentioned the portrait to Isis, Hillery saw that Isis had already drawn the same conclusion.

By this time their backs were aching with fatigue and the strain of the search. They quietly agreed to return to the kitchen. They had learned enough for now. As they reached the door, Hillery drew up short. She made a mad dash back to the trunk with the infant clothes, lifted the articles in question, and turned to confront Isis. "There are five," she said, her voice raw, as though she had received one too many shocks, "five of each individual garment. Each one is like the next. Each one was meant for a newborn babe. And none of them show any wear!"

They stared at each other. Marietta had borne five additional infants after Mariette's birth, and none of those babies had survived. Why? What happened to them? Isis looked on as Hillery wavered a moment.

It was as though she was looking at a ghost. The quadroon wondered what her charge saw that she did not, but she would wait for Hillery to confide in her. Isis was a wise woman. She simply took Hillery by the arm and steered her back downstairs to the warm kitchen where they found Ariel curled up in a ball. His tail thumped a greeting. When Hillery would have put the kettle on for a cup of tea, Isis pressed a glass of wine into her hands instead. "A little wine now and then won't harm the babe," she lectured gently. "You look peaked." Hillery's face had drained of color. She sipped the wine and stroked Ariel's rich fur.

# CHAPTER THIRTY THREE

he Condor glided swiftly over the murky waters of the Atlantic en route from England to the North Carolinian coast. Even in the gloom of night its proud lines were easily discernible. Aboard the speedy, three-funneled runner was the astounding sum of two thousand dollars in gold. The gold had been placed in the competent hands of a small group of dedicated Confederates in league with the Secret Service Bureau. As she neared the coast, the Condor was spied by the sites of a heavily armed Union gunboat. The race to shore had begun.

The Condor spent her rage and fury on the larger trailing vessel by sleekly attempting an escape within the mouth of the Cape Fear River. But fate had cast another obstacle into the vessel's path. Hidden in the darkened cove, the wreckage of another more untimely stockade runner loomed suddenly before them, affording it impossible to avoid the crunch of an ironclad collision. Though backed by the guns of Fort Fisher on the bluff, those entrapped in the wreckage were helplessly pinned between the conflicting assaults of shells. The Condor's greatest opportunity to serve her country was quickly slipping away! Its only hope was to be found in the form of a rickety lifeboat. With the Federal gunners boring down upon them, the captain had no choice but to relent to the persistent pleas of his top agents. They alone could see the gold safely to Rebel forces. Furthermore, their arguments were sound in that the three of them would know no mercy if they were taken captive. Unlike the captain and crew of the Condor, these agents were known spies. Each of them had at one point or another spent time in a Union prison camp.

With mixed emotions the captain watched the tiny lifeboat disappear into the churning current. It bobbed upon the stormy waves like a piece of useless cork. Drenched to the bone the trio clung to the upturned craft. The boat was tossed angrily about as though its punishment had been ordained by the great Neptune himself. It was much later when it reached shore. The two men staggered from the water, grateful for the feel of solid earth beneath them. It was then they noticed they were alone. Their companion, a female, was no longer with them. Anguish contorted their pale faces as they glanced at the craft they had used as a buoy. Defeat twisted like a blade in their vitals. They had lost their companion – and with her, the Confederate gold!

Later the lifeless body of a woman was washed upon the sandy shoal. Her face was turned to the earth, further obscured by the veil of streaming wet hair. There was something particularly eerie about the body. Perhaps it was the heavy mass of tangled black skirts, or the combination of dark hair and clothing that seemed to boast of death. Hands reached out from all directions to turn the now bloated body, bringing the face into view. The woman was no other then Rose O'Neal Greenhow. Upon closer scrutiny the golden sovereigns were discovered. This same gold which had borne the weight of the lady's death was the sole security of the South.

Hillery awoke with a start that fateful night in late September, the vision of Rose's corpse still fresh in her mind. She rose swiftly, closing the distance to the vanity in the master bedroom. Ariel followed in her footsteps, pausing to sit when she sat. Trembling, she reached for her favorite jewel box. It was an intricate box – a gift from Stuart – that contained only her most personal items of jewelry. Nervously, she lifted the clasp allowing her fingers only a moment's hesitation. A bead of sweat formed on her upper lip even as the tears slipped down her cheeks. Intuitively she knew what she would find before she raised the lid. There against the black velvet lining of the box was the delicate rose pendent – a gift from Rose Greenhow. The center ring of porcelain petals had become dislodged leaving the necklace broken in clean flowery slices.

Hillery had no idea how long she sat staring at the broken rose petals. She understood the significance only too well, for surely the necklace was an omen and the dream, real. She knew a deep, overwhelming grief. On October first Rose's body was washed ashore. On October second she was buried with full military honors. It was said she died a hero, and that she might have made it to shore but for the heavy bag of gold slung around her neck. After a service at the St. Thomas Church in Wilmington, the cortege proceeded to Oakdale Cemetery. A Confederate flag draped the coffin. It was believed the highly awaited dispatches she carried were lost at sea.

By mid-afternoon the following day Sherman's men fully occupied the city. Headquarters were quickly established in the old Neal house on Washington Street. Orders were soon issued for all citizens to make haste in vacating the city. Passes would be provided by the provost marshal to guarantee a safe escort. When Sherman arrived at the heel of his army, he closeted himself at Headquarters to outline his next crucial move. Most Atlanta families lived in fear of the awesome general as they knew him to be a man of callous intent. It was common knowledge he would seek revenge for his dead comrade, McPherson. Indeed, that was precisely what he planned. Major General William T. Sherman was certainly no fool. He was a hardened soldier whose mind was filled with rage. His eyes were mere slits in his craggy face. In this year of 1864 Sherman was sick to death of war. He felt no compassion for the people of the South. To put an end to the fighting, he was prepared to completely demolish the Confederacy. To his way of thinking they deserved no better. Because Atlanta was important as a leading railway hub in addition to its powerful manufacturing capacity, Sherman had no choice but to destroy the entire city. But the destruction would not stop with Atlanta. He would continue until he had burned a fiery path all the way to the sea. His deep devotion to James McPherson put to rest any qualms he might have had. McPherson's congenial features swam before him as he peered out the window overlooking the street. By God, he would have his revenge!

Meanwhile the men of the Union forces were enjoying a brief

respite. The result of such a successful siege left them frivolous in their pastimes. Although they lingered near the office of the provost marshal to watch the town's citizens turn out, most were cordial in manner. They played cards and placed bets, wrote letters and dreamed of days of old. Stuart thought of Hillery and wondered what he was missing. His mind had been so preoccupied with war for such a long time now that he somehow felt he was slipping – overlooking something otherwise quite obvious. He pondered this to the point of fatigue – and then it hit him! By God! She was with child! He knew it – felt it in his gut! How had he overlooked such a thing? His subconscious had tried to tell him, had he but listened.

Time fled. War consumed the present. The Union camp was thrown into turmoil as most of the troops were preparing to accompany General Sherman in their pursuit of the Confederate rival, Hood. This devastating opponent had launched a clever attack against Union rail lines running south from Chattanooga. It was with some misgivings that Sherman led his men out of Atlanta leaving the city only partially protected, but it was a decision in which he played only a minor role. Hood must be stopped and the damages reconstructed. There was no other choice.

Early the next morning, literally swarms of angry soldiers filed from the public square where their campgrounds had been maintained these past few weeks. They shook their fists at the building combining courthouse with city hall as if that single structure with the cupola capping its proud top was somehow a personal insult. Atlanta was a city many wished to see destroyed. The South would get her just desserts, the Union men vowed. It was an oath that would ring true, for much of her would perish in the days ahead.

Although a brisk battle was engaged at Allatoona, the major delay for the Union was discovered in an eight-mile break in the rail lines. This type of interference threatened all communication with the North. Spikes and rails were brought from Chattanooga to repair the needed tracks. Hood's men had performed their tasks well. Rails were bent at peculiar angles. Ties had been reduced to heaps of char. For one full week the Union forces labored to smooth the lines, thus enabling the army to re-enter Atlanta. As Hood altered his maneuvers, Sherman likewise redirected his. Now in the beginning of November, he strove to complete the drawings of a most important campaign – that notorious march that would be recalled throughout history as "Sherman's March to the Sea".

At his desk in Atlanta, Sherman plotted long and hard. After gaining the uneasy approval of General Grant he deliberately cut his troops from the vulnerable supply lines, thereby eliminating that particular threat in favor of foraging. If they were to crush Southern morale, foraging certainly bore a two-fold purpose. It was necessary to gain strong reinforcements for Grant in his struggle against Lee.

Orders in camp were brisk, but sure. Only the healthiest of men were allowed to embark on this heroic operation. Those who were ill or injured were sent north to hospitals in Nashville or Chattanooga. Stuart fell in the first category. Every single fighting man was stripped to the bare essentials. Meager rations of coffee, sugar, salt, and hardtack were carried for meals. Knapsacks were discarded as were any personal luxuries. Only mess plates and tin cups were allowed. It was indeed a stalwart army that marched from that dying city on the morning of November fifteenth.

Before the sun could rise on the following day Sherman had given the command to torch the city. By this time, the majority of the Union army had pulled out of Atlanta. Most, if not all of the Southern citizens, were installed at Rough and Ready. The flames spread quickly as vengeful arsonists displayed their magic. A bright orange bonfire of enormous magnitude burst through the dim twilight as the awakening sun reached its peak in the sky. Fire raced along the roof tops of train sheds and depots. Long smoky fingers wrapped around small businesses. Military installations were destroyed without exception as were all shops and food stores. Soon there was little of Atlanta left untouched as the flames licked a path down Peachtree to Decatur before thoroughly engulfing Loyde Street.

As the Union army reached the crest of the hill above the city they paused on the exact site where the Battle of Atlanta had been fought. Sherman, gazing into the copse of trees where McPherson had fallen, viewed a specter from the past. Tears welled in the shrewd eyes at the sudden image of his friend. He dashed them away only to find the specter had vanished. "Damn the city of Atlanta," he cursed beneath his breath. "Damn the entire South and all her belligerent people!"

"You never spoke about what you saw in the attic that day," Isis stated quietly. "Oh, I know, we discussed the five sets of newborn gowns, and we have both concluded that Marietta mourned five children. Your mother mourned them as well. That is why the garments are so well preserved. It must have been very difficult for her. Are you ready to tell me about it?"

Hillery shuddered, her face pale. She sat with one hand on her abdomen as if to protect the child within. The baby had been kicking for some time now. Though she was still quite slender, her abdomen was nicely rounded. She carried the babe high, Isis said, which meant she was to have a girl. Hillery shuddered again. She feared for her child. "I saw the face of the mamaloi – ancient, ugly, and mean. Then as if the years faded before my eyes, I saw her in her youth. And I knew her for what she was. *I think her name was Marie*, a voice whispered. *And she was Henry's placee.*"

After that conversation, the women's combined efforts were to dig up as much family history as possible. They searched the attic a second time, combed the house from top to bottom, and even rummaged the shelves of the library. They sat in the study in the evenings, mapping out the history of The Plantation. They added any new information they were able to gather no matter how trivial it might seem. They discovered a little more of a paper trail, but nothing concrete. In the end, they were still unable to fill in the gaps.

"Okay," Hillery picked up the thread of the conversation, "we know all of Marietta's babies were female. What about Aunt Allyson's? And if mama had no siblings how was she related to me?" Hillery's memories of the day her aunt died in childbirth were forever riddled with nightmares.

"Your Aunt Allyson was your mama's cousin, not her sibling," Isis confided gently. "Your mama had so longed for a sibling that she latched on to Allyson from the very beginning – or Allyson latched onto her! The two were inseparable, and Allyson adored her! Allyson wasn't able to conceive until later in life. She was so excited! But she never stopped mourning Mariette. She had loved her as a sister. She also loved to be called aunt. I don't believe it ever occurred to her to explain the difference. That is how she saw herself." Isis sipped a small glass of wine, warmed it between her hands. "And yes," she added sadly, "the infant she lost was female as well." There was more than a hint of worry in her voice.

"So," Hillery spread her hands, "it is as I feared. The curse is tied in with the family?"

"It would seem so," the quadroon replied. "The question is why?"

"So," Hillery mused, her brow furrowed, "where do we go from here? What's the next logical step?"

"I believe we must travel to the city," Isis offered. "I have access to places you do not. Perhaps we can shake up the past. It is still early enough in December," she continued. "I will leave Marta in charge of the house. Sukie will advise her."

"Yes, "Hillery nodded agreement. "That may be our best course of action. We can celebrate Christmas at the townhouse."

"Then it is set," the quadroon ventured. "We must make ready for our journey. In any case, it will be good to see Glory and her mother again! And I think we will find the answers we need."

"I hope so," Hillery agreed. "We are running out of time! My visions have me jumping at every little thing!"

"I know, ma d'or pearl," Isis slanted a look, aware of the protective stance Hillery had taken. She rarely saw her these days when her hands did not rest reflexively atop her abdomen.

# CHAPTER THIRTY FOUR

o it was on a brisk day in December Hillery and Isis arrived in the city of New Orleans. With the Battle of Atlanta a recent victory, Hillery felt her spirits should have risen, but her concerns for her husband and child overrode all else. Little did she know that at that precise moment, Stuart felt deeply connected to her, and was in fact attempting to sort through the multi-layers of visions he was experiencing. As they marched across the South he kept ever alert, but when they paused for provisions in a small town along the way his visions came back to haunt him and he saw an ancient voodoo queen involved in the destructive art of black magic. Her target was his wife – his very pregnant wife!

The women arrived safely at the house on Chartres Street and lost themselves in the immediate comforts of home and family. While they refreshed themselves, they caught up on all that was happening in the city, visited among themselves, and made plans for the morrow. Glory was so happy to see them, she wept. Helen, who usually pretended to be all business, shed a few tears as well. They took turns patting Hillery's swollen belly and hugging her while Ariel presided over all. That night they indulged in a peaceful evening, enjoying one of Helen's sumptuous repasts. Higgens smiled a slight smile, pleased to have his mistress home for the time being. Over all hung a cloud each and every one of them tried to ignore.

The following morning the women set out as planned. Ariel whined when he was left behind. Glory swept him up where she stood at the door and waved them off. They traveled the length of Chartres Street past the sprawling Pontalba Apartments which generously flanked the Place d'Arms on either side. Though barely older than a decade, the structure boasted a host of spicy tales which originated more from the lady behind the scene than from the building's opulent grandeur. The wealthy baroness was notorious for many things besides the construction of the apartments.

They passed familiar shops and restaurants without pause. When they grew hungry, they even passed their favorite place to dine. Located on the corner of St. Philips and Dauphine, the seafood there was amazing! But the women opted to continue on though Isis was acutely aware that her young charge must soon have something to bolster her strength. Her own stomach growled at the aroma wafting from the kitchens. "Which way do we go?" Hillery ventured in an attempt to quell her own appetite.

"North," Isis murmured, "though we must find a market where we can purchase sustenance. Are you sure you wouldn't care to stop for a spell? It's been a long day so far, and you must eat. The babe must be fed," she narrowed her eyes when she saw refusal in Hillery's own. It was difficult to come so far only to pause in their quest.

At length, Hillery cocked her head in thought. "I am starving," she admitted in all honesty. She was never a stubborn woman. "Why don't we see what's available at the market? It looks as if they have a wide variety of foods, even beverages. And we could take it with us."

"It would save time," Isis concurred, ready to take care of immediate needs. So it was they found themselves walking around the various stalls, collecting bread and wine, cheese and fruit. They even bought hot potatoes to warm themselves as there was a bitter wind. They covered their laps and drove on finding shelter in the buggy and feeling vastly comforted.

With strong determination they continued their search as they drove past the small white houses that lined Rampart Street. After a couple hours of careful exploration Hillery recognized one of the women from the market where they had stopped. The woman in question was entering a discreet house near the end of the street. Though this was a neighborhood no white lady should frequent, she saw the wisdom of Isis' suggestion. It seemed a likely place to find clues to her family history and therefore the curse. It was, at least, a good place to start and they had come along way.

Isis insisted on taking the initial steps. She secured the horses, hopped down and crossed to the front door, rapping with determination. A beautiful cream-colored quadroon opened the door. Black eyes clashed with tiger-gold. With a quick glance at Hillery in the background, the woman drawled in a practiced voice, "If she's looking for her husband, I'm sure I haven't seen him. My benefactor is single, wealthy, and completely unattached." With that she all but succeeded in closing the door.

Isis gave her pause with her ready tongue, "She isn't looking for her husband. We are looking for information about the Betaud family who originally owned The Plantation."

The black eyes widened. Her movements stilled. She sucked in her breath but continued to stare. "Why me?" she whispered. "Why did you come to me?"

"Mistress Hillery is the current owner. She is kind and good. She seeks only answers."

"But why did you choose me?" the other persisted.

"Mistress Hillery has the sight," Isis took satisfaction when the other recoiled. "She recognized you," Isis shrugged, "told me to pull up."

"Come back tomorrow, same time of day. I will see what I can do." The door closed immediately.

On the drive back Hillery had the odd sensation they were being followed. She turned and looked back down the street from which they had come. She saw no one. Still she thought, with a hand to her eyes, there was someone there!

That night Hillery soaked in a scented hip bath. She washed her hair and combed it dry, then dressed for the night in a warm nightdress the color of the scent she had chosen. She took the time to apply oils to her skin, rubbing her swollen belly calmly to soothe the babe. She and Isis had decided to set out early in the morning. They expected another long day. Her back ached from the long journey, so she took additional time with her grooming knowing a good night's sleep was essential. She decided against dinner in the dining room, calling instead for a tray in her room. Ariel sat beside the slipper chair where she relaxed with a steaming plate before her. He yawned widely as she took a sip of chamomile tea.

"I know Helen fed you," she murmured, slipping the pet a small morsel. "Did you miss me today?" She chuckled at the pup's enthusiasm.

Sometime later Helen tapped briefly. She turned down the bed as she warmed it. She wanted her young mistress to rest well, and there was nothing better than a warm bed. "I've a nice pot of chocolate," Helen indicated the cart in the doorway. "May I pour ye a cup?"

"You spoil me," Hillery giggled, feeling girlish. It was good to be pampered on occasion, and Helen took excellent care of her. Hillery knew that the staff was concerned for her. They were afraid of the curse, afraid for her child. She also knew that Helen, with her Scottish heritage, was of a superstitious nature. She believed in Hillery's gift as much as she feared it. It spooked her, this uncanny business of knowing. "It was a splendid dinner," she praised, and the little woman preened. Hillery grinned to herself, patted the bedside for Ariel and laughed as he complied. He circled once, curled up and propped his chin on her lap. Hillery sipped her chocolate, told Ariel a bedtime story, and then promptly fell asleep. Her dreams disturbed her that night. In them, she saw the pain in her mother's face even as she heard her soft apology.

They set out after breakfast. Helen packed a picnic lunch to make their day a bit easier. Hillery was beside herself. She couldn't shake her mother's words. Why would she apologize to me? Hillery wondered. She was quiet on the long drive along the river which had Isis taking occasional peeks in her direction. They took a short break at the riverside where they ate, drank, and stretched. By the time they reached the house in the Ramparts, Hillery was fit to be tied. This time she insisted on accompanying Isis to the door.

The beautiful quadroon with the wide black eyes answered on the first knock. It appeared at first she had lost her sass as she was both cautious and respectful around Hillery. She offered tea, but the ladies politely refused, preferring to get down to the business at hand. The quadroon who introduced herself as Antoinette drew a deep breath, released it, then began, "I will help you all I can," she said, her back as stiff as her manners. "Why have you waited so long?" she queried with an impudent toss of her curls. "Not to be rude, but much longer, and most of the information dies with the source."

"There was no choice," Hillery responded in kind, disliking the attitude that had crept into the other's voice. "My grand mére has been directing my movements," she said with a note of satisfaction. "My mother spoke to me again only last night." Isis shifted her gaze to Hillery's. Antoinette's eyes widened still more. She knew, like everyone else, the history of The Plantation. She was fully aware that the family members Hillery mentioned were long dead.

"I meant no disrespect," the woman murmured, suppressing a shudder. She had the sudden urge to cross herself.

"None taken," Hillery bowed her head before urging her on. Isis found the turn of events intriguing.

"I have arranged a meeting," Antoinette continued, careful to keep her tone respectful. It might not do to anger this lady, after all. "Be at the Saint Cathedral Church tomorrow at noon. I can't promise you anything," she hastily explained, "except that someone will await you. I believe she will have many of the answers you seek. That is all I know."

"Thank you," Hillery worked hard to mask her disappointment. She had hoped to learn more now. Instead she accepted the news with aplomb. Another day would make no real difference, she decided, and just may get them the facts they required.

Noon arrived quickly, and with it the engagement that had them on the edges of their seats. They arrived at the church, entered and sat down. As the bell struck half past, Hillery's eyes flew to the clock overhead, impatience stretching her nerves like salt water taffy. She sighed audibly, willing herself to calm. Isis nodded as if in agreement when suddenly the large double doors blew wide.

Hillery suppressed a gasp as an ancient woman in a black mantle appeared. She was escorted by a coachman who withdrew after seeing to her well-being. The lace netting around her face hooded her features. She was small, very short in stature, and obviously of French descent. In spite of her age she bore herself with grace.

The coachman had seen to the introductions. He referred to her only as Madame Genevieve. The trio sat together in a prearranged seating that was obviously meant to provide comfort. The lady allowed the netting to fall away from her face revealing fine skin stretched tight over exquisite features. If Hillery had wasted a single moment's worry on taxing the lady's strength, she needn't have. The eyes that stared back at her were sharp. They were so black as to be fathomless. The hands were tiny and heavily veined; the skin was taut. This lady had once been a beauty! Even now she displayed a great deal of charisma.

Madame Genevieve sat for a full minute without speaking. It was obvious she was appraising her audience. When she spoke, her voice was clear, "It has been brought to my attention, that you, young lady, seek wisdom. And rightly so! I see you find yourself in the family way. It is not such a safe thing." For an instant the woman's lips curled as though she found the situation intolerable. "What of your husband?" she resumed the conversation. It was impossible to read her thoughts, "Is he not at your side?"

"My husband is at war," Hillery conceded. She suspected the lady already knew as much.

"Ah," the lady nodded, "it is as it should be." She brightened slightly. "Men only get in the way in any case. They often interfere in women's work."

Hillery kept quiet. She did not voice that Stuart was not like that. In that moment the infant kicked and Hillery's hand absently strayed to her rounded abdomen, giving the child a comforting pat. The shrewd eyes missed nothing. "It is a girl child," she spoke with certainty then gave a nod of satisfaction.

Isis watched in concern. She knew when a cat toyed with a mouse. She kept her council for another minute, deciding if Madame did not come forth with an offer of help, she would need to rescue Hillery before this conversation became too disturbing. Her charge was in no position to play games.

Just as Isis was about to rise and steer Hillery from the church, Madame's tone softened. She became more animated, sat forward and without warning, placed a hand on Hillery's belly. Hillery jumped slightly as though shocked, but did not protest. Madame's words were spoken kindly. "Your grandfather was the cause of severe heartbreak," she said. "He was not an unkind man, but he was greedy. He took a dear friend of mine to wife, caused her to fall in love with him... just as he professed to be in love with her. She gave him a son, treated him like a king. But Henry fell in love with another. He chose to forsake his placee. And Marie could not endure this. She watched your grand mére closely and saw the love shine from her eyes...watched the two of them as they married in a traditional wedding of their own. I doubt in the beginning your grand mére knew about her rival, but she came to know..." Madame let the words hang and Hillery whitened. Isis took a shallow breath. "Marie was several years her senior," the old lady acknowledged, "and as is common in our tradition of placages, the arrangements may be broken at any time. Henry was not unfair to Marie. He actually left her well set. But Marie favored the dark gods... and she was strong." Again the elder paused as if to consider how to proceed. Hillery digested all she had heard, understanding that a placee was a concubine, but a well respected one. And that a placage was taken as seriously as any marriage. "Marie's heart became twisted, and the black arts knew no queen better than she. She steeped everything in hatred. Revenge became her motto and she sought to get even. This may sound absurd to you, but Marie cast a spell on Marietta, preventing her from carrying a child to term. I watched all this, and wondered what to do. I am ashamed to admit," here the elder showed true remorse as she dabbed a kerchief to her eyes, "that I did nothing. I was afraid."

Isis felt vast relief sweep through her. She was grateful to learn the lady had a heart. "You were a young woman yourself," Hillery whispered. "How could you know what to do?"

"But you see," Madame sighed, "Marie is my sister." She allowed her words to settle, *is* – not was. "I was afraid of her. I, too, had fallen in love…and Marie threatened my future happiness if I told anyone what I knew. Maybe I could not have changed the events that were about to unfold, but the fact is, I did not try."

"You are not the one who acted out. You did not cast the spell," Hillery's voice quavered and she straightened her spine. "Have you any idea what I can do?" She was open to assistance, yet was still weighing how much trust to put in this woman. She was Marie's – the mamaloi's sister – after all!

"There is more: the babies that your grand mére lost…she lost so that Marie could carry them to term herself," the elder's eyes were shadowed. "Do you understand how deep the magic? How intense Marie's work became to qualify such an act?"

"The girls…the infant girls," Hillery gasped, "Marie stole them for her own?"

"She did," Madame nodded, "Marie had discovered a way to steal the souls of infants. She cast a spell on Henry to bring him back to her. Like many men, Henry believed he wanted children and Marietta could give him only one. So, he returned to Marie's bed, and she did the rest. I don't believe your grand mére ever forgave him." Madame looked away for one distraught second before looking Hillery in the eyes. "I am sorry," she whispered. "I found my own happiness crumbling away. Greed can do a great deal of harm. My own child died, and my husband followed. I became intrigued with magic myself, but I called to a high god. And my god fights evil."

Hillery watched closely as the elder drew herself up, and then picked up the threads of the story. "Before I can rest in peace, I must make amends. Marie's soul is far too black to be saved, and only I know her weaknesses. I have come to help. You must give me your trust. Place your hands in mine. And let me proceed."

Hillery closed her eyes. She was slow to comply. Her thoughts whirled in her head. Isis was about to intercede again when Hillery nodded once, placed her hands in the elders, and drew a deep breath. What else was she to do? She could not win this battle alone! She sent a prayer to Saint Michael before she reopened her eyes and looked into Madame's dark gaze.

Madame shifted slightly and a light came into her eyes. It was eerie to watch the change that came over her. It was more than a mood or a change of mind. It was almost as if she shifted into a different personality. Her face relaxed, became more youthful. Hillery shivered visibly and Isis noted the entire church had grown ice cold. The voice that issued from the lady's lips had also changed. It was younger, more vibrant. "You must go to the mamaloi...in the ghost forest," she said. "You will take this with you. It and it alone, will see you there safely," her hands were cold as death as she pressed an amulet into Hillery's own. "If you cannot make the journey, you can send someone in your stead, but beware you bless them before they go! They must then wear the amulet. This will leave you vulnerable, and through you, your child. When your child is born to you, safe and whole...the curse will be lifted. In the meantime you must take care."

Hillery sat chilled all the way through. She remained still long after Madame Genevieve departed. Her fists were clenched tightly around the amulet. Before she stood, she fastened it securely about her throat dropping it into her clothing so that it rested between her breasts.

They talked all the way home. They had learned a lot that day. It was a chilling reality. "Now we know the beginnings of the curse," Hillery stated in as calm a voice as she could muster. "It's been grueling from the beginning."

"Yes," Isis acknowledged. "Who would have known of its origin if one had not been there?"

They both pondered this. "We were fortunate to find anything after all this time," Hillery ventured. "What I don't understand is how did mama give birth to me? I mean, she was dealing with the curse as well. So...what protected her?"

Isis hedged. Hillery sensed the hesitation in the other. "Your mother died, remember? She was not so well protected."

"There is more," Hillery stated without qualms. She had no doubt a piece of the puzzle remained missing. "What is it you are not telling me?"

"It is nothing that will save us," Isis spoke hurriedly, a trait that was totally out of character. Hillery gave a sideways glance. "Okay, I suppose it will not harm you to know," she said at Hillery's strained look. "She was desperate. She knew of no other way," she offered in apology.

"Say it," Hillery breathed. Already she could see what the other had been hiding. How had she missed it? How had she not known?

"In order to save your life, she agreed to sacrifice her own," Isis' hushed voice chilled them both. The winds roared just as Mariette's image flashed before them in the middle of the road. The horses bolted. It was then Hillery became aware of another presence, only this one was human. There in the shadow of the trees was a man. He was there one moment, then gone the next. But she knew that form. She had witnessed his scrutiny at other times. It was Tate! She was sure of it.

# CHAPTER THIRTY FIVE

here was another pair of eyes watching their adventures in the city, another watcher – Only this one meant them no harm. This one was female and very, very lonely. Eliza stood with her arms wrapped snugly around her waist for long minutes after Hillery and her mother were gone from sight. Oh, how she had longed for even just a glimpse of her mother! The irony saddened her. Eliza was just a ghost of the beauty she had once been, but she had learned the value of family. And she missed hers! She had roamed the streets of New Orleans for over a year now. At one time she had been engaged to a wealthy planter – had mingled with the cream of society at the top of her game. Then one day she was found out. That drop of Negro blood had betrayed her! As a result she lost her fiancé and her social position. She became the concubine of a cruel white man. She had had a long way to fall. Eventually, after so many heartaches she could no longer count, she found herself on the streets – a starving, penniless nobody. She had begged and scraped just to put food on her table, and then she had begged just to survive the streets. It was Antoinette who had remembered her kindly enough to direct her where she needed to go in order to catch a glimpse of her mother.

Eliza was ashamed. She did not know how to face her loved ones. She had only her mother and sister and did not even know what had become of Cynie. She, Eliza had been so selfish! She saw that now, saw all her many flaws and misconceptions. How harshly she had judged all the good people of The Plantation because she had believed she was better than they! Even the mistress had been nothing but kind, and she had thrown that very kindness back in her face! Eliza hung her head. At one time she believed she was the most beautiful of women. How foolish she had been! How young and stupid. Now she wanted nothing more than to see her mother, to hold her, and be held by her. She wanted to embrace her sister and apologize for all the hurt she had forced upon her. She wanted to belong, to be forgiven all her trespasses and accepted by her family. She secretly hoped and prayed her own people would welcome her back, but she would not blame them if they didn't. She had been a horrible person, and she had much to atone for. Eliza felt like she carried the weight of the world on her shoulders as she trudged back to the house on the Ramparts. While Antoinette could not offer her a steady home, the woman would spare her a hot supper, perhaps even a little coin. She had been a good and loyal friend. Eliza imagined she, too, had strayed from the path at one time or another. In any case, she was the only true friend Eliza had left.

Christmas at the house on Chartres Street was bittersweet. There was mail from the family in Washington with warm regards from everyone. And mail from Edie and Jenny and other friends as well. Most importantly there was mail from Stuart, including worried commentaries and loving wishes about the baby to come. Hillery hugged these close in the lonely hours of the night.

Helen served a tempting dinner with all the trimmings and everyone exchanged small gifts. The babe's time was fast approaching. Hillery's gait was more awkward now and filled with caution. The women had all made tiny garments for the baby including crocheted blankets and knit caps. The wassail bowl was piping hot and laced with spices. They shared a Holiday toast. It was long since dark when a knock sounded on the door. Ariel yelped in surprise. He was starting to snooze and was seldom caught off guard. He sniffed at the door, huffing low in his throat. Higgens set him aside earning a sharp yap.

He stared unseeing at the woman who met his gaze. She was poorly dressed with sallow skin and a hungry look about her. Though it was clear she had once been quite stunning, she had obviously fallen on hard times. His heart gave a painful lurch. He knew when someone was destitute. "The kitchen is around back," he said quietly, unwilling to disturb the mistress, yet still wishing to help the needy soul. "Why don't you go on around? I'll have Helen fix you up. A hearty meal will do much to restore you."

When the woman continued to stare up at him, he moved to quietly close the door. Isis approached on silent feet as if propelled by an unseen force. When she reached his side, she gasped aloud. She reached blindly for the younger woman, tears spilling from her eyes. Higgens heard his own breath escape as recognition set in. "Oh, dear Lord!" he managed, his words lost in all the commotion around him. Only when he witnessed Isis' stricken expression had he understood it was Eliza at the door! He had known she went missing some years ago, but he had since forgotten. The woman on the other side of the door hardly resembled the arrogant octoroon of days gone by. He held the door open as her mother ushered her in out of the cold, and suddenly everyone was helping the quietly sobbing women. Hillery had taken on the authority of her position. She put them all to work fetching and assisting, and in no time at all Eliza was settled before the fire with a meal and hot beverage. Hillery had her all tucked up in a cozy, bright colored blanket. He, himself, put another log on the fire. Helen ladled more wassail into her cup, topping it with a shot of whiskey. Anyone could see Eliza had gone into shock.

It was hypothermia from being exposed to foul weather for an extended period of time that had claimed Eliza. That and an overwhelming shock, most likely due to being reconciled with her mother after such a long and painful lesson. In all her wildest dreams, Eliza had never truly believed her family – even her own mother – would welcome her back. After all she had said and done, how could she expect this? Yet here they were speaking calmly to her, treating her like royalty until Eliza had simply lost her tenacious grip on reality. The world spun away in a numbing haze of freezing temperatures and ill health until her mother and the others reeled it back in. Eliza knew a wealth of gratitude she had never before known. This is where she belonged, she vowed – with her family, her people! She would never stray again!

When Hillery and Isis, with Ariel in tow, returned to The Plantation, Eliza went with them. She had rested, scrubbed herself clean of any lingering traces of dirt or cosmetics, changed into decent clothing, and insisted on holding her own during the journey home. Isis had been cast in a role almost foreign to her as doting mother to Eliza, something that had not occurred since Eliza was quite small. If she found herself shocked by the strange turn of events, she handled it quite well as any loving mother would. Hillery beamed in satisfaction.

Eliza regained her health quickly and offered her assistance on any household, or field position, earning the regard and respect of all. Those who might have looked askance at her reconsidered when they saw her willingness to correct the past. Her fierce loyalty to her mother, and to Hillery, gained her much. Soon the older women took her under their wings and Eliza bloomed. But even in this newfound joy, Eliza could see the strain everyone was under, especially her mother and Hillery.

When she addressed the issue she found herself swept away into a past of remembered curses and ancient haunts. Her mother appeared reluctant to speak of the matter. Hillery opened the conversation and told of her visit with Madame Genevieve. Isis sat silently observing them, her large expressive eyes trained on Hillery and her interaction with her daughter. Hillery looked at peace – that is to say, she appeared to have every faith in Eliza. Isis nodded to herself, cocking her head as the conversation continued. Ariel, sitting in the midst of them all, cocked his as well. He sat comfortably on one hip.

"But we made it safely through the New Year's celebration," Eliza considered, "and all is well. Does that not account for anything?"

"Sadly, no," Hillery murmured a reply, "it merely means we are running out of time. And I must act now."

Eliza looked momentarily horrified. "You are in no position to go into the forest...especially the ghost forest! Your baby is past due as it is!"

"That is a great concern," Isis chimed, her golden hoops swaying. "She refuses to allow me to go in her stead, and it is far too risky for her to make the attempt."

"Then I will go!" Eliza decided. "I am still young enough, strong enough. I can easily make the journey."

"You have barely recovered your health, daughter," Isis admonished, and Eliza felt a surge of pride that her mother had fondly called her 'daughter'. "I am not so sure it is safe."

"I am not so sure it is safe for any of us," Eliza agreed, "but I will have the amulet for protection, and I am the most likely candidate."

Before Isis could argue any further, Hillery raised her voice a notch, "She is right. She is recovered well enough, and we are out of time. Each day cost us. Have you not seen the fear among the people? You can smell it in the air!"

"Yes," Isis acknowledged, "you are right, of course." After Eliza left the room, Isis looked directly at Hillery forcing eye contact. "You are certain?" she probed. "Do you have any doubts or worries?"

"No," Hillery shook her head. "We can trust her completely. I have seen it. Besides Eliza is not only correct, she needs to prove herself. And we need to put the curse to rest."

"Very well," Isis nodded her approval. Her heart sang. "It shall come to pass."

So it was, with the cold winds buffeting her slim shoulders, Eliza dared the density of the forest. She drew in her breath sharply at the growl of an unfamiliar beast and carefully picked her path deeper into the ghost forest, shivering a little at the eeriness of the place. Traveling slowly through the swampland, she was cautious of the fallen logs knowing they could instantly transform into alligators. She clutched the amulet tightly to her breast. The trees were literally draped with coiled snakes. Had she not seen them, she would have known of their existence all the same. The air was alive with their ugly song. All this Hillery had seen... all this, she watched in flashes as the baby began to make her way into the world. Hillery cried out but once, and then clutched the sheets in her fists as the drums echoed in her ears. She was grateful Isis was here to tend her. She had made the right decision.

It had been many years since Eliza had made this journey. Now she relied largely on instinct. Still she was afraid. She feared these people as much as she respected them, for she had never actually participated in their craft. Her mother, however, was a devout follower of ritualistic white magic. Eliza knew she had learned many of her powerful remedies and elixirs from the cult, and had, in turn, passed them on to Miss Hillery. The house had reeked of herbs and other concoctions Eliza could not name when she set out. In her troubled state, Eliza's mind wandered back to the days of her childhood before her own corruption when she had accompanied Isis into these swamps. But her mother had known what she was doing. Now she, Eliza, must seek out the mamaloi – high priestess of the dark powers! That was a frightening prospect.

Eliza gave a nervous start as her large gray eyes flitted over the hidden recesses of the bog. From somewhere in the distance she heard the roar of a wild boar. Her throat constricted with fear. She flicked her tongue across the dryness of her lips, taking a sip of fresh water from a pouch she carried across her shoulder. She fervently wished she had not been forced to abandon the tiny pirogue a few miles back. Yet it had served its purpose well. Forcing herself to remain calm she tried to concentrate on the basics of the voodoo cult. The word voodoo was derived from voudou, a Creole word which sprang from the term vodu. Vodu, a pronunciation of the Fon language, was spoken by the Indian natives of West Africa. Eliza recalled her mother speaking of this group with grave pride and respect. The mamaloi was a descendant of this particular race. The magic word vodu was said to be the most powerful in the world.

Now as Eliza fought the decayed branches of the cypress, she felt an odd presence. For a fleeting moment her mind was filled with an image of Cynie. Unknown to Eliza, she had reached the copse of dead trees where Cynie and David had been captured years ago. While she knew nothing of this, she prayed her little sister was alive and well. To her, this place screamed of unexplained savagery. Her heart was in her throat as she hurried on her way. She was dimly aware of the distant rhythm of the drums.

Hillery, too, was aware of the drums and savagery of the place as she caught glimpses of Eliza's progress. The baby was coming more quickly now, the pains had increased their assault. Isis sponged her brow when she broke into a sweat, and tended her needs with a proficiency born of a lifetime of experience. Marta and Tanya hovered near the door afraid for their mistress. The women of The Plantation were mindful that the birth was overly complicated, and equally aware that the curse was wreaking havoc with Hillery. They prayed quietly among themselves. Outdoors the silence erupted into song. Hillery listened vaguely. She knew that her strength was waning. Sukie entered with a fresh pot of strong herb tea. She had followed Isis' instructions to the letter. She ducked her head as she set the pot where it could be easily reached. Her round face reflected her fear as she wrung her hands. Isis barely acknowledged her as she felt the positioning of the infant. Just as she feared, the child was breach.

Eliza slowed her pace, realizing that the drums had ceased their sporadic dance. They now echoed a slow, regulated pulse. It was an announcement of her arrival. This she knew for certain. Nothing escaped the notice of those who inhabited the swamps. The haunting rhythm echoed throughout the forest bouncing off the hollows of dead timber. The pulse grew louder as she approached. Eliza was numb with cold, but she knew the urgency of her mission. She feared for Miss Hillery, just as she feared for them all. She followed the compelling force, stumbling headlong into a clearing. Before her stood the dilapidated hut of the ancient one she sought. On the door of the hut was a five pointed star. In the center of the star was a crude rendering of a goat; it was drawn in blood. Only the head was depicted. Its evil eyes were overshadowed by its horns. The single, grimy window yawned like a cavity in the mud-caked walls. Eliza caught sight of a flickering black candle. A chill chased down her spine. With something of a start she realized the drums had ceased. As she raised her hand to rap on the door, an ancient voice beckoned. She eased the door open.

Once inside, Eliza paused to gain her bearings. It was a small structure. The light was poor after the harsh glare of the midday sun. Musty odors, accompanied by the stench of blood and decay, assailed her nostrils. In the middle of the dirt floor the ancient one huddled. She rocked to and fro on her haunches, and then drew herself up straight and tall. Any doubts Eliza might have had as to her identity were dispelled in that instant. This was the mamaloi she had sought. Her face was wizened, her skin resembling that of a shriveled apple. She did not look up, but continued tracing patterns in the dirt. Eliza could make no sense of the patterns, but noticed a particular symmetry about them. She sat when the elder gestured she should do so. And as she sat, she became aware of chanting in the near distance.

The ancient one crooned quietly to herself then set to work combining a potion. Eliza watched as the mamaloi's emaciated claws crumbled a dark chunk of powder into a black iron cauldron. Next she lit four candles, each of a different color. The black candle was placed at the left end of an arc the ancient one had scratched into the earth. A brown one was placed at its side, followed by a yellow, then a white. The white candle encompassed the right end of the arc while the cauldron blazed in its center. Its smoke curled up around them in the close confines of the hut, billowing out through a makeshift chimney in the roof. There were tools beside the mamaloi Eliza did not recognize. Instinctively, she knew them to be sacred.

The chanting outside grew louder. Heat swamped the hut, soaking her blouse and molding her clothing to her well rounded form. She had gained weight since her return home. She watched in mute curiosity while each tool was passed over the flame of every individual candle before being laid aside. When the ancient one was satisfied with the outcome of her work, she extinguished the flames of all but the white candle. She glanced at Eliza, a somber expression creasing her withered features then solemnly removed the cauldron. Its substance had evaporated until only a thickness coated the pot. Eliza made as if to move, but the ancient one indicated she should remain seated.

They sat together in the darkened hut. Neither spoke. The elder's gaze was fastened on the single remaining flame. Suddenly it began to sputter. Eliza's eyes widened. The flame shot all the way to the ceiling before it was doused by an unexplained gust of wind. Eliza sat transfixed, her eyes straining to adjust to the complete lack of light. Suddenly the door of the hut was thrown open by an unseen force! Eliza flinched, jumping visibly. The elder seemed oblivious to her reaction. Eliza was amazed by the brilliant light of the sun flooding, not only from the open door, but from the vent in the ceiling as well! Why had the opening been so dark only a moment before? And where had the strange burst of wind come from? It was clearly apparent there was no wind now. The very stillness of the air was eerie. Eliza drew in a breath as the elder's claw-like hand clamped down on her shoulder. She had not heard her move. A tremendous current flowed between them, much like a bolt of lightning.

"Etendez-vous! Etendez-vou!" The words were the first to leave the elder's mouth and sounded not unlike a command. Warily Eliza did as she was bid. The ancient one knelt beside her, and then proceeded to rub a vile ointment into Eliza's pale skin. Her gnarled fingers were roughly invasive, though Eliza took no offense. She gagged, choking back the bile that threatened to rise in her throat. The elder was fingering the drying entrails of a recently slaughtered animal. Without having to be told, Eliza knew the mamaloi was reading the future. What she didn't know was what kind of animal the entrails had once belonged to! Eliza felt strangely detached when the ancient one opened her mouth to speak.

"Damballah-wedo! Damballah-wedo!" the words grew in intensity. Eliza watched as if from above when the mamaloi reached for a large woven basket. The basket was covered with a lid of the same weave. It was an odd feeling looking down on one's self with the ancient one crouching nearby. She wondered fleetingly how she could feel so detached from the shell of herself just as the mamaloi raised the lid of the basket. Her movements seemed practiced, intentionally slow. "Damballah-wedo, Damballah-wedo," the chant filled the air like a living, breathing thing while the one outside escalated all around them. In one fluid motion, a rattlesnake uncoiled itself from the bottom of the basket. It slithered from the basket slowly entwining itself around the ancient one's arms in what appeared to be a loving gesture. Just as lovingly the high priestess caressed the reptile that was so ugly to Eliza. She raised it over Eliza's head swaying back and forth as she did so. The last thing Eliza witnessed before she slammed back into her still form was a clear view of the mamaloi scooping her gnarled fingers into the gaping mouth of the snake.

# CHAPTER THIRTY SIX

illery floated in an eerie cocoon of induced calm. Her pains had abated somewhat but were still sharper than they should be. While Isis gently forced a bitter tonic down her throat, Hillery watched spellbound as Eliza was met with the incantations in the hut. Her heart sank as she realized how close they were cutting it, for the baby needed oxygen. It was past time for her to emerge safely into the world! Hillery's brow furrowed in pain while she fought to remain alert. Sukie sniffed in the background as she tiptoed in and out. Marta and Tanya fought tears where they huddled near the door. And Hillery stifled a sob when she saw the priestess scoop the contents from the mouth of the snake even as she looked down upon the scene by the fire.

Eliza woke from a deep and dreamless sleep. Somehow, the priestess had managed to steer her away from the hut. As Eliza regained consciousness she found herself outside, her back resting against the bole of a huge, blackened tree. The mamaloi murmured ancient words, blessing the wisdom of Damballah, Saint of Bamboula. She pushed Eliza forward into a second clearing, then turned and walked away. Eliza knew a moment of true panic at the scene before her. There before the fire a second elder danced. She was far older than the ancient one. And she was garbed only in beads with ropes of bones draped about her throat, waist, and ankles. Her dusky skin was wrinkled with age, her face deeply lined.

The elder carried the authority of high priestess. Oh, dear Lord! Had she been mistaken? Or were there two of them? Eliza dug her nails into her palms to keep from calling out; she dared not utter a single sound. Suddenly, silence enveloped her. All movement ceased. The elder paused in triumph, her black eyes gleaming. As she stood there her posture straightened. Her skin grew young and supple. There was mute satisfaction in her pose as she thrust out her chest. Her breasts had firmed, the aureoles darkened. Her lips were full and ripe. Yet pure hatred poured from her very soul so strongly that Eliza had to fight to stand against it. In a state of shock she realized what the other was about. It was her intention to steal the child that Hillery carried! She would have its youth. And she was right on the precipice of completing the task! Pure venom emerged from her opened mouth. In a blur Eliza watched as the evil one reached out to Hillery's swollen abdomen as if to pluck the babe away! But the open cavity of her mouth spat dry venom. The necessary poison had been stripped away! The evil one recognized the ploy and set her shoulders. She would fight for what was hers!

Eliza struggled to stay erect for the evil that was spewed at her was fierce. She recounted the words of the mamaloi, hearing them again as if for the first time, then raised wizened eyes to this new threat before her. They stood glaring at each other, one as determined as the next. Yet Eliza had the weight of the ancient one with her, and her magic was strong. She stood facing the elder for what seemed an eternity. Then just as Eliza began to sweat, the beauty before her began to age. She shrieked as her pliant skin crinkled in ancient folds. And as she shrieked in defeat, the priestess stepped out from behind Eliza, her own lips stretched in a wide smile. She spoke in clear English for the first time since Eliza had met her. "There, mother," she said in great triumph, "your evil prevails no more! It is done." With that she turned and walked away and was never seen again. A hush filled the forest. The fire died before Eliza's very eyes, and then slowly sputtered out. With it, the evil one shriveled into a bundle of ancient bones which then turned to ash and were scattered by the wind. The winds came out of nowhere, and died just as suddenly. Eliza breathed in calm.

It was evening. The babe was positioned as well as could be. Hillery's brow was beaded with sweat. The bed clothes were soaked. There was a great deal more blood loss than was safe and Hillery's strength was waning. Her eyes were glazed as she watched the tableau before her unfolding. The second mamaloi, the one to be feared, reached out to pluck the child from her womb! She cried out in pain when the long nails gouged deeply into her flesh leaving bright red scratches in their wake. Her skin quivered dripping blood, which in turn ran like a river, pooling onto the floor. The attending women gasped audibly. Isis hushed them, hurrying them from the room. She bade Sukie clean up the mess that was blackened with the stench of evil. The black eyes of the elder gleamed at her and Hillery cringed, drawing upon an inner strength she had never known she possessed. This was her child's life! She must fight. She vowed she would die defending her baby, her love was that fierce. She sent a prayer to God and Saint Michael and in that instant the elder began to shriek in anguish. Hillery watched as she began to age. The bones about her neck and waist danced as she writhed in an agony of her own making. The open cavity of her mouth hissed an ugly rasping sound as it stretched wide enough to strike – a snake's mouth – gaping, yawning, as it sought its target. The sound died a gurgling death as the venom dried upon her tongue and her body withered into a pile of ash and bone. Hillery moaned, then drew upon that inner strength and pushed in earnest. Her daughter emerged into the world one fist at a time. And what a glorious bundle she was! Her head crowned and boisterous cries filled the room. Isis wept openly. She hugged Hillery and the babe close as the others poured into the room. This was an evening to rejoice.

She named the child Genevieve, spelling it Geneva and calling her Eve, in honor of the lady that made freedom from the curse more than a possibility. Now it was the new reality for those on The Plantation. Every day promised a new beginning. As word spread newcomers applied for positions, built homes, and joined the community. Soon The Plantation was bursting with new energy and a reputation for a free new way of life. New romances occurred. Couples made intimate promises and stepped out for strolls in the picturesque gardens. On Saint Valentine's Day more than one couple jumped the broom, and Hillery sighed in newfound contentment as she laid the novel *Robinson Crusoe* aside to suckle Eve. She smiled to herself as the fresh clean smell of talcum powder mingled with beeswax. They had carried the old cradle down from the attic, tucking it between the comfortable pair of Queen Anne Wingbacks in the cozy library. It had been scrubbed clean of age and grime then given a fresh coat of varnish.

Glory peeked at Hillery where she sat with the babe. She had come for an extended visit with the family after her lengthy stay in New Orleans. She would be forever grateful to Hillery for relocating her to the townhouse when her own child was stolen, then reuniting her with her mother. Hillery was a Godsend in Glory's mind and Glory was happily relieved about the birth of Eve. But Hillery had been plagued with nightmares of late. Too often she awoke in the night sobbing Stuart's name. Sometimes she talked in her sleep, the incoherent words sending chills down Glory's spine. The nightmares followed the same pattern night after night. Glory took to sleeping outside her mistress's door. Eventually she came to understand a few of the anguished words and she wondered if Miss Hillery knew what the dreams foretold. Glory thought they bespoke of Master Stuart's demise. She hoped not. She liked Stuart and worried for her mistress. But she knew one thing for certain, and that was the dreams bode ill for someone. To dispel her gruesome thoughts, she entered the library with forced cheer.

The baby gurgled and Hillery giggled. Ariel woofed quietly and wagged his tail. Glory felt a smile tugging at her lips. Miss Hillery looked adorable dressed all in red and white in honor of the holiday. Glory admired her fine new figure since the baby's birth. She could hardly believe only a few short weeks had passed! The dress she wore was adorned with tiny red bows. Ariel gave a little yip to regain Glory's attention and Glory patted his head. The little dog visibly preened causing Glory to laugh out loud. Laughter felt good, she decided.

Sukie announced it was time for dinner and Hillery realized she was starving. Even though she was regaining her strength nicely, the birth had taken its toll. Add to that, her dreams troubled her far more than she chose to admit. Because she didn't understand them, her concern for her husband grew daily. Dark smudges rimmed her eyes, testimony to her lack of sleep. She was grateful when Eliza swept Eve away allowing her the time and luxury of a hot lavender bath. Eliza had become an excellent nanny. She adored Eve and welcomed time alone with the infant. Eliza was surprised at herself. Who would have believed that she of all people had a weakness for babies? Eliza grinned at Eve who was busy making cooing sounds. She hugged her close enjoying the sweet new baby smell.

Stuart trudged on in the bitter destruction of the South. He, too, had been having dreams that warned of impending danger. Much like Hillery, he realized he would be targeted in the near future and that it was a separate thing from the circumstances of war. He knew a sense of doom and could smell a plot of some sort just as he sensed fowl play was at hand. For the life of him he had no clue as to what it pertained to. He did, however, recognize the urgency, the need for preventive measures. Thus he soldiered on knowing that he would climb any mountain to get home to his wife and child. It was only yesterday that he had received the news his daughter had been born. And in her letters, Hillery had enclosed a cross that had belonged to her mother. He wondered at the reason for it even as he slipped it over his head, wearing it close to his heart.

The budding of a new spring found the folks of The Plantation in the fields again. Hillery met the packet, eagerly accepting her purchases of new seed. While Old Jake drove, she sorted through them, excited to be a part of new life once again. This spring held promise. The scent of freedom was in the air. No matter how desolate war might be, she realized the end was in sight, and that lent an enormous measure of comfort. She knew that soon the men folk would be returning. This much she had seen in her dreams. Life would resume its natural course. She prayed Stuart would come home unharmed, and that he would conquer whatever else lay before him. She wondered if he had received the mail she had sent and if he understood her warnings. She prayed for peace across the land and the strength to cope with any further hardships.

With each new day the men and women of The Plantation labored. They planted new crops, watching them sprout and grow. While the crops thrived, the people fought rough weather and disease. In lieu of the curse that had long plagued the land a new prosperity blanketed the earth. Men and women rejoiced. Still more homes dotted the countryside. Couples smiled as they made new plans. They prayed for children and fervently believed that peace would prevail. Women laughed among themselves as they shared secret hopes and fragile dreams. Song erupted as everyone worked side by side. Hillery had assured them the war would soon be over and they had great faith in their mistress.

Eliza was startled to find that for the first time in her life she had fallen in love. She was truly amazed at herself. She had not believed she was capable of this emotion that seemed so normal to everyone else. She smiled as she recalled the words she and Patrick had exchanged. They were sweet words with honest intent. Patrick was still somewhat new to the area, but he fit right in. He liked everyone and everyone liked him. But it was Eliza with whom he had fallen in love, Eliza with whom he wanted to share a future! She believed she was the luckiest woman alive. She touched a slim hand to the jewel that nestled between her breasts. It was suspended on a delicate chain of pure gold. The chain alone must have cost a small fortune. There was a time when Eliza would have sneered at the simplicity of design. She would have been impressed only with jewels fine enough for a queen. But she was no longer that spoiled girl! She was a new woman, a down-to-earth female who worked hard, and dreamed of some day having a family of her own. Now it seemed that day was at hand.

Marta and Tanya too, were stepping out with beaus of their own. They whispered between themselves while they cleaned the big house, polishing the floors and furniture to a shiny gloss. Marta had never believed she would feel this way again after the harsh invasion of soldiers and the damage they had wrought. Part of her felt her body had betrayed her because even though she still feared the act of lovemaking, another part of her truly believed all would be well. She had talked to her beau about what had happened to her and the moisture that filled his eyes gave her the reassurance she needed. He vowed to be gentle and kind, and swore he would treat her with the utmost respect. Marta smiled and ducked her head. She knew in her heart it would be all right.

Glory watched all of this with unguarded jealousy. She was ashamed of this new emotion. Glory had never been jealous a day in her life! But she was now, and it hurt. Glory could only think of the rape of her young body and the painful birth of the daughter she had lost. Her child had been stolen away in the night, a product of the curse that had once ruled the land. She scowled at her own mood, disheartened. She would talk to Isis, she decided. Isis was magical. She would know what to do! For the life of her Glory was at a loss. The one thing she did know was that she did not want to become a jealous, mean-spirited person.

Isis listened to Glory's tale. The girl's shoulders slumped with defeat as she unburdened herself, and Isis' heart went out to her. She ran the situation through her mind, determined to help the poor child. Glory had always been a good soul. Though she was not nearly as pretty as many of the other girls, she had always been kind of heart. And she had carried an awful burden for one so young! Isis knew Glory's true beauty was in her goodness and quickly resolved to offer a solution. She told Glory exactly what she needed to hear, a reassurance of sorts. Glory listened with rapt attention determined to rid herself of her jealousy. She squared her shoulders even as she wiped her tears, and then solemnly promised Isis she would follow her advice to the letter. Isis smiled upon her saying that all would be well. She must simply allow a little time to pass. The rest would take care of itself. When Glory walked away there was a new spring in her step. Already she felt like a new woman.

# CHAPTER THIRTY SEVEN

sis and Hillery put their heads together. Isis had given Glory a pep talk in order to build the girl's shattered self-esteem. She had also promised her a talisman, one that would never fail her. Glory had smiled broadly when presented with the gift. It smelled of the sweet roses of the South plus something mysteriously intoxicating. Isis claimed it was jasmine. She said jasmine would draw the attention and adoration of the opposite sex, making the woman wearing the scent irresistible. Isis watched Glory's eager response. Her smile was radiant. Glory had many attributes besides a heart of gold. She had a beautiful smile, a strong, sweet voice, and a fine figure. Isis decided to use these attributes to heal the badly injured ego. Hillery was as always happy to assist. She quickly produced a fetching gown, made the necessary adjustments, and in a matter-of-fact manner informed Glory the gown no longer suited her. Upon reflection, she allowed, the dress would be far more fetching on Glory! Glory's eyes rounded in awe.

The dress was ivory, laced with warm gold tones, and trimmed in copper piping. Hillery judged it to be far more complimentary to Glory's complexion than her own. And when she tried it on, it was a perfect fit! Glory spent several long moments admiring her reflection in the looking glass. She thanked Hillery profusely then vowed to take excellent care of the generous gift. Hillery smiled as she ducked from the room.

A week later one of the women confided in Glory that she needed help with a family recipe. This recipe, she explained, was far easier to make with an extra pair of hands. The problem was, it was an old family secret. In return for her help, the woman was prepared to share the results with Glory who was extremely pleased by this turn of events. Not only was she privy to the recipe, she was given a large bottle of the tonic as well! One had only to rinse with the tonic to sweeten the breath!

Glory was in a fine mood when a woman named Irene approached her. Irene had been meaning to speak with her, she confided, and had been remiss in her duty. It would seem she was in charge of the church chorus and had forgotten to welcome Glory back into the fold. After all, Glory had been away a good, long while! It had not escaped her notice, she said, that Glory had a sweet, strong voice that deserved a place of honor in the choir. She offered Glory a front row position where she would be required to sing many of the church's finest solos. Glory happily accepted. By this time she had nearly forgotten the problem that had sent her crying to Isis. Glory was a new woman.

Hillery fought the prickle of fear that tingled along the nape of her neck like feathery fingertips. She struggled to reassure herself that she had warned Stuart, and no doubt he had received warnings of his own. He was sharp. He was intuitive. He would listen to the warnings. It was early morning and she had just awakened from another dismal dream. Her hand reflexively went to the small, golden cross that she wore about her slim neck. It had belonged to her mother, and it was not where it usually lay against her breast. She smiled as she remembered sending the cross to Stuart. She envisioned him wearing it, remembered the prayer she had blessed it with and told herself all would be well.

She padded downstairs with Ariel at her heels. She placed Eve in the cradle next to her favorite chair and rang for breakfast. Sukie was on top of things. Marta entered immediately bearing a covered tray. Hillery grinned as she accepted a fragrant cup of tea. There were triangles of buttered toast with fresh fruit on the side, and a hot plate of eggs and sausage to lift her spirits. While she ate, the newspaper arrived. Marta laid it next to her causing Ariel to glance up from his place at her side. Eve gurgled and Ariel's tail wagged. Hillery picked up the paper.

The war was over! The news spread rapidly. The Plantation came alive with joyous celebration. Isis and Hillery watched with contentment as the people broke into song. It was the day everyone had been waiting for. Gossip had preceded the arrival of the paper, and followed with varying details. Over the next few days, stories of Appomattox filtered along the wide expanse of the Mississippi River. Women wept with joy for those who would soon return home after eons spent away. Soldiers clad in contrasting hues of blue and gray met amiably on the mire roads. The suicide of Edmund Ruffin, the man who had fired the first shot over Fort Sumter back in 1861, was portrayed by some as the closing incident of a war too long between the states. Though Ruffin had taken his life after news of Lee's surrender, most of the citizens of the South – as well as the North – viewed the war's finale with a warm heart. The days and nights of terror were past. For many, there was nothing more than a fierce desire to reunite their scattered families. Husbands, sons, beaus, and brothers were sought in all the major cities. Daily news sheets were scanned with hopeful eyes. All were hungry for information that might prove vital in locating their loved ones. In the demolished lands of the South, lone females hid among the charred ashes of their homes to await the return of their men. In this, Hillery felt far luckier than most.

The merriment, however, was soon shattered by the force of Lincoln's death when the President was reportedly gunned down in his balcony of the Ford Theater during a performance of "Our American Cousin", a play starring the talented actress, Laura Keene. It was later discovered that John Wilkes Booth, a deranged actor and Southern sympathizer, had fired the derringer from a deadly range of five feet. The bullet that plowed through that worldly brain lodged in the area behind the right eye, leaving no chance of survival. While the slow process of death settled over the beloved president, hundreds of dignitaries accompanied by mobs of sobbing citizens spilled over the White House lawn. Millions more across the nation mourned this tragic loss.

News of the president's death hit The Plantation like a physical blow for Hillery had deeply admired Mr. Lincoln. Furthermore she was aware of her husband's honorable presentation to him at one point during the war. Stuart's heart would be ravaged, and she longed to be at his side. Wherever he was, her thoughts were with him.

Stuart was on the east coast when he received the devastating news of Lincoln's assassination. In a private salute with the remainder of his men, he stood grimly at attention. His jaw was set, his posture erect. He looked no less a man for the tell-tale moisture that threatened to impair his bright blue visage. The war had dealt many cruel blows, but this – the loss of such a great leader – must surely be the worst.

Now, as he spurred his mount wearily toward home, he faced the plundered stretch of land he had so long ago left behind. Luminous purple eyes shone before him. Magnolia white arms reached out to enfold him. He could almost hear the light tinkle of her laughter. He could almost feel the alluring pressure of her lips on his. He was unaware of the groan that escaped as he rode, unseeing. His thoughts were on one woman: the one magnificent flower of the South. It was she who had bestowed upon him the strength to endure these many years in hell. It was for Hillery his heart cried out. It was on her his thoughts were riveted.

When his path led into Atlanta, a lump rose in his throat. He had seen its ruin even from a distance. In the bitter aftermath of war, the air was stale – choked with a mixture of sulfur, blood, and gunpowder. He did his best to skirt the carnage. The sun beat down on his raven head, enunciating the new strands of silver that highlighted the blue-black crown. His uniform was badly tattered. Gone was the red captain's sash. In its stead he wore the gold braid of major. Gone, too, were the handsome white gloves that had covered those calloused palms. His hands were bare and rugged now. He spurred his mount toward home.

Hillery's visage was focused on Stuart as he rode toward home. He looked so handsome, her emotions became jumbled. Even as her heart throbbed for him, fear slid down her spine in tingly awareness as he approached the now familiar shelter of live oaks on the hill. She knew what lay in wait for him. She panicked as she felt the presence of uncoiled evil. She could feel it about to pounce. And Stuart was its target. The dream clouded, and with it, her vision. When it cleared, she bolted awake. "Oh, no!" she cried, waking Ariel who slept guarding her and the baby Eve. "Oh, no!" she repeated.

They passed each other on the road, all the many soldiers returning home from war. Some wore tattered gray, others threadbare blue. They nodded amiably, sometimes exchanging water for a bit of hardtack. Occasionally they shared a campsite or a stretch of road before moving on in their own individual direction. Stuart forged ahead, caring for his mount as would any good officer. Apollo snorted in appreciation. They passed water and woodland, small towns and farmland. There were endless miles of destruction, impoverished plantations that had somehow managed to survive. Finally, after innumerable days and nights, he approached a familiar grove of live oaks. As he crested the hill his senses heightened. A chill swept down his spine leaving goose flesh in its wake. He rode low in the saddle, the better to protect himself. He had to pass through the clump of live oaks to reach his destination. There was no going around it. He was near enough to The Plantation to taste it when evil spewed blackness across the land. His stomach churned. The sky belched. And day turned dark as pitch. Directly over the rise was a pall so dense it reeked. Stuart knew this was the evil of his dreams and it was the worst kind. It was manmade.

For perhaps the first time in his life he sent a prayer to Saint Michael. He didn't question his reasons, but cradled the small golden cross he wore for but a brief moment. He keenly felt his wife's energy wrapping around him like a mantle. His fingers flexed on the saddle, already feeling the weight of his firearms. He had a pistol at the ready, a rifle by his side, and he knew he'd need them. A long blade rode comfortably nearby. His senses were honed. The silence was broken in one single outburst. It was an ambush.

He fought long and hard against formidable odds. But he had known it would come to this, and he was fully aware of the numbers. The last man died in brutal combat, his throat nearly severed. Stuart shuddered, straightening in the saddle when a single bullet rang out. It creased his temple. A trickle of blood streamed down his face blinding him in one eye. His instincts were immediate. But a final man, a hidden man, had waited out the fight, keeping low to the ground. He was in prime condition while Stuart, himself, was exhausted, his horse lathered. The evil one, the likes of which he had rarely seen, stood tall before him. He gained height, standing several feet taller than any human could possibly stand. The face was grotesque, yet oddly familiar. Stuart could not help but stare as recognition dawned. It was Tate's cruel countenance gazing back at him. His skin was far darker than Stuart recalled. Their last encounter had been a couple of years ago when Stuart had looked him up in a bordello in New Orleans. He had hoped to put an end to him then, but the man had somehow eluded him, disappearing in a puff of smoke. He had wondered at the oddity at the time. He now realized there was something truly inhuman about the man. The smell of it washed over him. It was the cloying scent of putrid flesh like something long dead and buried. He knew that scent both from his visions and from the war. War had a way of changing men; of turning them into animals so depraved they would commit the most heinous crimes.

His hands were slick with blood and gore. The beast before him lashed out, and a wound so fresh and raw he never saw it coming, tore open his shoulder. His fingers tingled, and then went numb causing him to drop his blade. Before he could recover, another wound opened the leg of his trousers. His knee buckled. He went down, the pain horrific enough to stagger his movements. He raised his pistol, sighted briefly and fired. The beast before him shrieked in fury as his bullet struck home. The victory was sweet, but short lived. The beast roared, swinging an ax. It arced in midair, the sound of metal hissing. He ducked and rolled, refiring. This time his bullet went astray. It hit a tree spraying bark and earth in its wake. And in that second he saw the evil thing fire at him and knew he was doomed. The shot was delivered at close range and was directed at his heart. Time stood still. The air around him buzzed. The beast snorted in satisfaction. And just when he knew death was about to enshroud him, he witnessed the most peculiar vision. Hillery's mother, Mariette, loomed before him! She looked so much like her daughter, it truly staggered him. She opened her mouth to curse the beast, and then shoved him so hard he fell upon the blade of his own ax where it lay on the ground, his midriff cleaved clean in two. The bullet that whined straight for him struck the cross about his neck. The cross had suddenly grown in weight and proportion, creating a shield that not only protected him but took the blunt of the bullet. He sucked in a breath and gave into sweet oblivion. When he regained consciousness Mariette was gone and Tate lay dead at his feet.

Later Stuart was to forever question what had really transpired on that hillside near the copse of live oak. He had great faith and easily believed he had been saved by a miracle. He likewise believed without a doubt that Mariette had intervened and her actions had most probably spared his life. The rest he put down to loss of blood, the shock of battle, and his own ripe imagination. What he thought he had seen was too preposterous to have been real, and all soldiers knew what the mind could construe in the heat of battle.

Hillery was outdoors with Ariel when she spied a rider in the distance. Even through the vast cloud of dust she would recognize him anywhere. Dear Lord, it was Stuart! Time stood still for a full minute. She was rooted to the spot. Suddenly her feet grew wings and she ran, her legs eagerly swallowing the ground whole! Ariel yapped as he kept pace with her. When he drew close, Stuart slid from the saddle. Her arms wrapped tightly around him, helping to support his weight. A happy cry rang out from the people of The Plantation who were there within minutes to assist their journey home.

# PART FIVE

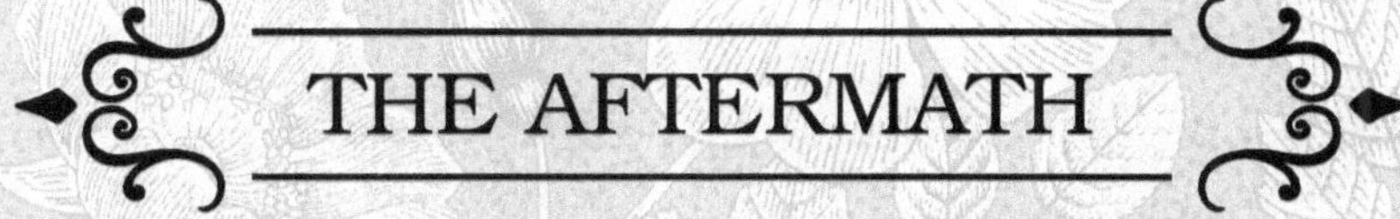

# CHAPTER THIRTY EIGHT

n the days and weeks that followed, the couple learned the detailed mystery of the curse. The story as told by Lady Genevieve brought a descendant of Marie's, the evil mamaloi, to their door. The kindhearted priestess, who had opposed her enough to stand strong against her, was actually her eldest daughter. Her name was also Marie, named for her mother, and the only one of the five girls who had the strength, knowledge and ability to not only stand up to her mother, but to put an end to her reign of terror. It was never said, however, what had become of her after her mother's demise, only that she vanished, never to be seen again. The second eldest of the girls was Sophia, and she was kind enough to reveal the rest of the story, putting to rest any doubts and fears that might arise. Sophia clearly spoke of her mother's love for Henry. Henry, she said, had taken Marie to wife in the Creole custom making her his placee. The placage between them was known in their culture as an honorable marriage, and Marie had refused to give this up even when Henry chose to marry in the custom of his own people. It was by law his choice whether to resume his relationship with Marie and any family he may have given her, or to terminate it on honorable terms. Henry chose to terminate the arrangement, generously providing for the future of his former placee and her family. The daughters, though fond of Henry, understood this to be common practice and accepted the terms with aplomb. They were,

however, preceded by one male sibling and this older brother, Marie's only son, was a fearsome young man who hungered after Henry's land and monies and when the plantation was handed down without regard to Marie or to him, he, like his mother decided to wage war against the family. And wage war they did! The son's name was Tate, and he entered into a pact with Marie to terrorize all of Henry's descendants, including anyone else who lived on the land they so coveted. In so doing, they truly felt the land would be restored to them.

Now Marie was an avid student of the black arts. She made it a point to excel at all she did, and soon her reputation preceded her. She struck fear into the hearts of all who crossed her, and before long The Plantation was known far and wide for the curse that plagued it. As Marie's strength grew, her heart rotted and her soul shriveled. She had sold it, you see, and with it, she had swept her son along in her wake. Tate became her eager accomplice, and she the queen of evil.

On the wedding day of Henry and Marietta, Marie set her hand at brewing the darkest part of the pact. She cursed their newfound happiness just as she cursed the children Marietta would bear. But Marietta was strong in her own right, she wanted children that badly. She managed to bring her daughter, Mariette, successfully into the world, but very nearly at the cost of her own life; the fact that she was willing to forfeit her life, and gladly, bestowed the necessary protection upon the daughter.

Upon learning this, Marie went a step further. She conjoined her soul with the prince of darkness. She mated and fornicated with the devil in such perversity that he granted her much. She was now the most powerful mamaloi – and possibly the most feared – in all the land! And there was nothing she wouldn't do to attain her goals. When Marietta again became with child, Marie greedily stole the infant from her very womb! Each consecutive infant met the same fate leaving poor Marietta bereft and alone, for Henry was not immune to her spells. He fell subject to Marie's cruel whims, and among her twisted goals was the stark desire to literally break Marietta's heart. In the end Marietta did indeed die of a broken heart, because aside from losing her five beautiful infants, Henry had returned to Marie's side. The grief was too much for poor Marietta. Henry did not come to understand his part in all of this until it was too late to save the life of his young wife, his one true love, and Marietta died unknowing of Henry's true feelings for her. The daughter, Mariette, watched, learned, and grew up understanding only that true love caused much pain. Coupled with this she also learned that in order to bring her own child safely into the world, she must give her life, and gladly. This she vowed, and by her own hand. But the souls of Marietta, and Mariette in turn, never slept, but roamed the land endlessly in pursuit of justice as the reign of evil went on for many more years.

All this only served to fuel Marie's twisted desire for still more power. She hungered for it until her appetite could not be sated, and the prince of darkness conjoined with her again in an orgy that was so wicked it set the pattern for a new level of perversity. Tate soon became his mother's own lover and between them they plotted to steal the first new female born to The Plantation each year in the pursuit of fulfilling a stronger and darker goal. In so doing, Marie gained the ability to enter into any one of these new souls and drain them of life. Likewise, she gained the ability to remain in each and every one of them as long as she so chose! This gave her the new means of choosing what life or lives she would live, and in which female body. It was then she decided to carry the experiment further still, allowing herself to enter other female bodies whenever she desired. These were, in general, weak souls prone to addiction. Marie knew how to manipulate these poor souls. Tate was in his element for this allowed him a wide variety of willing female flesh – all for the taking! He became so obscene that like his mother before him, his heart rotted and his soul burned in hell. Yet he did not notice. Both mother and son ruled the land with the sole belief that they were now immortal. And immortal they appeared to be! Each and every day was an awakening of pure poison, for they embraced the horrific choices they had made and there was nothing they would not do to preserve this lifestyle. Those who knew what they were about typically died a violent death or suffered the fate of becoming their full-time servants, which in general meant giving up their own souls in favor of maintaining a life of sorts. This they did willingly, life was that dear.

Tate's sisters watched all this in abject fear – all except one, and that was Marie, the eldest, and her mother's namesake. Young Marie took it to heart that if she studied hard enough, worked long enough, and was good enough she could overtake her mother and put an end to the madness. What she did not bargain for, however, was the incredible depth of Tate's black soul. She challenged her mother and met that challenge with success only to fall prey to her brother's evil ways. It was through her demise that Tate gained the strength and determination to eliminate Stuart, thus allowing him full reign and abject power, on and off, The Plantation. His own death was not a reality or a possibility he believed ever existed.

Now as Sophia ended her tale Stuart and Hillery looked to each other in awe. This was, indeed, the blackest tale they could have ever imagined. Hillery knew a wealth of grief for her family and descendants, those who had lived and lost on The Plantation. So many lives had been affected, lost, and permanently damaged. Stuart placed a protective arm about his seemingly fragile wife and thanked God for her and his daughter, both of whom had been fortunate indeed to have survived. The couple thanked Sophia for enlightening them. They would later see to it that she and her sisters received ample reward for their part in ending, and explaining, all that had happened. They, after all, had been victims themselves. Now was a time for the living, and Stuart vowed to give his beloved the life and family she so deserved. Together they would make a happy new future, full of promise, prosperity, and new beginnings. Hillery smiled a secret smile already aware of the new life she carried. This child would be a boy. She had seen it in her dreams and for the first time realized that her dreams were a budding awareness of her subconscious mind. God, did indeed, work in mysterious ways!

Eliza married her young man in the age-old custom of her people. She bore her first infant proudly and was an incredible mother. The couple made extensive plans to build on to their small cabin, including enough room for additional children.

Glory sang her heart out in the church choir where she met the love of her life, a handy man who admired her many attributes and most especially her pure heart. She accepted his pledge and they were happily planning their future. Glory had confided everything in him, and the fellow vowed to spend his life making her happy. Glory believed with all heart that there would be other children in her future, and though she could not replace the one that was stolen from her, she had plenty of love in her for as many children as the good Lord provided.

Old Jake lived his entire life on The Plantation and was still going strong to date. He was ninety-one years old.

Rachel continued to be the foundation of the family, welcoming each new grandchild in turn just as she welcomed each and every veteran home from the war. She put any and all who needed a home to work, graciously creating openings for them to ease their way back into civilian life. She carried Thomas' memory close to her heart, going so far as to begin a foundation in his name in order to feed and clothe all the brave soldiers. In this way she was able to help them reestablish themselves and find new value.

Among those who returned to society, Benjamin took up a brief position as veterinarian, but found he could not settle his unruly heart. His ventures took him into Mexico where he joined the company of Boyle and some of the gang from Libby.

Cricket accepted Hillery's invitation and decided to give New Orleans a chance. He met and courted Helen, Higgens' side kick and head cook of the townhouse. He took great delight in thawing her heart and was pleasantly surprised at the beauty he uncovered.

After being returned to Libby Prison that fateful winter of 1864, Colonel Thomas E. Rose did not remain a prisoner for long. He was exchanged in April of the same year. By this time, Provost Marshal John Winder wanted shut of the Union Officers, and Congress approved. Thomas went on to fight in the Atlanta Campaign and was belatedly promoted to Brigadier General on July twenty-second of 1865. Stuart would be forever proud of his friend and fellow officer. The men remained close friends for the duration of their lives.

Natalie married Randolph Wick, whom she fondly called Randy, but chose to build a career of her own in lieu of beginning a family. Natalie proclaimed there were enough urchins in the world to go around. It was her belief it took a village to raise a child. She therefore chose to spend her days writing children's stories for the many children of the world. By night, she studied the politics of the nation. It was the latter she someday aspired to write about, even venturing to go so far as to run for office. Someone had to bring women into their full potential!

Gran continued life in the Washington house where Stuart and Natalie had been reared. She was devoted to Rachel and the family and always managed to make herself useful. Gran had long ago decided to take Hillery under her wing and help her develop her abilities more fully. Young people, after all, needed a guiding light.

The Timberland's, like the Harlan's, remained close friends of the Michaels'. In the years to come, the couples would share many an adventure.

# THE END

# A summary of people, places, and events

The War Between the States was an active time of espionage packed full of real-life characters such as Rose O'Neal Greenhow, a notorious spy for the Confederacy, and Elizabeth Van Lew, a Union sympathizer who risked her life for the North. Both women are realistically portrayed. I have attempted to make note of many of the lesser known heroes on both sides of the war. Emma Sansom, another known, yet more obscure spy, is duly noted. Emma's last name appears in various spellings throughout the history books, as does Lily Mackall's, a messenger and companion of Rose O'Neal Greenhow's. In both cases I chose the most common spelling I could find. Mary Jane Richards Denman was known as Mary Bowser and was one of the Van Lew's former slaves whom Elizabeth freed upon her father's death. Knowing her potential, Elizabeth sent her to school in Philadelphia. John H. Winder was the provost marshal of Richmond, Virginia, just as Colonel John Letcher was the governor. Christopher Memminger was one of the founding fathers of the Confederate States as well as the principal author of the Provisional Constitution. He was also founder of the nation's financial system. Thomas Rose was realistically portrayed. Thomas McNiven was truly the owner of the Bakery in Richmond and active in his service to Elizabeth and the Union. Samuel Ruth was in the Richmond office of Richmond, Fredericksburg, and Petersburg Railroad. He carried information and gave aid to Federal fugitives along with his assistant, Lohman. Between them, they delayed supplies for the Confederacy. Laura Keene was the leading actress in the play

"Our American Cousin". Moses, who appears as the conductor for the Underground Railroad was in reality Harriet Tubman. Tubman was a former slave whose birth name was Araminta Ross. She changed her name when she escaped and did indeed manage to free hundreds of slaves. The voodoo scenes in The Plantation are loosely based on the life of Marie Laveau.

As for places and events, the Louisiana Starlette was an actual packet. All newspaper references were the factual ones of the day. The comment from a guard in Libby Prison beginning with "Hallow Bill" and regarding the noise of the escape was recorded in detail in the history books and I took this quote directly. And among other ploys, the reference to secret missives carried in egg shells as well as the method used for Elizabeth's ciphers, were factual.

# ACKNOWLEDGEMENTS

A special thank you to Barbara Bushong for her friendship, guidance, and continual encouragement through the years; Barbara was my all-time favorite English-Lit teacher and an incredible author in her own right.

Additional thanks to authors Jude Knight, Dawn Lee McKenna, Carol Roddy, Anita Rodgers, and Neal Davies for their insightful conversations, wisdom, advice, and friendships as well as a huge thank you to Kelly O'Dell Stanley for all her talent, patience, and meticulous work and for going that extra mile for me, and to Bobbie Gore for her guidance and experience in the world of Reviewers. I cannot give enough credit to my Arcs Dr. Robin R. West and Sheryl Gatliff Starnes without whom I may have lost my confidence. I sincerely thank you all.

9 781737 259602